MW01138977

The Last Time Traveler

Aaron J. Ethridge

Copyright © 2017 Aaron J. Ethridge

All rights reserved.

ISBN: 9781520189130

CONTENTS

CHAPTER 1: MORGAN

"So who are you again?" Morgan asked.

"As I've told you numerous times already," the young man replied, "I'm the last time traveler."

"And what do you mean by *the last time traveler*?"

"I mean," the time traveler said, waving his hands before him, "that out of all the time travelers that ever were, I'm the *last*!"

"Yeah," Morgan nodded. "But what if someone from the future..."

"No," he interrupted. "That's what I'm trying to explain to you. I come from a time where there is no future, and there never will be."

"That's not possible."

"I'm sure from your point of view, that's so," the young man replied. "But trust me, it's more than merely possible."

"Okay," Morgan nodded. "Let's say I believe you. Why come here?"

"*Why come now* would be a better question," he replied. "And I've come to try to undo all the damage."

"What damage?"

"I think I'm getting a headache," the young man said, rubbing his forehead. "All the damage done by the previous time travelers."

"Why would they..."

"Look!" the time traveler exclaimed. "In the not so distant future mankind figures out how to go back in time. First they start observing, then they start *correcting*. And before you know it, just a few thousand years later, the future is gone. Time travel was an unmitigated disaster and I'm here to fix it."

"So, are you like a cop," Morgan asked, "or a secret agent, or *Doctor Who*, or what?"

"Yes," he nodded. "Basically. Love *Doctor Who*, actually. It's ridiculous, of course. I mean, time travel: *as if*."

"But you said..."

"Yes," he nodded again. "Being funny. Try to keep up."

"Well then," Morgan began, a thoughtful expression on his face. "Isn't talking to me messing up the time-lines or something?"

"No," the young man assured him. "Because you don't matter."

"Everybody matters!"

"Not to the time-lines," the time traveler corrected. "Had history gone the way it was supposed to, you would simply be a missing person. A time traveler changed that and I'm here to change it back."

"Whoa!" Morgan exclaimed. "So you're going to make me a missing person? No thanks!"

"Let me ask you a few questions Morgan."

"Alright."

"Where do you work?"

"Taco Palace."

"How much do you make?"

"Minimum wage."

"You a manager?"

"Nope."

"How long you been working there?"

"Six years."

"Got a girlfriend?"

"No, but..."

"Right," the time traveler nodded. "Trust me, you're better off missing."

"Yeah, but..."

"Look, Morgan," the young man said shaking his head, "I said you were missing, I didn't say you were dead. Hasn't it ever struck you as strange that so many people go missing near the Bermuda triangle?"

"I guess..."

"Right. Well a lot of them aren't dead. They're working to save the future. This is your chance to be somebody."

"Alright," Morgan nodded. "So do you have a time machine?"

"Yep."

"What do you call it?"

"The Time Machine."

"It doesn't have a cool nickname, like *The TARD*..."

"Watch that!" the traveler interrupted. "The BBC is crazy zealous about copyright infringement."

"They can't hear us all the way out here."

"Why take chances?"

"Well, you just said *Doctor Who*," Morgan pointed out.

"That's just the name of a show," the traveler retorted. "I'll take my chances."

"Either way, does your ship have a nickname?"

"Nope."

"We should call it *The Morganatron*."

"No," the time traveler said, shaking his head. "We shouldn't."

"Well, I think..."

"Why don't we just call it *The Phone Booth?*"

"What does that mean?"

"How old are you?"

"Why? What happens in phone booths that I'm too young to know about?"

"We really don't have time for this, Morgan," the time traveler replied. "I'm Robert, by the way. Oh, and let me hold your jacket."

"Why?" Morgan asked, removing his coat and handing it to the traveler.

"Actually, just hold it up for me," Robert said, pulling something from his pocket. "You see, according to history - real history - *all that's ever found of you is a bloody jacket in the woods.*"

"Why do you say it like that?"

"I think it makes it sound *spooky*," the traveler replied.

The object he had in his hand was a switchblade, which he immediately snapped open before beginning to slash Morgan's jacket to shreds.

"What are you doing?!?!" the rather heavy set young man exclaimed. "Are you nuts?!?!"

"Oh," Robert replied, "I should have said *shredded bloody jacket.*"

"Don't say it like that... it is spooky... and you owe me fifty bucks for the jacket."

"No problem," the traveler replied. "But no way it was worth fifty. Now, throw it on the ground."

Immediately Morgan obeyed as Robert pulled a red aerosol can from his other pocket. He shook it vigorously before spraying the jacket thoroughly with it.

"No one, anywhere, ever, is going to believe that's blood," Morgan asserted.

"Why?" the traveler asked. "It is blood... In fact, it's your blood."

"What?!?!" he exclaimed. "What are you doing with a spray can full of my blood in your pocket? How much did you take? What's my blood-pressure right now? Everything's getting dark! I need to sit down!"

"Calm down!" Robert demanded. "I took a single cell from you while you were asleep and cloned the rest. I didn't even break your skin."

"You've seen me sleeping?" Morgan asked, slightly calmed, but perhaps more creeped out.

"Trust me, man," the traveler said, shaking his head. "It's nothing to write home about."

"Okay," the young man replied. "So, seriously, stop for a minute. Say that I believe this - which I don't for a second, by the way... And you're making me really nervous with the switchblade and everything."

"Here," the traveler said, folding up the knife and handing it to him. "I'm done. You hold on to it. Oh, and I've got the fifty with me; I figured you'd be like that."

The traveler pulled a wad of bills from his pocket, took a note from the top, and handed it to Morgan.

"This is a hundred..."

"Eh, keep the change."

"So seriously," Morgan said, glancing around the woods that surrounded them. "Are you like a thief, or a counterfeiter, or just some loony escaped from the crazy bin, or what?"

"I'm telling you the truth, Morgan," the traveler replied. "I'm the last time traveler. I really, honestly am. And, in fact, I can tell you a bit of the future. You're about to ask me *why was my shredded bloody jacket found out here in the middle of the woods?*"

"I wasn't," Morgan replied, shaking his head. "But now that you mention it: why was my shredded bloody jacket found out here in the middle of the woods?"

"Aha!"

"That's not predicting the future, you loony!" the young man chuckled. "That's tricking me into saying something."

"Okay, you're right," Robert admitted. "And enough of the parlor tricks."

As he said this, he glanced down at his watch.

"And so, in the spirit of that," he began, watching the time and slowly lowering his finger toward the woods, "there's your answer!"

The moment he said this, a giant grizzly bear strode into view.

"What do we do?" Morgan whispered.

"Well," Robert replied. "I plan to run."

The last time traveler was as good as his word. He had no sooner finished speaking when he burst into a run in the opposite direction.

"No way we can outrun a grizzly bear!" Morgan screamed.

"Don't need to!" the traveler replied. "I just need to outrun you!"

"What?!?!"

"Just kidding! The ship's not far!"

"Don't you have bear tranquilizer in the future?" Morgan asked.

"You have it in the present, Morgan. However, as neither of us thought to bring any, that hardly matters now!"

"I'm not going to make..." Morgan began.

At that moment, he struck something with such force that it knocked him to the ground. His eyes rolled around in his head, searching for whatever had hit him, as the time traveler grabbed him by the ankles and dragged him into an invisible chamber. As soon as they were inside, Morgan could see that the room appeared to be a box made of glass.

"What is this?" he asked, slowly sitting up.

"The loading platform," Robert replied, before pushing a button causing them to rise into the air.

"What did I hit?" Morgan asked.

"The loading platform," the traveler chuckled. "Anyway, we weren't really in any danger. I actually did bring..."

As he said this, he jammed his hand into his jacket pocket.

"Meant to," he nodded. "I meant to bring a tranquilizer pistol."

"You what?!?!"

"I'm kidding," the traveler said, drawing the weapon from his coat. "I'm just kidding. You need to lighten up, Morgan."

"I'll try," the young man replied, clutching his chest. "But are we likely to end up chased by any more bears?"

"Eh..." the traveler replied, rotating his hand back and forth.

"Well, if you had a tranquilizer, why didn't you just use it?"

"I had to get you to the ship," Robert replied. "You thought I was crazy, remember?"

"I still think you're crazy!" Morgan said.

"Maybe I am," the traveler chuckled. "Either way, let's get on board."

Robert helped the young man to his feet before brushing him off and leading him into the cargo bay of his ship. The interior was a rather audacious shade of aquamarine that somehow didn't seem to match Morgan's idea of how a time machine should look.

"What color is this?" he asked, gazing around with a puzzled look on his face.

"No idea," Robert replied, shaking his head with a wink. "I've always just called it *spanking mermaids*."

"What does that even mean?"

"No idea. Let's go."

The last time traveler marched over to the door and pushed a button. It immediately vanished, only to reappear after they stepped through the portal. The pair made their way silently through a long hallway of green to reach what appeared to be the bridge of the ship. Brightly colored buttons glowed along every panel and the displays were filled with information that Morgan couldn't make heads or tails of.

"Dude..." he said slowly.

"Yes?"

"This is seriously like *Star Trek* or something," Morgan asserted, gazing around in awe.

"You think that's something?" the traveler asked, pushing a button and pulling a silver cylindrical object from a concealed drawer. "Check this out!"

"Oh! My! Goodness!" Morgan exclaimed. "Is that a *light saber*?!?!"

"What?" the traveler chuckled. "No! It's a flashlight that looks like a *light saber*. Still, pretty cool isn't it? I picked it up at a convention for next to nothing."

"Wait! Can we say *light saber*?"

"Just say it as two words and we should be cool," Robert smiled. "I don't think *Disney* will come after us over that."

"Can they hear us here?"

"Never underestimate *Disney*."

For a few moments, Morgan stood there staring silently at the traveler.

"OK," he said after some thought. "I was originally killed by a bear."

"I didn't say that. I said: *all that's ever found...*"

"Yeah, yeah," Morgan replied. "But I mean, hasn't saving me altered time or something. I mean now the bear's hungry. And I'm not complaining! I'm just asking is all."

"Oh yeah," the traveler replied, snapping his fingers. "Follow me!"

Robert leapt to his feet and quickly made his way back to the cargo bay.

"Voilà!" he said, pressing a button which raised a shield covering a tank filled with glowing red liquid and Morgan's body.

"That's me!" the young man exclaimed.

"That's a clone," the traveler explained.

"We can't just kill him and feed him to a bear!"

"It's not alive," Robert said, shaking his head. "It never was. It's just a bunch of *you* meat."

"Well... *it's* naked!"

"Don't worry," the traveler smiled. "I didn't look."

"This is crazy!"

"True," Robert nodded, before pressing another button that flushed the clone out of the ship. "Now, let's head out. We've got places to go and things to do, Morgan, my boy."

"You're not that much older than me," Morgan said, turning to follow the traveler back to the bridge.

"Oh... I wouldn't say that," he sighed.

"Well then, you look good for your age," Morgan observed.

"Thanks!" he replied, taking a seat at the controls and punching a number of buttons. "I try to take care of myself."

"Quick question."

"Lay it on me," Robert said, turning his eyes to his companion.

"Why couldn't I see the ship?"

"Oh, I should have explained that," the traveler replied. "It's invisible."

"And how does that work?"

"Right, right," Robert nodded. "Should have explained that, too. It can't be seen."

"Yeah but..."

"Morgan," the traveler chuckled. "I don't have the time to explain every technological advancement that's been made over the past five thousand years or so. We've got all of time to save, man. So, just sit back, relax, and maybe get yourself a drink. We got a ways to go before the sun sets."

"One more thing," Morgan replied. "So, our quest is to undo everything every other time traveler ever did, right?"

"*Quest?*"

"Yeah," the young man nodded. "It's a quest isn't it? Anyway, is that what we're doing or not?"

"Well..." the traveler said thoughtfully, rocking side to side in his seat. "*Everything* is one of the *big words* Morgan. And we may have a talk about the *big words* one day. But, for the moment, it's enough for you to know that we plan to undo *most* of it."

"If time travel was such a disaster," Morgan began, "why not undo everything?"

"Wow!" Robert exclaimed. "You're already beginning to think. This is awesome! That is seriously ahead of schedule!"

"Could you just answer the question and stop patronizing me?"

"*Patronizing?*" the traveler said, shaking his head. "You're so serious that you're breaking out *your* big words. In that case, I guess I'd better answer. To begin with, we're not sure that we can undo any changes that led directly to the construction of my time machine. If we did that, I might not have a ship to go back and undo things with. And that would be a paradox. And, if we create a paradox..."

"These monsters show up eating people until the universe is destroyed!"

"No," Robert replied, gazing at his companion from under a single raised eyebrow. "No, Morgan, that's not what happens. The universe is too well put together for that. You see, there are certain random elements that are *always* random. A lot of scientists in your day didn't understand that, but that's hardly surprising considering how long ago that was."

"How does that help?" Morgan asked.

"Well, it means that the *exact* same thing almost never happens twice," the traveler explained. "So, if we went back and undid my ship, that would undo our changes - which would give me a ship that would allow us to undo my ship. You with me so far?"

"I think so..."

"Good," Robert nodded. "Now, if there weren't any truly random elements, this would create a never-ending loop. But, those very elements prevent that. Because of them, at some point in the loop, I would fail to undo my ship or it would never be created. In either case, however, we'd have done something we shouldn't have done. So, we need to make sure that we don't accidentally do that!"

"Like what?"

"Like what, what?"

"I mean," Morgan said, "what can't we change?"

"Alright," the traveler replied. "That's a fair question. And I have the perfect example. One of the first time travelers, the third actually, felt that mankind wasn't emotionally prepared for a number of things that happened in the twenty-second and twenty-third centuries. She wanted to help prepare the mind of man for what it was about to encounter. So, she took a bunch of history books, reworked them as fiction, and introduced them subconsciously into the imaginations of a number of writers throughout portions of human history. Didn't it ever strike you as odd that a guy wrote a book called *The Time Machine* years before the first airplane ever flew, or that a book about electric powered submarines was published in 1869?"

"Whoa!" Morgan said, leaning back in his seat and gazing at the traveler. "Whoa! So, like, some of our fiction is history?"

"Some of it is based on..."

"Whoa!" the young man interjected. "Whoa! Are you trying to tell me that: *A long time ago in a galaxy...*"

"I'm not saying that, Morgan," Robert chuckled. "I'm just saying..."

"So, seriously!" Morgan said leaping to his feet. "Is *Captain Kirk* real?"

"Morgan," the traveler said, raising his hands, "I'm not going to tell you..."

"Oh! My! Goodness!" he exclaimed. "They brought *Spock* back from the dead! That is crazy!"

"I'm not saying..."

"One thing!"

"Morgan..."

"One thing!"

"Try to focus, bro."

"One thing!"

"Oh alright!" the traveler exclaimed. "What?!?!"

"Green women," Morgan said with a wide smile. "Are there any green women?"

"What difference does it..."

"Just answer the question!"

"Yes! As amazing as it may seem, the universe is rather replete with green women."

At this Morgan bit the first knuckle of his index finger and bounced around the room on one foot for several seconds.

"I knew it!" he exclaimed. "I mean I *knew* it! That's why I never had a girlfriend. Fate was saving me for this!"

"Mmmm," the traveler hummed slowly, nodding his head and staring at his companion through squinting eyes. "I'm not sure that's exactly what it was there, Morgan. It could have more to do with the neck beard and the fact that you're wearing socks and sandals, in spite of the fact that it's October..."

"Whatever!" Morgan said, dropping back into his seat. "You just get me to the green women and stand back, bro."

"Mmmm," Robert replied, nodding once again. "I get the feeling this is going to be an interesting trip..."

"Where to first?" Morgan asked, spinning around to gaze at the controls in front of him.

"Good question!" the traveler said, turning his own seat. "First, we've got some prep work to do. We got to get the universe ready for you, Hoss."

"Well, I'm ready!" the young man said excitedly. "We gonna start by saving Abraham Lincoln or something?"

"No!" the traveler said, turning his seat once again toward his companion. "And, before we go any further, I need to explain about that."

"About what?"

"I never," Robert began, "and I mean *never* allow anyone to touch any history they know anything about."

"Why is that?" Morgan asked.

"OK," the traveler said. "That's a fair question. Here's the answer: have you ever heard of Hiroshima?"

"Of course," Morgan replied rolling his eyes. "Everyone has."

"Right," Robert nodded. "Well, what if I told you that the bomb was dropped because of the changes a time traveler made. Would you be willing to help me undo those changes and stop the bomb?"

"Absolutely!" the young man nodded. "I mean, think how many lives..."

"Right!" the traveler said, nodding his head slowly. "Now suppose I told you that the bomb that hit Hiroshima *didn't* go off because of changes a traveler made. Would you help me undo them?"

"*Undo them*?" Morgan asked. "As in: we change things so the bomb *does* go off."

"Exactly!"

"We couldn't..."

"Exactly, Morgan!" the traveler said, staring into the eyes of his companion. "That's what I'm telling you. I haven't come to save lives, or to rescue men, women, and children. I'm here for one reason: It's my job to save the future. I fix history, I don't judge it."

"Well, I..."

"Everybody dies, Morgan," Robert explained. "You'd been dead for thousands of years before we ever met. But people can die the way they were meant to, or the way we make them. I'm here to make sure that things happen the way they must; not the way we want them to. That's the golden rule, Morgan. It's the one absolute. We do what has to be done because we have to. That's the only way it can be."

"I see where you're coming from," Morgan replied.

"Good!" the traveler said. "That's why we're not going to be messing with Earth history much. It's also why we work with missing persons. Your fate from now on has very little to do with the time-line. Oh, and I might have been a little overly assertive... There are points in history where you can safely save all the men, women, and children. And if we run into one of those, we'll do our best."

"Sounds good," the young man smiled. "Well, if we can't go see Abe, where are we headed?"

"Like I said, we need to prep you up," Robert replied. "In order to do that, we need to go see Sister."

"Sister?" Morgan asked.

"Yep," the traveler nodded. "And you might want to hit the bathroom and, you know, shave off that neck beard."

"Nah, man," Morgan replied, shaking his head. "I'm cool."

"Suit yourself," Robert replied. "But, I've got a feeling you're going to regret that decision before the day is over. Either way, let's get going."

As he said this, he punched a number of buttons in rapid succession. The entire front of the ship became transparent as it rose slowly into the air. There, below them on the ground, Morgan could see the bear and his clone. He quickly looked away, but it was too late; that image was burned into his memory. For the rest of his life, it would flash before his eyes every time he saw a bear. As a result, he never enjoyed going to the zoo as much as he once had.

The ship rose quickly and, in a matter of moments, it was sitting in space.

"Shouldn't we be floating around?" Morgan asked.

"Gravity generator," the traveler replied. "As much sci-fi as you watched, you should know that."

"I actually figured," Morgan said with a nod. "Just wanted to make sure. So, how does this thing work? Are we just going to disappear here and reappear there?"

"Nope," Robert said, shaking his head. "We're actually going to jump into hyper-space, engage our warp engines, and head for the nearest wormhole."

"Seriously?"

"Nope," the traveler smiled. "I'm a time traveler, Morgan, not an engineer. I push the buttons and the ship goes. Now, the truth is that I *do* know a lot more about it than that, but I certainly can't explain it to you. Since this is going to take a few minutes, you may want to at least put on some other clothes. I've got a bunch of stuff in your size, from several different periods in history."

"Nah, man," Morgan replied, shaking his head. "I'm cool."

"Wow," Robert replied. "Just going to go with the: *I hate it when my schwartz gets twisted* T-shirt then? Alrighty."

"It's what's on the inside that counts," Morgan said with a knowing grin.

"Yeah," the traveler chuckled. "You keep telling yourself that. Anyway, let's see here... North Star... Second to the right... Go time!"

Suddenly, the cockpit once again became opaque as the ship jerked into motion. The view outside the windows turned jet-black and Morgan sat, gazing into the apparent nothingness ahead.

"Where did everything go?" he asked.

"Oh, it's still there," the traveler explained. "It's just that we're not. We're in what you might consider non-space or the space between space."

"What does that mean?"

"Who knows?" Robert asked. "Does it matter? We're going where we're going and we are where we are. Call it whatever you want."

"Alright," the young man nodded. "That's cool."

"You know, Morgan," the traveler said glancing at his companion, "you're actually handling this pretty well. Not everyone can go from walking around in the woods alone to being on a time machine with a guy they've never met before over the course of, like, twenty minutes without puking their guts up. Well done, man!"

"Yeah," Morgan nodded. "Well, I've already worked it all out."

"I..." Robert began. "No, actually... I don't... You've got what worked out?"

"Oh," he replied. "All this. You see, one time I was at this frat party and I noticed some guys smoking... I guess it could have been a hand rolled cigarette, but I'm thinking now that it was probably weed..."

"Okay," the traveler nodded.

"Yeah," Morgan continued, "so as I was walking through the room some of that smoke - some of that second hand smoke - got in my lungs, right?"

"Sure..."

"Well, I don't know why, but something out in the woods must have activated it. So now I'm having a *major* flashback.

"Mmmm," Robert nodded. "I do see some problems with your theory there, man. For one thing you have to have a *flash* before you can actually have a *flashback*."

"Well, of course you'd say that," the young man laughed.

"And why is that?"

"Well," Morgan explained. "You're part of the hallucination; so you have to try to convince me that it's real. It's all part of your *survivor instinct*."

"Mmmm," the traveler said again. "But, do "flashbacks" have *survivor instincts*?"

"Yeah... Actually, that is a fair point..."

"And how did you end up at a frat party?" Robert asked.

"It was a giant order," Morgan replied. "Like, three-hundred tacos or something."

"Yeah... that makes sense. You get to drive?"

"Nah," the young man said, shaking his head. "The assistant manager drove."

"Yeah... that makes sense." the traveler replied. "This is gonna take an hour or so. You hungry?"

"I could eat. You got a replicator on here or something."

"No, but I stopped at Wendy's before I picked you up. You like cheeseburgers, right?"

"Oh yeah," Morgan nodded. "No ketchup?"

"Crap!" Robert said, shaking his head. "I forgot about that. Sorry, man. You want mine? I got a chicken sandwich."

"Nah, it's cool. I can just wipe it off. Hand me a napkin. Did ya get some sodas?"

"Dude, I got a soda fountain on this bird!" the traveler smiled.

"Awesome! You got Baja Blast?" Morgan asked hopefully.

"Man!" Robert replied. "You've got a gift... I ain't got that. You want a coke?"

"Sure."

Morgan still had a fair amount of confidence in his flashback theory as he watched the traveler step from the room only to return a moment later with their drinks. After all, Robert certainly seemed more like something from a *trip* than a time traveler. At least, he did to Morgan. Of course, Morgan had never actually been on a *trip*, so he wouldn't have known.

Either way, Morgan was fairly certain that none of this was happening. For one thing, the traveler was shorter than him. Like, a lot shorter. Morgan was six-foot one, so a lot of people were shorter than him, but Robert couldn't have been more than five-foot six. People that saved the universe were usually tall in his experience; and not so common. The traveler had plain brown hair just like Morgan - he didn't even appear to have a five-hundred dollar haircut or anything.

Also, he was way too young. He couldn't have been over twenty-five by any stretch of the imagination. Unless, of course, he was one of those "ancient young guys". But, who could tell? And even though he was well-enough-dressed, the traveler's choice of sneakers, blue jeans, and a Lynyrd Skynyrd T-shirt weren't likely to get him on the cover of GQ. He just didn't have the fashion sense of a super hero. All things considered, he seemed a very unlikely guy to be charged with saving all of everything.

For close to an hour, they sat at the controls discussing music, movies, and television. Morgan would have asked more questions but, as none of it was happening anyway, there didn't seem to be much point. Finally, Robert glanced up at one of the monitors before pressing another series of buttons.

The ship quickly dropped back into normal space.

"Well, Morgan," the traveler said, smiling over at his companion, "welcome to Never Never Land."

The view that met the young man's eyes was an odd one to behold. Directly ahead of them was a massive star ship (or so Morgan supposed) floating above what appeared to be a section of ocean adrift in space. In the middle of this ocean was a large tropical island. A small sun hovered over the scene, flooding it with light; while a number of smaller craft seemed to be making their way to and from the star ship as well as the island.

"So, where is this?" Morgan asked after a brief silence.

"Nowhere, Morgan," the traveler replied. "Nowhere, no time. To the best of my knowledge, it's the only place like it in the universe."

"If there's no time, how is anything happening?"

"Wow!" Robert smiled. "Another great question. Time generators, my friend. They work just like the gravity generators. Well... no they don't, but I'm not going to be able to explain either of those to you."

"How did time generators get here?"

"This is our *base*, Morgan," the traveler explained. "We built this place very near the end. We could see it coming, but we couldn't stop it. We built Never Never Land so we could survive until everything could be fixed."

"So... Is this the "real" Never Never Land?"

"It's the *only* Never Never Land," Robert replied. "Anyway, I'm requesting permission to go straight to induction. We don't have time to play around, and I don't want to end up in a thousand conversations."

"Why would you end up in a thousand conversations?" Morgan asked.

"I'm not surprised you don't know," the traveler nodded. "You see, Morgan, I'm popular. Like, *super* popular. Hardly shocking, what with me being the potential "savior of the universe" and all. Don't worry though, if we manage to succeed, some of my popularity may just rub off on you. Who knows? You might even get a date. I mean, after you lose the sock-sandals, obviously. Either way, we've got clearance."

"What's *induction*?"

"It's where we take new missing persons who are about to go into active rotation," Robert replied. "Like I said, we've got to get you prepped. Oh, and last chance: I'll give you ten minutes to shave and change clothes."

"Nah, man," Morgan replied, shaking his head. "I'm cool."

"Suit yourself."

Minutes later, Robert docked his ship in the small landing bay used by induction. The pair stepped down the gangway before heading directly toward the nearest door. Everything looked very much like Morgan had expected. The place was remarkably well lit, immaculately clean, and simply brimming over with science. As soon as the door opened, the young man's eyes fell on an unexpected sight.

Standing in the middle of the room was, perhaps, the most beautiful woman Morgan had ever seen. She was completely green, with bright blue eyes and lips. Raven black hair ran down her back, almost reaching the floor, and her figure made the young man's heart skip several beats. She looked to be somewhere between thirty and forty and, if Morgan had thought that he had any chance at all, he would have asked her to marry him right then and there.

The traveler said something to her in an unknown language and she responded in kind, turning a wide smile to him as she spoke. Morgan started to pass out, but bit down on his index knuckle until the pain kept him conscious.

"I believe!" he exclaimed, his voice filled with passion. "This is all real! It's all happening! And she's *green*!"

"She also speaks archaic English, Mr. Sock-sandals," the woman replied, shooting a glance at the young man.

"I warned you," the traveler whispered before stepping boldly up to the woman. "You can't blame the kid, Sister. You know the effect you green women have on all us mere mortal males."

"Not all," she laughed.

"On me," he said with a wink.

"Liar."

"Sometimes, love, but never to you."

"Liar."

"True."

"What do you want, Rob?"

"Oh, I think you know what I want," he grinned.

"Rob..."

"Right, right," he sighed. "I need Morgan here programmed for Common."

"Anything else?" she asked, gazing at the young man as she spoke.

"Nope," the traveler replied. "Not at the moment."

"You know best, I guess," she smiled. "Hook him up, if you would."

"Sure thing," Robert replied. "Morgan, take a seat in that chair."

The young man obeyed and the traveler pulled a metal ring down from above him and slipped it around Morgan's head. He then took a pair of glass lenses, held in a thin wire frame, and lined them up perfectly with Morgan's eyes.

"Let's see what we have here," Sister said, punching a few buttons on a nearby panel. "Hmmm... That's a mistake. Hold still, sock-sandals..."

15

"My name's Morgan."

"Alright," she replied with a smile. "Then hold still, Morgan."

Again, she pressed a series of buttons.

"Something's wrong, Rob," she said. "We're going to have to recalibrate this machine."

"Nah," the traveler said, shaking his head. "It's fine."

"What is it?" Morgan asked, leaning forward and attempting to see the screen they were looking at.

"Whoa! Don't move!" Robert exclaimed. "That thing can fry your brain!"

"Seriously?!?!"

"Nah," the traveler laughed. "I just like messing with ya. Anyway, this wouldn't mean anything to you. Just sit back and let us handle it."

"But honestly, Rob, that can't be right," she insisted.

"It is," he nodded. "Can we clean out some more space; maybe erase some of his memories?"

"You want to what?" Morgan said.

"*More* space?!?!" Sister replied at the same instant.

"Yeah," the traveler said. "I want just a tad more space. Can we wipe out the memories of like every time he wanted to talk to a girl, but was scared to? You don't want those memories, do you?"

"I want all my memories!"

"Up to you, I guess," Robert replied. "Can we back 'em up, Sister? Then we can put 'em back after the mission."

"I guess so..."

"Is that OK with you, Morgan?"

"I guess," he sighed.

"Alright," she said, shaking her head before rapidly pressing buttons. "There. It's done."

"Can you speak common?" Robert asked, turning his gaze to Morgan.

"Nope," he replied in common.

"Awesome," the traveler smiled.

"So, I do speak common?" Morgan asked, stunned at his own cognizance of the tongue.

"You do now," Robert nodded. "Thanks, Sister."

"Anytime, Rob," she replied. "You need anything else?"

"I think you know what I need," he grinned.

"Rob..."

"Right, right," Robert replied. "I need Cleo."

"No way, Rob," she said, shaking her head. "Sorry, not this time."

"I have to have her, Sister."

"You can't, Rob. She's taken herself out of rotation. That's it for now. You know the law."

"*The law*," he laughed. "What does that even mean?"

"I think it has something to do with *the prison*, Rob. I'm serious, she doesn't want to see you. She's gone back home."

"Mmmm," he said slowly. "That is bad... *back home*... Ouch..."

"You left her on the island for a *year*, Rob. What did you expect?"

"That wasn't my fault!" the traveler exclaimed. "I got back as fast as I could."

"Don't tell me, love, tell her," Sister replied, shaking her head.

"You're right," he sighed. "Just tell me where and when she is so I can."

"No way!"

"Sister, the fate of the universe is on the line."

"Then make an application," she replied.

"I don't have time," he insisted. "Seriously, just one more bend of the rules. She won't complain. She won't say anything, trust me. You know, as well as I do, that she wants me to come get her."

"Rob..."

"You know it," he said, gazing directly into her eyes with a smile on his face. "She was mad. She's over it by now. Don't do it for me, do it for Cleo."

"This has got to be the last time, Rob," Sister sighed.

"Absolutely!" he said, placing one hand over his heart and raising the other.

"I'll send the coordinates to your ship."

"Thanks, Sis," the traveler replied, leaning over and kissing her on the cheek. "I owe you one."

"You owe me a lot more than that," she said, a trace of a smile on her lips. "And, Rob, be careful."

"Always, love, always," he replied, helping Morgan to his feet.

"And Morgan," she said, turning her gaze to the young man, "lose the neck-beard."

"One last thing," Robert said as they were headed for the door. "How long has she been there?"

"Two years now," Sister replied.

"Wow!" he exclaimed. "Where was I?"

"If you don't know, I can't tell you."

"Two years... geez..."

"That's bad?" Morgan asked as they stepped back in the docking bay.

"Yeah, Morgan," Robert nodded. "That's *real* bad."

CHAPTER 2: CLEO

"How's this?" Morgan asked, leaning his head back.

"No neck beard," the traveler nodded. "It's a start. And you grabbed a pair of sneakers. You're certainly heading in the right direction."

"How much longer before we get there?"

"About ten minutes or so," Robert replied.

"How long will it have been for her?" The young man asked.

"I plan to give her about fifteen minutes," the traveler said. "That'll have given her a little time to cool off. You can be sure she was getting more and more angry the entire trip back. Fifteen minutes is, like, the minimum *safety* window. It's kind of the ideal time. Any sooner, and she'll scratch my eyes out; any later, and she's going to want to know where I was."

"You think she's expecting you?"

"No," Robert replied with a smile. "That would imply that she didn't know. But she does. She *knows* I'm coming for her. She only left to make a point."

"Sister said she'd been gone two years," Morgan pointed out.

"Yeah," the traveler nodded. "But we're going to fix that. When we're done, she'll have only been gone fifteen minutes."

"Will she know?"

"Only if she figures it out."

"Will she?"

"Yep," Robert sighed. "Now hold on for a sec. We gotta land."

The ship entered real space above a beautiful ocean planet dotted with countless islands. The entire world seemed like a tropical paradise and the color of the water ranged from aquamarine to deep sea green. Once again the cockpit became transparent as they descended into the atmosphere. They made their way to a small isle surrounded by hundreds of miles of empty ocean before touching down on its tree covered surface.

"You might want to stay here," the traveler said. "This may not be pretty."

"Nah, man," Morgan replied. "I got your back."

"Cool."

Side by side, the pair strode down the gangway and stepped out onto the verdant soil that made up the island. In the distance, on the beach, a single figure sat; back turned, head down, arms wrapped around her knees. The last time traveler marched forward with complete confidence.

"Hey Cleo," he said as soon as they were in speaking distance. "Long time no see, sweets."

In response, the figure reached up, quickly rubbing one cheek and then the other with their hand.

"How long?" she asked.

"Like, maybe fifteen minutes," Robert chuckled.

"No," Cleo said, turning to glare at him. "I mean how long was I *really* here before you showed up?"

The moment her face entered his view, Morgan's heart stopped. Until he had seen this woman, he'd thought Sister was as beautiful as a woman could be. Now, however, he realized that poor Sister was past her prime. This woman certainly wasn't.

Her features seemed fragile and almost unreal, as if she were a perfect porcelain doll. Her large eyes were a bright violet and her jet-black hair was pulled back in a ponytail that hung down to the middle of her shoulders. Her skin, which was also green, was a slightly darker shade than Sister's had been. And her lips were also a darker, and somehow more living, blue. The young man hoped that this *was* as beautiful as women could get, because any more than this would kill him. As it were, he wished they had brought a portable defibrillator, just in case.

At the moment, she was wearing long pants and a long sleeve shirt. He wondered if she had tans lines or not, but was afraid that finding out might cost him his life. Under the circumstances, it was hardly surprising that he lost control of his mouth.

"*Another one*," he said, straining as if he were about to burst a blood vessel.

"Another what?" she asked, turning her gaze to the now neck-beardless young man.

"Ponytail!" the traveler instantly replied. "Another ponytail. It's the second one he's seen today. They were *very* rare in human culture and he's just a little overawed."

"I know all about human culture, Rob," she said, glaring at him once again.

"Oh, yeah..."

"She's *green*!" Morgan interjected excitedly.

"Rob, who is he?" she asked. "And what's his problem?"

"He's the new guy," Robert replied. "He's just excited to be here. You'll like him once you get to know him. He's like a laugh a minute."

"I'm not going to get to know him," she said. "Because I'm not going with you this time!"

"You have to come with me," Robert pleaded, pulling the young woman to her feet. "I *need* you, Cleo!"

"You don't mean it, Rob!" she replied, tears welling up in her eyes. "You never mean anything you say!"

"I do," he said, taking her by the chin and turning her face to his. "I meant *everything* I've ever said to you."

"How long, Rob," she replied. "How long did you wait before you came to get me? And keep in mind that I'm going to ask Sister!"

"Two years," he confessed.

"Two years!" she screamed. "Rob, you filthy..."

"Excuse me," Morgan interjected, his eyes locked on Cleo. "If I could be allowed to interrupt for just a moment. I'd just like to say that you are the most beautiful creature I've ever seen. You are *at least* ten or fifteen times hotter than all of my wildest fantasies."

"Thank you, Morgan," the traveler replied, shaking his head. "That's really helped a lot, man. I had no idea that losing the sock-sandals would so increase your confidence level."

"Either way," Cleo said, turning her gaze back to Robert. "You left me here for two years *after* you left me on *the island* for a year!"

"The first year totally wasn't my fault!" he explained. "You can ask Vox!"

"What's the point in asking Vox?" she replied, putting her hands on her hips. "He agrees with everything you say!"

"That's not true!" Robert asserted. "You know he would *never* tell you a bald-faced lie."

"No! I agree with you there," Cleo replied. "That's one *real* difference between the two of you!"

"Wow..." he said. "I should have thought that out better."

"You should have thought a lot out better," she said, shaking her head. "But, it's too late now, Rob. I'm not going with you. Not this time. Not again."

"Cleo," he said, taking up one her hands. "You have to. We need you. I *need* you."

"He's right!" Morgan exclaimed. "We really do need you."

She glared at the young man silently for a moment.

"If I did come with you," she said, her voice filled with venom, "I'd want a lock on my door!"

"Whoa!" Morgan yelled. "Whoa! I find that *highly* offensive! You don't know me, lady! I was just trying to be nice! I mean, yeah! Okay! You're fine! You're real fine! But, I don't have to take crap like that from you! The universe is - what word did you use, Rob? Replete? - replete with green women! I don't need ya, honey!"

"*Replete with green women*," she said, turning to Robert with fire in her eyes.

"That's been taken *way* out of context!" he explained.

"Oh, I'm sure!" she yelled. "Either way, I'm not going anywhere with the two of you!"

"Cleo..."

"No!" Morgan interrupted. "Let her go, man! Who needs her?"

"We need her!"

"No!" Morgan yelled again. "There is no way I'm going to be on the same ship with a... a... a green woman like that! It's me or her, man! Take your pick. You want to take her, that's fine by me. I'll stay here and live out the rest of my missing personhood on this island. I ain't gonna have a problem with it. I've watched I don't know how many survival videos on *YouTube*!"

"Look Morgan," the traveler said, pointing at Cleo as he spoke. "Before you make up your mind, there's something I want you to think about: this is, like, the most clothes I've ever seen her wear. She must have been about to freeze to death right before she got here."

"Whoa!" Cleo yelled. "Now *I* find that offensive! You think I'm going to..."

"It was a joke!" Robert interrupted. "I was just joking! I was trying to lighten the mood. You two have gotten way too serious!"

"Forget it, Rob," she said. "It's not working this time. You had three years to make it right. You didn't."

"Cleo," he sighed. "It's only been a year and fifteen minutes. Well... and your trip time which was probably what? Four hours, maybe?"

"That's not how it works, Rob," she replied, tears once more in her eyes. "You left me here, alone, for two years. Then you flew back in your magnificent time machine to make it all right. That doesn't change the fact that you deserted me."

"Not to be argumentative," he said, "but it does. That's *exactly* what it does. I wouldn't have left you hanging if I hadn't been able to fix it all."

"And what about the year on *the island*, Rob?" she replied.

"I'm sorry," he said. "I really am. And I'll explain after we pick up Vox. That way you'll know I'm not stretching the truth even a little. I really am sorry, Cleo. I would *never* do anything to hurt you on purpose."

"Close, Rob," she laughed. "Really close. But, not this time."

"Okay," he sighed. "I didn't want to do it like this, but you've left me no choice."

Having said this, he dropped to his knees on the sand and took both of her hands in his. He stared up into her face, the sunlight sparkling in his bright green eyes, the warm tropical breeze blowing around them.

"Cleo," he said, pausing dramatically for a moment before continuing, "would you please just get on the ship so we can get out of here?"

"Rob," she replied, gazing down at him. "Sometimes, I could just scratch your eyes out."

"What if I buy you Krispy Kreme?"

"Bear claws?"

"Absolutely," he smiled. "A whole box. No, two boxes. We should *live* a little."

"Starbucks?"

"Pumpkin Spice Latte," he replied. "It was even October the last time I was on Earth."

"This has got to be the last time, Rob," she smiled. "If you ever do this to me again, don't come get me. Because, if you do, I'll kill you in your sleep the first chance I get. I can't take any more of this."

"I don't blame you," he replied, leaping to his feet before bending down to kiss her on the forehead. "I'd do the same if I were you."

"I'm glad you understand," she said softly.

The trio quickly made their way back to the ship and prepared for lift off. Having had a few minutes to cool off Cleo decided to extend the olive branch to Morgan - who would, after all, be one of her traveling companions.

"I'm sorry about that *lock* comment," she said, smiling at the young man. "I was just so mad at Rob that you're supporting him in any way made me want to kill you, burn your body, and dance around on your ashes. I'm sure you understand."

"Certainly," he chuckled. "And, I'm sorry about the staring, and the drooling, and I'm *really* sorry for some of the things I was thinking back there on the beach. Can you forgive me?"

"Sure..."

"Maybe we should have, like, a friendly makeup hug."

"No," she said. "No, I think it'd be better if we didn't. In fact, honestly Morgan, I think we need to keep a really friendly six foot distance between us, if you see what I mean. Good fences make good neighbors."

"I see where you're coming from," he smiled.

"I'm so glad."

"I do have a question, Rob," Morgan said.

"Who said you could call me that?"

"But I already..."

"I know," the traveler laughed. "I'm just messing with ya. What would you like to know?"

"Well," the young man said. "If you're *the last time traveler*, how did Cleo end up in the past without you?"

"He's not *the last time traveler*," Cleo laughed. "He just likes to tell people that."

"No!" the traveler replied. "That is *not* true! I am *the last time traveler*."

"And, he's very sensitive about his title," she giggled.

"Don't do that," Morgan said, gazing at Cleo.

"Don't do what?" she asked.

"Don't giggle like that," he replied, clutching his chest. "You're going to give me a heart-attack?"

"Does it scare you?" she asked, one eyebrow raised.

"No..." he replied, shaking his head. "No, it doesn't... Anyway, he's not *the last time traveler*?"

"Yes I am!"

"No, you're not," she said, stifling another giggle.

"Look," he said, obviously agitated. "An automated delivery pod that is *only* used for insertions and removals is *not* a time traveler."

"Do they travel in time?" she asked playfully.

"Yes," he sighed. "But they don't count."

"Why not?" Morgan asked.

"They can't affect the time-lines," Robert explained. "I mean, you might as well call commercial airliners time travelers. They take people to a certain place at a certain time just like the delivery pods do."

"But commercial airliners can't travel through time," the young man pointed out.

"No," the traveler admitted. "But the point is that they *can't* effect time. A pod brought Cleo to this island because, no matter what happened to her here, it couldn't change the time-lines. She would simply have gone back to being a missing person. That's not what I'm going to do. I'm going to fix things."

"Going to?" Morgan asked.

"Well, yeah," Robert replied. "We haven't actually done a job yet. Up to this point, it's all been prep work. Just think about that, Morgan. You're on the ground floor of this one, man!"

"That's good, I guess," he smiled. "One more question."

"Shoot."

"Why couldn't you just go back in time and pick Cleo up on *the island* without her having to wait a year? And what is *the island*, anyway?

"Yeah, Rob!" Cleo said, her voice filled with emotion. "Why don't you explain that to him?!?!"

"Thank you, Morgan!" the traveler replied, his own voice edged with excited agitation. "How in all the universe could I have *possibly* forgotten to bring that up again?!?! Especially so soon?!?!"

"Just answer him," she barked.

"Right," he sighed. "You see, Morgan, *The Island* is... well... the island... the one in Never Never Land. It's were all the survivors live. And it's a *really* nice place! I mean, you've got super high-speed internet, twenty-four hour shopping, an almost endless number of five-star restaurants, a huge ice-skating rink, amateur theater, year-round ladies' beach volleyball, and countless other entertainments. So, really, some might say that being abandoned on it really wouldn't be..."

"Just get on with it, Rob," she said, tilting her head to the side as she spoke.

"Don't do that," Morgan insisted.

"Don't do what?" she asked.

"Don't tilt your head like that," he replied clearing his throat. "You're going to give me an aneurysm."

"You have a lot of medical problems..."

"I didn't until recently."

"Right..." she replied rolling her eyes. "Either way, explain it, Rob."

"Okay," he continued. "Like I told you before, Never Never Land is *nowhere* in *no time*. So, whenever you get there it's *always* the same time; it's no time at all. However, the time generators create a bubble of fluid time around everything. And that time passes in its own stream. So, even though I got back as quickly as I *possibly* could - in spite of countless hardships, and dangers, and asteroids, and pirates, and giant blood-sucking space-bats -"

"Rob!"

"Right! Anyway, a year had passed for Cleo -"

"Yes!" she replied, glaring at the traveler. "A *year* had passed for me, Rob. A year, all alone on the island..."

"There are millions of people on the island," he interrupted.

"You *know* what I mean!"

"Kidding..."

"Well, don't" she replied, raising her voice slightly. "It's nothing to joke about. I wasted a year of my life waiting for you!"

"I'll give it back to you," he smiled.

"You can't."

"Sure I can," he chuckled. "You hop in the regenerator, I'll make you a year younger."

"I'm not worried about my age, Rob."

"Okay," he shrugged. "Two years younger."

"That's not the point," she said, shaking her head. "I'll still have the memories."

"You don't have to," he pointed out.

"You see, Rob, that right there's your problem," she said, gazing into his eyes. "You just don't get it. I don't want to be abandoned for a year and then have you come do some patch up job because, suddenly, you want me for something. You *never* think about the consequences; you just do things and then *fix* it all later using a time machine, or a regenerator, or a brain scanner..."

"It's better to beg forgiveness than ask permission," he grinned.

"No, Rob," she sighed. "It isn't..."

"So, you don't want me to make you a couple years younger?" he asked.

"Well," she replied, the trace of a smile on her soft blue lips, "I suppose that wouldn't hurt."

"Perfect," he nodded. "We'll take care of that in no time. So, am I forgiven?"

"No!" she exclaimed, before softening her tone. "But, you're heading in the right direction."

"So, you can make people younger?" Morgan asked.

"Oh yeah," the traveler replied with a smile. "No problem. Either way, Cleo, you want to get Vox or Krispy Kreme first?"

"Krispy Kreme," she replied thoughtfully. "Let's surprise him."

"Good idea!" he agreed, before pressing a sequence of buttons.

The ship quickly lifted off and made its way back into orbit. Seconds later, they were in the complete blackness of non-space.

"Oh, and one thing before we regenerate you, love," Robert said, turning his eyes to Cleo.

"Don't call me that," she sighed. "Not for while at least..."

"No problem, Cleo," he smiled. "Could you put yourself back in active rotation and contact Sister to let her know that you're not pressing charges?"

"*Pressing charges*," she repeated wistfully, "what a beautiful phrase... Oh well, maybe one day... Sure, Rob, I'll let her know."

"Thanks!" he said, rising from his seat. "Come on, Morgan. We'll prep the regenerator while she handles that."

The pair quickly made their way to what Morgan assumed was the medi-bay. At least that's what it looked like to him. There were a couple of tables, plenty of light, a tank just the right size to hold another naked floating clone body, and numerous instruments that might be used for various kinds of probing.

The traveler stepped over to something that looked almost like a large *future coffin* and began pushing buttons on its cover.

"So, this is the regenerator?" Morgan asked.

"Yep."

"And, it can make anyone young again?"

"Yep," Robert replied.

"And, it does that by regenerating whoever it is?"

"Yep."

"Doesn't that make them like addicted and power mad after a few uses?" the young man asked.

"Nope," the traveler shook his head. "This is reality, Morgan, not an episode of *Stargate SG-1*."

"Right..."

"Are you ready for me?" Cleo asked, stepping lightly into the room.

"Always," Robert smiled, holding his hand out to the young lady.

The lid of the regenerator opened, releasing plumes of white gas that Morgan felt were very sci-fi looking. Cleo took the traveler's hand before stepping into the chamber and lying down. Robert pushed a few buttons and the container sealed itself before a gentle hum filled the air.

"Okay," Morgan began, "So, when Cleo gets out of this thing, she's going to be two years younger?"

"Yep."

"Do you have a defibrillator in here?" the young man asked.

"Yes. Why?"

"How long is the regenerator going to take?"

"Like, five minutes. Why?"

"Could I hold the defibrillator for a minute?"

"I guess," the traveler shrugged, before stepping over to the wall and pushing a button.

A drawer opened, from which Robert drew a small case. He opened it on one of the tables and turned to Morgan.

"There it is," he said, waving his hand at the open box.

"Alright," Morgan replied, looking down at the device. "So, I guess I would put one of these pads on each side of my chest?"

"The patient's chest, yes," the traveler nodded. "You want them kind of on each side of the heart. And they're self-adhesive, so you just stick 'em on there."

"Kind of like this," the young man replied, putting one and then the other of the pads under his shirt.

"Sure... I guess... I mean, if you were going to defibrillate yourself..."

"And, I guess this button..." Morgan began, taking up the small cylinder in the case and jamming his thumb down on it. "Ahhh!!!!"

The young man collapsed on the floor, writhing in pain.

"You know, Morgan," Robert laughed, "I am seriously glad I picked you, man."

"Right," Morgan replied, climbing slowly to his feet and gazing down at the regenerator. "Now, I'm ready. How much longer?"

"Seconds."

The lid of the chamber slid back, releasing even more clouds of the white vapor. Cleo sat up, immediately taking the traveler's outstretched hand and climbing from the device. The result wasn't what Morgan had expected at all. Oh, she was still the most beautiful woman he had ever seen. There was no doubt about that. But, she simply wasn't what she had been five minutes before. It seemed that the next two years were going to be really good to her. He just hoped he'd be around to see her blossom into her former glory.

Robert headed back to the bridge while Cleo made her way to her room to get a change of clothes. For his part, Morgan carefully put the defibrillator away. As he strolled back toward the bridge, he heard rather unusual singing.

"*With a rebel yell she cried more bear claa-aa-aaws!*" Robert sang forcefully as Morgan dropped back in his seat.

"You know sometimes, Rob," Morgan said, "I think you're not altogether normal."

"That's good of you to say," he smiled.

Morgan just nodded and stared into the nothingness outside the ship.

"You seem pensive," the traveler chuckled. "What's up?"

"It's Cleo," the young man sighed. "The whole regeneration thing... It didn't go exactly how I thought it would. I mean, she's still so hot I feel like my eyes are going to burst into flames every time I look at her; but she's not as hot as she was. You know what I mean?"

"Oh, I agree," Robert replied with a knowing grin. "I just like watching her grow into that *super-ultra-mega hot* again and again."

"I see where you're coming from," Morgan nodded slowly.

"Oh, and while we're talking about it," the traveler said, turning to look at the young man. "I just want to make sure you know the score. Cleo is *spoken for* - if you follow me."

"Spoken for by who?"

"Don't worry about that," Robert grinned. "It's a guy you can't complete with."

"We'll see about that," Morgan replied, puffing ou

"You can try," the traveler chuckled. "But trust m won't get anywhere. You'll just end up with your eyes scratched

"Maybe..."

Right after they finished this short discussion, Cleo stepped back onto the bridge. She had changed from her long sleeve shirt into a camisole, but had covered that with a black leather jacket. In Morgan's humble opinion, she was even *more dressed* than she had been when they picked her up.

For the next couple of hours, the trio talked about this and that and nothing-in-particular. Finally, they emerged from non-space above Earth on October 31st, 2017. The traveler had carefully selected the date as it would make their current quest much simpler. As soon as they arrived, he leapt from his seat and marched off the bridge.

"Where's he going?" Morgan asked.

"No idea," Cleo said, throwing her hands in the air. "But, he usually has a plan."

Minutes later, Robert stepped back into the room dressed entirely in black and wearing a long black overcoat and dark sunglasses.

"Call me *Neo*," he smiled.

"What?" both Morgan and Cleo asked.

"It's Halloween," he explained. "This way Cleo doesn't have to wear a holo-emitter or anything."

"Good idea," the young man agreed. "Where's my costume?"

"Oh yeah, here," the traveler said, throwing Morgan a rainbow colored clown wig.

"I'm not wearing that," he replied, tossing it back to Robert.

"Well, the only other costumes I have are Trinity and the cowardly lion," he explained. "Which one do you want?"

"Hand me the wig..."

"So, what am I supposed to be?" Cleo asked.

"Well," the traveler said, stepping over to her seat and pulling her up to his chest. "If anyone asks, just tell them you're my *Orion love slave*."

"I have to admit it," she said, rolling her eyes. "You dream big."

"You know those tiny points on your ears kind of make you look like a little devil."

"If there's a devil around here, Rob, it's you."

"You might be right," he winked. "Let's go."

"Where have we landed?" Morgan asked.

"Winston-Salem, North Carolina, man," the traveler smiled. "Where it all began. If you're going to go, go first class."

The trio made their way out of the ship and headed for the nearest road. The traveler had landed in one of the city's parks and he hoped to catch a cab fairly quickly.

"So this is what the future's like," Morgan said, looking around with a contented sigh.

"Well, yeah," Robert replied. "But I picked you up on the 6th and it's only the 31st."

"Right," Morgan nodded, "But, that means we're twenty-five days *into the future*."

"I guess that's true," the traveler laughed. "You know, you really are a lot of fun to run around with."

"Thanks!"

The group had only been walking along the road for perhaps five minutes when a passing cab slammed on the brakes before backing up so the driver could speak to them.

"I don't know who did you're makeup, ma'am," he said, staring at Cleo, "but that's the best costume I've ever seen. Y'all need a lift?"

"Sure enough," the traveler nodded, stepping over to open the door. "Hop in, Cleo."

Robert helped her into the cab and then climbed into the middle seat, Morgan following right behind him.

"Where y'all headed?" the cabby asked.

"The nearest Krispy Kreme," Robert replied. "And then the nearest Starbucks."

"Y'all going to a party or something?" he asked.

"Something like that," the traveler smiled.

"Well, buckle up and we'll get rollin'."

Each of the trio fastened their belts and the taxi pulled off, heading into the city.

"I get *The Matrix* and I guess I get the clown wig, but what are you supposed to be, ma'am?"

Cleo sighed before saying, "I'm his *Orion love slave*."

"Lucky him," the cabby laughed. "But, exactly what is that?"

"It's a *Star Trek* thing," Morgan replied.

"Yeah," the man nodded. "That makes sense. We got a lot of *Trekkies* around here."

"Well, she's the *Trekkiest*," Robert grinned. "I can't keep her out of conventions."

"Really?" the cabby said. "I've never been to one. But I think I might have to check out the next one that's around here."

"You might find it worth your time," the traveler chuckled.

Over the course of the next forty-five minutes, they bought three boxes of bear claws (Robert decided to *really* live it up) and various other donuts and donut-related products, as well as a couple of trays full of Pumpkin Spice Lattes. With these comestibles in hand, they had the cabby take them back to the park.

"Let's see," the man said, "According to the meter..."

"Here," the traveler interrupted, handing the man a bill.

"Alright," he replied. "Out of a hundred..."

"Eh, keep the change," Robert said.

"Thanks, man!" he smiled. "Much appreciated!"

The trio left the taxi behind them as they made their way back into the park and then into the ship. Next stop: pick up Vox. As they sat eating bear claws and drinking coffee, another thought occurred to Morgan.

"A thought just occurred to me," Morgan said.

"That's remarkable!" the traveler replied. "What is it?"

"Well," the young man said. "I mean, I like bear claws, and coffee, and counterfeit money as much as the next guy - maybe even more - but aren't we junking up the time-lines when we do stuff like this?"

"I never said it was counterfeit," Robert replied. "And, in all honesty, Morgan, the time-lines have a certain amount of flex to them."

"Like underwear elastic?"

"Sure... I guess," Robert chuckled. "That's what I love about you, Morgan. You say that to a thousand people and not one of them is going to say *underwear elastic*. They say rubber-band or springs or even Glad trash bags maybe; but not you, man. I'm surprised you didn't say: *like garter belts*."

"Well, actually..."

"Never mind," Cleo interrupted. "How long before we reach Vox?"

"About an hour and a half," the traveler replied.

"Alright," she smiled. "I'm going to take a nap. Wake me when we get there."

"Gladly!" Morgan exclaimed.

"With the call button," she replied, rolling her eyes, before stepping briskly out of the room.

"She's something, isn't she," Morgan observed.

"Morgan, my boy," the traveler replied, "she's a lot more than that."

CHAPTER 3: VOX & THE DOC

"Wake up time," Robert said, pushing a button on the panel in front of him.

"We've still got about half an hour to go," Morgan observed.

"Well done!" the traveler exclaimed. "You managed to read the monitor."

"Well, yeah," the young man replied. "But, it's just the trip timer you set..."

"True," Robert nodded. "But, you have to start somewhere."

"Either way, we've still got half an hour."

"Yeah," the traveler said. "But, Cleo's gonna want to brush her teeth after she wakes up. And she'll probably want to grab a shower, too."

The next thing Morgan remembered was Robert shaking him vigorously by the shoulders.

"You in there, man?" he asked, gently slapping him on the face. "You alright?"

"Yeah," he replied with a start. "Yeah, I'm fine."

"We were talking and, all the sudden, you just got this vacant expression on your face."

"I think I was having a waking dream..."

"Weird," Robert replied. "You get 'em often?"

"I don't think I've ever had one before..."

"You probably just need some sleep," the traveler suggested. "After all, it would be... around eight... your time. That's not that late... What time do you normally go to bed?"

"Around eleven, I guess..."

"Hmmm... Probably just the stress of time travel."

"Must be, I guess."

A few minutes later, Cleo stepped into the cockpit wearing high heels, black stockings, a black leather mini-skirt, a fresh gray camisole, and her leather jacket. She also happened to be vigorously rubbing her head with a towel at that moment.

"What's with him?" she asked, carefully considering Morgan's slack jawed grin.

"Crap!" Robert replied, once again shaking the young man. "This is the second time this has happened in, like, twenty minutes. You think he's hypoglycemic?"

"Filled with bear claws and Pumpkin Spice Latte?" she replied. "I don't think it's low blood sugar."

"Man..." the traveler replied. "You don't think we've put him into a diabetic coma do you? I mean he ate, like, five of those things..."

"I doubt it," she giggled. "I ate three and I'm fine."

"I just didn't think to check if he was diabetic... Of course, I guess it could be because of that defibrillator..."

"What?"

"Nothing..."

"Whoa!" Morgan said with a start. "Where are we?"

"You alright?" Cleo asked, gazing down at him with a smile.

"Oh, yea," he nodded. "I'm just dandy."

"Good," Robert replied, returning to his seat. "We're almost there. Fortunately, this shouldn't take long. When we get back to the ship, I want you to head to your room. You need to get some sleep."

"Boy, do I!" Morgan nodded. "I *seriously* have some dreams to finish!"

"Right..." the traveler replied. "Now, I need to warn you: Vox is *not* a missing person. He just happens to be one of the best mechanics and technicians that *ever* lived. So, when we pick him up, we'll be surrounded by all kinds of things that could potentially change the time-lines. We have to grab him without causing any car wrecks or anything like that."

"You didn't seem overly concerned when it was Krispy Kreme time," Morgan observed.

"Well, no," the time traveler admitted. "But, that was kind of a one off. I never get donuts from the same place twice. However, I end up at Vox's place a *lot*. So, we just have to be careful. Of course, we still have the *underwear elastic factor* working for us. Anyway, we just need to be careful. That's all I'm saying."

As he finished speaking, the ship dropped into real-space above a very Earth-like planet.

"What's this world called?" Morgan asked.

"What difference does it make?" Robert replied. "It's where Vox lives at the moment. That's all that matters."

"I just want to know."

"What if I told you it were called Duck à l'orange?" the traveler asked. "Would it matter?"

"No," the young man admitted. "But, I think it's cool to know. Duck à l'orange... Duck à l'orange … It seems vaguely familiar and yet, at the same time, it's so completely alien..."

"You were right," Cleo laughed. "I think I am starting to like him."

"I told ya," Robert said, smiling at her. "He's a riot."

Minutes later, the ship landed a short distance from Vox's house. In order to lessen the chance of discovery, the traveler had them exit the ship by way of the loading platform.

"The thing I like about this," Robert said, carefully scanning the scene, "is that we can see out, but they can't see in."

"Well don't we need disguises or something?" Morgan asked.

"It's amazing how smart you can be," the traveler mused. "And, how dumb... Anyway, good question. No. No, we don't. At this place and time, interstellar travel is pretty common. Even rare aliens like humans don't attract much attention. Let's go."

As he said this, he stepped quickly from the loading platform, crossed the street, and made his way toward a large house that seemed much like the others that surrounded it.

"This doesn't look very *futury*," Morgan observed.

"No, it doesn't," Robert agreed. "This is what's called a *retro suburb*. That's another thing about Vox: the man's got money. Anyway, be quiet for a minute."

The trio walked up the driveway until the traveler was standing beside what seemed to be a rather ordinary, and definitely large, car.

"Vox, man," Robert said. "You still under there?"

"Uuuuhhh," a voice replied from under the car. "Rob, you have got to be kidding me... It's been, like, fifteen minutes, man..."

"No it hasn't," he replied, glancing down at his watch. "It's been like twen... No, you're right, actually, it's been exactly fifteen minutes..."

"I know I'm right," the voice chuckled. "And you said you'd give me at least a week to get this thing running."

"I know that's what I said," Robert agreed. "But, we don't have time."

"You have all the time there is."

"Yeah, but you don't," the traveler replied. "You get to live in a real time-line, but it comes at a price, Vox. You ain't getting any younger, man."

"You're not kidding," Vox replied, sliding his head out from under the vehicle. "Oh, hey small-girl!"

Several things struck Morgan about Vox all at once. His skin was raven black, while his short facial hair was snow white. His head seemed extraordinarily large, and his eyes - which matched his skull for size - were a very unique kind of milky blue. In point of fact, as he stared up from under the car, they looked like a pair of giant star sapphires. One thing was for sure: Morgan would be able to spot him in a crowd, no problem.

"Hey, Vox," Cleo replied with a smile. "How are ya?"

"Good," he smiled. "Been missing you."

"For fifteen minutes?" she laughed.

"Nah, small-girl," he replied shaking his head. "Me and Rob were trapped on the ship for, like, a year. Right, Rob?"

"A little over a year," the traveler nodded.

"I wanted to track you down and fill you in as soon as we got back, but..." he began, his eyes moving from Cleo to Robert as he spoke. "But, something came up."

"You mean Rob wouldn't let you," she speculated.

"Yeah, small-girl," he sighed. "I guess I do. You know how he is. There ain't no arguing with him."

"No," she agreed, shaking her head. "Or reasoning with him."

"You're right," he smiled. "Who's the new guy?"

"Morgan," she replied. "He's a laugh a minute."

"Sounds good."

"Either way, Vox," Robert replied. "We got to get going man."

"How long we gonna be gone this time?"

"I don't know..." the traveler replied. "Maybe a week."

"Okay," Vox said thoughtfully. "Last time you said it would take an hour and it took a year. This time, you think it'll take a week... I better go kiss my wife goodbye and tell her to remember that I loved her right up 'till the end."

"Very funny, man," Robert replied. "You know that wasn't my fault."

"I know," he chuckled. "Either way, we got to take care of some things. First, we have to tell my wife we're going. And, I ain't lying to her anymore so I'll let you do the talking."

"That's probably best."

"Also, as soon as I walked back in the house, she told me I needed to be careful where I went with you. She said it looked like that fifteen minute drive had put a year on me. Well, Rob, it did put a year on me..."

"Regenerator."

"Right," Vox nodded. "And lastly you're going to have to get me back faster this time for real."

"I got you back in fifteen minutes."

"No, Rob, you got me back in a year. I don't remember what's wrong with this car anymore. And I can't just walk in there and ask Celeste what's wrong with a car I been working on for three days. She'll want me to see a doctor, man..."

"Right, right," Robert nodded. "No problem. Let's go."

Vox climbed from beneath the vehicle and got to his feet. He was at least six inches taller than Morgan. This gave the young man a feeling of hope: here was a man who was tall enough to save the universe!

"Come here, small-girl," Vox said, bending down to kiss her on the forehead.

She grabbed his massive head in her seemingly diminutive hands and, standing on her tiptoes, kissed him in return.

"Let's get inside," he sighed. "And, Rob, make it good."

"Not a problem!"

The band of four made their way to the front door before the traveler grabbed the nob, threw the door open, and marched confidently inside.

"Hey, Celeste!" he called out, stepping through the door.

"You're back already, Rob?" she cried from the kitchen. "Dinner's almost ready, but I thought you said you'd be an hour."

"I thought you said you'd be a week," Vox whispered.

"She made me promise to come back for dinner," he whispered in reply, before continuing at full volume. "Yeah, but we forgot the part!"

"Forgot the part," Celeste replied, stepping into the living room. "Rob, how you... Oh, hey Cleo."

Celeste was slightly taller than Morgan. She also had jet-black skin and long white hair that hung down to the middle of her back. While her eyes were similar to her husband's, they were red, giving them the appearance of star rubies.

"Hey, Celeste," Cleo replied. "How are ya?"

"Great," she smiled. "I'm glad to see you, but what are you doing here, girl?"

"I came to check on, Rob," Cleo replied. "He was gone *way* longer than he said he would be."

"Sounds like him," Celeste laughed. "And, who is this handsome young man?"

"He's Morgan."

"Nice to meet you, Morgan."

"And, you as well," the young man smiled.

"Are you Cleo's new boyfriend?"

"He is *not* her boyfriend," Robert replied.

"I don't know, Rob," Celeste said shaking her head. "Seems a shame for a pretty little girl like that to just sit on the shelf waiting for her expiration date to come up."

"It is a shame," Cleo sighed. "It's a very real shame."

"Still, girl," Celeste continued. "I don't think you got much to worry about. I swear, you look younger every time I see you."

"It's the makeup," the traveler asserted. "She wears a lot of makeup."

"I don't wear *any* makeup! Can you imagine me wearing lipstick?"

"Yes!" Morgan interjected. "Yes, I can! Just hold on for a minute, everyone. I don't want to lose this image!"

"Is he alright?" Celeste asked.

"Yeah," Cleo nodded. "He just has a few medical conditions..."

"Oh... That's too bad," she replied. "Well, both of you are more than welcome to stay for dinner."

"Thanks, Celeste!" Robert replied. "They'll do that. And, actually, I told Doc you might have room at the table for him."

"Always!" she replied with a smile.

"You invited Doc?" Vox whispered.

"Not yet," he replied.

"Either way, if you need to go get that part, then hurry," she said. "If Doc shows up, I'll tell him you'll be back in a few minutes. Of course, I don't know how you forgot to get the part you went up-town specifically to get."

"We got to talking," the traveler replied. "You know how Vox and I are when we're talking."

"Yeah," she laughed. "I do. Anyway, go on and get it. Cleo, you and Morgan can stay here with me if you want."

"Thanks!" Cleo replied. "But, I think we'll ride along. I don't want to let Rob out of my sight again."

"I can understand that," she laughed once more. "Either way, be quick."

"Don't worry, Celeste," Robert replied. "We will. We'll be back in about fifteen minutes."

The four made their way quickly and cautiously back to ship before slipping onto the loading dock. Minutes later, they were enjoying another round of Krispy Kreme with reheated Pumpkin Spice Lattes while moving through non-space, heading directly for the place and time where Doc could be found. The last time traveler decided it would be best to put the ship in orbit for about eight hours to give them enough time to get a good night's - or day's... or whatever it was's - sleep.

He then led Morgan to a small room that contained everything the young man would need for both rest and hygiene. A bed was situated along one wall that, in spite of its rather mundane appearance, was unquestionably a *future bed*. There was also an in-room shower, sink, toothbrush, comb, neck-beard razor, etc. In addition, there were drawers simply packed with clothes - especially underwear... In fact, there were several drawers filled exclusively with clean underwear. Robert explained that Morgan might *really need it* before the trip was over. The young man figured he was right... he hadn't seen a laundry room on this bird.

"Well, goodnight, Morgan," the traveler said with a smile, drawing a small cylinder from his pocket and spraying the young man with a silvery mist. "And, turn around real quick."

"What is that?" Morgan asked, obeying the command.

"Stuff," Robert replied. "It won't hurt you at all, but your clothes are going to dissolve in about a minute and a half."

"What?!?!"

"The schwartz is no longer with you, man," the traveler chuckled. "And take those shoes off. I don't want them turning to goo, they're brand new. Anyway, just rinse off in the shower. Tomorrow, you can put on some real clothes."

After just over forty-five minutes, Morgan figured out how to turn the shower on. Two minutes after that, he was lying in bed wearing brand new, extremely clean, *future underwear*. He was still so excited with everything that had happened to him that he knew he wouldn't be able to sleep for days. Thirty seconds later, he was in a coma.

The next morning, he stumbled to the sink, the wakeup call still echoing through the room. He brushed his teeth, amazed that mint flavored toothpaste had remained popular for thousands of years. Morgan then took the time to floss and use mouthwash. This time, he planned to be *Cleo Ready* when he marched onto the bridge. The young man even took the time to eradicate every trace of sprouting beard, neck or otherwise, that had adorned his face.

In the spirit of complete preparation, he spent a good deal of time selecting his clothes. Robert had been right. He really should have made better wardrobe choices yesterday. However, this was a new day and another chance to get it right. For what felt like eons, he dug through the drawers and closets trying to put together the perfect outfit. When he glanced at the clock, he could hardly believe his eyes... He had spent almost twenty minutes getting dressed! His mother would never believe it.

After a quick look in the mirror, he strode confidently onto the bridge.

"What's with the jean jacket and the leopard pants?" Cleo asked as Morgan stepped into view.

"Oh wow..." the traveler replied, turning around to gaze at the young man. "I just put that Bon Jovi stuff in there as a joke... Why didn't you wear the wig?"

"I didn't see it..."

"Yeah... that makes sense. Anyway, go change."

"No," Cleo said. "I don't know why, but that outfit seems really *him*. You know what I mean?"

"I think I do," Vox chuckled.

"So," Morgan said, smiling widely, his eyes locked on the fair maiden, "Does it do something for you?"

"Oh yeah!" she nodded. "I think it's hilarious! Rob, where'd that clown wig get to?"

"That would be epic," Vox laughed.

"I think I'll go change..." Morgan sighed.

Minutes later, he returned in the much more suitable attire that was old-fashioned blue jeans and a white tank-top. He had also grabbed a black leather jacket. It was his hope that it would plant the seed in Cleo's mind that they had some things in common.

"Is it time?" Vox asked.

"Almost," the traveler replied, glancing at one of the displays.

"This is a time machine," Morgan pointed out. "We don't ever have to wait."

"Maybe," Robert replied. "But I'm not firing up the engines over fifteen minutes."

"Well, what is it we're waiting for then?"

"Doc," the traveler replied. "He's a very special kind of missing person and he and I have an agreement. It was the only way I could keep him in active rotation."

"What makes him so special?" Morgan asked. "And what's the agreement?"

"Well," Robert began, "Doc is kind of a self-made missing person. He wandered into the no-man's-land of his home planet in search of spiritual enlightenment and never wandered back out. For the rest of his considerably long life, he never had a direct effect on the time-line again. So, he could just move to Never Never Land and live with the rest of the survivors, but he won't. He's still out here searching away."

"Alright," Morgan nodded. "That makes sense. And the agreement?"

"Every time I pick him up," the traveler continued, "I have to get him at the exact same time in the morning; I have to get him on *consecutive* days; and, when we're done, I drop him off ten minutes later on the same day - after I've regenerated him for the *exact* amount of time he was with me. Also, because it was the morning when I picked him up, I have to let him sleep on the ship and get up well rested to face the day he hasn't lived yet."

"Seems like a pain," the young man observed.

"It might be for some," Robert admitted, "but I don't mind. Doc sees our time together as *visions* that the universe has given him to help him understand the true nature of all things. And you'll never find a gentler, more compassionate companion."

"That's a fact!" Vox replied with a smile.

"And, it's time," the traveler said. "Let's go."

The entire cockpit became transparent as the ship descended toward a world of red stone, smoking volcanoes, and rivers of molten rock.

"People live down there?" Morgan asked.

"Millions do," Cleo replied with a smile.

"How?"

"If you're curious, ask Doc," Vox chuckled.

The ship dropped onto a large plateau that was connected to a nearby cliff face by a natural stone bridge.

"Is this safe?" Morgan asked, as they stepped out onto the impressive arch. "If this thing gives way, that's gonna be a long drop."

"Don't worry," the traveler said. "It's been here for thousands of years and will be here for thousands more. *It's made of wood, it's real sturdy.*"

"It's made of..."

"A quote, Morgan," Robert sighed. "Just a quote. Didn't you ever see *Happy Gilmore*?"

"Oh yeah," the young man nodded. "*Chubbs.*"

The four quickly made their way to a large cleft in the cliff face from which smoke and steam were continually rising.

"Doc," the traveler shouted. "Doc, I'm here. Are you ready to go?"

As soon as Robert said this, a massive, red, black-taloned claw reached out from the cleft and grabbed hold of the cliff face. From its shadows stepped a monster that was the stuff of nightmares. The creature was over seven feet tall, and muscles rippled beneath the short, black tunic that it wore. What appeared to be ram's horns sprang from its head and the tops of two giant wings could be seen just behind its shoulders. Its orange eyes seemed to burn with their own unholy light, and its grinning mouth was filled with long, dagger-like fangs. Before the beast's cloven hoof had touched the bridge, Morgan sprang into action.

"Demon!" he screamed, tackling Cleo and doing his best to cover every inch of her body with his own flesh.

"Get off of me, you idiot!" she screamed in rage. "That's Doc!"

"Who's the new guy?" Doc chuckled, with a deep booming voice.

"Morgan," Vox replied. "You'll like him. He's, like, a laugh a minute."

"Sounds good."

Immediately, Morgan climbed from atop Cleo and the traveler helped her to her feet. She very vigorously brushed her entire body off before shaking all over spastically, waving her hands wildly in the air in front of her.

"Morgan," she said, her voice filled with emotion. "If you ever see me about to get killed and the only way you have to save me is by covering me with your body; Let! Me! Die!"

"Ouch!" he replied shaking his head. "I mean, you cut me deep just then. I was just trying..."

"Look, Morgan," Cleo interrupted, staring directly into his eyes. "I'm sorry. I really am. But, I'm just setting ground rules! That was *not* the very friendly six foot distance we agreed on, was it?"

"Well, no, but..."

"Right!" she exclaimed. "Good fences, Morgan! Good fences! Now, let's get back on the ship!"

Cleo stormed off in the direction of the time machine, her male companions following a short distance behind. As Vox and Doc strolled along, side by side, laughing and talking, Morgan and the traveler fell into the rear.

"I tried to tell you," Robert chuckled. "She's spoken for, man. Not to mention, *way* out of your league."

"I was just..."

"It's cool," the traveler smiled, slapping him on the back. "I know why you did it and I appreciate it. You did the right thing. And, if it comes up again, make sure you *don't* let her die."

"Yeah..." Morgan sighed. "I wouldn't."

As soon as they were all on board, Doc got right to work.

"We need to get the checkups out of the way," he said, waving his hand in the direction of the medi-bay.

"We can skip it this time, Doc," the traveler replied.

"No, Rob, we can't," he said, shaking his head. "After all, *the doctor is in.*"

"You just like saying that," Robert chuckled.

"True," Doc smiled. "But, that doesn't alter the fact that we're going to get the checkups out of the way."

"Alright," the traveler sighed. "Let's just hurry."

The five companions quickly made their way to the medi-bay where Rob leapt up on one of the tables and laid down. Doc stepped over to the station and began pushing buttons.

"As always, Rob," he said slowly, "you're in perfect physical condition. And, it seems that you're now using ninety-seven point eight percent of your brain. You're progress is truly amazing, my friend."

"Thanks Doc," he replied, before jumping from the table and helping Cleo up.

"Let's see, my dear," Doc said, punching another series of buttons. "You're also in excellent condition and, if memory serves, it seems you're actually a year younger than you were during your last checkup."

"I am," she giggled.

Morgan grabbed his chest.

"I thought so," Doc sighed. "Well, of course, that's your own affair, my dear. However, I would ask that you consider the fact that the universe has us age for a reason. We have to be very careful when we defy nature... In any event, you are currently using eighty-three point two percent of your brain. I suppose that does show that, although you're younger, you may still be a little bit wiser."

"Thanks Doc!" she said, climbing down from the table.

Vox was the next to lay down and await his checkup.

"Very good," Doc observed. "However, Vox, you're no longer a child of forty. I know you're still young, but you need to start being more careful about what you eat. I'd also suggest you do a little more in the way of exercise. It looks like you've been sitting around the ship for a year."

"I was..."

"That explains it," Doc nodded. "And, you're using eighty-five point one percent of your brain. Wonderful progress."

As soon as Vox climbed down, Morgan climbed up.

"Hey, Doc," the young man said, leaning back on the table as he spoke. "Sorry about that whole *demon* thing."

"Think nothing of it, Morgan," he smiled. "I get that a lot."

"Really?"

"No," he chuckled. "Now, lay still."

Doc pushed a series of buttons, shook his head, and pushed more buttons.

"Hmmm," he said, his deep voice echoing around the chamber. "Rob, this can't be right. We need to recalibrate this machine."

"It's calibrated," the traveler replied.

"Look at this, Rob," Doc replied, pulling one of the monitors away from the wall and turning it toward the traveler. "That *cannot* be right. It's not medically possible."

"It is," Robert replied.

"What are you guys talking about?" Morgan asked.

"Rob, man," Vox said shaking his head. "I mean, I know that normally you're right, but I got to go with Doc on this one."

"I agree," Cleo nodded. "I mean, he's not a genius or anything, but that's just not possible."

"What are you guys talking about?" Morgan asked.

42

"Robert," Doc said, gazing at the traveler with one raised eyebrow, "it's my medical opinion that we should recalibrate this machine."

"Alright," the traveler laughed. "You're the doc, Doc. Knock yourself out. Me and Vox will get the ship moving while you do that."

"Yeah," Cleo said. "And, I'm going to take a bath and change these clothes. They smell funny..."

"Has he gone like this before?" Doc asked staring down at the stunned young man.

"Yeah," Robert nodded. "He did that twice yesterday. I figured he just needed some sleep. Either way, you might want to check that out, as well."

"I think I will," Doc nodded.

In less than an hour they were all gathered in the medi-bay once again to see the results of Doc's re-calibrated tests.

"You know, it's weird, Doc," Morgan said, stretching himself out on the table. "I mean, your name being Doc and you being a doctor and everything..."

"My name isn't Doc," Doc chuckled. "My name is Malas Tryffin Dassmock. Everyone just calls me Doc."

"You're first name is Malice?"

"No," Doc replied, shaking his head. "My first name is *Malas*, which means *child of peace*. And, I'd better check your hearing while we're at it. Now, lie still."

Once again Doc pressed a sequence of buttons, before shaking his head and pushing even more buttons.

"Well, Robert," he said, turning his gaze to the traveler. "It seems I was mistaken. I apologize."

"Not at all," Robert replied. "You were just doing your job, Doc."

"Mmmm," Cleo said, gazing at the display and biting her lower lip thoughtfully. "That's not good."

"Don't do that," Morgan insisted.

"Don't do what?" she asked.

"Don't bite your lower lip like that," he explained. "You're going to give me a stroke."

"A stroke?" Doc asked.

"Oh yeah," Cleo replied. "We should have mentioned that. He's got some medical problems. Yesterday he said he thought he was having a heart-attack and, like, fifteen minutes later he thought he was going to have an aneurysm."

"I didn't say that," Morgan said.

"You *did* say that!" she replied.

"I just meant..."

"I'll take a look," Doc interrupted. "Either way, he does have a number of issues that we need to address. Morgan, you're slightly overweight and, as a result, your heart is slightly older than the rest of your body. Your blood sugar is also a little high. It looks as if you had nothing but coffee and donuts for breakfast..."

"I did," the young man interjected.

"Ah. Well, that's probably alright then. Are you a smoker?"

"Never."

"Well then, your lungs are in bad shape. Do you ever do any walking, jogging, or running?"

"Never."

"That explains that, then. It also explains your rather lackluster muscle development. And, it may have something to do with that touch of acne, as well. For that, however, I have a cream that should fix you up in no time."

"Thanks..."

"Not at all. Now, that brings us to the brain..."

"What's wrong with my brain?"

"Nothing's *wrong* with it, exactly. It's just that you don't appear to be using much of it. You see, Morgan, the average human from your time used roughly ten percent of their brain."

"No," Morgan replied, shaking his head. "That was a myth. Scientists way back in my day were able to prove that wasn't true."

"No, Morgan," Robert replied. "They were able to prove that humans use one-hundred percent of their brain cells. And that means almost nothing. The scientists of your day had no idea that you could measure brain *potential*, much less *how* to go about measuring it. Didn't you ever think it was odd that *nobody* ever knew where that ten percent rumor started? There was no paper, or theory, or famous quote they could trace it back to for certain. That's because it was an idea inserted into the subconscious of many, many people over the course of early human history by a particular time traveler."

"Why would they have done that?" Morgan asked.

"Because, Morgan," the traveler explained. "That idea, that belief, is exactly what people need in order to reach more of their potential. That's where it all starts. The brain's abilities increase almost exponentially as more and more of that potential is unlocked. The living brain is capable of things that the people of your time simply couldn't imagine. And, Morgan, you're seriously brimming over with potential, man. At the moment you're only using about five percent of your full capacity."

"Five percent!" Morgan exclaimed. "I have to be the stupidest person that ever lived!"

"I wouldn't say that," Doc smiled. "Of course..."

"Of course, what?"

"Well..." Doc sighed. "Technically speaking, no one has ever been found that used less than ten percent of their brain. Still, you're living proof that it's possible. You're a medical marvel and may help us redefine the way we look at brain potential."

"Glad I could help," Morgan sighed. "So, Rob, if all this brain power is exponential and all, you must be, like, a super-genius."

"I wouldn't say that," Robert smiled, pulling out his false modesty for its annual airing.

"In point of fact," Doc replied. "Robert is the most intelligent human being that has ever lived. Of course, there is a great difference between intelligence and wisdom."

"Can you, like, bend spoons with your mind?" Morgan asked.

"No," the traveler replied. "But, I can juggle six things at once. Well... Five. But, I'm working on it."

"So, be honest," the young man sighed. "Am I just here as your pet or something?"

"What?" the traveler asked, knitting his brows. "No way, man! You're a member of my team - of our team - one of the most elite teams ever assembled in the history of the universe. I spent years of my life searching for you, Morgan. And, I'm very glad I found you."

"Well then, what part of the team am I? Like, the red shirt or something?"

"No!" Robert exclaimed, a wide smile on his face. "You're our jester!"

"Really?"

"Eh," the traveler replied, rotating his hand back and forth. "Sort of. But, you won't always be! Trust me, man! Either way, now that the checkups are over, it's time to really get started. To the conference room!"

As Morgan followed the traveler along the corridor, he considered his potential. He sincerely hoped that he'd be able to work his way up to at least ten percent in time. At least now he understood why he'd never made assistant manager at Taco Palace. Of course, now he was the Jester of what was possibly the most elite team that ever existed. The wheel of fate had certainly turned in his favor!

The addition of Vox and Doc also filled him with a great deal of confidence. Between the two of them they had brought the party's average height up to just over six-foot one. All things considered, it looked like the universe was in good hands.

CHAPTER 4: A PLAN OF ACTION

"If you'll all take a seat, we can get started," Robert said, stepping around the conference table and pulling Cleo's chair out for her.

As soon as his four companions had seated themselves, the traveler took up his place at the head of the table.

"As all of you already know," he began, "we're here to repair the damage done to the universe by my predecessors. The order in which we do this is absolutely critical. And so, it should come as no surprise that our first target is the next-to-the-last time traveler; the infamous time-thief Marcus Delmont. His short-lived career was the greatest example of time-abuse in the history of the universe. Of course, what he did stopped time, and that fact kept anyone from being able to be even worse than him in the now non-existent future."

"Question," Morgan said, raising his hand.

"Sure!"

"How did he stop time?"

"Well," Robert replied. "The first thing the idiot did was steal a prototype time drive and sell it to another culture that hadn't discovered time travel yet! According to history, he didn't think it would hurt the time-lines much because he left both the plans and the creator of the drive alone. And, he figured since the universe was full of time travelers anyway, a few million more wouldn't hurt anything. However, what the moron didn't count on was the fact that the creator was going to have a heart-attack and fall over dead as soon as he noticed the drive was gone. As a result, it was never completed."

"Question," Morgan said, raising his hand.

"We're not in grade school, Morgan," the traveler replied. "What is it?"

"How did that break time?"

"It created a series of paradoxes... Morgan, you don't need to raise your hand, man. What?"

"What about the *random elements*? Why didn't they repair the paradoxes?"

"Wow..." the traveler replied. "You've actually been paying attention. You're going to break the five percent barrier in no time at this rate. Either way, you're right. Under normal circumstances, at least according to everything we understand about time travel at this point in time, they would have. However, the plain fact is, they didn't."

"Why not?"

"We can't be sure, but the current theory is that what Marcus did was like setting off the time-equivalent of a hydrogen bomb. With a single action, he undid countless changes - out of sequence - and created countless new ones. As a result, time was *seriously* scrambled. Roughly a thousand years after that happened, time just stopped. Apparently, the universe's self-repair system couldn't handle it."

"Or perhaps," Doc said thoughtfully, "we're part of that self-repair system."

"That's certainly possible," Robert nodded. "Depending on your philosophical outlook."

"So, no problem," Morgan smiled. "We just go back and blast his machine before he can use it."

"No," the traveler said, "we don't. Haven't you been listening? We don't know why this happened in the first place. But, what we do know is that making drastic changes is a bad idea. If we just went back and blasted his machine, he wouldn't make the changes and, so, we wouldn't go back. Making more paradoxes is what we want to avoid. So, even though we can't do that completely, we want to keep our paradoxes as small as possible. What we have to do is undo his changes while causing as few of our own as we can. And, in order to do that, we need to work backwards."

"What do you mean?"

"I mean, we have to start by un-stealing the last thing he ever stole and returning it to where it should be in the time-line. Well, that's not exactly true. The very first thing we need to do is disable his time machine..."

"That's what I just said!" Morgan interrupted.

"Well, no," the traveler replied. "I mean we have to disable it *after* the last time he ever used it."

"What's the point of that?" the young man asked. "If he never used it again, why go to the trouble of disabling it."

"Let me explain," Robert said with a smile. "He never used it again *before*, but he might use it again *later*. If he figures out that someone's un-stealing all his junk, for instance, he might want to try to find out how and why. You see, when we make these changes they might just affect him. It's a remote possibility, but all he's got to do is stumble on a history book that shows something somewhere that he thinks shouldn't be then and there and he might put the rest together. The odds are billions to one, but we can't take any chances."

"Okay. So we disable it, then what?"

"We un-steal the Orb of the Gods at a point in time after it's dropped out of the time-line and return it to where he stole it from about five minutes after it's gone. That will undo most of the damage he did without creating any more. Then, we disable his ship again and see what happens."

"What do you mean?"

"Just that! After we've returned the Orb, we disable his ship right before he went to steal it and see what happens. The universe will either start to heal or not or blowup or something. We'll just have to see what happens."

"That's your plan?!?!"

"You got a better one, Morgan? If so, let's hear it."

"Well, no... But, I can see some problems with this one!"

"Like what?"

"Okay... Okay... We un-steal the Orb and disable his ship so he can't steal it, right?"

"Right." the traveler nodded.

"Well... BAM! I mean, paradox! If he didn't steal it, we won't go back to un-steal it."

"If he didn't steal it, we won't need to."

"Okay... but, we won't even know it happened because it won't have." Morgan pointed out.

"Normally, that's true. But, we'll be in Never Never Land in an independent time stream - with our memories quite intact. How do you think we can tell what *should* happen in history, Morgan?"

"Okay... but, how do we disable his ship from Never Never Land?"

"He does ask good questions," Vox observed, rubbing his chin thoughtfully.

"He does," Doc agreed. "I wonder if I should try to recalibrate the machine again..."

"Excellent, Morgan!" the traveler laughed, a wide smile on his face. "Truly excellent! That's right where I was headed. Cleo and Vox are going to build a device that will allow us to disable his ship from any place at any time. Then, we go back to before he ever used his ship and install it. The device will be there the whole time but he'll never know it until it's too late, too late, too late, etc."

"Rob," Cleo said, gazing at him, her eyes filled with awe. "You really are a super-genius."

"I know, right?" he replied, with a grin. "Now, to get started, we're going to need to collect a Dorvient power crystal. I'm sure Vox and Cleo will need one to build the device."

"We might be able to do it without that," Vox said, shaking his head. "I don't like the idea of having to go get another one."

"Why not?" Morgan asked.

"Well, several reasons," Vox replied, turning to look at the young man. "But, mainly because the planet they come from is crawling with Kalasks."

"Not crawling," Robert chuckled. "And, we've got to have one. We can't chance using a less-reliable or less-powerful energy-source. We can't let this go wrong."

"What exactly is a *Kalask*?" Morgan asked.

"Imagine a giant boa-constrictor," Doc began, "with ten pairs of powerful legs, eyes placed so that it can see in three-hundred and sixty degrees, and a hinged mouth filled with great white shark teeth. Then, make it very hard to kill and very, very angry. That's basically a Kalask. The reason we can safely take Dorvient power crystals without effecting the time-lines is because no advanced creatures ever managed to colonize the planet. And, the reason for that is the Kalasks. Which, of course, means that it's perfectly safe to collect the crystals - provided you don't get eaten alive."

"Okay," Morgan nodded. "But, that raises another question."

"What's that?" Doc asked.

"How is it you guys know to reference things I'm familiar with?" the young man asked. "I mean, I'm not complaining or anything, but *great white shark*? Shouldn't you be using some *space shark* or *asteroid snake* as a reference point?"

"Wow..." Cleo said. "He does ask good questions sometimes. Maybe the machine is wrong. I mean, I've seen him walk and talk at the same time myself."

"Well, Morgan," Doc replied. "It's because we travel with Rob. For some reason, he's obsessed with Earth culture between the nineteenth and twenty-second centuries. So, unless you know all about that time and place, you won't be able to understand half of what he says. Movies, television, plays, music, history, you pretty much have to know it all."

"How long did it take you to learn all that?"

"Probably not quite as long as it took you to learn common..."

"Oh... right..." Morgan nodded. "So, anyway, we're off to get some power crystals and avoid super snakes. Is that about the shape of it?"

"Yep," the traveler nodded. "That's about it. And, under the circumstances, we need to be completely kitted out."

"What does that mean?" Morgan asked.

"It means we need weapons and armor," the traveler smiled.

The five companions all rose and made their way to the ship's armory. Morgan stood in the middle of the empty room feeling less-than-impressed.

"This doesn't seem to be much of an armory," he said. "For one thing, there aren't any weapons in here. Or anything else."

"One sec, Morgan," the traveler replied. "I think we'll start with the armor."

As he said this, he pushed a series of buttons on a nearby panel causing a long shelf filled with gray clothing to slide out of the wall."

"Cool!" Morgan exclaimed.

"Indeed, it is," Doc smiled. "Now, grab a set in your size and go change."

Morgan selected a pair of shoes and pants, as well as a shirt, a jacket, and a baseball cap. Minutes later, he was staring at his all gray wardrobe in the full length mirror in his room, shaking his head. He couldn't imagine why they wanted him to change... Unless the planet they were heading to was really muddy or something... As soon as he had taken a good look, he headed back to the armory.

He arrived to find that all of his companions were dressed exactly the same and was amazed at just how good Cleo carried off the *all gray* look.

"What was the point of changing clothes?" Morgan asked.

"Oh... This!" Robert replied, spinning around and kicking Morgan right in the gut.

Instantly, the cloth solidified, protecting the young man from the force of the attack.

"That's amazing!" he exclaimed. "I had no idea you knew Karate!"

"*I know Kung-Fu,*" the traveler chuckled, nodding his head. "And also, these clothes are actually armor."

"Oh yeah!" Morgan exclaimed glancing down at his stomach. "Awesome!"

"It is," Vox agreed. "Of course, normally we'd use personal shield generators. But, we can't on this mission. Which is another reason I'm not fond of this plan."

"It'll be fine, man," Robert replied. "Now for some weapons!"

After another series of button presses, a number of weapon covered shelves sprang from the surrounding walls.

"Oh! My! Goodness!" Morgan exclaimed. "This is like something out of *The Matrix*! Do I get a blaster?"

"We don't called them that," the traveler replied.

"Well then, do I get a phaser?"

"We don't call them that, either."

"What do you call them?" Morgan asked.

"Well, as amazing as it may seem, we call guns that shoot lasers *laser guns*."

"Awesome!"

"And no, you don't get one," Robert said.

"Aw man…"

"Besides, on this mission we need to use what you might call *conventional weapons*," the traveler explained.

"Which is yet another reason that I don't like this, Rob," Vox replied.

"Sorry, but there's no other way," Robert pointed out.

"Well, if we're doing *conventional weapons*, can I get a .357 magnum?" Morgan asked. "*Do you feel lucky? Well… do ya, punk?!?!*"

"Morgan," Robert chuckled, "of all the things I'm not going to do, giving you a .357 magnum is right at the top of the list."

"Why not?"

"For one thing, you haven't been out on the range enough," the traveler explained.

"You mean like *home on the range*?" the young man asked.

"You see, Morgan," Robert replied, shaking his head, "that's why you don't get a gun."

"Well, can I have a sword?"

"Are you serious?"

"A knife?"

"Do you still have that switchblade?" the traveler asked.

"Yeah. It's in my pocket," Morgan replied. "Why?"

"Let me hold it for a sec," Robert said, holding out his hand. "Thanks! And, no, you can't have a knife."

"What can I *pack* then?"

"You can *pack* this with medical supplies," the traveler replied, taking a backpack from one of the shelves and handing it the young man. "And hurry up."

"What should I grab?"

"Good point," the traveler nodded. "Doc, show him what we need, please."

"Not a problem, Rob," Doc replied, before leading the young man from the room.

A short time later, the ship was touching down on a forest covered planet. As the members of the band prepared to exit the ship, they certainly seemed a good bit more *martial* than they had up to that point.

Robert looked like something out of an *Arnold* action movie. He had a forty-five caliber pistol hanging from his belt, a high powered automatic rifle slung over his shoulder, and a P90 in his hands. Vox could have been one of the cast of the *Dirty Dozen* as he was carrying a chain fed thirty caliber machine-gun with bullets draped all over him. Doc had almost gone the *Hellboy* route with dual sixty caliber – yeah, sixty - revolvers hanging from his hips. He also had another gun slung up on his back. Cleo looked, if possible, even more attractive with an automatic pistol hanging under each arm and a crossbow in her hands. There was just something of *The Fifth Element* about her at that moment. As he gazed down at the medical bag in his hand, he realized that, if anything, he was ready for a guest spot on *Doc McStuffins*. Next time, he was going to have to get a gun...

"So, what planet is this?" Morgan asked as they marched down the gangway.

"Bouillabaisse," Robert replied.

"Cool. And what planet is Doc from? You didn't tell me before."

"Baguette," the traveler said.

"Awesome... And, where did we pick up Cleo from?" the young man asked.

"Escargot."

"Man! I'm going to be, like, a walking encyclopedia of the universe by the time I'm done," Morgan asserted.

"I'm sure you'll be an interesting read," the traveler chuckled.

"Thanks!" the young man replied with a smile. "One more question: why is it everywhere we go, the plants are all exactly the same?"

"How many plant types were there on Earth in your time, Morgan?" the traveler asked.

"I don't know..." Morgan replied.

"Well, there were a few hundred thousand," Robert pointed out. "Name ten trees."

"Let's see..." Morgan replied thoughtfully. "There's Apple, Orange, Plum, Apricot... Pine... How many is that? Oh, and *number one... the Larch... the Larch*."

"Okay," Robert said. "So, you got four fruit trees, the most common tree in the area where you grew up, and the *Monty Python* tree. You're not a botanist, Morgan."

"Yeah... I see what you're saying," the young man nodded.

"If you pay careful attention, Morgan," Doc said, smiling at him as he spoke. "You'll begin to notice the differences."

For the next few minutes, they pressed through the dense undergrowth that seemed to cover the planet. After about a quarter of a mile of marching and a quarter of a gallon of sweat, Morgan decided that they had to be doing it the hard way.

"Why didn't we park closer?" he asked.

"We couldn't," was Robert's simple reply.

"Why not?"

"The power crystals can junk up the engines if we get too close," the traveler explained.

"For, like, a year," Vox added.

"At least," Robert sighed. "That's also why we couldn't use personal shield generators, or stealth fields, or laser guns, or the car."

"It's also the reason we shouldn't have come," Vox pointed out.

"No choice," the traveler replied.

"I know," Vox nodded.

"Well, okay," Morgan replied. "But then, why didn't we just use the transporters and beam down."

"Those aren't real Morgan," the traveler replied, pushing a limb out of Cleo's path. "I keep trying to tell you, this is reality; not *Star Trek*. There is no *beaming down*. And, even if there was, we'd never get through all the interference even if I was *giving her all she's got*."

"Weird…" the young man mused. "What else doesn't exist in the future?"

"Seriously?" Robert replied. "You want me to go down the list, man? Even if I was willing to (which I'm not), and I had the time (which I don't), you might not want to hear it. How would you feel if I told you mermaids weren't real? Even if they weren't, I wouldn't tell you! I'm not about to dash a man's fantasies."

"Mermaids *better not* be your fantasy!" Cleo said, glaring at Robert from under a single raised eyebrow.

"What?!?!," he exclaimed with a forced laugh. "No way! My heart is *way* too full for crap like that."

"You're a terrible liar, Rob," she replied with a coy smile.

"That's not true," he asserted. "I'm a *stellar* liar. Like, an unbelievably incredible liar. In fact, I'm so good at lying that, if you ever suspect I'm lying, you can be sure I'm telling the truth. If I were actually lying, you wouldn't have a clue."

"Then, how can I tell if you're lying to me?" Cleo asked playfully.

"It's easy for you, girl," he smiled. "I never lie to you."

"You're a terrible liar, Rob," she said again.

"Actually, Rob," Morgan said thoughtfully. "If that is the case, about the mermaids I mean, not the lying... Why do you call that one color *spanking mermaids*?"

"What color does he call *spanking mermaids*?!?!"Cleo asked, raising her voice and turning her eyes to Morgan.

"I have *no* idea what he's talking about!" Robert exclaimed.

"Yes, you do!" the young man replied with a grin. "That color in the cargo bay!"

"So, that's why you repainted it!" Cleo said, turning her glaring gaze back to Robert. "I wondered why you did that even after Vox insisted that it didn't need it."

"It did need it!" he counter-insisted. "And, I honestly have *no* idea what Morgan's talking about."

"When I first got on the ship," Morgan explained. "You told me that's what you called it as soon as I stepped in the bay. I asked you what color it was and you said: *No idea, I've always just called it spanking mermaids.*"

"Did he?" Cleo asked, her voice edged like a knife.

"Of course I *didn't!*" the traveler replied.

"But, Rob..." Morgan began.

"Look, Morgan!" Robert interrupted, turning around to face his friend. "You had just run *full tilt* into the loading platform. I think you have to admit that you *might* be mistaken."

As he said this, he ever so slightly moved his head in Cleo's direction.

"Well, I suppose you could be right," Morgan replied thoughtfully, completely oblivious to the reason behind Robert's head twitch. "Things are kind of blurry."

"You see?" the traveler said, turning his eyes to Cleo. "Even poor old Robert should be presumed innocent until *proven* guilty."

"I guess you're right," Cleo sighed. "I'm sorry... Will you forgive me?"

"You first," he replied with a smile.

"Not yet," she said, shaking her head.

"So..." Morgan mused. "You've got me thinking. I'm not sure what I actually remember and what's just head injury... Do you or do you not have a *light saber* shaped flashlight that you got for a song at a convention?"

"What convention?" Cleo asked, glaring at the traveler. "Did you go to *another* convention without me?"

Several minutes later, Robert had managed - once again - to talk his way out of trouble as the band made its way ever nearer their goal. As they traveled along, Cleo and Morgan ended up side by side among the shades of the forest for a moment. The young man leapt on the opportunity.

"Cleo," he said with a sigh, "be completely honest. Would you ever consider going out with me?"

"It all depends on what we were *in* at the time," she replied thoughtfully.

"No, I mean like on a date," he explained.

"Oh…" she said. "Well... No... Never..."

"Aren't you even just a little bit curious?" he asked.

"Not anymore," she replied, shaking her head. "You see, I had a lot of different pets as a child."

"You know just how to crush a man's dreams," he nodded.

"I'm just keeping it real, Morgan," she replied smiling at him. "I'm just keeping it real…"

"I suppose that's best…" he sighed again.

"It will be in the long run…"

As Cleo brought this conversation to an end, Robert brought the party to a stop. They were standing just outside the mouth of what appeared to be a large cavern. Morgan could feel *something* in the air. It was as if all the hair on his body was thinking about standing on end any minute now. All things considered, he was glad he had shaved the neck-beard.

"This is it," Robert said. "All we need to do is grab a couple of crystals and then head back to the ship. Like I said: no problem."

"We're not back in the ship yet," Doc pointed out.

"That's what I'm saying," Vox agreed.

The group quickly made their way inside the cavern. All of Morgan's arm hair stood straight up the moment he entered cave. An almost eerie blue glow emanated from its shadowy recesses.

"What's with this?" the young man asked, glancing down at his arm.

"It's *the power*," the traveler said quite spookily. "And, that's nothing. Pull your hat off."

Immediately Morgan obeyed. Each of his hairs shot out as far from each other as they possibly could. In a universe that had been filled with many a fine 'fro over the eons, the young man's stood proudly amongst the most bodacious.

"Now, that is epic," Vox chuckled.

"It is!" Cleo grinned. "It's even better than that clown wig."

Morgan reached up to feel it only to receive quite a powerful shock.

"Ow!" he exclaimed. "What was that?"

"*The power*," the traveler chuckled. "Anyway, I should have warned you about that. Don't touch your hair until we get back outside."

"So what do I do with my hat?"

"Eh, just put it on top of your hair. Carefully."

Once again Morgan obeyed, cautiously setting the ball-cap atop his sphere-o-hair.

Moments later, the entire band was standing at the back of the cave staring at a wall of glowing blue crystals.

"Grab two of 'em, Vox," Robert said, kneeling down beside the nearest crystals.

"Are you sure, Rob?" Vox asked, turning his eyes to the traveler. "That's a lot of power, man. And remember what happened last time. I don't want to spend another year…"

"Nah, man," Robert interrupted, shaking his head. "The crystals weren't the problem. I never should have trusted those guys. They were *way* out of their depth. And anyway, I spent another year reworking that box. I think it was one of those two years I wasn't picking Cleo up with…"

"You don't remember?"

"Eh…" the traveler replied rotating his hand back and forth. "It gets a little fuzzy. But logic dictates that I had to have improved it *after* the first one failed."

"Alright, Rob," Vox sighed. "You're the boss, man."

Vox slipped on a heavy looking white glove and pulled a pair of pliers from his belt. Quickly he reached out and snapped off one of the crystals. As he did so a blue electric arch shot between the broken crystal and the face it had been taken from. A moment later, the second crystal had been collected and the pair of them were placed in a small metal box.

"That's it!" Robert said, with a wide smile. "Piece of cake! Let's go."

"That wasn't so bad," Morgan replied, as the party started its journey back to the ship.

"I said it wouldn't be," the traveler pointed out.

"Well honestly, I was a little bit worried," the young man admitted. "I didn't like the phrase *crawling with Kalasks*, I guess."

"I understand," Robert replied, as the pair stepped back outside the cave mouth. "But it's like I said, the planet's not really *crawling* with them. If I had to guess, I would say that the odds of us actually running into a Kalask are about one to…"

"Rob!" Cleo screamed.

"One," the traveler continued, following the green maiden's pointing finger to the ridge above them. "Well… At least it's a small one…"

Gazing down at the party was a creature that very much matched the description Doc had given. It was pure white, with a body that appeared very much like a large snake, perhaps twenty feet in length. It had ten pairs of legs, and its mouth was huge, open, and filled with rows of razor sharp teeth.

Instantly, the well trained band leapt into action. Robert unleashed roughly nine-hundred rounds a minute at the creature; hot brass flying from his P90. Vox followed suit with the thirty cal, while Doc jumped into the air, taking to the sky, at the same time drawing his revolvers. Cleo took careful aim with her crossbow, firing at the creature as it rushed down the valley toward them. Her bolt exploded when it struck the ground, knocking the creature to the side and blowing a huge, smoking hole in the earth. The monster then ran momentarily back into the woods as Cleo flew to Morgan's side.

"Cock this," she cried, throwing the crossbow to him. "I'm not strong enough!"

"Then how did you cock it in the first place?" he screamed.

"I didn't," she yelled. "Vox did it before we left!"

"Can't he do it now?!?!"

"He's busy!"

"Right!" he replied, grabbing the string in both hands and pulling back as hard as he could.

The creature shot out of the undergrowth, heading straight for the traveler as Doc rained down sixty caliber slugs on it from above. Vox did his best to cut the monster's feet out from under it, but only managed to shatter four of its legs along one side. Robert emptied his magazine into the beast as it got nearer and nearer.

"Not like that, you idiot!" Cleo screamed. "Use the winch!"

"Right!" he replied, staring down at the weapon. "The winch..."

"That handle thing, you moron!"

The traveler pulled his pistol with one hand, and he grabbed a nearby branch with the other. He jerked himself up into the tree as he fired shot after shot into the monster's face. The creature reared up to the traveler's height preparing to strike as Robert squeezed off his last round. At that moment, Doc fell from the sky like a thunderbolt. He grabbed the beast by the throat with one of his massive hands, one of his revolvers gripped in the other. The monster threw him to the ground, raking him with its terrible talons. After a little more than a second, one more shot rang out. Doc sent a slug through the creature's brain. Its massive corpse instantly collapsed on top of him.

"Got it!" Morgan cried triumphantly, handing the crossbow to Cleo.

"Thanks..." she said, shaking her head. "Just in time..."

"Are you alright, Doc?" Robert cried, leaping down from the tree. "Did it get you?"

"It did *get me*," Doc chuckled, crawling from under the beast. "But not badly."

The monster had actually managed to tear its way through Doc's armor. He was bleeding profusely down one side.

"Hey, *Doc McStuffins*," Robert yelled, gazing at Morgan. "Get those supplies up here."

"Are you psychic?" the young man asked, as soon as he reached them.

"Not that I'm aware of," the traveler said, opening the bag and handing it to Doc. "Why?"

"Why did you call me *Doc McStuffins*?"

"I don't know," the traveler replied, shaking his head. "It just seemed to fit somehow."

"Right..." Morgan said slowly. "Anyway, that crossbow is a *conventional weapon*?"

"Well," Robert replied, rocking his head from side to side, "I guess I should have said *semi-conventional*."

In less than five minutes, they were once again on their way to the ship. Fortunately, they didn't encounter any more Kalasks along the way. As it turned out, Morgan didn't need clean underwear. But it had been a close thing. All things considered, he was glad to have drawers full at his disposal should he need them.

"Piece of cake," Robert smiled, dropping into his seat on the bridge.

"I'm not sure that's how I'd put it, Rob," Doc pointed out, gazing down at his ruined and blood-stained cloth-armor.

"Well... Piece of ultra-hot barbeque chicken, then. The main thing, is that we're all here and mainly uninjured. I'm sure you'll have yourself fixed up in no time, Doc."

"Yes," he replied, settling down into his seat. "And I'll take care of that in a minute but, I think I'll take a breather before I do."

"Alright, Rob," Vox said. "We got the crystals. Now, what?"

"Well," he replied, rubbing his chin as he spoke. "I want to recalibrate the magnetic bubble."

"That's a good idea," Vox nodded.

"And, I guess you and Cleo should go ahead and get to work," he continued. "I've got everything you need here already – including complete schematics of Marcus Delmont's ship."

"Perfect," Cleo smiled. "While we're working on that Morgan can hit the gym."

"You have a gym?" the young man asked.

"We do," she nodded. "And, you need to spend some time in it. If I had been able to get a second shot off, Doc wouldn't have gotten injured."

"That wasn't a matter of strength!" he pointed out. "I just didn't know how it worked."

"Hmmm," she said, gazing at Morgan, her head tilted to the side.

The young man bit his lip until he almost broke the skin. Cleo used the winch to carefully uncock the crossbow before handing it to Vox.

"Could you cock that please?"

Vox grabbed the crossbow in one hand and the string in the other. He then simply pulled it back and cocked it.

"I don't know if it's even possible for me to get that strong!" the young man exclaimed.

"It is, Morgan," Doc replied. "But, we don't have to make that our immediate aim."

"What should our *immediate aim* be, then?" Morgan asked. "Buff?"

"Oh, I don't think I'd aim for that," Cleo replied, shaking her head. "Not right at the start. Shoot for something simpler."

"Like what?" the young man asked.

"I don't know..." she mused. "Like *less pudgy* maybe?"

"Oh, very nice," he nodded. "*While you're at it, why don't you give me a nice paper cut and pour lemon juice on it?*"

"What?" she asked.

"It's a quote," he replied. "Rob ain't the only one that can do that crap, you know..."

"Either way," Robert said. "That's the plan: I'll work on the bubble, Vox and Cleo will work on the device, and Doc and Morgan will work on depudgifying Morgan. Any questions?"

"What's *depudgifying?*" Morgan asked sarcastically.

"Don't worry," the traveler grinned. "Doc'll show ya!"

CHAPTER 5: TO KILL A TIME MACHINE

"Can I come in?" Morgan asked, standing just outside the door.

"Sure," the traveler replied, not lifting his gaze from the panel he was staring at.

"I won't pop the bubble or anything will I?"

"Nope."

"I've got lunch with me. Can I bring it in?"

"Yep."

"I've got a fork."

"Is it plastic?" the traveler asked, glancing up at the young man.

"Yeah."

"Come on in."

Morgan instantly obeyed and stepped across the floor taking a seat at one of the tables in the magnetic bubble chamber. He opened his MRE and stared at it with a certain amount of disdain as it heated up.

"I'm getting sick of these MREs already," he sighed.

"Really?" the traveler asked. "I like 'em. And, you've only been eating them for like three days."

"Yeah," Morgan nodded. "But, I eat all the time now."

"Hardly surprising," Robert observed. "Doc's got you burning billions of calories. And, even with the non-stop eating, you're looking less pudgy already."

"Thanks..." the young man said, using his fork to toy with his food. "Why do we only have three different meals?"

"They're my favorites."

"What about everyone else?"

"They don't care."

"Well, I do!" Morgan replied, shaking his head. "Are you sure there aren't any replicators on board?"

"Why? You want an *earl grey hot?*"

"I don't know," the young man sighed. "I never had one. What are they like?"

"No…" the traveler said, shaking his own head, "we don't have any replicators."

"Do replicators even exist?"

"Not like that."

"Then, how do they exist?"

"In a way I'm not going to explain about right now," Robert chuckled.

"Got ya..." Morgan sighed.

"What's wrong, man?" the traveler asked, having taken note of the sullen tone in the young man's voice.

"I'm just suffering through the agonies of unrequited love…" he sighed again.

"*Unrequited?*"

"Yeah," he nodded. "That's what Doc said it was anyway. I think that's a real word. Either way, it's supposed to be good for my soul. But, I'll tell ya, it ain't no good for my self-confidence."

"Yeah," Robert replied, gazing at his companion "I know what you mean."

"You do?"

"Nah, man," he replied, shaking his head. "No idea…"

"I figured that," he said, with yet another sigh. "I'm just a loser, man."

"No," Robert said, locking his eyes on those of his friend. "No, you're not. You're an essential member of perhaps the most elite team ever assembled in history. Try to remember that."

"So, *Jester* is an essential role?"

"It is in this team," the traveler laughed. "And, anyway man, Cleo's not the only *bird* in the universe. She's just not for you. I told you that early on. I was trying to spare you some pain."

"I know, man," he nodded. "And, I tried to resist her."

"You did?"

"Nah… Not even a little. In fact, I think I worked at trying to fall even more in love with her just to prove you wrong."

"I thought as much," Robert chuckled. "So, how goes the training?"

"Good, I guess," Morgan replied. "But, don't we have some kind of machine that could make me buff in like minutes?"

"Oh yeah."

"Then, why can't I just use that?"

"Because, Morgan," the traveler explained, "we don't have a machine that can give you character."

"What do you mean?"

"I mean, we can't just program you to keep pushing even when it hurts or keep at it even when you fail, man. The regenerator could give you the body of *Arnold Schwarzenegger*, but it couldn't give you the resolve that it took him to get that body. You follow me?"

"I guess so," he said with another sigh, "but the future's not all I thought it might be."

"What about the green women?"

"You're right! In fact, the future is way *better* than I thought it would be. Especially my own personal future! I'm just a little down about the whole *Cleo* thing..."

"That's understandable," the traveler said, pulling the not-a-light-saber flashlight from his pocket.

He laid it on the table before opening the case that held one of the Dorvient power crystals. After slipping on a single heavy white glove he lifted one of the crystals from the case, opened the flashlight, and snapped it into place.

"You're putting a battery like that in a flashlight?" Morgan asked.

"No," the traveler replied. "I'm *hiding* a battery like this in a flashlight."

"What's the point of that?"

"Well, I don't want to lose our only spare crystal. And now, if pirates attack the ship or sneak on board and go to looting all our precious swag, they're not likely to find it are they?"

"Have pirates ever *looted your precious swag?*"

"No," Robert replied. "But, why take chances?"

"That doesn't even make any sense."

"Why not?"

"You know where all the pirates in time are. Can't you just avoid them?"

"*Random Elements.*"

"So you're worried that a wild pack of swag-obsessed pirates might just cross your path *randomly?*"

"Be prepared, Morgan," the traveler said with a nod. "That's the motto of the Boy Scouts, you know?"

"I was never a scout," the young man replied. "But, I think you're over-thinking this one. I mean, why don't you keep the MREs in a *space-weevil* proof container?"

"*Red Dwarf?*"

"Yeah..."

"Anyway, Morgan, I can always go pick up more MREs. You want to go get more of these crystals?"

"Not especially. Not until I can get a gun anyway."

"Right," the traveler nodded. "And that won't be for a while. So, let's keep the ones we've got. Oh, and don't touch this flashlight. With that crystal in it you could blind yourself."

"No problem man. I outgrew playing with flashlights like two or three years ago."

"I'm glad to hear it!" the traveler nodded. "Either way, Vox and Cleo just finished a few minutes ago, so we need to head to the conference room. We've got a time machine to disable."

"Sounds good."

The pair left the chamber the moment Morgan had finished his meal. With the push of a button, Robert summoned the rest of the crew and, in minutes, they were all seated around the table once again.

"Alright, guys," Robert began, "we're up to the first, and arguably the most important step. The device is ready thanks to Vox and Cleo. Well done, by the way."

"Thanks!" they replied in unison.

"Now, all we need to do is go back to the point in time where Marcus Delmont had completed his machine, but had yet to take it on a test flight, and install the device. This is going to be a little tricky because he was extremely wealthy even before he started his time-thief career. As a result, he had the money to build a vault of solid cormax to store it in."

"Cormax?" Morgan asked.

"One of the most durable substances ever created," the traveler explained. "At the time, it was believed to be indestructible."

"So, we need to break in through the front door?"

"No, Morgan," Robert replied, shaking his head. "I actually have another plan. In any event, one thing that will make it a little easier is the fact that we'll be able to use personal shield generators and stealth field generators. We're also going to take tranquilizer guns as well as one *deadly force* firearm each."

"Including me?"

"No."

"Why not?"

"Range time, Morgan," the traveler replied. "Now, let's keep in mind that we don't want to have to tranq anyone and we really don't want to kill anyone."

"Right!" Morgan agreed.

"However," Robert continued, "we can't be stopped - no matter what. And, if we have to kill anyone, they should be un-killed when we finally manage to wrest the machine out of Delmont's hands before he ever gets it. So, we have to do whatever we have to do. Everyone got that?"

Everyone did...

"The plan is simplicity itself," the traveler said. "We know we have hours of empty time in the bay and the device will only take twenty minutes or so to install. So, we turn on our stealth field generators, sneak in, Cleo disables the security in the bay, we go in the bay, Cleo disables the security on the ship, we go in the ship, Vox and I install the device, Cleo enables the security on the ship and in the bay, and we get out of there. Any questions?"

"How do we get in the bay?" Morgan asked.

"I'll show you when we get there," the traveler replied.

With their plan laid out, the ship was put in motion and each member appropriately equipped. Several hours later the ship touched down on a distant - depending on where you were looking at it from (it was certainly a fair distance from Earth, I can tell you that) - but very Earth-like - you know, a lot of them are - planet. They had landed near what looked almost like a military base built into a mountain - Again, that's a fairly common thing if you consider all of space and time - Before exiting the ship, they activated their very effective - and very stylish - stealth field generators.

"These invisibility belts are incredible!" Morgan exclaimed, as they marched away from the ship. "I feel like the *Predator.*"

"That's funny," Cleo said thoughtfully. "I've felt that way about you for a while now."

"That was completely uncalled for!"

"I'm just teasing," she giggled. "You don't really. You actually remind me more of a bald, dumb *wookie* or something."

"Thanks…" he sighed. "That's much better."

"At least wookies are nice guys," she pointed out.

"Sometimes," he chuckled. "But, you better watch your step. What if I decide to *tear your arms out of their sockets*?"

"If I were you, I wouldn't try it," she replied.

"No…" he admitted. "I wouldn't if I was me, either."

"Would you two try to keep in mind that we're saving the universe here," Robert said. "We'll have plenty of time on the ship for mindless chatter."

Moments later, a slap echoed through some of the surrounding trees, causing several birds to take flight.

"What was that?" the traveler asked.

"Nothing!" Cleo replied. "Morgan just needs to watch where he puts his hands!"

"How am I supposed to do that, Cleo?" he asked defensively. "My hands are invisible and I can't see you!"

"Well then, put your hands in your pockets!" she demanded.

"When I do that, I can't walk!" he explained.

"Morgan, what in the universe is wrong…" she barked. "You know what? Never mind! Wherever you are, get in front of me!"

"I don't know where I am!"

"Would you two shut up!" the traveler said quietly. "You're going to get us caught!"

"Cleo…" the young man said after a few moment's silence.

"What is it Morgan?"

"What did I touch?"

"Would you shut up?!?!" she exclaimed. "Oh and Rob, I want a lock put on the stealth field generator cabinet."

"I find that *very* offensive, Cleo!" Morgan replied.

Shortly after this exchange, the entire band was very carefully making its way through the front gate. Before them was a massive cavern just filled with *future security guards*. Fortunately for the party, however, most of them were more interested in hot space-coffee and their planet's equivalent of Dunkin Donuts than they were in keeping a group of invisible would-be heroes out of their base. As a result, the entire band reached the control panel to the bay in less than five minutes.

As soon as Cleo started punching buttons, Morgan decided to help her.

"Dun dun dun... dun dun... dun dun dun...," he whispered. "Dun dun... dun dun dun."

"The theme song to *Mission Impossible* isn't going to help her, Morgan" the traveler pointed out.

"It couldn't hurt."

"Unless, of course, it gets us caught and killed!"

"Oh... right."

"Got it," Cleo said triumphantly.

The vault that held the time machine was actually a large box of cormax set in the middle of a huge and mostly-empty cavern. Robert moved the party behind the structure before switching off his stealth field generator.

"We should be perfectly safe here," he nodded. "Nobody walks back here for the next year-and-a-half or so."

"Great," Morgan replied, switching off his own invisibility cloak. "Now, all we have to do is break into the un-break-into-able box."

"Exactly," the traveler smiled, pulling the it-wasn't-actually-a-flashlight from his pocket.

He flipped a switch on its side and a long blade of orange light shot from the silver cylinder.

"I thought you said it wasn't a *light saber*," Morgan said, staring at the traveler from under knitted brows.

"And it isn't," he explained. "*Light saber* is a copyrighted term. This is a *light sword* or *photon saber* depending on who you ask."

"Be that as it may," the young man said, shaking his head, "you said it was a flashlight."

"Yeah, I know," he nodded. "I lied. I didn't want you playing with it."

"It didn't have a power crystal," Morgan pointed out. "What harm could it have done?"

"You could still have lost it," Robert replied. "Either way, we can argue about it back on the ship. For the moment, we've got work to do. Stand back."

"Hiding it from *swag-mad pirates*," the young man muttered under his breath, as he obeyed the command.

Vox stepped up and stuck a pair of handles to a section of the wall as Robert jammed the light blade into it. Slowly, but surely, the *photon saber* sliced through the not-quite-indestructible cormax. In roughly twenty minutes there was a hole in the vault large enough for them all to pass through.

"Okay," Morgan said, gazing through the opening. "How are we going to put that back when we're done?"

"Have some faith, bro," the traveler replied, slapping him on the back. "Let's go."

In less than three minutes Cleo's magic fingers had disabled the ship's security and opened its hatch.

"Doc," Robert said. "You and Morgan keep a lookout. This shouldn't take twenty minutes."

"Keep a lookout?" Morgan asked. "Don't you know whether or not anyone's coming?"

"Yes," the traveler nodded, "and they're not for about twelve hours. But, *random elements*, Morgan! Never underestimate the *random elements!*"

"Right," the young man nodded. "Well then, me and Doc here will keep a look out for any bands of *swag obsessed pirates* that happen to just *randomly* pop into existence here in the un-break-in-able vault..."

"I would appreciate it," Robert chuckled before turning to make his way into the ship.

"Why are we out here, Doc?" the young man asked as soon as the traveler was out of earshot. "I've spent enough time around Rob to know he's full of crap about half the time."

"No quite that much," Doc chuckled, "but I take your point."

"Right," Morgan nodded. "And, I can tell you this, we ain't out here just in case of random pirate attack."

"That's almost certainly true," Doc nodded.

"So, why are we out here, then?"

"Well, when Rob lies - which is often enough - he *always* does it for what he believes is a good reason. Because of that, you can often figure out what the truth is by looking at what's going on and what his motivation for lying might be."

"Okay, let's pretend I understand what you just said for a minute."

"Alright," Doc nodded.

"So, why are we out here, then?"

"Well, it could be that Rob is lying about no one being around. For instance, there could be patrols of guards marching all over this place that may or may not notice us."

"Why would he lie about it?"

"To keep us from being nervous," Doc explained. "At the moment, we believe no one's coming. As a result, we're not on edge."

"*Weren't*," Morgan corrected. "We *weren't* on edge. Now that I know we're surrounded by guards, I'm *very* nervous!"

"We don't know that we are," Doc pointed out. "It could be that Rob was telling the truth about that. Instead, he might have been lying..."

"Stop," Morgan demanded. "I don't want to know anymore. The guards are bad enough. I'll just keep on keeping a lookout for them!"

"Very well," Doc smiled.

"Let's talk about something else."

"Alright," Doc replied. "What would you like to talk about, Morgan?"

"Tell me about Baguette."

"About what?"

"Your home world, Baguette," Morgan explained. "Did I say it wrong?"

"No," Doc chuckled. "You said it fine. What would you like to know?"

"How do you live on a planet with no water?"

"There's plenty of water," Doc explained. "It's just below the surface of the world."

"Weird..."

"Well, it seems weird to us that people could thrive on a planet the surface of which is mainly covered by water."

"Yeah," the young man replied. "I can see that, I guess..."

For the next fifteen minutes or so, Doc and Morgan discussed the differences between Earth and Baguette, as well as the rather fascinating culture of the Baguettians. As the twenty minute mark drew near, Doc sent Morgan to check on the traveler's progress. As the young man neared the bridge, his ears were met by more of Robert's singing. Once again, he was filling the air with familiar eighties lyrics.

"Do you ever sing anything but *Billy Idol* songs?" Morgan asked as he stepped into the chamber.

"Yes," Robert said, sliding out from under the console. "Yes I do, Morgan. And do you know why?"

"Why is that, Rob?"

"Because I'm a simple kind of man who was born on the bayou, right down the road from the house of the rising sun. But then I ran, I ran so far away. And after that Morgan, I walked five hundred miles and I walked five hundred more. All to get away from that tainted love."

"That is weird..." the young man mused. "I mean, you being born in New Orleans. What year was it?"

"Ten Sixty-six."

"That's crazy! I mean, that was... Oh... I see... Are you about done?"

"No," the traveler replied. "We're *completely* done. Let's go."

In less than five minutes, the ship's security was re-activated and the entire band was standing outside the massive hole in the vault.

"Check this out, Morgan," the traveler said. "I think you'll like it."

Doc and Vox opened a tripod and set a small device on top of it. Into this they fed the end of a very long coil of material that exactly matched the color of the vault wall.

"Is that cormax?" Morgan asked, glancing down at the material.

"No," Vox replied. "It's dullex."

"What's the difference?"

"A lot of things," Vox replied. "For one thing, dullex is a lot easier to work with. Of course, it ain't near as strong."

"No, it's not," the traveler agreed. "You could probably break through the dullex patch we're about to put in with nothing more than a sledge hammer and a cold chisel in a week or so. Well... if you worked in shifts. Anyway, do you think it will hold, Vox?"

"I'm pretty sure it will," Vox nodded before pushing a series of buttons on the dullex fed device.

Immediately, a red laser scanned the area of missing wall. Within seconds, the machine was filling the void with flying dullex that hardened almost instantly. In just over two minutes, the opening was gone.

"Well," Morgan said, gazing at the now seemingly undamaged wall, "I'm impressed."

"Yeah," Robert nodded. "It's kind of the ultimate in 3D printing."

"Do they still call it that?"

"No. Let's go."

Vox and Doc attached both a stealth field generator and a gravity reducer to the section of cormax wall laying on the floor. Moments later, it was invisible and practically weightless. Both of them grabbed one of the handles Vox had attached to it earlier. Then, the entire band fired up their invisibility cloaks and started making their way out of the cavern. They stopped just long enough for Cleo to turn the security back on in the bay. Fifteen minutes later, they were on the bridge. The job completed perfectly, and their ship was headed toward the heavens.

"Alright," the traveler said thoughtfully. "Should we go ahead and try it?"

"No, Robert," Doc replied, shaking his head. "We should head back to Never Never Land."

"Well, this shouldn't change the time-lines much," he replied. "If at all."

"True," Doc nodded. "But, I see no reason to take chances."

"You're right," Robert sighed. "Cleo, love... Love?"

"I guess, Rob," she replied, a coy smile on her face. "You've been a *fairly* good boy lately."

"I'm glad," he smiled. "In that case, Cleo, love, second star to the right."

"No problem," she replied, punching a number of buttons on the console.

"That was easier than I was afraid it would be," Vox pointed out.

"Agreed," Doc smiled.

"It's what I call a job well done," Cleo said, leaning back in her seat and putting her hands behind her head.

"Don't do that," Morgan insisted.

"Don't do what?" she asked.

"Don't lean back and put your hands behind your head like that," he explained. "You're going to kill me stone dead."

"What is wrong with you, Morgan?" she asked, a tone of annoyance in her voice. "Do you want to tie me up in a straightjacket? Would that make you happy?"

"Whoa!" he exclaimed, clutching his chest. "Whoa! No! Do *not* ever say... No! No! Do *not* ever even *think* anything about anything that has anything to do with you, me, and a straightjacket! Do you hear me? I mean... Unless - for some *bizarre* reason - we end up married."

"Don't worry, Morgan," she sighed. "That ain't gonna happen!"

"Right!" he cried. "Exactly! Cleo! Engage!"

"*Engage* what?"

"It means *go*..."

"Oh, right! *Next Generation.* But, we're already going..."

"Right," he replied, nodding his head. "Exactly. Well... I'm going down to the medi-bay to check my blood-pressure."

Roughly half-an-hour later, Morgan made his way back to the bridge to find Robert sitting at the controls alone.

"How's the old blood-pressure?" the traveler asked with a grin as Morgan lowered himself into a nearby seat.

"It's good," he nodded. "And, I finally figured out, bro…"

"Figured what out, Morgan?" Robert asked.

"It's you…"

"What's me?"

"You're the *other guy*," Morgan pointed out.

"Yeah, I am," the traveler sighed. "So, how'd you figure it out?"

"Doc told me," the young man explained. "He said he thought I should know because it might help prevent any more *little episodes*. Whatever he meant by that."

"Ah…" Robert nodded. "You know, Morgan, that's not actually figuring it out."

"No… I guess it's not…" Morgan mused. "I never did have any kind of a chance, did I?"

"Well… no, man," the traveler said shaking his head, "you didn't. But it ain't exactly like it was an even playing field."

"What do you mean?" the young man asked.

"I mean, Cleo's *addicted* to me," Robert explained.

"*Addicted to you*? You really are a megalomaniac."

"No, I'm serious, Morgan," the traveler chuckled. "You see… Well… First of all, I guess you should know that there's more than one kind of green woman in the universe."

"Oh! My! Goodness!" Morgan exclaimed.

"Breathe, Morgan. Try to stay with me. Anyway, the women of Cleo's people."

"You mean the *Escargotians*." the young man pointed out.

"Yeah… I guess I do. Either way, their women feel emotions on a level we can't begin to comprehend. All their love, hate, rage, envy, jealousy…"

"Most of those are negative."

"Well, I get those from Cleo a lot for some reason," the traveler explained.

"Yeah, I can see that."

"Like I was saying," Robert continued, "all their emotions are more powerful than anything we can imagine. Then, there's the body chemistry. They're like little pheromone factories. I'm sure you've noticed how good Cleo smells."

"Boy, have I!" Morgan exclaimed, deeply snuffing the lingering *Cleo* in the cabin.

"And, that's just her mainly sitting around on the ship," the traveler explained. "If she were to go for a jog or play tennis or something, it might kill you."

"I believe it might," the young man speculated.

"Then, there's the fact that their sweat tastes like maple syrup to human men."

"So far, I get why I love her," Morgan replied, nodding his head, "but, not why she's addicted to you."

"Right, right," Robert said. "Well, when they're attracted to a man, they become *receptive*."

"*Receptive*? You mean like *Kif*?"

"*Kif*?"

"From *Futurama*."

"Oh… Well, no, not *that* receptive," the traveler said thoughtfully. "But, it's actually kind of similar. Either way, the point is that she and I had been working on a project together for a couple of years. During that time she became *very* receptive to me. Well, we finally succeeded right after she turned eighteen…"

"Which is what she is now," Morgan replied.

"Yeah, but that was the first time she turned eighteen," Robert explained. "Anyway, we were both really excited and jumping around and cheering and she got all hot and sweaty and I wasn't nearly as strong as I am now and… I kissed her."

"You kissed her?" the young man asked sitting bolt upright in his seat.

"Yeah…" the traveler nodded. "I believe I meant to just give her a little peck on the cheek or something, but she turned into me and… I think I went temporarily insane. It's all like a blurry flash of ecstasy."

"So, you kissed her?"

"Yeah. I mean like, I really kissed her," Robert explained. "Like, 'picking her up, spinning her around in the air, panting for breath when we were done' kissed her."

"Like with your tongue?" Morgan asked, his voice overflowing with excitement.

"You know what," the traveler replied, shaking his head. "I don't want talk about that. We're saving the universe, man! I ain't got time to get distracted. However, *after* the universe is saved… Boy, do I plan to set aside some time to *get distracted*!"

"So, that made her addicted to you?"

"Well, yeah," Robert explained. "When they're receptive, their bodies will pull bodily chemicals from the male they're receptive to."

"And your kiss gave her body that opportunity?" Morgan asked.

"My kiss gave her body a gold engraved invitation, a bottle of champagne, and room keys!"

"Yeah, I can see that," the young man nodded.

"Anyway, her skin soaked up my sweat…"

"And her mouth soaked up your saliva," Morgan speculated.

"Don't say it like that…" the traveler said, shaking his head. "You make it sound nasty… Either way, yes. Yes, it did. In a matter of minutes, her body chemistry had completely reworked itself. We became biologically custom made for each other. If you think she smells good to you, you should smell her through my nose."

"Wow!" the young man exclaimed "How do you think about anything else?"

"It's not always easy…" Robert admitted.

"So… she really, truly, honestly, is addicted to you," Morgan said thoughtfully.

"Like crack," the traveler replied.

"She's a Rob head…"

"Basically."

"And you've known that the whole time?" the young man asked.

"Yep."

"And yet you treat her like you do? Rob, sometimes you're a real piece of…"

"I know," the traveler sighed. "You're right, I am. But nobody's perfect Morgan, and I'm working on it. Trust me, Cleo will get her happy ending."

"She had *better*," Morgan replied, his brows knitted.

"The way you said that, it almost sounded like a threat," Robert observed.

"No, Rob, it was a *warning*," the young man explained.

"Wow. Big, bad Morgan Harker. You know man, I liked you the moment I met you, but I've never been prouder of you than I am right now. And honestly, bro, I'm so in love with her that my heart aches from it. But we ain't gonna have no future together in a universe that ain't got no future at all."

"I see where you're coming from," Morgan nodded.

"I'm glad."

"One last thing," the young man said.

"Yeah?"

"What does their saliva taste like?"

"…………Honey," the traveler replied after a long silence.

"Oh! My! Goodness!" Morgan exclaimed.

Half-an-hour after this - let's face it - rather intriguing conversation, the ship re-entered normal space on the very outskirts of Never Never Land. The entire crew gathered on the bridge for the maiden usage - if that's the phrase I'm looking for - of the time machine disabling device.

"Alright Vox," Robert said, taking a deep breath. "Hit it."

"Done," Vox replied, pressing just the right series of buttons.

"Cleo?" the traveler said, turning his attention to her.

"It worked!" she exclaimed, glancing down at one of the monitors. "Twenty minutes after the last time Delmont used the ship, it mysteriously exploded. Effects on the time-lines: nominal."

"Exploded?" Morgan said. "I thought you said the thing would *disable* it."

"That was *maximum disability*," Robert explained. "Trust me man, it ain't getting any more disabled than it is right now. Well... *was right then* is probably a better way to put it..."

"Cool," the young man nodded. "So, what do we do now?"

"Take a break!" Vox exclaimed. "I haven't had time on the island in more than a year."

"True," Doc nodded. "I think you'll agree that we've earned it, Rob."

"Absolutely," the traveler replied. "But, just a few hours. We got a lot of work to do."

"Rob," Cleo said softly, a beautiful smile on her soft blue lips. "Give me a hand up."

"Sure thing," Robert replied, reaching out to take her hand.

In less time than it takes to blink - maybe even, like, half-blink - Cleo snapped one handcuff on the traveler's outstretched wrist and the other on one of her own.

"Handcuffs?" he asked, gazing down at his wrist as Vox and Doc howled with laughter and Morgan fanned himself vigorously with his hand.

"Yes, Rob, handcuffs," she smiled. "I've got some shopping I want to do and I'm not going to end up left behind again."

"I told you," he replied, shaking his head. "I'm *never* going to leave you behind again."

"You're right, Rob," she giggled. "You *never* are."

Morgan fanned even more vigorously.

"Alright," Robert sighed. "What are we shopping for?"

"Feminine hygiene products," she said firmly.

"Oh, that's funny," he replied, nodding his head.

"We'll see if you feel that way at the checkout," she said. "You've got a little *payback* coming, Rob."

"Well, I can tell you one thing for sure, I ain't shopping for no *feminine hygiene products*!" Morgan pointed out. "So, what am I supposed to do?"

"Let's go out for something to eat," Vox suggested. "I'm sick of Rob's stupid MREs."

"I thought you said they didn't mind," Morgan said, gazing at his friend.

"They don't... Well... most of the time," the traveler sighed. "And where did you get the handcuffs from, Cleo?"

"Oh, I bought them about two weeks after you deserted me here, Rob," she explained. "I had a year to practice my *quick snap*."

"Well," he sighed again. "You're really good at it, I'll give you that."

"Thanks," she smiled. "I've practiced a lot."

Shortly after the ship set down on a private landing pad reserved for VIPs, two cabs were heading to two different points on the island. Morgan, Doc, and Vox were all going to some restaurant while Robert and Cleo were on their way to pick up the... *supplies*... Cleo needed. Well, the *supplies* she wanted Robert to have to stand in line with at the checkout. The plain truth is that she planned to buy a lot of stuff she didn't even need just because he didn't like doing it. She figured it was good way to teach him a lesson and would help get him ready to get married someday. After all, what kind of husband can't go up town to get *supplies*? And let's be honest, she had a point, didn't she?

And while it might be interesting to watch the traveler stand in line with boxes of this and that, our tale follows Morgan, Vox, and Doc instead. Now, you might be a little disappointed about that at the moment, but trust me, what happens with them is *way* funnier...

"Where should we go?" Vox asked, as the cab flew along just inches above the ground in an unquestionably *futury* type way.

"I was thinking *Paris on the Half-Shell*," Doc replied.

"I don't know, Doc," Vox said, shaking his head. "I'm not that big a fan."

"Trust me," Doc smiled, "I think you'll enjoy your meal today."

"Alright," Vox nodded, "I trust you. That all right with you, Morgan?"

Morgan didn't answer. He was too busy staring out the window at the odd combination of tropical paradise and sci-fi movie set that was *The Island*. And, as he didn't seem to care one way or the other, the trio soon found themselves at the famous five star restaurant *Paris on the*

Half-Shell. As they stood waiting for a table, which Robert's friends never had to do for long, Morgan was amazed at all the many *Escargotians*, *Baguettians*, and even *Duck à l'orangians* he saw. And there were countless other species of alien that Morgan couldn't even imagine the names of. That's hardly surprising, however, since he didn't have Robert's vivid imagination and knew next to nothing about French cuisine.

In just minutes, the friends were sitting at one of the best tables and browsing over some rather impressive menus written in French.

"Doc," Vox sighed, shaking his head. "I just don't see anything I want. I mean, I can get a steak and potato anywhere, bro."

"Give it two minutes," Doc replied with confidence. "If you want to go after that, we'll go."

"Okay, Doc," Vox said. "But I don't see what two minutes..."

From the moment the menus had been handed to them, Doc had been carefully watching Morgan. As the young man drew a breath to speak, Doc grabbed Vox by the arm in order to temporarily silence him.

"This is weird..." Morgan mused.

"Here it comes," Doc whispered with a smile, before continuing at full volume. "What's weird, Morgan?"

"Some of this stuff is named after planets," the young man pointed out.

"Is it?" Vox asked, gazing over the menu, a puzzled look on his face.

"You think that's gonna work?" Morgan replied, glancing up over the top of his menu. "I may still be the new guy, bro, but I've learned some things over the last few days. In fact, Vox, the name of your home planet was one of the first things I learned after I got here. That's *day one info,* man. And there it is right at the top of the menu: Duck à l'orange."

"Okay, mister savvy space-time-traveler," Vox replied with a grin. "What does it mean then?"

"Hmmm," Morgan said thoughtfully. "Well, my guess is that each of these is like the *planetary dish* of each of these different planets."

"I've got to say," Vox nodded. "I'm impressed, Morgan."

"Oh, there's no doubt about it," Doc replied. "Morgan leaves an impression."

"So," Vox continued, "based on that, what are you going to order?"

"Well," the young man replied taking a deep breath. "I don't know a *lot* about the universe yet, but I think I'm going to go with the escargot. Anything *Escargotians* eat has got to be good."

"Doc," Vox said.

"Yes?" Doc replied.

"I'm glad we came here to eat."

Shortly after Morgan had made his decision, their food was ordered and on its way. Vox just got a steak and potato, Doc went with Sole Meniere, and (as you already know) Morgan thought he wanted escargot.

"What is this?" Morgan asked as soon as their waiter had stepped away.

"Escargot," Doc replied.

"Very funny," the young man said. "Did you have to bribe the chef to do this?"

"No," Vox said, shaking his head. "That really is escargot."

"It can't be," Morgan replied, staring down at his dish. "I mean, this ain't even food, man, it's just a plate covered with dead, steaming snails. I may come from the past, but we had snails back then too, ya know. I mean, no way *Escargotians* are gonna eat garbage like this!"

"I'm beginning to believe you about fate, Doc," Vox said, staring at a nearby table.

"What do you mean?" Doc asked.

"Morgan," Vox replied. "Look at that table over there. Tell me what you see."

The young man immediately did as he was asked.

"Okay," he sighed. "It's a couple of *Escargotians* eating a couple plates of dead, steaming snails..."

"Try it, Morgan," Doc suggested. "You may like them."

"Maybe..." the young man replied. "But, what am I supposed to do with this tiny little fork?"

"Well..." Vox began, before having to pause a moment to keep from laughing in Morgan's face. "I would suggest that you might want to try putting it in your food and then putting that in your mouth,"

"So, what you're saying," the young man replied, pointing at Vox with the fork, "is that I should put the fork in a snail, and then put a snail in my mouth."

"Basi..." Vox started before busting out laughing.

"Yes, Morgan," Doc replied, still having mastery of his own composure. "That is escargot and a lot of people like it. Just try to look past the fact that it's snails."

"Alright," Morgan sighed. "But I'm asking Cleo about this when we get back to the ship. I just don't see her sitting at a table with white wine and candles, jamming hot snails in her mouth."

Roughly half-an-hour later, the three companions were finished at the restaurant. In truth, Morgan had enjoyed the escargot, but he still refused to believe that Cleo had ever eaten a snail. After picking up a couple of things that the young man wanted, they made their way back to the ship. It was very unlikely that Robert would fly off without them, but Doc and Vox had known him long enough not to take chances.

Cleo and the traveler arrived perhaps an hour later, carrying numerous boxes and bags - very few of which actually contained *supplies*. Most of them turned out to be new clothes... Go figure...

"Cleo," Morgan said the moment she stepped on the bridge.

"Yes?"

"You ever eat escargot?"

"Yeah. It's alright."

"See," Vox said. "We told ya."

"Nah," Morgan replied, shaking his head. "That ain't gonna work. Cleo, describe escargot."

"It's cooked snails..."

"Wow..." Morgan said, nodding his head before turning to make his way to his room muttering to himself. "So I guess *Escargotians* just like to eat dead snails... I don't know... the future is a crazy place... Maybe they didn't have cows, I guess..."

Having taken a little break, it was time to get back on the move. With the press of several buttons, the traveler got his ship back into space and his team back on the job.

CHAPTER 6: ACH, ZOMBIES

"So," Morgan said, dropping down in a seat on the bridge. "Where are we headed?"

"To get the Orb of the Gods," Robert replied. "Well, for the moment, we're just getting close. We need a good night's sleep before we tackle this one."

"I feel ya," the young man nodded. "So, I got a question."

"You got all the questions, Morgan. I think you must be like a young Buddha or something."

"What does that mean?"

"Nothing, Morgan," the traveler replied. "Ask the question."

"What happened after you kissed her?"

"Kissed who?"

"Wow!" Morgan exclaimed. "How many green women have you kissed?"

"You didn't specify *green*."

"Wow! Wow!" Morgan double exclaimed. "How many women have you kissed total?"

"One."

"Then why did you…"

"Is this still the same question, Morgan?" Robert asked.

"Yes!" Morgan replied. "What happened after you kissed Cleo?"

"Bad things, Morgan."

"*Oh Really?*" the young man asked.

"You don't need to say it like *Ace Ventura*, man," the traveler replied, shaking his head. "I mean *bad things* not… I don't know… *naughty things*, I guess… Some bad, bad, bad stuff went down."

"Man…" Morgan said. "Like what?"

"Well…" Robert began, "I think the truth is that she and I started falling in love the minute we met. Well, no that's not true, because she was actually a baby when I first met her…"

"How old are you, bro?" the young man asked.

"Are you changing questions?"

"No!"

"Anyway," the traveler continued, "as soon as she was grown, I had her assigned to work on the ship. You know, she rewrote all the code that runs this bird? Well, most of it… I guess in all fairness, *we* rewrote it…"

"I haven't changed questions."

"Right, right," Robert nodded. "Anyway, it's fairly obvious that I'm pretty much the poster child for *Teenage Girl Fantasies*…"

"I don't see it…"

"*And that is why you fail.*"

"What do you mean?" Morgan asked. "And that was a good *Yoda*, by the way."

"Thanks," Robert smiled. "I've had time to practice. Either way, it's equally obvious that Cleo is pretty much at the very core of the human male's most inner and basic desires."

"Way *more* obvious!" the young man observed.

"Well, to men I'm sure that's true…" the traveler admitted. "So, there we were, both pretty much the living, breathing fantasy of the other, spending every single waking hour together for two years straight. During that time, what started out as physical attraction had a great deal more added to it…"

"What more is there, man?!?!" Morgan exclaimed. "I mean, her sweat tastes like maple syrup!"

"You see, Morgan," Robert sighed, "this is why you're not ready for a girlfriend. I mean, Cleo is the finest girl I've ever seen…"

"Cleo is the finest girl that's ever existed!" the young man insisted.

"Well, I feel that way, sure," the traveler replied. "But, I'm not sure you always will. All of space and time is a big place and *everyone has different tastes, you know?*"

"Who said that?"

"*Strong Bad.*"

"Oh yeah!"

"So, to continue," Robert said. "Over those two years, I came to realize that Cleo is also one of the best people I've ever met. She's sincere, honest, self-sacrificing, considerate…"

"Like, all the things you're not…" Morgan mused.

"Right…" the traveler said slowly. "We really complete each other. Anyway, the point is that we fell very sincerely in love."

"And that was a problem?" the young man asked.

"Well, yeah, kind of," Robert explained. "I'm trying to save the universe here, man! And she's part of my team! We're like a family, you know."

"Well, the family that plays…" Morgan began.

"Shut up, Morgan!" the traveler interrupted. "What I'm saying is that I can't be distracted and neither can Cleo."

"Right, but what happened next?"

"Well, she collapsed…" Robert replied.

"Collapsed?"

"Yeah! She collapsed!" the traveler said, throwing his hands up. "And I almost did! I mean two years' worth of built up wild carnal fantasies suddenly ripping their way into reality through your mouth and nose and wildly throbbing…"

"Whoa!" Morgan interrupted. "Whoa! Take five, bro! You're giving me chest pains!"

"Yeah… me too…" the traveler admitted. "Either way, she collapsed. You have to keep in mind that her body immediately started rewiring itself to be my perfect mate. It can put a bit of a strain on 'em. When I saw her lying there I realized what I'd done. So, I stumbled to the comm panel and called for Doc."

"For Doc?" the young man asked.

"Yeah, Doc!" Robert exclaimed. "I needed medical attention, man! I was still half-crazy and my blood pressure had to be, like, a million over five-hundred or something. He arrived in seconds… Doc's a good man and realized there wasn't any time to waste. He hit me up with a tranquilizer and got her safely to bed."

"That don't sound so bad…" Morgan shrugged.

"That wasn't," Robert replied. "But then me and Doc had a real talk. I was poisoned, bro…"

"Poisoned?" the young man asked, a touch of disbelief in his voice.

"Sort of…" the traveler replied, rocking his head side to side. "And I really mean Cleo and me both were. We had started something we couldn't finish…"

"Oh, I think I could have finished it!"

"Watch your mouth!" the traveler barked, a flair of anger in his voice that Morgan had never heard before.

"Sorry!" Morgan immediately replied. "Honestly, bro, I'm sorry! I just get excited."

"It's cool," Robert nodded. "Just don't do it again."

"No worries, man."

"Cleo's a girl you marry, not one you play with," the traveler pointed out. "And I don't *play*."

"Neither do I, man…" the young man said almost sincerely. "Not that I've ever had the chance… I mean, I guess if I did get the chance…"

"Do you want to hear the story, Morgan?"

"Yeah, sorry. But why couldn't you just get married then?"

"One question at a time," Robert replied.

"Right!"

"So, as things were me and Cleo couldn't be left in the same room alone together," the traveler explained. "She was pumping out pheromones chemically designed to attract me specifically, and the moment her *transition* was complete…"

"*Transition?*"

"That chemical change the *Escargotians* go through," Robert replied.

"Oh, right?"

"Anyway, as soon as that was complete, my pheromones did the same thing to her. And, of course, my sweat..."

"And saliva!" Morgan exclaimed.

"What is it with you and saliva, man?"

"Sorry... But what does your sweat taste like to her?"

"I don't know, Morgan..." the traveler sighed. "She hasn't tasted me..."

"Well, how about..."

"Krispy Kreme Bear claws," Robert answered before the question was complete.

"But, that means..." Morgan mused.

"Yeah..." the traveler sighed again. "I try not to think about that. But I do eat a lot of honey when I'm alone..."

"So... you were poisoned?"

"Right! Can you imagine us trying to work together after that?"

"Oh, I can imagine..." Morgan asserted.

"Well don't!" Robert demanded. "Anyway, me and Doc decided that we would have to leave Cleo in Never Never Land for a few months to let the two of us cool off."

"Makes sense, I guess," the young man admitted.

"Yeah, but it ripped my heart out," the traveler said, his voice filled with emotion. "Not for my own sake... I mean, I felt like I had kind of brought it on myself and I could deal with that. But, Cleo..."

"You alright, man?" Morgan asked.

"Yeah..." Robert sighed. "I just have a real good memory, Morgan. Some things I have to work hard not to remember. Anyway, Cleo thought I was rejecting her. I promised to call her for three hours a day every day. And, I did that for a week or so. But, you know me. I'm always trying to *save the universe* and what have you. So... before long it was two hours, then an hour, then every couple of days, then once a week..."

"Rob, sometimes you really are a total piece of..."

"We've been through that remember?" the traveler said, shaking his head. "And if it makes you feel any better, consider the fact that part of the reason I work so hard trying to save all of time is so that she and I can be together some day."

"I feel ya," Morgan nodded.

"So, one day she didn't pick up," Robert continued. "I checked and it had been fifteen days – her time - since I had called. Me and

Doc fired up the engines and went to pick her up. It was obvious I couldn't handle the responsibility of keeping up with her like I should. We were going to have to be on the ship together and just learn to control ourselves."

"What happened when you showed up?"

"Well, to start with, she tried to kill me."

"Really?" Morgan asked.

"Kind of…" the traveler replied, rotating his hand back and forth. "I mean, I don't think she honestly thought she could beat me to death with those tiny fists, but she certainly made the attempt."

"Then, what happened?"

"I held her in my lap for like two hours while she sobbed into my chest and Doc rubbed her back," the traveler replied, gazing off into nothing, his mind in the past. "Every few minutes, she would pull back, slap me in the face as hard as she could, and go back to sobbing. They got a lot of powerful emotions, ya know?"

"Yeah…" the young man said softly.

"Finally, she tried to scratch my eyes out," Robert said, rubbing his chin. "She was actually really fast too. I jerked back, but she ripped my cheek up pretty bad. When she saw the blood pouring down my face she went into a full blown hysterical fit…"

"Wow…"

"Yeah…" the traveler sighed. "We got her back on the ship and got her in bed. After a few days, we had her nursed back to health. Since then, we've had a rather stable *she's basically always mad at me* relationship. Of course, things had softened up a bit before the whole ship-break-down thing… Either way, that may actually be for the best right now."

"Man… that *was* rough."

"Yeah…" Robert replied slowly, almost speaking to himself. "Their tears smell like honeysuckle... Did you know that? Every time I smell it now I get a little sick to my stomach. Sometimes I wonder if it's like my own inner commentary on myself… you know what I mean?"

"I think I do…" Morgan nodded. "Man, no offense, but you've bummed me out a bit. I'm gonna go grab some space ice-cream. You want some?"

"Yeah…" the traveler sighed. "Yeah, I think I do…"

After a few servings of chocolate space ice-cream, Robert and Morgan each went to their rooms to get some rest. The one consoled himself by laying on his bed, eating honey out of a plastic bear, while the other satiated his hunger with a hot ham MRE smothered in maple syrup. The following morning – I guess it was morning... It's actually a little hard to tell when you're floating out in space-time - the entire party gathered once again in the conference room.

"Alright guys," Rob began. "So far we've done very well. We've disabled..."

"Exploded," Morgan corrected.

"Just so," the traveler nodded. "We've exploded Delmont's time machine and set the stage to start going back to undo some of the damage he's done. Now, as you know it's imperative that we try to make corrections one step at a time. This isn't always going to be possible, but we're going to do the best we can. If we can reduce the number of paradoxes, then the universe may be able to handle the rest and finish the job for us."

"Right boss," Vox nodded. "What's the next target? I don't want to be out here for another year."

"True," the traveler nodded. "Our next target is the *Orb of the Gods*. It was a religious relic that the original owners claimed was given them by deities. It was supposed to prove the worth of their people. For centuries their religious leaders felt it was meant as a prize that only the strongest could hold. As a result, their planet was thrown into complete and total war for hundreds of years."

"That's insane!" Morgan exclaimed. "What kind of idiots were these people?"

"Morgan," Doc said, turning to the young man. "Are you certain the gods didn't give it to them?"

"Yeah!" the young man replied, turning his own gaze to the traveler. "Rob, where did it really come from?"

"Two brothers created it hundreds of years before it had any religious significance," Robert replied.

"There ya go," Morgan nodded.

"What inspired them to make it?" Doc asked. "And where does inspiration come from, Morgan? What's the next part of the story, Rob?"

"Well," the traveler continued, "During the period of global war, a group of peaceful religious leaders started a movement to leave the world - and the war - behind them. To a certain extent, they succeeded. A large portion of the population left the planet to start a new splinter colony. This event triggered global talks that eventually ended the wars. The orb was then lost to history for a time. However, roughly a thousand years later, when their world was once again on the verge of global war the orb was rediscovered. The people took it as a sign and put down their arms. As a result, the orb indirectly gave birth to two of the most peaceful civilizations in history."

"If you choose to criticize a religion, Morgan," Doc said with a gentle smile, "at least take the time to learn something about that faith before you condemn it."

"I see where you're coming from," Morgan nodded slowly.

"And that's where Delmont comes in," Cleo speculated.

"Exactly!" Robert replied. "He went back in time to just before the orb was lost and stole it. As a result, it was never rediscovered and so the second war was never stopped. Billions of people died and it created a huge number of paradoxes. However, to complicate matters, the genius sold the orb to someone at the splinter colony as a religious relic from their original home world. The people took it as a sign from the gods and it kicked off a war that should never have happened, killing billions more. Which, of course, created loads more paradoxes. With one theft Delmont managed to make two of the most peaceful societies that ever existed into two of the most violent."

"Wow..." Morgan said. "What a jerk!"

"Well, 'thoughtless, selfish, idiot' might be a more fitting description," the traveler mused. "But, your point still stands."

"So what do we do about it?" Doc asked.

"Simple," Robert replied with a wide smile. "We go to the point in the current time-line where the orb is truly lost forever. We then grab it just moments before that happens. Once we have it, we go back to around ten minutes *after* Delmont stole it and return it. It'll be a little older than it was, but no worse for the wear, I'm sure. Then it *will be* found when it's supposed to be. That will undo a lot of the damage. Once the time-lines have settled, we disable Delmont's time machine a second time. And, voilà we'll have un-stolen the orb and corrected even more of the time line."

"Brilliant," Cleo smiled. "Where do we go to get the orb?"

"Ahhh," the traveler replied, his eyes flashing. "That's the really *exciting* bit."

"Oh no," Vox said, rubbing his hand across his face. "Please Rob, for the love of life, tell me it's not actually going to be *exciting*."

"I like excitement!" Morgan exclaimed.

"Well, you see Morgan," Doc explained, "Rob likes to use the word *exciting* as a euphemism for *suicidal*."

"Euphemism?" the young man replied.

"So, where is it, Rob?" Cleo asked.

"The where isn't important!" he exclaimed. "The important thing is that the orb is lost as the result of two simultaneous apocalypses... Apocalie? What's the plural on that Doc?"

"Apocalypses," Doc sighed. "But, I'm not sure why it has a plural. It only ever takes one."

"Two apocalypses?!?!" Vox exclaimed. "Are you serious, Rob? Have you gone crazy? I mean, have you gone even crazier than the kind of day to day crazy you are all the time?"

"Oh come on, Vox!" he replied excitedly. "It'll be fun!"

"And just what are these apocalypses, Rob?" Doc asked.

"Well," the traveler replied, "it all takes place at the very end of the war on the splinter colony. The two main factions had *each* developed a completely working doomsday device. And, within just minutes of each other, they both set them off."

"What?!?!" Vox exclaimed.

"Wait..." Doc said, shaking his head. "Wait just a second, Rob. What were these devices?"

"Oh, they were crazy brilliant!" Robert replied, clearly impressed. "The first was a group of self-replicating nanobots that broke living creatures down to make even more nanobots. The result was a planet filled to the brim with electro-zombies in just hours! The second doomsday device was a little more ham-fisted, though... It just blew the planet up."

"Whoa!" Morgan exclaimed. "Whoa! So, we're going to a planet covered in zombies to recover a religious artifact right before the planet explodes?"

"That's about the shape of it, man," the traveler admitted.

"Awesome!" the young man nodded excitedly. "I'm going to be like *Indiana Jones* on crack!"

"Rob, this is completely..." Vox began.

"Don't worry, man. We got it!" Robert injected confidently. "Oh, but we can't use shield generators... the nanobots would just feed off of 'em."

"What?!?!" Cleo exclaimed. "Rob, this *is* insane. Why don't we just make a copy of the orb and leave it in place of the stolen one?"

"I'm afraid we can't do that, *sweetheart*," he replied, pulling a toothpick from his top pocket and putting it in his mouth.

"Sweetheart?" she replied.

"Yeah," the traveler nodded. "The people were technologically advanced enough to make a molecular imprint, *see?*"

"Could we make a fake that matched the imprint?" Morgan asked.

"Nope," the traveler replied. "As much as I like faking things..."

"Like money," the young man interrupted.

"I never said it was counterfeit," the traveler replied before continuing. "Not even *we* have the technology to do that. We would need the exact molecules it's made of to make a fake."

"Couldn't we just change the records?" Cleo suggested.

"*No chance*," Robert replied, sounding a good bit like *Humphrey Bogart*. "It was verified thousands of times over the years. We'd have to make thousands of corrections, each one possibly changing the time-lines, and a single mistake could *blow the whole gaff*."

"*Blow the whole gaff*, Rob?" Doc chuckled. "Why are you talking like that?"

"I always talk like this when we pull a *job*. This is a *job*, and you all are my *gang*, and Cleo... Well, Cleo's my *moll*."

"I'm not your *moll*, Rob," Cleo corrected, as if she were fooling anybody.

"Yeah," Morgan sighed nodding his head. "Yeah, you are..."

Vox and Doc merely nodded in time.

As completely insane as Robert's plan obviously was they had no choice but to see it through - or die trying... Personally, I don't think I've have gone myself. Time would have just had to *take one for the team*. Of course, I'm just a writer, not an action hero... Just minutes after the decision had been made, the ship was set on autopilot and the entire team was assembled in the ship's landing bay. There, in its very center, was a rather bodacious eight-seater, convertible, *future car* that was capable of some serious high-speed maneuvers and full-on flight.

The party was very well - even crazy well - armed. However, they had neither shield generators nor invisibility belts. From the point of view of shielding and visibility, they were having to do this one *au naturel*. And, of course, Morgan still didn't have a gun.

"Where did you get that bat?" the traveler asked, staring the young man straight in the bat.

"I found it," Morgan explained. "I'm not going without a weapon again."

"Where did you find it?" Robert asked. "I didn't even know I had a bat."

"I don't remember," the young man replied. "I wander around the ship when I'm bored."

"That makes sense," the traveler replied. "Anyway, don't hit anybody with it."

"I may have to hit some electro-zombies."

"Yeah, that'll be fine."

The five of them had just piled into the car when a sudden thought hit the young man.

"What is this called?" Morgan asked.

"It's called a *car*," the traveler explained.

"We should call it the *Morganmobile*!"

"No... No, we shouldn't. Everybody ready?"

"Put the top up, Rob," Vox said.

"Nah," the traveler replied. "The weather's awesome!"

As he said this, the ship reached its destination, hanging roughly a hundred feet above the ground. With a quick series of button pushes, he opened the landing bay and allowed the car to plummet into the sky below them. As they made their rapid descent toward the temple that was their target, Morgan threw his hands into the air.

"Wooo!" he screamed, wildly waving his arms in the wind. "Cleo! Put your hands up!"

"No, you moron!" she replied.

Seconds later, they crashed through the roof of the temple. Robert quickly brought the car to a stop roughly ten feet above the floor. The building was, as promised, just crawling with e-zombies. However, with a few more button presses the traveler caused the car to power up its weapons and pull something along the lines of *Death Blossom* from *The Last Starfighter*. Within moments, all of the zombies that filled the chamber were nothing but nanos with every last bit of bot blasted right out of them.

Instantly, the traveler landed the car and the entire party hopped out. Robert pressed the security button on his keyring causing the car to rise out of the chamber and hover a short distance from the giant hole in the roof.

"So far, this is going well," he said. "Which is really great, because we have exactly twenty minutes before the planet explodes."

"Rob!" everyone screamed.

"No time! Let's go!"

Just ahead of the band was a staircase leading into the bowels of the temple. The lights filling the building flickered on and off like something out of a horror movie - specifically one with zombies in it - as the band made their way down the stairs.

"We have to get to the holy vault as quickly as we can," Robert pointed out just as they reached the foot of the stairs, entering another chamber filled with nano-nightmares. "We're going to have to have time for Cleo to unlock it."

The entire band opened up some serious auto-fire laser action on the zombies that were making their way very quickly toward the party. A dense pack edged ever closer through the fire, however, making steady headway against the constant stream of *not-blaster not-bolts*. Doc pulled the gun from his back, took careful aim, and blasted a massive hole in the not-really-undead pack.

"What is that?" Morgan asked.

"It's basically a shotgun," Doc answered. "But, for super-elephants."

As most of the party's attention was focused on the swarm of electro-zombies in front of them - particularly on the one that had its legs blown off and was crawling toward them on its hands hoping for some revenge - something attracted Morgan's attention. It was the terrified scream of a woman.

Morgan jerked his head to the left. In the corner of a not-so-distant adjacent chamber stood a truly voluptuous blue female who was about to be accosted by a single automated-corpse. The path between them was clear and Morgan's inner hero filled his mind with a single primitive thought: must save woman!

"*Crom!*" he screamed at the top his lungs, lifting the bat above his head and boldly charging his nano-fied foe.

In moments, he reached the enemy, who had evaluated him as just slightly more threatening than an unarmed woman using its powerful computerized e-brain. And so, as Morgan swung his bat with all his might, it was prepared. The nano-zombie grabbed the steel improv-weapon in its vice-like grip and began crushing it before the amazed eyes of the young man.

"Wow..." he said. "That didn't go at all..."

That was as far as he got before the thing grabbed him by the throat, lifting him from the ground, his well-sneakered feet kicking wildly in the air. Before the life was completely choked out of him, a massive volley of laser fire cut his enemy to pieces. Immediately Doc was at his side, scanning the area where the zombie had touched him with a device emitting a bright blue beam.

"That will deactivate the nanobots," Doc explained, before turning his eyes to the woman. "Ma'am, you may want to follow us."

The chamber had been cleared of most of its less-than-living occupants and the band quickly finished off the last stragglers before moving on. Two minutes later, the party was standing just outside the holy vault with Cleo pushing buttons as fast as she could think to. More and more zombies appeared each moment and the surrounding floor was slowly covered by the dust of broken down nanobots.

"Shoot!" Robert yelled, handing the rifle he was holding to the blue woman before pulling a pistol.

"She gets a gun, but I don't?!" Morgan screamed.

"Yes!" the traveler replied. "She knows what she's doing! She's been in the middle of a war for just over a decade!"

Robert seemed to be right about that. At least, the blue woman certainly had no trouble ending the e-lives of their enemies.

"Cleo, honey," Robert said. "I don't want to rush you, but we ain't got a lot of extra time."

"Well, Rob," she replied, "had I known I was going to have to do this, I could have studied up. However, you didn't tell me!"

"I didn't want to make you nervous."

"Well, I'm nervous now!"

"That's a fair point," the traveler admitted. "I'm going to have to make the briefings more informative in future."

"Got it," she cried triumphantly as the vault opened.

"Morgan, grab the orb!" Robert yelled.

Immediately the young man obeyed.

"And whatever you do, don't drop it! It's filled with explosives!"

"What?!?!" Morgan screamed.

"Just kidding! Let's go!"

"Rob!" everyone but the blue woman screamed.

As the party was making its way up the stairs, Vox made a rather important observation.

"I don't want to upset anyone," he yelled, "but we're into minute twenty-two of our twenty minutes!"

"That's no problem," the traveler replied. "I lied! We had twenty-five minutes; I just wanted you guys to hurry."

"Rob!" everyone but the blue woman screamed.

In not-quite-three-minutes, the party had reached the top of the stairs. They blasted their way through another group of e-zombies and piled into the car on exactly the twenty-five minute mark. Fortunately for them, Rob had lied again. They actually had twenty-seven minutes. That was just enough time to get to the bridge and fire up the engines before the planet exploded. As the ship flew from the world, wrapped in flames, and the flying debris of a dying world, Vox made yet another observation.

"This ain't no good for the shields, Rob!" he yelled as the ship was slammed one direction, then the other.

"Eh," he said, gazing down at the console and wildly pushing buttons, "they'll hold."

Seconds later, they were safely in non-space with the orb in their possession.

"See," the traveler said, spinning his chair around to face his crew. "What did I tell ya? Piece of cake."

"Doc," Vox said. "Head down to the medi-bay with me. This time, I need to check my blood pressure."

As soon as they stepped from the room, both Robert and Morgan turned their attention to the blue woman, who was clearly in a state of shock. The young man now agreed with Robert wholeheartedly; everyone did have different tastes. As beautiful as Cleo was, he found this girl even more attractive. Of course, part of that was probably the fact the Cleo had already so completely, totally, and unequivocally rejected him. Besides, she was really Rob's girl...

Morgan felt that *voluptuous* truly was the only word that could describe her. Well, that or *stacked* depending on where you grew up. She was just under six feet tall and had dark purple hair that hung down to the center of her back. And her eyes, which were staring blindly ahead, were a breathtaking shade of aquamarine. She was a *well-developed* woman in every sense of the word and the young man had to work very hard to stare at her without getting caught.

"I'm sorry, miss," Robert said, his voice filled with sincere sympathy. "You've just witnessed something no one should ever have to see: the death of your home world. But I promise you, it's not as bad as it seems."

"I'm not sure how it could be worse," she replied softly, her breathing quick and shallow.

"What's your name?" he asked.

"Azure," she replied.

"Well, Azure, I'm Robert," he said with a smile, "the last time traveler. Your world was never meant to be destroyed. And, before I'm finished, it won't have been."

"What do you mean?" Azure asked, turning her eyes toward him. "That's impossible."

"I'm certain it seems that way," the traveler replied. "However, I assure you it's more than merely possible. In fact, it was a time traveler that destroyed your world. I've come to undo the damage he did. And, very shortly, I will have."

"Am I dead?" she asked, slowly gazing around her.

Morgan turned his eyes to the floor. He couldn't help but find the woman attractive, but something about that struck him as *very* wrong at the moment.

"No," the traveler replied. "You're certainly not dead. You are, however, in a severe state of shock."

"Where am I?"

Robert reached down and pushed a button on the console. "Doc, we're actually going to need you back up here pretty quick. She's not in great shape."

"I know. I'm just grabbing some things," Doc replied. "I'll be back up there in a minute."

"Where you are is here," Robert said, kneeling down by the young woman and taking her hands in his. "You're with friends. And you're safe. Very soon this is all going to be nothing more than a bad dream."

"I'm not sure I'll ever wake up..." she whispered.

"You will," he nodded. "And, once you have, you won't even remember this nightmare. Now, this young lady is Cleo, and she'll take care of you. Just let her know if you need anything at all. Me and Morgan here have to have a quick chat, but we'll be right back."

Robert and Morgan immediately rose and made their way silently toward the young man's room.

"What's up?" the young man asked.

"Sit down," Robert commanded, opening Morgan's door and pointing toward his bed. "I have a question."

"Alright, bro," the young man replied, quickly obeying the command. "What is it?"

"I want to know what you were thinking when you saved Azure," the traveler replied. "Walk me through your thought process."

"Well," he said, taking a deep breath. "It was clear she was about to get killed. So... I tried to save her. I know I didn't exactly..."

"Morgan," Robert interrupted, "do you remember that conversation we had when I first picked you up?"

"I think so."

"Good! We're not here to save men, women, and children, Morgan. We're here to save the universe!"

"We couldn't just let her..."

"Yes!" the traveler interrupted again. "Yes, we could have let her die. That's exactly what we could have done. And it's exactly what you should have done!"

"What?!?!" Morgan asked, rising to his feet. "Are you nuts?"

"Everybody dies, Morgan," Robert replied. "We're over a thousand years in the past. Azure's been dead for a *long* time, man."

"But, still we couldn't..."

"You're not listening, Morgan!" the traveler replied rather loudly. "Yes, we could! That's exactly what we could have done! We can't mess this up, man! We can't afford to! There ain't no cavalry coming to our rescue. No time traveler from the future is going to go back and fix our mistakes. We just can't make any! What if saving her had caused a paradox that kept us from fixing the future? We can't take chances, Morgan. You think I like that? I believe all life is sacred! You think I want to stand there and do nothing while I watch a young woman get killed?!?! No, I don't! I *hate* it! But we don't have a choice, Morgan! We do *not* have a choice! Do you understand me?!?!"

"I'm trying to..." Morgan, sighed. "It's just not..."

"No! It's not easy! But you need to wrap your head around it right now! We can't make any more mistakes! And Morgan, you also need to think about the fact that, because you *saved* her, she's up on the bridge in a state of shock right now, instead of peacefully dead with the rest of her people. Just think how she's going to feel for the next few hours."

"You're right," the young man sighed again. "I messed up."

"Thank you, Morgan," the traveler said, stepping over to sit down on the bed. "And it wasn't all your fault. I should have warned you guys that there might be survivors. I was just hoping they'd all be dead before we reached them."

"Yeah..."

"Either way, there's no harm done this time. Well, not to the time-lines. But, you might have done a little to yourself."

"How do you mean?" Morgan asked.

"Well," the traveler began, "When we un-steal the orb, Azure will vanish and we'll have never rescued her. So, your big heroic moment saving a beautiful woman will be undone."

"That doesn't matter," Morgan replied, a slight smile on his face. "We'll have saved her whether or not she ever knows it."

"You're right about that, man" the traveler replied, with a nod. "And don't worry, we may run into other opportunities where you actually *can* rescue the damsel in distress. But, either way, from now on, no more mistakes, right?"

"Right!" Morgan agreed.

CHAPTER 7: AZURE

"Well Azure," the traveler said, stepping back onto the bridge, "how are they taking care of you?"

"Very well," she replied. "But, I'm really nauseated."

"That'll pass in a moment, dear," Doc said with a smile. "I've already given you something for it."

"And in just a few hours," Robert added, with a smile, "none of this will have ever happened."

"Days," Vox replied, gazing down at one of the consoles.

"Days?" the traveler asked.

"Two or three, yeah," Vox nodded. "The ship took a bit of a beating, Rob. It wasn't exactly made to fly through the exploding remains of dying planets."

"I can't believe this is happening," Azure whispered.

"Just try to pretend it isn't," Cleo said, rubbing the young woman's back. "It'll be over soon."

"Are you sure, Vox?" Robert asked, stepping over to the console himself.

"Well," he replied, waving toward the screen. "You tell me what you think."

"You're right," the traveler sighed, rubbing his forehead. "Still, it's not too bad."

"No," Vox agreed. "But, I don't want it getting that way. It's all minor stuff and should be easy to fix. At least, it will be if we don't let it get any worse."

"True. Drop back into real space, I guess, and we'll get to work," Robert replied, before turning his attention back to the young woman. "Well, Azure, it looks like it's going to be a few days. After that, however, you're going to wake up safe and sound on your home world. I know it's hard to understand, but you need to accept it. It'll make the next couple of days a lot easier on you. Just forget what you've seen and try to keep in mind that none of it ever happened."

"Thank you," she replied, tears welling up in her eyes. "Thank you all. You saved my life, even if you couldn't..."

Here the young woman was overcome by grief. She began sobbing into her hands as tears of sympathy began to flow down Cleo's cheeks. Slowly, the scent of honeysuckle filled the cabin.

"Doc," Robert said, "you got any more of that nausea medicine on ya? I ain't feeling a hundred percent myself."

The next twenty-four hours were rather difficult for Morgan. Robert and Vox were both working on repairs, only stopping for food or sleep, while Cleo and Doc were doing their best to make Azure as comfortable as possible. The young man would have been willing to help with either task, had he been able. However, he didn't know enough about the ship to reliably use the intercom, much less make repairs and he had a hard time being in the same room with Azure without *caressing her with his eyes*, which even Morgan knew was inappropriate at the time...

As a result, he spent the rest of the day and a good portion of the following morning reflecting on what he had done. The suffering Azure was going through really was all his fault. If he had just let the electro-zombie kill her, it would have all been over in minutes - if not seconds. Now, she was going to have to go through several days of mental anguish all because of him. He had wronged her. And, there's only one thing a man can do when he's wronged a woman. He has to apologize.

Around ten the next morning, - I guess... It's hard to do the time-math. Either way, it was late for breakfast, early for lunch - Morgan found Cleo and Azure having a couple of MREs on the bridge. Neither of them were crying, so he figured their spirits had picked up at least a little bit. He knew he had to leap on the opportunity.

"Look," he said with a deep sigh, gazing down at Azure. "I'm really sorry. I hope you can forgive me."

"Sorry for what, Morgan?" she asked, her aquamarine eyes staring up at him.

"Oh," he said, with a touch of embarrassment. "I mean for saving your life..."

"What?" both women replied at once.

"Well," he sighed again. "I know you'd probably rather be dead right now. I just..."

"No, actually," she interrupted, one eyebrow raised slightly. "No, I wouldn't. What would make you think that?"

"Well," he explained. "If I hadn't saved you, that thing would have killed you in like seconds, and so you wouldn't be so upset right now."

"No..." she replied. "I suppose I wouldn't be, but on the other hand, I would be *dead*, Morgan."

"Right..." he nodded slowly. "So... You're saying you'd rather *not* be dead?"

"Is he crazy?" Azure asked, turning her gaze to Cleo.

"No... Well... maybe actually, it's kind of hard to tell," she replied. "Morgan, sit down."

Immediately, he obeyed.

"Alright," Cleo said. "Try again. And, maybe start at the beginning."

"Okay," he said, pausing a moment to collect his thoughts. "What I'm saying is that, after we un-steal the orb, Azure's home world is never going to be destroyed, right?"

"Right," Cleo nodded.

"So," he continued, "that being the case, all the people on her home world that were killed by e-zombies won't be killed by them, right?"

"Right," Cleo again agreed.

"So," he explained, "by saving Azure I didn't actually *save* her, because we're really going to *save* her by un-stealing the orb, right?"

"I see what you're saying."

"And, since I didn't *save* her by saving her because we're actually going to *save* her later, all I've done by saving her when I did is put her through days of pointless suffering and Rob's crappy MREs, right?"

"I guess you could make that argument."

"Right," he nodded. "So, it would have been a lot easier on her if I had just minded my own business and let the zombie do its work."

"Well," Azure said shaking her head, "I'm glad you didn't..."

"Oh," he said with a smile. "In that case, you're welcome!"

"So you guys are really serious, then?" Azure asked.

"About what?" Cleo asked.

"The whole time travel, saving the universe thing," Azure replied.

"Yes," Cleo nodded. "Of course. What would make you think we weren't?"

"Mainly the fact that it's impossible, I guess," Azure explained. "I mean, it certainly doesn't seem possible..."

"Well, it is," Cleo smiled.

"I'm beginning to believe it," Azure replied. "Well... I believe Morgan believes it anyway..."

"Oh, I do," he nodded. "I didn't at first, I thought I was having a *flashback*, but I finally came around."

"You've done drugs?" Cleo asked.

"No!" Morgan exclaimed.

"Then, how could you have a *flashback*?"

"Well, ya see..."

"You know what, Morgan," Cleo interrupted. "Never mind, it doesn't even matter. The point is that we are serious and none of this is ever going to have happened to you, Azure."

"That's just... weird..." she replied. "I mean, you're going to save my life, my world, and I'll never even know it."

"You'll never even meet us," Cleo smiled.

"That's kind of sad," Azure said thoughtfully. "Obviously I wouldn't want to meet you under *these* circumstances, but I wish I could meet you. I wish I could thank you!"

"You already have," Cleo replied.

"I guess that's true," Azure said. "But, you know what I mean."

"So," Morgan said with a slight smile. "Are you feeling better?"

"Much," Azure replied. "I know it's crazy, but I actually believe you. For one thing, this ship is like nothing I've ever seen before."

"It is," Cleo agreed.

"Okay," Morgan said. "I just want to double check. Azure, you now realize that we *are* time travelers, that we *are* going to save your world, and - all things considered - you're feeling pretty cool about it. Is that right?"

"Basically... I guess," she replied. "I mean, it's still a lot to take in, but I'm beginning to wrap my head around it."

"Close enough," Morgan replied before settling comfortably into his seat for a prolonged *eye caressing*. "You two carry on."

For the next few minutes, the girls sat there talking, laughing, and enjoying their MREs. Morgan, for his part, just enjoyed himself watching them enjoy themselves.

"So..." he said thoughtfully, after the girls had finished their meals. "I've been thinking."

"That's unfortunate," Cleo said.

"Awww," Azure replied. "Be nice to him. He did risk his life to save mine."

"Alright," Cleo sighed. "But I have a feeling you'll regret that in a minute. What is it Morgan?"

"Well," he said with a knowing wink, "In a couple of days we're going to make it where Azure was never on board."

"Right," Cleo nodded. "We've been through that more than once now."

"Right, right," he agreed. "But, that means she can do whatever she wants and there will be no consequences for her."

"Morgan," Cleo replied, a tone of warning in her voice, "what are you suggesting?"

"Well," he said with a grin, "to start with... space ice-cream. She can eat all she wants and not worry about any of the calories."

"I suppose that's true," Cleo laughed.

"I'll go get some!"

The young man returned a few minutes later with a variety of space ice-creams and syrups. Surprisingly, although Rob only really liked three kinds of MREs, he loved a wide range of ice-creams. Of course, they didn't have double fudge MREs, so maybe it's not really all that remarkable.

"What is that?" Cleo asked, glancing over at Morgan's *space bowl*.

"Oh..." he said, a slightly guilty look on his face. "It's... just... pistachio ice-cream with maple syrup on it..."

"Is it any good?" she asked.

"Oh yeah!" he replied.

"Let me try it," she said.

"Oh yeah!" he replied.

"Not yours!" she exclaimed. "I'm not eating after you... I'm never sure where your mouth has been lately..."

Both she and Azure fixed themselves a small portion.

"This is good!" Azure observed.

"Oh..." he said slowly. "You're right about that... it is *very* good..."

"Morgan," Cleo said with a contented smile, "sometimes, you're a genius."

"Thank you," he replied, before lifting a plastic bear in his hands. "Maybe you girls would like to try a little honey on it? Or we could even try that with the blueberry ice-cream..."

"Hey guys, what's up?" Rob said, stepping quickly into the room.

"Whoa!" Morgan screamed, throwing the plastic honey bear into the air. "Nothing! Nothing's up, man! What could be up?!?! *Why* would anything be up?!?!"

"Right..." the traveler nodded, catching the falling honey bear in his hand. "And where did you get this, Morgan?"

"It's mine," he replied defensively.

"Yeah... but where did you get it from?"

"Vox bought it for me when we were on the island. Doc didn't really want him to, but after Vox explained that it was an *entertainment investment*, whatever that meant, Doc went along with it."

"Mmmm," Robert nodded slowly. "And what else did Vox buy you?"

"Nothing..." Morgan said, his eyes wandering around the room. "I mean... there was a... a ten gallon... ten gallon jug of a... of maple syrup..."

"Mmmm," the traveler replied.

"What difference does it make, Rob?" Cleo asked. "He's putting it to good use. You should try this! It's pistachio ice-cream with maple syrup! It's delicious!"

"Oh, I'm sure it's good!" Robert replied. "I'm surprised he didn't have you try the blueberry."

"Yeah," she smiled. "We were going to try that next."

"I'm sure you were, love," the traveler said. "But, unfortunately, Morgan's already had enough ice-cream. Haven't you, Morgan?"

"More than enough!" the young man replied.

"That's good!" Robert nodded. "Too much ice-cream can be bad for your health, Morgan."

"I had heard that!"

"Well, it's absolutely true!" the traveler assured him. "Besides, you've got something else you've got to start working on."

"And what's that?" Morgan asked.

"Learning to use a gun," Robert replied.

"Awesome!"

"Indeed," the traveler replied. "We can't keep taking you on missions without you knowing something about weapons. I didn't want to take the time before but, now that we've got a couple of days, you shouldn't waste them. Besides I'm afraid that, under the circumstances, too much free time might just get you into trouble."

"It might at that," the young man agreed.

"So," Robert continued, "go get Doc and have him take you down to the range. I want him to walk you through the basics and let you get some shooting time in. In fact, I think it would be best if you basically spent all of the next two days shooting."

"Right," Morgan nodded.

"Can I come?" Azure asked.

"Sure," the traveler replied. "If you feel up to it."

"I do," she nodded. "I'm actually feeling a lot better now. And honestly, I think it would be better for me to have something to focus on."

"Good point," Robert replied. "In that case, I could use some help, Cleo. Are you up for it?"

"Always," she smiled.

Immediately, Morgan and Azure went to find Doc while Robert and Cleo went to help Vox. Doc got Morgan out on the gun range – Which was on the ship. How cool is that? – and laid out a small assortment of weapons for him to practice with. For roughly an hour, he went over the basics - and a lot of gun safety. Finally, Morgan got to take his first practice shots.

"That's not very good, is it?" he asked after he had fired off his third round.

"Oh, I don't know, Morgan," Doc said, shaking his head. "None of them hit us, and that makes me feel really good at this point."

"True..." he sighed. "But, none of them hit the target either."

"That's hardly surprising," Azure pointed out. "You're holding your gun all wrong."

"How do you mean?" he asked.

"I mean," she said, taking his hands in hers, "that you need to hold it more like this. Then, put one leg out a short distance ahead of you and lean forward slightly. Now try."

He tried. To his own amazement, he hit the very edge of the target.

"Wow..." she said. "You're really bad. I don't know that I've ever seen anyone with less natural talent."

"Thanks," he said nodding. "And I don't even have to try."

"Azure," Doc said, "do you think you can help him?"

"Absolutely."

"Would it be alright if I left?" he asked. "I have some things I want to take care of in the medi-bay if you can handle this."

"Sure," she said with a smile. "I'd be glad to. It gives me something else to think about."

"Excellent," Doc replied. "In that case, I'll leave him in your capable hands."

For the next half-an-hour or so, Morgan went through all the different guns and tried a number of multiple aiming techniques. He was equally terrible with all of them...

"This is going to take more extreme measures," Azure asserted, shaking her head almost in disbelief. "Look, Morgan, I'll be right back. Do *not* touch any of these guns while I'm gone. Okay?"

"Oaky."

"Promise?"

"Promise."

"I'll be right back."

For a few minutes, Morgan stood alone on the range, his eyes moving from the firearms laying on the table to his basically unscathed target. After what seemed like quite a long time to the young man (although it was really only about five minutes) Azure strutted back into the room wearing a pair of black stiletto boots.

"Wow!" Morgan exclaimed. "Where did you get those?"

"My room," she replied. "This ship is surprisingly well stocked..."

"It sure is!"

"Anyway, Morgan," she said, pointing down range, "pick up a pistol and aim it at the target."

He instantly obeyed.

"Alright, with these boots on I'm just a tad taller than you," she said, stepping up behind him and covering his hands with her own, before setting her head on his shoulder. "Pull in tight, like this... Put your foot a little further out... Now, lean slowly forward..."

"Oh! My! Goodness!" Morgan exclaimed.

"What is it?" she asked.

"I've just fulfilled one of my childhood fantasies," he explained.

"What fantasy?" she asked, a touch of confusion in her voice.

"Well," he lied, "I always used to fantasize about going down to a gun range."

"But, we've been here for over an hour."

"I know," he lied some more. "But I had forgotten about it."

"Oh..." she said. "Well, I'm glad you're living your dreams. Either way, pull it up like this... and slowly... pull... the... trigger..."

This time, the shot at least hit the scoring section of the target.

"Score!" he said appropriately.

"It's a start," she sighed. "But, it's going to take a lot more work to make you any kind of a shot."

"Oh," Morgan grinned. "I got time..."

For the next two hours, Azure stood behind the young man helping him learn how to hold his body while shooting. All things considered, he did pretty well. I mean, her hot breath on his neck just about made him drunk, not to mention her hands on his, and it's probably best not to even think about what was pressed against his back the whole time. After a while he got an idea - Well, let's face it, he got a lot of ideas, but we're only going to hear about one of them...

"I've got an idea," he said surprisingly.

"What's that?" Azure asked innocently.

"What if we approach this from a psychological angle?" he suggested.

"What do you mean?"

"I mean, like a *rewards* system," he explained. "I mean, to give me motivation, you know?"

"Right..."

"So, maybe we should, like, kiss every time I hit a bulls-eye or something..."

"Wow... Cleo said you were a crazy optimist," she replied. "But, I have to admit I like the general idea."

"You do?!?!"

"Sure," she replied. "I just think the execution part needs work."

"What do you mean?"

"Well, instead of us kissing when you do good, maybe I could punch you in the back of the head when you do bad."

"You're right," he sighed. "The psychological angle is no good. I just need to put in more practice..."

"That's the spirit, Morgan!"

After roughly five more hours of practice, they decided to call it a night. Morgan had at least gotten to the point where he wasn't a danger to himself or others with a gun in his hands. And, he could shoot without Azure holding his hands. The young man saw both sides of this, however, and was thrilled and bitterly disappointed at the same time.

"Well," Azure said as they reached her door, "I'm gonna take a quick shower and then maybe head up to the bridge for a few minutes... Morgan..."

The young man was staring into nothingness, his mind trapped in a fantasy universe. Azure shook him gently by the shoulder.

"Morgan," she said. "Are you alright?"

"What?" he said, suddenly jerking back to reality. "Yeah! I'm great! You know if you need any help..."

"Thanks..." she interrupted, "but, I think I got it."

"Right," he nodded. "Well, remember, the offer's on the table."

"I'll see you in a few minutes, Morgan," she replied, closing the door in his face.

The young man took a deep breath and made his way slowly to the bridge where he found Rob sitting alone.

"Well!" he said, sliding down into one of the seats. "I've got a new favorite color!"

"Let me guess," the traveler said, turning to look at the young man, "it's blue."

"Indeed, it is!" Morgan nodded. "Of course, to be fair, blue was my original favorite until that *Star Trek* episode made me switch to green. Anyway, it reminds me of that song."

"*I'm Blue*?" Robert suggested.

"No. *Rock the Cradle of Love*. I think you singing it all the time has just got it stuck in my head."

"I guess I can understand that," Robert admitted.

"Either way, I'm *really* in love this time."

"So, you're over Cleo?" the traveler asked.

"Oh yeah, bro. She's your *bird* and I'm past that."

"That's for the best," Robert nodded. "What about the honey and maple syrup?"

"I'll try to wean off over the next few days," the young man suggested. "Good enough?"

"That'll do."

"Anyway, this is the *real* thing this time," Morgan asserted.

"I have my doubts," the traveler confessed.

"What makes you say that?"

"Maybe it's the fact that you don't really know her."

"It was love at first sight," Morgan insisted.

"There's no such thing."

"You're wrong this time, Rob."

"Okay. What do you love about her?" the traveler asked.

"Well, for starters she's got huge…"

"You see, Morgan," Robert interrupted, "that's not love. What you've got there, my friend, is *lust* at first sight."

"I was going to say *personality*." Morgan lied.

"No, you weren't," the traveler pointed out. "That's a *lie*. You weren't even going to say *huge tracts of land*. You've been hanging around me too much. You're picking up bad habits."

"No… you're right," Morgan confessed. "I wasn't going to say *personality*… And, I don't want to pick up bad habits. However, I do want to pick up good habits. What should I say to her?"

"As little as possible?" Robert suggested.

"That's no help, Rob!" the young man replied. "I've got to get to know her. I just *have* to go out with her. And, you know why?"

"Why is that?" the traveler asked.

"Because she's stacked! That's why!"

"You see, man," the traveler chucked, "this is why you're not ready for a girlfriend."

"Help me get ready!"

"I don't have the time."

"You have all the time!"

"It's not enough…" Robert insisted. "And besides, Morgan, she's not going to be with us long, man. Day after tomorrow she's gone forever. Even if you were a *grand master*, you couldn't get far with a girl like that in so little time."

"How far could you get?" Morgan asked.

"Probably no further than a couple of hours into our honeymoon."

"That would be enough for me," Morgan replied. "In fact, I'd settle for ten minutes into the honeymoon."

"You'll never make it!"

This inane conversation continued for perhaps twenty minutes and was only brought to an end by the appearance of Azure and Cleo. Both of them had wet hair, but neither was wielding a towel. As a result, Morgan was able to keep his head.

"Is there any way I could come with you?" Azure asked as she and Cleo sat.

"Come with us where?" Robert asked.

"I mean *come with you*," she explained. "Like, become part of the crew."

"Well, no," he replied, shaking his head. "Because when we un-steal the orb you'll have never been here in the first place."

"Oh," Azure replied. "And, there's no way around that?"

"No," he said. "What would make you think there might be?"

"Well..." she said thoughtfully. "It just seemed to me that if you un-steal the orb then you wouldn't need to un-steal it and if you didn't need to un-steal it then it would get stolen so you would have to un-steal it. Is that right?"

"It's hard to say," he chuckled. "You sound like Morgan."

"Hey!" both she and Morgan replied at the same moment.

"Let's see," Robert replied. "I *think* you're trying to ask how we get around the *paradox* that is the fact that our own actions will remove the cause of those actions. Is that right?"

"Right!" Azure replied excitedly. "How do you get around that?"

"We have ways," he winked.

"Can't I use those ways?" she asked.

"Yeah!" Morgan said, his own voice filled with excitement as well. "What if we took her to Never Never Land?!?!"

"It might work, Rob," Cleo pointed out.

"It might," he admitted. "However, it might blow up the universe. She's not a memory Cleo, she's a person. Who knows what would happen. Why do you want to come with us, anyway, Azure?"

"Are you kidding," she laughed. "You guys are, like, the saviors of the universe. Who wouldn't want to be a part of that?!?!"

"Well... it's *mainly* me," he corrected. "However, I do see your point. But, no Azure, I'm sorry, there's just no way. You have your fate and we have ours and *never the twain shall meet*. I hate it for you, but console yourself with this: you'll never know what you're missing."

"Yeah," she sighed. "I figured that was the case. But, I thought I'd better ask while I had the chance."

"I completely understand," he smiled. "I'd gladly take you with us if I could."

The following day Morgan resumed his training with Azure by his side. This time, however, Doc stayed at the gun range with them for several hours. He and Azure talked a good bit about fate and what her future might be like. Then, he excused himself and left the two of them alone. Hours later, Morgan's two day crash course was complete and, as Azure took another shower, he made his way back to the bridge.

"How goes the gun play?" the traveler asked as Morgan took a seat.

"Good," the young man replied. "I'm getting better all the time."

"Glad to hear it," Robert smiled. "Next time, you'll get a gun."

"Awesome!"

"Rob," Doc said stepping onto the bridge. "We need to talk."

"Talk away, Doc," the traveler replied.

"Do you believe in fate?" Doc asked, taking a seat beside the traveler, their eyes locked together.

"I don't know, Doc," Robert replied, shaking his head side to side. "I mean, you're one on my best friends..."

"And you're one of mine," Doc interjected.

"Well, I don't want to upset you," the traveler continued, "but I don't think I believe in it like you do, no. Why do you ask?"

"It's about Azure," Doc replied.

"What about her?"

"She wants to come with us."

"Well, she can't."

"Ah, but Robert, she can," Doc corrected.

"What do you mean?" the traveler asked.

"I mean," Doc explained, "she's a missing person."

"That is epic!" Morgan replied.

"One sec, Morgan," Robert said. "What makes you think that, Doc?"

"I checked with Sister."

"What made you do that?"

"Several things," Doc replied. "I simply found the idea that Azure had managed to accept her fate and fit in with our crew in roughly twenty-four hours truly remarkable..."

"It was, but..." Robert injected.

"And then, of course," Doc continued. "I found her sincere desire to go with us curious..."

"I suppose..."

"Also, her faith is similar to my own, Robert," Doc explained. "She told me she felt as if destiny had led her here. She couldn't understand why fate would show her what she wanted - a true purpose - only to take it away."

"So, then you called Sister?" the traveler asked.

"I did," Doc nodded. "It seemed the sensible thing to do."

"It certainly was," Robert nodded. "And, I already told her she could come if we could find a way. Maybe you have Doc... How'd she go missing?"

"She headed into the mountains near her homeland on a spiritual retreat," Doc explained. "There was an avalanche. Her body was never found."

"That'll do," the traveler replied.

"Robert," Doc said taking a deep breath. "What are the odds that we would rescue someone during an apocalypse, who would then end up stranded on our ship just long enough to realize that they wanted to join our cause, who also just happened to be a missing person?"

"Slim," Robert admitted.

"Just consider it, Rob," Doc smiled. "Just consider it."

"What are you guys talking about," Cleo asked as she and Azure stepped in, their hair still damp.

"Azure," Robert replied.

"She can come with us!" Morgan exclaimed.

"I can?" she asked excitedly.

"Maybe," the traveler said, before reaching over to the com. "Vox, how go those repairs? You about done?"

"Almost, Rob, Why?"

"Can you come to the bridge for a few minutes?'

"On my way."

Five minutes later, Vox stepped in the room, completing the party.

"Alright guys," the traveler said. "Here's the situation: Azure wants to come with us and I think she's already proven she can be an asset. And, as it happens, she's also a missing person..."

"What does that mean?" Azure interrupted.

"Just what it says," Robert smiled. "According to real history, Azure, you went into the mountains seeking enlightenment. There was an avalanche and you were never seen again. That means, we can pick you up just before you're lost and you can come with us."

"Awesome!" Morgan exclaimed.

"However," the traveler continued, "sometimes it can be difficult to retrieve people. And, I hate shooting them with tranq-guns because it tends to start the relationship off on a bad foot. So, I figured since we have you here with us, you could help us make it easier on you."

"How?" Azure asked.

"Do you have any secrets?"

"What do you mean," she giggled. "Almost everyone has secrets."

Morgan grabbed his chest.

"I supposed that's true," the traveler chuckled. "But, do you have a secret you could share with us? Something no one else knows?"

"Oh!" Morgan said, sitting bolt upright. "That's a good idea! *Real* good."

"I think so," Robert smiled. "It will help prove that we know her even though she doesn't know us. It can be something you did, or always wanted..."

"Or always wanted to do," Morgan suggested. "Like some *really* wild fantasy, maybe. Really, the *wilder* it is, the better because then you'll *know* you *never* told *anybody*. You know what I'm saying?!?!"

"Thanks, Morgan," the traveler replied. "I think she's got the idea."

"Well," she replied with a slight purplish blush, "there was one thing. But, it was kind of crazy."

"Don't worry about that!" the young man assured her. "We *all* have crazy desires sometimes. And, I mean *crazy!*"

"Calm down, Morgan," Cleo said, "before I ask Doc to give you a tranquilizer."

"I mean..." Azure replied. "It's still a little embarrassing."

"What?!?!" Morgan said. "You ain't got nothing to be embarrassed about. We're all friends here! Maybe it would, like, ease the tension if we all shared a fantasy. Cleo, get the ball rolling would you?"

"Ignore him," Cleo replied rolling her eyes. "What was it, Azure?"

"Well," she said, "when I was in my early teens..."

Morgan began biting his index knuckle in anticipation.

"I always wanted a monster truck..." she confessed.

"A... a what?" Morgan said, leaping to his feet. "A monster truck?"

"Yes," she replied with a nod. "It's basically like a regular truck but it's..."

"I know what it is!" he said. "And that's your big embarrassing fantasy?"

"Well... Yeah..." she replied. "I mean, I don't know about where you come from but, where I was raised, most teenage girls wanted horses or convertible cars."

"Man..." Morgan said sitting back down. "If you find that embarrassing, some of *my* fantasies would kill ya!"

"I'm sure that's true," Cleo replied, shaking her head.

With a plan in mind and a secret in hand they all went to bed. The ship repairs were almost complete and, on the following morning, they would be able replace the orb; then drop Azure off somewhere; then unsteal the orb; and then pick Azure up. All things considered, it promised to be a rich, full day.

CHAPTER 8: PICK UP & DELIVERY

"What are you wearing?" Cleo asked as Morgan stepped onto the bridge.

"They're called *clothes*, little lady," the young man replied, adjusting his cowboy hat, and putting his ostrich booted foot up on one of the seats.

"What's with the gun belt?" the traveler asked.

"Well, partner," Morgan replied, pulling the toothpick from his mouth, "you said I could have a gun for the next mission. And, this here's the next mission."

"We're not gonna need guns," Robert pointed out.

"Well," Morgan replied, "That don't seem to matter much now, does it? I earned a gun, I get to wear a gun, d'ya get me?"

"Sure..." the traveler chuckled.

"So, where are we headed?" Morgan asked.

"Planet A," Robert replied. "We need to replace the orb and see what happens with the time-lines before we do more."

"Planet A?" the young man replied. "That's an idiotic name for a planet."

"Right..." Cleo said, slowly nodding. "That's not actually the name of the planet, Morgan. It's just that Rob doesn't care enough to tell you what its actual name is."

"What?" Morgan said, obviously incensed. "Why not?"

"Because, man," Robert replied. "There are billions of planets in the universe and sometimes they have different names depending on the date. And, the name doesn't matter anyway. It's the *where* and the *when* that really counts."

"Well, I'd still like to know."

"Then look it up. I ain't your personal encyclopedia, Morgan."

"I don't know how."

"Then learn."

"I don't know how."

"We can argue about it later," the traveler replied.

"Well then, I want you to tell me just one more."

"Why?"

"I want to know the name of Azure's home planet," Morgan explained.

"Okay, man," Robert replied, "that's fair. Her world is called Ratatouille."

"Thank you!" the young man said. "Don't you feel better for being helpful?"

"You know, Morgan," the traveler smiled. "I kind of do... Oh, and seriously, you have to leave that gun here."

"Why?"

"We're heading for a planet of borderline pacifists, man," Robert explained. "You might attract a bit of attention strutting around in a gun belt."

"I got ya," Morgan sighed. "But next time, *it is on baby*!"

A few minutes after this truly mind-expanding conversation, the ship dropped into real space a short distance above Planet A. Fortunately for the band, this was a rather nothing-to-it drop off situation. In truth, it was so simple a job that Vox and Doc opted to stay on board and guard the ship from any swag-mad pirates that might suddenly pop into existence in the cargo bay.

The really exciting - or *suicidal*, depending on your point of view - bit was rescuing the orb from the e-zombies. This was just a matter of wandering around in an almost abandoned monastery and avoiding the time-doofus Marcus Delmont.

"Remember," Robert said, staring out of the transparent walls of the loading platform. "The important part of all this is avoiding the time-doofus Marcus Delmont. Other than that, this one really is a piece of cake."

"Couldn't we have just landed an hour or so after he left?" Cleo asked.

"Sure," the traveler replied. "Why not?"

"Then, why didn't we?" she asked, quite logically.

"I just like the idea of returning it five minutes after he takes it," Robert explained. "It's kind of like: *in your face*!"

"But, he'll never know you did it," she pointed out.

"Yeah," he agreed. "But, I will!"

"Rob, you're a lunatic!"

"Agreed," he nodded. "Let's go!"

The four companions stepped from the interior of the quite invisible loading platform and headed straight for an old monastery that was roughly a mile down the road. As they strolled along Azure gazed around her, apparently amazed.

"So this is my people's original home world?" she asked, almost speaking to herself.

"It is," Robert smiled. "This is where your people got their start."

"Do we ever reunite?"

"Not up to the point where time stops," he replied. "However, who knows what will happen once time starts up again."

"I would like to help it happen," she said thoughtfully.

"Well," the traveler replied, "you'll soon belong to our time. And, if there's ever a future again you'll be able to work toward that in the then present, if you see what I mean. Wow... that'll be weird..."

"What will?" Cleo asked smiling at him.

"When people ask me 'when did that happen?' and I say 'like, just now!' and actually mean it."

"Yeah..." she mused. "You're right. That will be weird."

"So..." Azure sighed. "When is this?"

"Mmmm," Robert replied. "It's a little more than ten years before your home world's destroyed."

"So, at this exact moment my people are still safe and happy?"

"Yep," he nodded, turning a wide smile toward her. "Even you."

"This is crazy," she replied. "I mean, to think that ten years from now..."

"Don't think about it," Robert replied. "It never happened. Oh! There he is!"

Marching down the road toward them was a very handsome man in his mid-thirties. He was over six feet tall and had long blond hair pulled back in a ponytail. He was also built like a brick chicken house.

"That's Delmont?" Morgan asked.

"That's Delmont," the traveler replied.

"He doesn't look like I expected," the young man pointed out.

"What did you expect?" Robert asked.

"I don't know..." Morgan replied. "Fat, balding, thick glasses..."

"Sock-sandals?" the traveler suggested.

"That's hurtful, Rob," the young man observed. "But either way, he doesn't look anything like I thought he would."

"Me, either," Azure admitted. "I mean, he's *really* good looking. Like a nine, or maybe even a nine-and-a-half."

"You couldn't have waited an hour could you, Rob?" Morgan asked accusingly.

As Delmont drew near, Robert spoke to him.

"Good morning," the traveler said with a slight bow.

"Good morning," Delmont replied before continuing quickly down the road.

"You said we were supposed to avoid him!" Morgan pointed out.

"I meant," Robert explained, "we weren't supposed to run up and punch him in the gut or anything."

"Well," the young man said, "you've changed the time-lines by talking to him!"

"*Underwear elastic*, Morgan."

"What?" Azure asked.

"I'll explain later," the traveler replied. "Let's get in the monastery."

Just minutes later, the four of them were standing in a shadowy corner in the back of a room filled with forgotten relics. A single cask, on a shelf loaded with boxes, was no longer completely covered with dust.

"That's it," Robert said, nodding toward the small chest. "Azure, would you like to do the honors?"

As he said this, he held out the orb to her. She took it gently in her hands, opened the box, and carefully placed the relic back in its case.

"And, that's that," the traveler smiled. "Azure, you just saved billions of lives. How do you feel?"

"Amazing!" she said with a wide smile, and tears in her eyes.

"Get used to it," he replied. "You're going to feel that way a lot. Let's go!"

As soon as they reached the ship, Robert had Cleo check the time-lines.

"Yep," she nodded. "The war never happened. And, the paradoxical side-effects are minimal."

"Awesome!" Robert replied. "Now, we need to drop Azure off someplace nice."

Having said this, he jumped in his seat and started quickly pressing buttons. The ship lifted off and, in almost no time, was once again flying through the void of non-space.

"Azure," he said turning his seat to face her. "This may be a little difficult for you. We've got to drop you off so we can un-steal the orb. And, I've got to leave you some place completely alone. But, you'll be safe and, after about an hour, you'll have never been there at all. You think you can handle that?"

"I can," she nodded.

"Great!" he replied. "However, there's something I want to take care of first. Let's you and me head to the medi-bay."

Roughly an hour later, the ship dropped back into real space above a familiar world.

"*Escargot*," Morgan said with a contented sigh. "Beautiful, isn't it?"

"What?" Cleo asked.

"Your home world, Cleo!"

"Oh," she giggled. "Of course."

Morgan stared at her from under a single raised eyebrow.

"Sorry... I forgot," she said.

"No..." he said slowly. "It's cool. I've got to get used to it, ya know?"

"That might be best," she smiled.

At that moment, Robert, Azure, and Doc stepped onto the bridge.

"Alright," the traveler said, dropping into his seat. "Let's land this bird."

Before the ship touched down on the very same island they had picked Cleo up from, Vox joined the rest of the group.

"I been thinking, boss," he said, settling down in a nearby seat.

"What about, Vox?" the traveler asked.

"Well," he replied, "We've just saved billions of lives, the next part of the mission is just pushing buttons, and I've barely gotten to speak to Azure."

"All true."

"So," he continued, "since we got to leave her down here all by her lonesome, why don't we have a little party? A bit of a sendoff before we go pick her up. Ya feel me?"

"Absolutely," Robert nodded. "It's a brilliant idea. Let's do it."

"Azure," Cleo said, turning her eyes to her companion. "Do you like swimming?"

At this question, Morgan bit his index knuckle in eager anticipation.

"What's the water like?" Azure asked.

"Eighty degrees year-round, crystal clear to about a thousand feet, filled with brightly colored fish and coral even at shallow depths, and nothing dangerous. I figured we could go snorkeling for an hour or two. It's been ages since I've gotten to."

"Sounds great," the blue maiden said with a smile.

Minutes later, the ship landed and the girls went to change into their swimsuits. Morgan nervously paced the bridge trying to psych himself up to face *tan lines*.

"Rob," the young man said, wiping his brow, "will you hold my hand."

"No, Morgan," he replied, shaking his head. "I think you're getting a little over excited."

"Rob," Morgan replied, staring his friend in the eyes, "this is one of those situations in life where there isn't enough excitement in the universe to get *over excited*."

"If you say so, Hoss," Robert replied.

"Doc," the young man said thoughtfully. "If I collapse make *sure* it's one of the girl's that gives me mouth to mouth."

This evoked a glaring stare from Robert.

"Azure, Doc," Morgan corrected. "Make sure Azure gives me mouth to mouth."

The young man's ears caught the sounds of the approaching young women, causing him to jam his knuckle once again into his mouth. Seconds later, the moment arrived. It wasn't the moment he had been waiting for...

Both of the young ladies were unquestionably dressed in *swimsuits*. They were not what Morgan had been hoping for, however. They were full body diving jumpsuits. They even had gloves on... The young man stared in disbelief. This was *absolutely* the *most* dressed they had been since he had met either of them.

"What is this?!?!" he asked, a stunned tone in his voice. "What are you two wearing?"

"*Swimsuits*," Cleo replied shaking her head.

"Those are not..." he said, before throwing his hands in the air and dropping his head on his chest. "Rob, is this for real?!?! Are those considered *standard* swimsuits?"

"Well... Yeah, Morgan," the traveler nodded. "They're very functional and..."

"Man, the future really stinks sometimes!" Morgan interrupted. "Rob, is there any *period* swimwear on this ship?"

"Yeah, I think," Robert replied. "There should be some trunks in the bottom of one of your underwear drawers."

"Right!" the young man exclaimed. "Wait right here, ladies!"

A short time later, Morgan returned wearing nothing but flip-flops and a pair of blue and white swimming trunks.

"This is a swimsuit!" he explained, turning around slowly to give them the full effect.

"It's also blindingly white!" the traveler pointed out. "Doc, you've got to add *get some sun* to his fitness routine."

"So it would seem..." Doc mused.

"You'll notice ladies," the young man said, pointing at his chest with his open hands, "that *at least* eighty percent of my flesh is *completely* exposed."

"*At least!*" Cleo exclaimed.

"Wow..." Azure replied, a look of mild embarrassment on her face.

"So, why don't you girls try again," Morgan suggested, pointing over his shoulder with his thumb. "I think you might enjoy *kickin' it old school* for a change."

"What's the point of swimsuits like that?" Azure asked.

"Oh, this is gonna be *good*," Robert chuckled. "Go on, Morgan, explain it to her."

"Well..." the young man replied thoughtfully. "They help to..."

"Help to what?" the traveler asked.

"Okay," Morgan said nodding, "First off, they help to get vitamin D."

"Extraordinary," Doc replied. "He's actually right."

"Exactly," the young man said. "*And*, they help to get rid of any tan lines you may have."

"I don't have any tan lines," the girls said in unison.

Morgan swallowed.

"And, anyway, Morgan," Cleo pointed out, "these suits are *tan through*."

"Yea, Morgan," Robert chuckled. "What about that?"

"Okay," Morgan replied confidently. "Okay. But, you have to think about the fact that our bodies are mostly water."

"Again," Doc said, "that's true."

"And, so," the young man explained, "when our skin comes into direct contact with the water it's like a return to nature. It's like being back in our mother's wombs."

"Wow," Robert said. "I can't believe you used the word *womb*..."

"Well, I did," Morgan replied. "It's natural, Rob. You need to grow up. In fact, the more the skin; the more the nature. So, if you want to go really natural..."

"Either way, Morgan," Cleo interrupted, her head cocked to the side. "That suit of yours isn't gonna do anything to protect you from the sun."

"She has a point," the traveler nodded. "Doc, we got any sunscreen?"

"I have some SPF85 in the medi-bay," Doc replied.

"Eh," Robert replied. "I guess that'll knock the edge off, anyway. You girls go ahead and get started. We'll be along after we've fireproofed Morgan."

"Why did you do that, Rob?" Morgan asked as soon as the girls left the room. "I had 'em on the ten yard line, man."

"No," the traveler replied, shaking his head. "No, you didn't. Anyway, you gotta help me carry the cooler and setup the volleyball net. Oh, and I got a surprise for ya."

"What is it?"

"A surprise," Robert pointed out. "Vox, Doc, what are you guys wanting to do?"

"Nothing!" Vox immediately replied. "I'm sitting in the sun, watching the waves with my toes in the sand, and *not* fixing the ship!"

"And you, Doc?" the traveler asked. "You hanging out or what?"

"I'm going fishing, Rob," Doc smiled. "And, I'm going fishing on the other side of the island where your inane chatter won't frighten the fish. Then, I'm going to catch a whale that we will eat later tonight."

"Sounds great, Doc," Robert chuckled.

After they had practically dipped the young man in SPF85, Robert and Morgan grabbed the cooler and the volleyball net and headed for the beach. Once they had setup a few chairs and dug a bit of a fire pit, the traveler revealed his surprise.

"Voilà!" Robert said, throwing open the cooler.

"Baja Blast!" Morgan exclaimed. "Awesome, bro! Thanks!"

"Not a problem, man," the traveler smiled. "So, you want to dig some clams or something while we wait for the girls?"

"Sure. Why not?"

For roughly three hours, the traveler and his companion wandered the beach digging up *space clams* as the warm, but not hot, breeze fluttered around them. The air was scented by countless flowers and Morgan sampled some of the local and very *alien* fruit. It was pretty good. All things considered, the young man felt this had to be one of the most peaceful places in the universe.

Shortly after the girls joined them, the volleyball net was put up and a quick game of guys vs. gals started.

"Look, Morgan," the traveler whispered, on their edge of the court, "to the best of my knowledge, Cleo has *never* beat me at volleyball. But, she's *about to* if you don't get your head in the game, man!"

"I can't help it!" the young man exclaimed. "I keep getting mesmerized by Azure's giant..."

"Morgan!" Robert barked under his breath. "This is exactly why you don't need a..."

"I was going to save *serves*," Morgan lied.

"No, you weren't!" the traveler pointed out. "How stupid do you think..."

"Are we going to play or what?" Cleo shouted. "What are you two talking about?"

"Rob's mad 'cause we're gonna lose!" Morgan shouted back.

"We're not going to lose!" the traveler lied.

"Yes, you are," Cleo smiled.

They lost. For several minutes, Cleo sang *We Are the Champions* at Rob before the four of them strolled over to Vox. One by one, they dropped down into beach chairs.

"So, Vox," the traveler said, gazing at his friend. "What are you thinking about?"

"My wife..." Vox replied, staring into the distance.

"I'm sorry, man," Robert nodded. "I'm going to get you home as fast as I can."

"I know..."

"There ain't nothing for it..."

"I know..."

"Anything I can do?" the traveler asked.

"I don't know, Rob," Vox replied. "We may just have to tell her the truth, man."

"I've been for that since the very beginning."

"You're a liar, bro."

"Yeah..." Robert sighed. "Yeah, I am. Still, I can see some sense in telling her the truth when we get back. It might make things easier in the long run."

"I don't know, bro," Vox said shaking his head. "She loves you like a son, but if she found out about that whole e-zombie thing, she might just choke the life out of ya..."

"Yeah..." the traveler said thoughtfully. "But I could probably lie my way out of it."

"True," Vox chuckled. "You probably could."

"And, really," Robert continued, "if we had her on the ship, she'd be in *easy lying distance,* if you see what I mean."

"I think I do," Vox laughed.

A few hours of relaxation later, Doc showed up with several massive fish. They cooked these along with the clams they had collected and a few lobsters the girls had caught. All in all, it was a truly delicious non-MRE meal. The sun began to set as they finished eating and twin blue moons slowly rose on the horizon.

"Morgan," Robert said, pulling the young man aside. "I have a serious favor to ask, man."

"Ask away?"

"Well," the traveler began, "I may be the *last time traveler* and *the savior of the universe* and all, but I'm also a man."

"What's your point?" the young man asked.

"My point, Morgan," Robert explained, "is that we're in one of the most romantic places in the universe with two pale blue moons slowly rising into the sky."

"I guess I'm with you so far."

"So," the traveler continued. "I want to go for a moonlit walk down the beach with my not-exactly-girlfriend."

"Makes sense."

"Right," Robert nodded. "But... I also want to hold her hand."

"So," Morgan replied with a shrug. "What's the big deal?"

"Did you pay any attention to those stories I told you?"

"Dude," the young man said quite seriously, "I've got 'em completely committed to memory."

"Well then," the traveler said raising his hands, "you should see the danger! Me and Cleo could go from holding hands to who-knows-what in like ten seconds!"

"Yeah..." the young man sighed. "I suppose that's true..."

"What's wrong with you?"

"I don't think me and Azure could go from holding hands to *who-knows-what* in like ten years..."

"Ahhh..." Robert replied. "Well, we can work on that later. But, tonight, I need your help, man."

"I'm in," the young man nodded. "What do you need?"

"You've got to watch me like a hawk," the traveler replied. "If I look like I'm getting *distracted* even a little bit - you're going to have to run up and punch me in the head or something."

"I'd be glad to."

"I'm serious, man!" Robert explained. "If I go to kiss her, you *have* to stop me - no matter what!"

"Trust me, Rob," Morgan replied, nodding his head. "If I see you going to kiss her, I'll very happily break your jaw."

"Thanks, man! I owe ya big time!"

"Not at all," Morgan grinned.

The two young men stepped over to the two young ladies.

"So..." Robert said slowly. "Me and Morgan were thinking that you two might want to take a stroll in the moonlight. And, don't worry, we can protect you from any wild animals."

"Are there any wild animals?" Azure asked.

"Only the two of them," Cleo giggled.

"If you will," the traveler said, offering his hand to Cleo.

She took it as Morgan offered his hand to Azure. The four began strolling across the sand in the moonlight side-by-side. After just a few minutes Robert ran his finger down Cleo's arm and took her by the hand. Cleo stepped nearer and, for a second, Morgan thought he would have to spring into action. She only laid her head on his shoulder, however. For the moment, the danger had passed.

"This is so strange," Azure mussed as they sauntered along.

"I've been surrounded by strange lately," Morgan pointed out. "Could you be more specific?"

"I don't know," she replied. "This just seems surreal. I mean... You guys show up out of nowhere - just as my planet's exploding; I end up trapped on your ship; I'm a *missing person*; and so, I can come with you... This is all just crazy!"

"It is," the young man agreed, "but it's true, none-the-less."

"I know!" she replied. "That's the crazy part! If this were a dream I could understand it..."

"Well," he said, "If you want to think about *strange*, consider this - in a few hours, I'll be trying to convince you that we know each other because you'll have never met me."

"Yeah..." she agreed. "That is strange..."

"And..." he said slowly, "So... if you wanted to do anything to show how much you appreciate all the effort we're about to go through in order to pick you up; now would be the time to do it. I'll remember the absolute rapture of it, but you'll never have gone through the terror of it. It'll be nothing more than a sweet memory of mine."

"You don't give up, do you?" she giggled.

"I don't see any point," he confessed. "Getting nowhere is getting nowhere, whether you're trying or not..."

"And, do you plan to keep trying after we meet again?"

"Oh yeah," he sighed. "I figure I've learned enough about you to make a better first impression. Maybe it'll give me half a chance."

"I doubt it," she laughed. "But, I honestly wish you luck."

"Thanks," he nodded.

"I'll tell ya what," she said, stopping him and turning him toward her. "You did get this far."

As soon as she said this, she kissed two of her fingers and then pressed them to his lips.

"Eh," he smiled. "I'll take it. Who knows, maybe I really will have a chance."

"I doubt it," she replied shaking her head. "I only did that because I knew I never would. And, even with that in mind, that was as far as I could go..."

"I see where you're coming from," Morgan replied.

The rest of Morgan's stalk-Robert evening was lovely, but unremarkable. Robert and Cleo controlled themselves completely and all

Azure was up for after the finger-kissing thing was conversation. When they got back to the fire pit, they made a couple of improvised-beds for the girls out of large tropical leaves. They then lay down, gazing up at the stars together, until both Azure and Cleo fell asleep.

"Let's go," Robert whispered. "She'll never even know we left."

As he said this, he bent down to pick up Cleo. He stopped before he did so, gazing at her for several seconds.

"Vox, bro," he sighed, "you better carry Cleo."

"Not a problem," Vox replied, gently lifting her from the ground. "Hold on, small-girl, we got to get you to bed."

"Doc," the traveler said, "you got it?"

"I do," Doc replied. "I'll meet you on the ship in five minutes."

"Thanks," Robert replied. "Come on, Morgan, let's get our stuff."

"Alright," he sighed. "You know, I'm really gonna miss her."

"Not for long, you won't," the traveler smiled.

Fifteen minutes later, the ship was in non-space headed for Never Never Land.

"So is sci-fi the only real history?" Morgan asked, leaning back in his seat, his hands behind his head.

"What do ya mean?" the traveler asked.

"I mean, like is *Lord of the Rings* or *The Prydain Chronicles* real?"

"I keep trying to explain…"

"Yeah, but I mean are they based on real history?" the young man interrupted.

"Why?" Robert chuckled. "You afraid of the *Horned King*?"

"Yes," Morgan admitted. "But I have other, better, more practical reasons for asking."

"Well, even if there are elvish chicks, and I'm not saying there are, I ain't going to pick any up."

"So, you're *not* saying that there *aren't* any elvish chicks?"

"Look, Morgan," the traveler said, turning his gaze to the young man, "you stumble across more than enough women to offend and/or annoy. We don't need to go looking for more."

"Yeah…" the young man sighed. "I guess that's true… You ever notice how all the spells in Harry Potter were just, like, Latin or something?"

"I guess."

"I've always wanted to know how to say *make woman* in Latin," Morgan said.

"Ake-mae Oman-wae," the traveler replied.

"That's pig-Latin."

"I got the feeling it would work for you, bro."

Not quite an hour after this - I guess you could call it a *conversation* - the ship emerged from non-space on the outskirts of Never Never Land. Cleo was awakened just long enough to join in the honors. As soon as she was on the bridge, they *got the party started.*

"Time to take out a time machine," Robert nodded. "Hit it, Vox."

"Done!" Vox replied, having pushed a series of buttons on the console.

"That's it," Cleo said with a yawn. "Fifteen minutes after everyone left the dock, Delmont's machine exploded."

"That was *proximity disability!*" the traveler replied with a grin.

"The orb was un-stolen," she added, "and the time-lines are very close to corrected."

"Perfect," Robert replied. "Now let's all get to bed. First thing tomorrow we pick up Azure."

Early the following morning, Morgan stepped onto the bridge. He had shaved, brushed his teeth, flossed, used mouthwash, had cinnamon chewing gum in his pocket, had on clean pants, and had cleaned his shoes up. He had even put on a very special shirt for Azure's pick up.

"What's with the shirt?" Robert asked, glancing over his shoulder.

"Oh," the young man replied, looking down at his chest. "I figured it would help us convince her that we know her deep dark secret."

"Yeah..." the traveler replied. "But, that's a *Big Foot* shirt, man. How's that supposed to help?"

"Well," the young man said with a knowing smile, "she always wanted a monster truck, right?"

"Yes..."

"Well," he continued. "*Big Foot!*"

"Right, Morgan," Robert said shaking his head. "But, again, that's a *Big Foot* shirt. It's not a monster truck shirt."

"What do you mean?" Morgan asked. "*Big Foot* was like the most famous monster truck ever..."

"No..." the traveler explained. "*Big Foot* was the most famous monster truck on *Earth*."

"I don't follow."

"Wow..." Robert replied. "Okay. I get your idea there. What I'm telling you is that she's not going to think *monster truck* when she sees that shirt. She's going to think *Sasquatch*. That is, if she thinks anything of it at all..."

"Ah..." Morgan said. "Well, do we have any monster truck shirts on board?"

"Good question! And, yes, we do actually. I'll get one for you."

"Epic," the young man said. "And, by the way, is that *common?*"

"Is what *common*, Morgan?"

"Monster trucks?"

"Basically," the traveler replied. "It's kind of like shoes."

"Monster trucks are like shoes?" Morgan asked.

"I mean," Robert explained. "That very *few* societies that discover space travel don't discover shoes."

"Like how many."

"Like none in the history of the universe."

"Yep. That qualifies as *few.*"

"And," the traveler continued, "since a monster truck is just a big truck, and a truck is just a modified car, and *all* advanced societies develop cars; monster trucks are really pretty common."

"So, in reality," Morgan said thoughtfully. "The universe is replete with green women *and* monster trucks."

"Pretty much."

"Man, the universe is an awesome place!" Morgan observed.

"That it is, Morgan," the traveler agreed. "That it is."

Over the next few minutes, the ship landed at the pickup zone and Morgan changed into a clearly *monster truck themed* T-shirt. The two young men strode side by side through the thick grass and flowers that filled the valley that currently contained Azure.

"It's hard to believe this place is about to be hit by an avalanche," Morgan observed.

"Well, it is," the traveler pointed out. "And we got like ten minutes, tops."

"There she is," the young man said excitedly. "And, I think she's younger!"

"I believe she is."

"She's not quite as hot as she was, though..."

"It happens," Robert nodded. "Now, shut up man. It's show time!"

The two men quickly approached the fair blue maiden.

"Hey, Azure!" the traveler said with a wide smile. "It's good to see you!"

"Do I know you?" she asked, clearly surprised by his knowing her name.

"Now, that's a fair question," Robert chuckled. "And, yes, you do. Or more accurately, you *did*."

"What do you mean *did*?" she asked.

"Well," he replied. "I'm the *last time traveler* and you knew me in a future that no longer exists."

"So..." she said. "Are you, like, some nut escaped from a loony bin or something?"

"I get that a lot," he laughed. "But no, I'm not. My name's Robert, by the way."

"And, I'm Morgan!" the young man interjected. "You knew me, too!"

"So... you're both loonies?"

"Azure, do you know what you always wanted when you were in your early teens?" the traveler asked with a smile. "You didn't want a horse or a convertible car like all the other girls, did you? No... You wanted a monster truck."

"And, that's why I'm wearing this shirt!" Morgan pointed out.

"Yes it is," Robert replied. "And, do you know how we knew that about you?"

"How?" she asked, gazing at him under knitted brows.

"You told me in a past future."

"That's impossible," she replied.

"No," he corrected. "That's improbable. But, it's also absolutely true."

"Okay," she said. "Say that I believed you, which I don't, so what? You knew me. And?"

"Well, I know why you're up here," he replied. "You're looking for enlightenment, searching for a purpose."

"So?"

"So," he said staring into her eyes. "I'm the *last time traveler* and it's my job to save the universe. And, I want you to help me do it."

"You really are nuts!" she exclaimed. "And you're kind of scaring me."

"Here," he replied, pulling a tranq-pistol from his jacket pocket and handing it to her. "That's a tranquilizer gun. I could have just shot you with it. I didn't. Now, you could just shoot me with it. Please, don't, though. So, can I keep talking?"

"Talk," she said.

"Azure," he replied, pointing toward the nearby mountains. "In a few minutes, an avalanche is going to sweep through this valley. Your body will never be found. According to history, you're a *missing person*. Now, it's up to you whether you go missing because you came with us or because you got killed in an avalanche. But, either way, we have to start heading back to our ship."

"We can walk and talk," she said. "So, how exactly are you saving the universe?"

"We're going through time undoing all the damage other time travelers did," he said, walking quickly toward the ship with Morgan and Azure following at his heels. "In fact, just yesterday... well... sort of... you helped us save billions of lives."

"And, how did I do that?" she asked.

"Well, actually," he said increasing his pace and glancing at his watch. "Actually, we may want to jog at this point... And it's complicated *time stuff*, Azure. But trust me, you helped save your people's original home world as well as this planet."

"Rob," Morgan said excitedly, "what's that sound?"

"Run!" he replied.

All three burst into a mad dash as snow began pouring down from the mountains. They reached the loading platform before the avalanche reached the ship and stood panting in the cargo bay just seconds later.

"We made it," Robert smiled. "No way the snow will get through the shields."

"Take me home now," Azure demanded, aiming the gun at Rob.

"Azure, you can't..." Morgan began, taking a step toward her. The maiden fired, shooting the young man right in the chest. "Ow!" he screamed. "Rob, can you believe..."

The next thing Morgan remembered was Doc staring down at him.

"He's fine," Doc said, glancing at a monitor on the wall. "And, awake in just three hours. Not too bad."

"Morgan," Azure said, taking him by the hand. "I'm sorry I shot you. I honestly didn't mean to. I'd never even held a gun before. I had no idea what I was doing with it."

"It's cool," he said, trying his best to focus on her face. "Are you alright?"

"I will be, I think," she smiled. "I've had a long talk with Doc. It's just really hard to wrap my head around, you know."

"I see where you're coming from." Morgan replied.

Doc kept the young man in the medi-bay for a few more hours, just for observation. Morgan grabbed a pen and pad and began talking to Azure, who had decided to sit with him until he had completely recovered. He intended to make *very* good use of the time. Well, from his point of view anyway...

"So," Morgan said, dropping down in a seat on the bridge, "in order to prove you wrong, I've made up a little list."

"Prove me wrong about what?" the traveler replied. "And what list?"

"You see what it says right there at the top?" the young man replied, holding out the pad and tapping the top of it with his pen. *"Morgan's Love List.* And, that's just what it is. It will prove that I really love her; not just lust after her. So, you want to see how Azure measures up?"

"Sure," Robert replied. "Hit me with it."

"From the top down: Is she blue?"

"When did that get on your love list?"

"The *when* doesn't matter, Rob," Morgan asserted. "The point is that's it's at the very top of the list."

"If you say so..." Robert chuckled.

"Check!" Morgan replied, making a check mark as he spoke. "Has she got huge..."

"I believe you've missed the point of this, man."

"Check!" the young man continued. "Could you crack an egg on her..."

"Morgan, this is actually more of a *lust list*," Robert pointed out.

"Check!" Morgan said again, checking off the point with great flourish. "Does she not throw up when she's in the same room with me?"

"Actually, that's a good one," the traveler agreed.

"Check!"

"Morgan, can we skip to the chase?" Robert asked. "Now that you've made your list up, is there any line where Azure doesn't get a check?"

"Right here, doubting Thomas!" Morgan replied, shoving the list under Robert's nose. "Does she like *Monty Python's Flying Circus*? No check!"

"Ouch!" the traveler exclaimed.

"Yeah..." Morgan sighed. "But, I figure I have to make some sacrifices."

"Sure... but, that's a big one."

"I figure I'll work on it after we're married."

"That's always a bad idea in my experience."

CHAPTER 9: TEA FOR TWO

"So..." Morgan said, stepping onto the bridge and lowering himself into a seat. "Have you seen Rob lately?"

"No," Cleo sighed. "Not for three days, six hours, and twelve minutes."

"Yeah," the young man replied. "I haven't seen him for, like, four days. What's he working on?"

"*Saving the universe*," she asserted. "That's what he's always working on..."

"Yeah..." Morgan replied.

"Can I help you with something?" she asked.

"Cleo, what do you think I'd look good in?"

"Another room?" she suggested.

"You know," he said nodding, "it hurts when you say things like that."

"I'm just teasing," she giggled.

"Yeah… Anyway, I've come to accept the fact that you're Rob's bird."

"I'm not anyone's *bird*, Morgan."

"Right…" he replied slowly. "Either way, that doesn't mean we can't be friends."

"Oh, trust me, Morgan, that's *all* we'll ever be."

"I know!" he exclaimed. "That's what I'm saying! So… Help me Cleo!"

"How?" she asked.

"I don't know how to dress myself," he explained.

"I've noticed that…"

"So, help me!"

"How?" she asked again.

"Come dress me."

"That is *well* beyond the realm of friendship, Morgan."

"No…" he explained. "I mean: come pick out my clothes."

"That I can do…" she replied. "Provided you stand outside the room while I do it."

"That's not very friendly…" he pointed out.

"You know I'm teasing," she replied, giggling again.

"Do I?"

"Well, you should by now."

"Alright," he replied. "I'll keep it in mind. And, you keep in mind that I *know* we'll never be *anything* more than friends. Honestly, all I want from you Cleo, is friendship. I mean, sure, I'll always cherish the countless fantasies you filled my imagination with. They took me to places…

"Morgan!" she interrupted. "That's not friendly! That's stalkerish and creepy!"

"Oh, sorry…" he replied. "I meant it as a compliment... Either way, my point is that I'm past that. I'm really wanting to make something happen with Azure. I mean, I actually have a chance with her."

"I think you may be overestimating your abilities," she observed.

"Okay!" he replied. "In that case I'll just have to settle for stalking you for the rest of my life."

"Let's go get you some clothes!"

"Awesome!"

The two of them rose and quickly made their way to Morgan's room. Leaving the door as open as she possibly could, Cleo began laying out clothes on the young man's bed. Mainly, she stuck to different shirts. It was pretty obvious that he was a *jeans* type of guy and she really didn't want him pulling off his pants at any stage of this whole affair. As a result, one shirt after another went on and then off the young man's still-very-pale back.

"Do you actually think any of these look good on me?" he asked.

"Some do…" she admitted. "I mean Morgan, it's not that you're bad looking…"

"Really?"

"Really," she replied. "It's just that you're… well... *bad* in every other aspect that might allow you to someday attract a mate."

"But, I'm good looking?" he asked.

"No. You're just not bad looking."

"Oh…"

"Look Morgan," she said. "I'm not the only woman in the universe. I'm sure *somewhere* there's a woman that would think you look great. Everyone has different tastes, you know?"

"That's what Rob said…"

"That you're not bad looking?" she asked.

"No…" he replied. "He said that everyone has different tastes."

"Well, they do. Who knows? Maybe Azure even thinks you're handsome. I find it hard to imagine, but…"

"Well, looks aren't everything," he observed. "Not to women anyway. I'm mean, you're crazy about Rob and he's like five-foot six!"

As he said this, he turned his back and started pulling off his current shirt. Cleo turned around as well. She had already seen more than enough of his back just a few days ago on the beach.

"They care a lot more about a man's qualities than his looks," he continued. "Well, the ones that I've got any chance with do anyway."

"That's certainly true," she agreed.

"Right! And, that's exactly why I *do* have a chance! I'm *never* going to give up, Cleo. I'm going to prove to Azure that I love her. I'm always going to be trustworthy, loyal, helpful, friendly, courteous…"

"That's the boy scouts, Morgan."

"I figured it was a good place to start," he asserted.

"It kind of is, I guess…"

"Right!" he replied. "Anyway, I'm going to keep working until I get her. Nothing will stop me. I'm going to keep buffing up, learn to dress myself, learn how to talk, learn how to act, learn how to dance, I may even learn to play the…"

At that moment, Morgan noticed the scent of honeysuckle filling that cabin. He turned around to see Cleo's head down and her shoulders shaking slightly.

"What's wrong?" he asked.

"Nothing, Morgan," she lied.

"Something's wrong!" he exclaimed. "Did I say… Look I'm sorry, I was just teasing. I know Rob's a great guy even if he's not six feet tall."

"Rob is *not* a great guy, Morgan…"

"But, you love him."

"I *hate* him, Morgan," she asserted.

"You hate… But why?"

"The main reason, Morgan," she replied, turning to face him with tears running down her face, "is because I *love* him."

"So, you do love him?"

"With everything I have!" she almost screamed. "With everything I am! With every fiber of my being and to the furthest depths of my soul. I love everything about him. Except for one small flaw…"

"And, what is that?"

"He *doesn't* love me…" she explained.

"Oh yes he does!" Morgan exclaimed.

"Don't say that!" she yelled. "If you want us to be friends, Morgan, *never* say that again. He *does not* love me! He *owns* me!"

"What do you mean?"

"It's like you said," she laughed bitterly, "I'm just Rob's *bird*."

"I didn't mean…"

"Yes, you did!" she exclaimed. "Oh, you didn't mean to mean it, but you did mean it!"

"What?"

"You know why I'm here, Morgan?" she asked. "Why we're all here? Because Rob needs us. He doesn't care about me any more than he cares about the rest of you. To him we're just a bunch of tools in a box. His heart is way too big to love meaningless individuals. The only thing he cares about is the entire universe. Nothing smaller than that can attract his attention. Of course… who can blame him? He *really is* the savior of all of time. And I honestly am glad to be one of the tools he uses to save it."

"Well…" the young man replied. "He kissed you."

"Of course he kissed me!" she screamed. "I tricked him!"

"You tricked Rob?"

"Yes!" she laughed again, tears falling from her face. "I'm one of the few people in the history of time that has ever *outwitted* him. And, had I known how *truly* terrible his vengeance could be, I would never have dared!"

"Vengeance?" Morgan asked, his brows knitted.

"Without even trying…" she sighed, rolling her eyes. "I'm destined to spend the rest of my, perhaps immortal, life in my own personal purgatory with the thing my soul most longs for just out of reach. Where I can touch it, but never grasp it."

"How did you trick him?"

"He's a man!" she snapped. "He may seem like a god…"

"I don't see it…" the young man replied, shaking his head.

The green maiden glared at him, daggers in her eyes, her breathing quick and shallow.

"I'm sorry…" he said softly. "Please continue."

"He's a human male," she replied. "I knew what my body could do to his. And, for two years, I did everything I could to get him trapped with me in hot enclosed spaces. I tried my very best to get him to kiss me. I just *knew* that, if he did that, I would *have* him. He would love me. He would have to. I would become his perfect mate and he would finally surrender, he would finally be *mine*. But, in spite of all I could do, he never would…"

"But, you said…" he began.

"He went to kiss me on the cheek!" she screamed. "As if I was his niece or his little sister! But, I stopped him! I turned my mouth to his and caught him in the trap I had worked two years to lay. I had no idea I would be the one it actually caught… *Whoever digs a pit will fall into it; if someone rolls a stone, it will roll back on them.*"

"Where's that from?"

"The Bible, Morgan…" she replied, shaking her head and rolling her eyes once more. "I've spent a great deal of time reflecting on those words…"

"Well…" the young man said slowly. "He's never kissed anyone else."

"Of course not," she laughed. "Things like that are beneath him. He plays with love the same way a child does with a ball. It entertains him, but it doesn't mean anything to him. The only reason he doesn't kiss every woman that ever lived is because he doesn't want to do to them what he accidentally did to me…"

"But Cleo, he *told* me he loves you…" Morgan assured her.

"And, what does that mean?" she scoffed. "*Liar* is Rob's quintessential descriptor. Sure, he's a man, he's a human…"

"He's five-foot six…"

"Right, Morgan…" she sighed. "But, my point is that *liar* is the most important one in the list. He's more a liar than he is a human being. The truth, lies, love, lust; all of them are just more tools in his box. He's above them!"

"No one's above those…" Morgan asserted.

"Why don't you tell him that?" she asked, honeysuckle tears streaming down her face.

"Well, what about that moonlight walk down the beach?" he asked.

"For Rob, that was like giving a sugar cube to a horse or a treat to a dog that's done some cute trick," she replied. "It was my *reward* for being a *good girl*."

"Ouch…" Morgan said, gazing down at her, sincere sympathy in his eyes.

"Yeah, Morgan…" she replied, nodding slowly. "Ouch… Anyway, he doesn't even know what love is. Not like we do. Look at you! What you're doing is at least sort of like love. You're trying to win the girl you… well… *lust after*, but at least it's a start! All Rob has ever done is push me away. Oh, there are times I manage to forget, times I manage to deceive myself into believing he cares. I even make plans, Morgan! How sad is that? I've picked out wedding dresses and thought about what I want to name our children! But, then, something like this happens… Rob gets busy and it reminds me of my place: I can only ever be near him when I'm *useful*; when I'm part of the *mission*. He's not even capable of feeling what we do, Morgan. And, he never will be…"

"Cleo," the young man sighed. "I'm going to go grab some space ice-cream. You want some?"

"Please," she replied, wiping the tears from her eyes.

In less than an hour, five of the ship's six crew members were sitting in Morgan's room, listening to 80's music, and feasting on space ice-cream. Cleo's mood lightened noticeably as they sat talking and laughing about the many insane things Robert had done over the years.

"What's going on?" the traveler asked, sticking his head in the doorway.

"Just having an improv celebration," Vox said with a smile. "Small-girl's been teaching Morgan to dress himself and, so far, the results ain't too bad."

"Well, that's great," he smiled, "but we got work to do. Everybody ready?"

They were. Minutes later, all six were seated around the conference table.

"So," the traveler began, "you may or may not have noticed that I've been a little busy over the past few days..."

"We've noticed," Cleo interrupted.

"Right," he nodded. "Well, the reason for that was the lock on the holy vault."

"But, Cleo already broke into that," Morgan pointed out.

"Yeah... I know that, Morgan," Robert replied. "But the point is that I didn't let Cleo get ready for it. I was confident that she could handle such an old system and I was *right*. It was still sloppy of me, however, and I should have done better. So, for the last few days I've been working on *doing better*. I think I've got all the details we'll need for the rest of this job in my head now. We shouldn't have any more unpleasant surprises."

"Good to hear, boss," Vox replied.

"One thing before we go on," the traveler said, turning his gaze to Azure. "How's your training going?"

"Well..." she said, a look of confusion on her face.

"We felt she should have a little time to adjust, Rob," Doc pointed out. "All of this is a lot to take in."

"Of course," he smiled. "However, as soon as you feel up to it I want you weapons trained."

"I'm not sure about using weapons," she replied.

"You'll be great at it!" he replied. "In fact, you were."

"I just don't like the idea..."

"Here's the great thing about our work, Azure," he interrupted, "even if we do have to shoot anyone (which we basically *never* do), we get to un-shoot them at the end of the job. So, it's really not a big deal. Besides, you don't want any of us to get killed, right?"

"Of course not!" she exclaimed.

"Great!" he nodded. "Then, you'll need to learn to shoot soon. Morgan, you've been practicing, right?"

"Every day."

"Awesome," the traveler replied. "Do you think you could teach Azure?"

"Oh! My! Goodness!" he exclaimed. "Yes, Rob! Yes, I can!"

"Great!" Robert replied. "Now, on to business. This next mission is a little odd because it involves a person. The idiot Delmont..."

"Who Azure thought was *very* unattractive," Morgan interjected.

"What?" Azure asked.

"Oh," Morgan replied. "You saw him in that future that never happened. You said he made you want to puke..."

"Morgan," the traveler said, gazing at the young man in disbelief, "may I continue?"

"Please do."

"Right... Anyway, Delmont kidnapped Calvin Rex, who was one of the most skilled bio-engineers in history. Rex was unappreciated in his own day, but his son Theodore Rex invented the cure for the common cold, which then brought his father's name into the historic limelight as it were."

"What changes did his kidnapping cause?" Doc asked.

"Well," Robert began, "like most, if not all, of Delmont's idiotic thefts, it caused a number of different ramifications. First off, Rex never had a son, and so the cure for the cold had to wait thirty more years. This caused literately billions of lost man hours due to a sickness that should have been cured already. This alone actually created a number of paradoxes. However, the moron then sold Rex to a private weapons development company that worked outside the laws of any individual government. Using techniques we won't go into, they *persuaded* Rex to develop one of the most powerful biological weapons ever created. The result: billions of lost lives, including a number of time travelers. And, of course, even more paradoxes."

"So, what do we do?" Azure asked.

"A few things," the traveler replied, his eyes filled with excitement. "Step one: we go back in time and get a DNA sample and brain scan from Rex. Step two: we grow a fully functional clone and program it to pretend to be Rex. Step three: we break into a classified military weapons research facility with the clone in tow. We then swap the clone for Rex, bring Rex back here for a bit of regeneration and a little memory wipe, and then drop him off at home five minutes after he's kidnapped. Step four: we disable Delmont's machine again and defeat the doofus for a second time!"

"Why is it so convoluted?" Azure asked.

131

"It always is," Morgan replied. "I mean, I think it always is..."

"The reason, Azure," Robert explained, "is because of the way the time-lines are laid out. We have to undo the damage of the cold not being cured *before* we undo the damage of the weapon. So, we have to put Rex back *before* we un-kidnap him."

"Okay," Morgan nodded. "But, in that case, why don't we just drop the clone off at his house?"

"What?" Cleo asked.

"Well, I mean, we wouldn't have to break into that base if we just let the clone have the kid and..."

"What?!?!" both Cleo and Azure exclaimed.

"Morgan, what is wrong with..." Cleo said, a look of disgust on her face. "Rob, I want a lock put on the cloning tank!"

"What did I say?" Morgan asked, gazing at the girls. "I'm just trying to keep us all safe."

"Well," the traveler replied, a wide grin on his face, "you've accidentally hit a bit of a taboo subject there. Clones aren't people, Morgan."

"What's the difference?"

"There are a number of differences," Robert asserted. "But the big one is that they don't have *souls*. At least, if you believe in souls... But, whether or not you do, *trying* to have children with them is *very* taboo. Do you follow me, Morgan?"

"I'm not sure..."

"Mmmm," the traveler nodded, squinting at the young man. "*Trying*, Morgan. *Trying*... You see? To have children. *Trying* to have children. With me? It's taboo. It's like being a *baaad* boy in your time. You see what I did? *Baaad*. Like baaa, baaa... You see what I'm saying?"

"I'm not..." Morgan said thoughtfully before it struck him. "That's just nasty, Rob! What is wrong with you, man?!?!"

"You see, Cleo," Robert said, smiling at her. "He's not a pervert, he just didn't know."

"I suppose," she replied, rolling her eyes.

"Either way," the traveler said, shaking his head, "we replace the man, not the clone."

"Right!" Morgan wholeheartedly agreed.

"The first part of this mission," Robert explained, "me and Morgan can handle. Vox, I want you and Cleo to go over all the schematics I've put together on that base. I want to be able to just walk in and walk out without them ever knowing."

"You got it, boss," Vox replied with a smile.

"Doc," the traveler continued, "you can start teaching Azure some of the basics of field medicine. The more she knows, the better."

"Agreed," Doc nodded.

"And, that's it," Robert said. "We'll be in position in just a few minutes. Me and Morgan shouldn't be gone long."

"Awesome," Vox replied. "Come on, small-girl, we got work to do."

"Sure thing," she smiled.

In less than an hour, the ship was settled down in an area of farmland a few miles from Calvin Rex's country home.

"So," Morgan mused as they strolled down a long country lane in the moonlight. "How many planets have moons?"

"A lot of 'em."

"Are they all romantic?"

"A lot of 'em."

"Do you think we should go for another moonlight stroll?"

"We're already on one," the traveler pointed out.

"I meant with the girls," Morgan explained.

"No," Robert replied. "I can't take any more right now. In fact, I had a couple of close calls the other night."

"You did fine!" the young man said encouragingly. "I'm sure you can handle it! And besides, it may give me a chance to get somewhere with Azure..."

"It's going to take a lot more than moonlight to do that, Hoss."

"Oh," Morgan sighed. "Do we have any wine on board?"

"Be quiet, Morgan," the traveler replied. "We're almost there and I need to concentrate. Try not to speak until I've given Rex a little night-night gas."

"What's that?"

"Try to figure it out from the context, man!"

"Right..."

A short distance from the house, both young men switched on their stealth generators - vanishing completely from sight - as they approached the door.

"Get off me, Morgan," the traveler whispered.

"Sorry," the young man replied. "I didn't expect you to stop so suddenly."

"What did you expect me to do? Walk through the door?"

"No, I just..."

"Never mind!" the traveler said, slowly turning the handle. "Crap... It's locked."

"Use the *sonic screwdriver*," Morgan suggested.

"I don't have one," Robert explained. "This is *still* just the future; not a television show."

"So how do we get in then?"

"I pick the lock," the traveler explained.

"You can do that?"

"Are you kidding me?" Robert replied, sliding a set of picks into the lock.

"Rob," Morgan whispered. "Sometimes, you are really cool, man."

"*Sometimes?*" the traveler replied, before slowly opening the door.

The two made their way quickly into the house. Morgan immediately knocked over a table with a rather elegant lamp on it, but Robert managed to catch the lamp with his hand and the table with his foot before they hit the ground.

"Morgan," he said softly, a hint of annoyance in his voice. "Why do I bring you with me on things like this?"

"I was actually wondering about that myself..."

"Well," the traveler sighed, "the truth is, I just like hanging out with you... But, don't tell anybody."

"I won't!"

The pair moved quickly across the room and made their way to Rex's bedroom. There he lie, very much asleep; his sheets and pillows in a complete mess, and drool pouring from his mouth. The traveler pulled something from his pocket and sprayed it a short distance from Rex's open mouth.

"Done," he said, switching off his stealth generator. "Now, we just take what we need."

"Do I look that bad in my sleep?" Morgan asked.

"At least once."

"What do you mean?"

"I mean, I've only ever seen you asleep *once*," Robert explained, pulling a scanner from his pocket and pushing buttons on it. "And, that was enough. You looked *at least* this bad. And, you were wearing those goofy *X-Men* pajamas."

"You've seen those?"

"They're nothing to write home about Mr. *Wolverine*. Anyway, we're done!"

"We're done?" the young man asked in surprise. "That was fast!"

"What did you expect?" the traveler chuckled. "It's been a long time since we had to take people's brains out of their heads to scan them."

"You had to..."

"No, Morgan," Robert replied. "It was a joke. Let's get out of here."

The two made their way quickly back to the ship. They were back in non-space shortly after; with a perfect *clone bud* blossoming in the clone tank.

"Alright," the traveler said with a contented sigh. "That's that for a few days. Morgan, I've got to dive back into work for the moment..."

"I thought you said you were done," the young man interrupted.

"I lied," he admitted. "But, not by much! There are just a few more burs to knock off. We've got to seriously not mess up, you know?"

"I do."

"So," Robert said with a knowing grin, "maybe you'll want to take Azure down to the range for the next few days."

"Oh! My! Goodness!" he exclaimed. "Do I?!?!"

"Well then, you're in luck," the traveler replied. "Because those are orders. Now, get to it soldier!"

"Yes, sir!" Morgan replied, snapping a salute before flying from the medi-bay in search of Azure.

Minutes later, the young man and young lady were all alone on the gun range - which was *still* on the ship - with a number of weapons spread out before them.

"That's not very good, is it?" Azure asked, staring at her unscathed target.

"Well," he sighed, pretending very hard to seriously consider the question. "I think you're holding the gun wrong."

"How should I hold it?"

"More like this," he replied, taking her hands in his and correcting her grip.

"Thanks!" she replied, before staring at him out of the corner of her eyes for several seconds. "I think I've got it now, Morgan..."

"Shhh..." he replied. "Don't rush it... You need to be one with the gun..."

"I'm one *enough*," she replied, jerking her hands away.

"You're probably right," he said with a nod. "Try again."

She did somewhat better; but still needed a lot of work. Morgan was patient. He knew this was only ever going to happen once. Taking his time would pay off, he just couldn't rush it...

"I don't feel like I'm making much progress," she sighed, after about a half an hour.

She was right. Of course, part of the reason for that was because Morgan had set the target as far down the range as he could. You see? He wasn't always an idiot!

"Well... I suppose I could..." he said thoughtfully. "No. No, never mind. You're just not quite ready for that yet..."

"Ready for what?" she asked.

"Some advanced training techniques I know," he replied with complete confidence. "But, you're just not ready for 'em."

"Alright," she sighed, "If I'm not ready..."

"Hold on!" he exclaimed. "Just hold on for a second now. I admit I see a lot of potential in ya. But, you would have to do *exactly* what I tell you. I don't want either of us getting hurt."

"Okay," she smiled. "I'm willing to give it a try if you are."

"Oh..." he said slowly. "I'm willing..."

"Then, let's get started."

"Yes. Yes, let's," he replied. "Now, remember, I'm kind of like a doctor in this situation. This is all just like clinical training, so try not to get *too* excited."

"I think I can handle it..."

"I'm glad," he said, stepping up behind her and covering her hands with his own, before setting his head on her shoulder. "Pull in tight, like this... Put your foot a little further out... Now, lean slowly forward..."

"Like this?" she asked.

"Oh! My! Goodness!" Morgan exclaimed.

"What is it?" she asked.

"I've just fulfilled one of my childhood fantasies," he explained.

"What fantasy?" she asked, a touch of confusion in her voice.

"Well," he lied, "I always used to fantasize about teaching someone to shoot."

"But, we've been here for over an hour."

"I know," he lied some more. "But, I had forgotten about it."

"Oh..." she said. "Well, I'm glad you're living your dream."

"Me, too," he replied "Either way, pull it up like this... and slowly... pull... the... trigger..."

She hit the target in the very center.

"Bull's eye!" she said excitedly.

"Oh... Yeah..." Morgan replied slowly. "Bull's eye."

"You know, you're a really good teacher," she said.

"Well," he replied. "I learned from the very best."

"Who taught you?"

"You did," he smiled.

"Really?" she asked, a touch of disbelief in her voice.

"Oh yeah," he nodded. "The truth is Azure... and I hadn't planned to tell you this... not for a while anyway... but you and me had quite a little thing going on."

"Really?" she asked, gazing at him from under a single raised eyebrow.

"Absolutely," he replied. "In fact, just before we undid that other future, you and I had *quite* an evening out on a beach on *Escargot*."

"*Escargot?*"

"Cleo's home planet."

"Are you serious?" she asked, "I mean about *us*, not about *Escargot*."

"Deadly serious," he sighed. "I hated to give you up girl... but, I had to... the universe was counting on me... So, I've had to start all over. But, it's all good. You're the girl you were and I'm the man I am. It'll all work out."

"So we..." she said, taking a few steps back. "We were *involved?*"

"Do you know how you got me to shoot as well as I do?" he asked.

"No..."

"You said we needed to approach it from a *psychological* angle," he lie-explained. "Every time I hit the bull's eye, we would kiss."

"Did you hit it often?"

"All the time," he said. "But, to be fair, you were always moving the target closer."

"I was?"

"Oh yeah!"

"Wow... I must have *really* believed in self-sacrifice..."

"Well, either way," he smiled. "I was thinking the same thing might work for you. You know, when you hit a bull's eye, like you just did, we should kiss."

"No," she replied, taking another step back. "I think a better motivator would be for you to kiss me if I miss..."

"And, what should I do if you hit a bull's eye?" he asked, his grin getting even wider.

"I don't know," she said, throwing her hands up. "Punch me in the back of the head or something!"

"Wow..." he replied, shaking his head. "That's just weird..."

The next few days were filled, at least from Morgan's point of view, with hours and hours of non-kissing shooting practice with a beautiful young woman. By the end of this period, she was at least as good a shot as the young man was. Which was really great timing as the clone was just ready to come out of the oven. As a result, Robert called them all together in the conference room.

"Alright, ladies and gentlemen," the traveler began. "Oh, and you too, Morgan."

137

"Witty," he smirked. "Really witty. Some of your best material..."

"Moving on," Robert continued, "This part of the job is going to take some exact movements, but it should be easy enough in reality. Cleo, I need you and Vox to make their security systems fail strategically to give us a clear path in and out."

"Easily done," she smiled.

"Perfect," he replied. "It might also be a good idea to fire off a false alarm or two. The place is crawling with soldiers and the more you can get out of the base, the better."

"Not a problem," Vox replied.

"Under the circumstances," Robert continued, "it would be best to be ready to pick us up if things go south, Doc. We *do not* want to get caught by these guys. In an emergency, I think you could bust in with the car to grab us. I don't think it would get too hot, as it's got its own shield and stealth field generators. But, I only want to do that as a last resort."

"One suggestion," Vox said. "I want to put transponders on you so we can track you. These guys don't have the technology to see the signals, so it shouldn't add any risk."

"Good idea!" Robert replied. "Anything more?"

No one had anything more.

"Let's do it!" the traveler said excitedly.

Just minutes later, the ship set down less than a mile from the not-quite-a-military-base that was their target. Robert and Morgan marched quickly through the woods with the clone in tow; all three of them invisibled up by stealth belts. They quickly made their way to the main entrance and patiently waited. Suddenly, the gate began to open on its own.

"That's it," the traveler said. "Let's go."

"I still think this is stupid, Rob," Morgan asserted.

"I've already explained. We have to hold hands. We can't afford to get separated."

"Well, the clone's hand is clammy."

"Maybe he's nervous."

"Really?" Morgan whispered.

"No..." the traveler replied. "And, what's with all the cinnamon chewing gum all of a sudden?"

"It's part of my *get Azure* plan."

"What part?"

"*Be Prepared.*"

"How so?" Robert asked.

"I figure I need to be ready all the time; just in case she decides to kiss me on the mouth."

"I have to admit, Morgan, that I really respect your optimism..."

The trio passed through the gate and entered a courtyard filled with military equipment and personnel. Alarms began sounding moments after they entered. The front gate closed again as soldiers began to run one way and another.

"Mmmm," Robert said, as they streaked across the distance that stood between them and the elevators, carefully avoiding the guards. "They seem to have triggered some kind of *lock down*. Still, I'm sure Cleo will have it sorted before we're ready to head out."

The elevators opened just moments before they reached them.

"Man, I love that girl," the traveler said with a genuine tone of admiration as the elevator automatically selected the correct floor.

The elevator opened on a long hallway with doors along each side. The guards for the floor were beating on the entrance to the guardroom, which had mysteriously locked just moments before, in an attempt to get out. The two companions and their pet clone flew to the correct chamber and found it unlocked by the time they arrived.

"Hello, Calvin," Robert said with a smile as he stepped into the cell and suddenly became visible.

"Who are you?" the man asked.

"Does it matter?" the traveler replied. "We're here to rescue you."

Having said this, he handed the man a belt with both a shield and a stealth generator on it.

"Put that on quick," he said before turning to the clone. "Clone, activate program *Calvin Rex*; authorization *last time traveler*."

"I'm not a clone, Robert," the clone replied, "as you know very well. Now, if you gentlemen will excuse me, I'd like to get some rest. Oh, and good luck!"

"Why did it say it wasn't a clone?" Morgan asked as they rushed back up the hall.

"All part of the program, Morgan," the traveler explained. "They'll never know what they've got."

"This is crazy!" Calvin said under his breath.

"It is," Robert agreed, "but the universe is a crazy place!"

When they got back in the courtyard, the lock down was still in place and the gate still very closed.

"Mmmm" Robert said. "We can't sit still long. If Doc thinks we're stuck, he'll come to get us. And, I don't want that."

"What do we do?" Morgan asked.

"Okay," the traveler replied. "We have to split up, Morgan."

"We what?!?!"

"No choice!" Robert barked quietly. "Now, listen! In roughly two minutes, one of those tanks is going to bust through the wall. After it does, let it get about a hundred feet out and then make a run for the ship. Don't stop for *any* reason and *do not* lose Calvin. Clear?"

"Clear!"

"I'll meet you back at the ship, bro!"

Roughly a minute and a half later, one of the tanks cranked up and started driving straight for the wall. Gun fire rained down on it, but the massive machine paid it no respect. In just moments, it had plowed into and then through the wall. Morgan took off running, holding Calvin by the hand. Seconds after he stepped beyond the gap, several missiles hit the vehicle all at once. It exploded, knocking both Morgan and Calvin to the ground.

"What happened?" Calvin asked.

"Nothing," Morgan replied, his heart pounding in his chest. "We have to get back to the ship!"

"But your friend!"

"No time," the young man said, dragging Calvin into a mad run.

"What about your friend?"

"He's not dead!"

"I didn't say he was."

"Look!" Morgan shouted as they ran along hand in hand. "None of this happened! Do you understand me?!?! None of that just happened. In a matter of hours, you'll be home in bed and then you'll be un-kidnapped and this will all be undone."

"What do you mean?" Calvin asked, panting for breath as they reached the loading platform.

"I mean," Morgan replied, his own breath deep and heavy, "that when we undo all this, Rob won't have died because we'll have never even come here."

"You're right," Robert replied, turning off his stealth generator.

"Ahhh!" Morgan screamed, clutching his invisible chest.

"You're not dead?"

"Not yet! Get on the platform!"

Immediately, Morgan and Calvin obeyed. In seconds, they were on the ship and the ship was in the sky.

"Wow, Morgan!" the traveler said, slapping the young man on the back. "Wow!"

"What?"

"You would have just saved my life!" he exclaimed. "I mean, if I had just gotten killed back there, you would have actually managed to save me!"

"Awesome!" Morgan replied, a huge smile on his face. "Oh, and how didn't you get killed?"

"Man, I *never* get killed," the traveler explained.

CHAPTER 10: WHAT IS LOVE

"So," Morgan said as he stepped on the bridge, "we heading out?"

"Looks that way," Robert nodded. "Doc's wiped Calvin's memories of what happened, regenerated him back to where he was when he was picked up, and has him sedated. Now, all we need to do is drop him off and head to Never Never Land."

"Awesome," the young man nodded. "How long we got?"

"About forty-five minutes or so."

"Good, 'cause we need to talk."

"About what?" the traveler asked.

"A couple of things."

"Alrighty. Go."

"Let's start with that other question I had…"

"What other question, Morgan?" the traveler asked. "How am I supposed to know what you're talking about, man? You're like the star of a movie entitled *The Never Ending Questions*."

"*The Never Ending Questions… ahhhahahhahahaha,*" Morgan sang.

"Not bad…" Robert nodded. "You're a little flat but, all things considered, not bad. What's the question, Morgan?"

"Why not just get married?"

"We haven't known each other long enough."

"You two have known…"

"It was a joke, Morgan," the traveler interrupted. "See, you were supposed to think I was talking about you and me and then you were supposed to say: *I don't mean us! I mean you and Cleo!*"

"What?"

"Repeat the question, Morgan…"

"Why not just get married?"

"Several reasons," Robert replied.

"Such as?"

"Well, first off, Morgan," the traveler explained, "when a man and woman say *I do*, the woman's mind immediately rewires itself. Well… it may actually be that moment when the ring slips on her finger. I'm still doing research…"

"Rewires how?" Morgan asked.

"Well, invariably, they start seeing houses set upon neatly trimmed lawns surrounded by white picket fences in their mind's eye. And, whereas I've got no problem with the whole *settling down* crap in the long run, I sure ain't got time for it now. If I married Cleo, she would be under the constant strain of trying to get me into a mortgage."

"You wouldn't need one," the young man pointed out. "You could just buy a house with that *Monopoly Money* of yours."

"I never said it was counterfeit."

"Okay, that's one reason," Morgan nodded.

"Reason two: when a female manages to bind a man in *the irrevocable shackles of wedded bliss...*"

"What?"

"*Futurama.*"

"Oh yeah!"

"Anyway," Robert continued, "it's only a matter of time before she hits you with the old *I want to have your baby!* Of course, I get that a lot anyway..."

"I never get that," Morgan admitted.

"Yeah..." Robert nodded. "I can see that. Either way, I obviously want Cleo to have my babies and all..."

"Oh yeah!" the young man exclaimed.

"Focus, Morgan!"

"Sorry..."

"So, my iron will would only be able to resist for so long..." the traveler explained. "After that, I'd have to give her children..."

"I don't think I could use the phrase *have to* in that context," Morgan pointed out.

"Well, you know what I mean..." Robert replied, lifting his hands. "Right now, I'm a barely passable not-exactly-boyfriend. What kind of father would I make?"

"Yeah... Actually, I do see what you mean... More?"

"Oh yeah!" the traveler exclaimed. "Then there's the crackling electrical energy of non-stop sexual tension!"

"I *can't believe* you just said that. You usually don't talk like that."

"That's not *naughty*, Morgan," Robert pointed out.

"I know," the young man explained. "That time, I was messing with you. See? I'm learning!"

"So you are!" the traveler smiled. "Anyway, Morgan, at the moment we're basically immortal. There's no hurry, no reason in the universe to rush anything. I'm one of the few men in the history of all time that can watch his not-exactly-girlfriend blossom into her full glory and then rewind it and watch it again."

"I guess I see that."

"And, that means that she and I can live on the very edge of raw animal passion, staring over into the paradise that is complete and total carnal fulfillment..."

"You could write books, you know that?" Morgan interrupted. "I mean; you could write books that I'd be embarrassed to read!"

"Yeah…" Robert sighed. "I have to be careful. My heart's in perfect condition, but I could still give myself an attack if I really tried. Anyway Morgan, it's like taking that moment when your lips brush hers, but you haven't actually kissed her yet and stretching it out for years. It's unbelievable, man. And, maybe one day, you'll know what I mean."

"I'm going to have to get to the *lip brushing* stage before I completely understand," Morgan confessed, "but I think I get the general idea. You want it to last."

"Absolutely!" the traveler exclaimed. "I'm the kind of man that would sit at a table for decades gazing down at a perfectly cooked steak, letting my eyes revel in its perfection and smelling every glorious, juicy scent it had to offer before I ate it."

"It's funny that you picked that image, because…"

"Morgan!" Robert warned.

"Right…" the young man sighed. "You know, for a guy determined to resist temptation, you sure seem to revel in it."

"What else have I got right now?" the traveler chuckled. "And, I've learned to sail pretty close to the wind, Morgan. Trust me, it makes the trip a lot more exciting."

"What does sailing…"

"It's an expression, man," Robert explained. "I just mean that I can dance right up to the edge with Cleo, and then dance safely away. I mean, provided I take precautions, like having you ready to punch me in the head."

"Well, I just hope you don't ever trip while you're a little too near that precipice."

"*Precipice?*" the traveler asked.

"It's like the edge of a high cliff."

"I know that! I just didn't expect you to know it."

"Well, I do," Morgan replied. "But, that's really beside the point. You've led me to another question."

"What's that?"

"Why not get engaged?" the young man asked.

"Well because…" Robert began.

"No, hear me out," Morgan interrupted. "I mean, you plan to marry her like it's a done deal. If that's really the case, then you already are engaged; you just haven't made it *official*. So then, why not make it official? Why not show Cleo that you love her and that you want to spend the rest of your life with her? I mean, what's holding you back?"

"Wow!" the traveler exclaimed. "I mean, like, seriously! Wow! You're *absolutely* right, Morgan! I don't think it's even possible to be *righter* than that! And, you thought of that before I did… I mean, you thought of that with comparably no time to think about it. You're going to break the six percent barrier!"

"I'm not sure about that," the young man said, shaking his head. "There's a difference between *intelligence* and *wisdom*."

"Wow!" Robert replied. "Zing! Two in a row! Slow down, Morgan, you're gonna blow a gasket!"

"Thank you, thank you!"

"And, seriously…" the traveler sighed. "You're right. I'm going to ask her."

"When?" Morgan asked.

"Who knows, man?" Robert laughed. "I got all the time in the universe!"

"Maybe, bro," the young man replied, shaking his head again, "but, I wouldn't take chances if I were you."

"What do you mean?"

"I just mean," Morgan explained, "*engagement* or not, you better start showing Cleo that you really care for her. If you actually do, that is."

"What do you mean by that? She knows I love her!"

"I wouldn't bet on that, bro," the young man pointed out, staring his friend in the eyes. "I *really* wouldn't."

"Well…" the traveler said slowly. "No. You know what? You're *right* about that, too! I'm going to start. In fact, I'm going to start *right now*. Where is she?"

"Hold on a sec," Morgan chuckled. "I'm glad you're excited and all, but I said *a couple of things*, remember?"

"Okay," Robert replied, leaning back in his seat. "You're right again. You're forming a habit, man. Anyway, go on with *part two*."

"Alright," Morgan said, taking a deep breath. "I'm getting *nowhere* with Azure and I can't understand it."

"I think I can…"

"Well, I can't!" the young man exclaimed. "I mean; I've done everything you do! I've bragged and lied all over the place!"

"There's a little more to it than that, Morgan," the traveler chuckled.

"Well, if there *is*, I sure don't see it…"

"The core problem is that you don't even know what love is."

"Well… " Morgan said slowly, before beginning to sing *I Want to Know What Love Is.*

"Okay, Morgan!" Robert laughed. "I'll help you! Just stop singing."

"Done!"

"Alright…" the traveler said, leaning forward in his seat. "Let's start at the very beginning. From our many previous conversations, I can tell that the whole *love/lust* line is really blurry for you. So, we'll start by turning up the contrast a bit."

"Sounds good."

"Now, I feel confident that you've got a whole pocketful of fantasies about Azure…"

"More like a hot tub full!" Morgan exclaimed.

"Mmmm," the traveler nodded. "That's part of the problem right there, but I have to admit your imagery was really good that time."

"Thank you!"

"Either way, do you have a fantasy - that involves her - where the two of you don't actually *touch* at all."

"Yeah…" the young man nodded. "I got a couple of those."

"Well, that's a start. Tell me about one."

"Alrighty. Now, keep in mind, it's a *fantasy*; so not all of it makes sense."

"I would have expected nothing less," Robert replied.

"Okay. Well, for some crazy reason, Azure ends up trapped in this large plastic pool…"

"Large plastic pool?" the traveler asked.

"Yeah," the young man replied. "It's like a kiddy pool, but it's bigger, so the top of it is up to Azure's chest."

"Mmmm."

"And, for some reason, she's in a French bikini," Morgan continued. "You know what I mean?"

"I do, Morgan," the traveler said, pinching the bridge of his nose. "And, I'm beginning to lose hope. But, I guess I might as well finish the ride now that I'm on it. Please, go on…"

"Okay. So, the pool is filled with marshmallow cream," the young man explained, "and so everything's really slick."

"Right…"

"So, Azure can't get out no matter how hard she tries," Morgan continued with a huge grin. "She just keeps slipping and falling back in."

"Mmmm," Robert nodded. "And, you don't touch her *at all* in that fantasy?"

"No!" Morgan exclaimed. "I just sit in a deck chair eating marshmallows."

"Yeah…" the traveler sighed, "that makes sense, I guess. We'll have to try again…"

"Alrighty."

"Do you have any fantasies where you and Azure are watching the sunset or walking through a park holding hands?"

"I have some that *start* that way," Morgan asserted.

"Clearly, I'm going to have to take a different tack," Robert replied, shaking his head. "Tell me, why did you save Azure?"

"Well, she was about to die!" the young man explained. "What could I do?"

"Sure…" Robert nodded. "But, you didn't save her because you thought that one day you and she might…"

"No!" the young man interjected. "Is that what you think of me, bro?!?! I'm not a monster, man!"

"I don't think anything like that," the traveler assured him. "I just wanted to make sure. Remember, I'm trying to help you."

"Right."

"So, if Azure had been a little old bald man you would have done the same thing?" Robert asked.

"Well… I probably wouldn't have yelled *Crom*, but I still would have tried to save him."

"Okay…" Robert sighed. "I'll bite… Why wouldn't you have yelled '*Crom*'?"

"Well, I admit I wanted to plant the idea of *Conan* in Azure's mind," Morgan confessed. "So she'd, you know, kind of link me and *Arnold* on a subconscious level."

"But… She didn't know anything about human culture… So, that really wouldn't have meant anything to her…"

"Oh yeah…"

"Either way, Morgan," the traveler continued, "that's kind of like love. In fact, it is love. It's a love for life, love for another creature that doesn't expect any carnal gratification in return."

"Hmmm," the young man replied, clearly confused.

"Okay, Morgan," Robert said. "What would you do if Azure was crazy in love with another guy? Like, so in love with him that she ached over it."

"Well…" the young man replied, taking a deep breath. "I guess, honestly, I'd try to help her get him and then, try to persuade you to take me to meet some of those elvish chicks as a reward for my good deed."

"I never said there were elvish chicks," Robert pointed out, "but, I think we're making headway. Why would you help her get another guy?"

"I want her to be happy," Morgan explained. "She deserves it, man."

"Bingo!" the traveler exclaimed. "We've had a breakthrough! That is *love*, Morgan."

"Man…" Morgan said thoughtfully. "It's not quite as cool as *lust* is it?"

"Two steps forward, one step back…"

"Anyway," Morgan replied, "how does that help me?"

"Well," the traveler explained, "try to hold onto that feeling when you talk to her. Always try to keep in the very front of your mind that her happiness is what matters most in the universe to you."

"Is that what you do with, Cleo?" Morgan asked quite sincerely.

"Well, ye…" Robert began before stopping. "No, Morgan. No, that's not what I do. It's what I *try* to do, it's what I *want* to do, it's what I *should* do, but it's not what I *actually* do…"

"Okay," the young man nodded. "So, we've both been going about this the wrong way?"

"Yeah," the traveler sighed. "I guess we have…"

"So, what do we do about it?"

"I think we should start by spending more time with them," Robert replied. "Together I mean. I certainly can't be left alone with Cleo at the moment, and I don't think Azure would be alone with you without a gun in her hand…"

"So, we should, like, go on a double date?"

"Maybe…" Robert replied thoughtfully. "If we can get Azure to go out with you…"

"We can," Morgan nodded. "Well, you can. You'll just come up with some brilliant lie or something and there we'll be at dinner with her having no idea how she got there."

"You're probably right," the traveler agreed. "But, we have to start small."

"Quick question."

"Yes?"

"We're dropping Calvin off on the same night we scanned him, right?"

"Yeah," the traveler replied. "A couple of hours later."

"Well, what about that moonlight stroll I was talking about?"

"Nah, man," Robert replied. "It'll be a while before I can take another one of those. Like, seriously!"

"What about all that *close sailing/edge dancing* you were just talking about?"

"Well, it's easy to talk like that when it's just you and me sitting on the bridge," the traveler replied. "It's another when I'm strolling down some moonlit lane with Cleo's head on my shoulder..."

"So, you were lying?"

"Not *exactly*," Robert replied. "I mean I *really* do feel pretty much constant tension and sometimes I can safely *pump up the volume*, if you follow me. I mean, I can get *all* up in her face if we're in a seriously crowded room. I could probably even dance with her."

"A quick kiss maybe?"

"On the cheek, I can handle sometimes," he replied. "I think I even did that in front of you once."

"You kissed her on the forehead," Morgan pointed out. "Either way, no moonlight. So, what do we do?"

"Let's drop Calvin off while I'm thinking," Robert suggested. "I'll have a plan when we get back to the ship. I mean; *all* you care about is spending more time with Azure, right?"

"Right!"

"Alright then," Robert smiled, "we'll just start *really* small."

A few minutes later, Robert, Morgan, and Vox were making their way to Calvin's house with Calvin's unconscious body slung over Vox's shoulder. They dropped him in bed, locked the door, and headed back to the ship. A quick time-check showed that the common cold had been cured right on schedule and billions of people had gotten back to work in the future... or past... or whenever it was... With this accomplishment under their belts, they pointed the ship back toward Never Never Land and jumped into non-space.

"I'll do all the talking," Robert said, as he and Morgan wandered through the ship in search of the girls.

"That's probably for the best," Morgan admitted.

They didn't have to look for long, as both beautiful maidens were sitting in Cleo's room just talking and giggling away. Morgan asked Robert to give him a moment to steady himself before they made their presence known. After about ten seconds of hand fanning, a quick brow wipe, and a fresh stick of gum, Morgan was ready.

"Knock, knock," the traveler said, stepping just within the portal and doing his best *sexy lean* against the door frame.

Morgan thought he did it pretty well. He decided to start practicing that himself once he got back to his room for the night.

"May we come in?" he asked with a devilish smile.

"You already are," Cleo replied, glancing up at him, but refusing to turn her head.

"Well then," he said, pulling himself upright and strutting into the chamber. "I'll take that as a *yes*."

Morgan took this as *yes* as well and followed behind on Robert's heels.

"Just what is it that you two want?" Cleo asked, the slightest trace of a smile on her lips.

Morgan had a very hard time not telling her *exactly* what he wanted. But in the end he felt it better to leave the conversation to Robert.

"Well," the traveler replied, leaning against the dresser directly across from Cleo's bed, which was what the girls were sitting on, "*we* two want *you* two."

"And, what exactly do you mean by *that?*" she asked, a single eyebrow raised.

"Well," Robert replied, moving slowly nearer, "Me and Morgan here were just *lamenting* the fact that we couldn't spend the next hour or so in the company of the two *most beautiful* women we had ever seen. We had almost given up hope, when I just *happened* to remember you two were on board. After a quick discussion, we realized that you two *were* the two most beautiful women we had ever seen. That struck us as an act of *fate*. So, we decided to drop by and see if you felt the same way about it."

"So, you want to spend an hour with us?" Cleo asked.

"Oh yeah," Robert replied, stepping right up to her, gazing down into her eyes. "That's *exactly* what we want. We want *you* to come up to the bridge with *us*."

"And, why is that?" she asked staring up into his face.

"It's a *micro-date*," he explained.

"What, exactly, is a *micro-date?*"

"It's like a *date*," he replied, gently taking her by the chin, "but it's *tiny*."

"Sorry," Azure replied with a cruel smile, "but, there's not a date *small* enough for me and Morgan to go out on."

"Ow!" Morgan said.

Cleo giggled.

"Rob," she said, a slight blue tint turning her cheeks teal. "What's this really all about?"

"Well..." he replied, turning around and stepping back into the center of the room. "I mean, after all, you are my..."

"Your what?" she asked, both eyebrows raised.

"I mean," he continued, drawing a deep breath, "I am definitely your..."

"My what?"

"Don't play coy with me," he chuckled, shaking his head.

"What's *playing coy?*" she asked with a coy smile.

"Cleo," the traveler said quite seriously, "you are my *girlfriend*, aren't you?"

For several seconds, she sat silently staring at him, her breath slightly more shallow and her tint slightly bluer.

"Yes..." she said finally. "I *am* your *girlfriend*, Rob."

"And, that makes me your *boyfriend*?"

"I guess it does, Rob," she sighed, rolling her eyes.

"And, we've never really been on a *date* as *boyfriend and girlfriend*, right?"

"No... We haven't."

"Well," he said, "that's what *this* is. I want us to *date*, but we need to start small. In fact, we need to start *micro*. Hence *micro-date*."

"What's wrong with you, Cleo?" Morgan asked.

"What do you mean?" she replied.

"I mean; you're changing color!" he observed.

"No, I'm not," she insisted, turning ever-so-slightly bluer.

"Yes, you are! You're turning blue!"

"I am not!"

"She's fine," the traveler replied.

"I ain't sure about that, man!" Morgan said. "She looks like she's asphyxiating! We need to call Doc!"

"She's blushing, bro..."

"She's..." the young man began before it dawned on him. "Oh! Right! That's why your lips are blue! You've got blue blood!"

"That's right," Robert nodded.

"Azure must have purple blood!"

"Yep. She does."

"We have red blood," Morgan explained.

"They know, Morgan" Robert pointed out. "They already know. So, girls, you'll be up there in a few?"

"Yes, Rob," Cleo sighed. "We'll be up there in a few."

Moments later, the guys were sitting on the bridge waiting for the girls.

"So, what are we gonna do when they get here?" Morgan asked.

"Talk," the traveler replied.

"About what?"

"About whatever, Morgan," Robert said. "We talk to them all the time."

"Then, how is this a *date*?"

"*Micro-date*," Robert pointed out.

"Whatever!"

"Look," the traveler said, "didn't you just tell me that I should make things *official* with Cleo?"

"Yeah," Morgan nodded.

"Well," Robert replied, "that day on the beach wasn't a *date* because we didn't call it one. This *is* a date *because* we're calling it one."

"*Micro-date*," Morgan pointed out.

"Whatever!"

Shortly after this truly astounding intellectual exchange, the girls stepped onto the bridge. They had both changed into miniskirts, stockings, stiletto heeled boots, and long sleeve shirts. Morgan's heart skipped several beats.

"I wish I had brought the defibrillator," he whispered.

"Me, too," Robert agreed softly, "that was a lot of fun."

As soon as he said this, he leapt to his feet, followed instantly by Morgan.

"You changed," he smiled, stepping quickly across the floor and offering his hand to Cleo.

"You didn't," she observed.

"Well," he said, glancing down at his shirt, "I thought seeing me in my *action gear* might do something for you. Does it?"

"A little," she half-smiled. "But, next time try to make a little more of an effort."

"Absolutely," he replied, leading her to the seat she always sat in.

"Okay," Azure said, staring down at Morgan's outstretched hand. "I want to make one thing clear from the get go. You two are on a *micro-date*. Morgan and I, however, are on two completely separate and unrelated chaperoning missions. And, I want to *stress* the fact that I'm *only* here because Cleo asked me to be."

Having made her position clear, she took Morgan's hand and followed him to her seat.

"So, Rob," Cleo said, gazing at him from the sides of her eyes, "what are we doing on this *micro-date* of ours?"

"Well," he replied, glancing over at the clock, "we have about forty-five minutes and I thought we could talk about something *other* than saving the universe for a change."

"You'll never make it forty-five minutes," she pointed out.

"I'm willing to try for you," he smiled.

"If you say so, Rob," she replied, rolling her eyes. "What else do you have planned?"

"I thought we might have a little space ice-cream," he suggested.

"Oh no," she replied, shaking her head. "I don't know if I could stand any more. Do you know how much I've eaten lately?"

"Not exactly," he admitted, "but I have noticed that you guys have been having a *lot* of ice-cream parties without me."

"Like, when?" Morgan said.

"Well," the traveler replied, "we could go back as far as three or four days ago when you guys were all in your room."

"Oh yeah," the young man said. "Well, that one was your fault anyway."

"What?" the traveler chuckled.

"Nothing," Cleo replied, blushing teal again, "Morgan's just an idiot."

"She's right," Morgan nodded. "I am."

"Alright..." Robert replied. "Well, just days before that the three of you were up here eating ice-cream without me."

"No, we weren't," Azure said.

"Actually, we were," Cleo corrected. "It's part of that future that never happened."

"Yeah," Robert said, "it is. What was that great combo you came up with, Morgan?"

"I don't think I remember..."

"It was pistachio with maple syrup," Cleo reminded him. "And, that was actually really good."

"Oh, I'm sure it was!" the traveler replied. "But, I didn't get any. What was it you wanted to have with the blueberry there, Morgan?"

"I just can't seem to..."

"It was honey, Morgan," Cleo replied. "Don't you remember?"

"Ooooh," Azure said, "That does sound good."

"I'll go get some!"

"No, no," the traveler replied, "I think we'll save that for a second date. Don't you, Morgan?"

"Absolutely!"

"You know," Azure began, "it's crazy to think that I've sat up here eating ice-cream with you guys even though it never happened."

"I guess it is, a little," Robert admitted.

"How did I end up on the ship, anyway?" she asked. "The day you guys picked me up, for the second time I guess, Doc said he'd tell me more when I was ready, but he hasn't yet."

"It's actually a rather interesting story," the traveler replied, excitement flashing in his eyes. "We'd gone to collect the Orb of the Gods just as two different apocalypses were destroying your home world simultaneously!"

"So, how did that get me here?"

"To start with," Robert began, "you were basically this priestess-warrior..."

"I was?" she interjected.

"Oh yeah," he replied. "Anyway, you served at one of your people's most holy temples. The very temple, in fact, where the orb was kept. Well, our little party - led by me, naturally - broke into that temple by crashing my car through the roof..."

"Seriously?"

"Absolutely," he nodded. "I then did some of my magic and, in seconds, there was nothing but e-zombie dust filling the floor of the foyer."

"E-Zombie?"

"Think zombies made out of robots!" he smiled. "Nightmarish! Man, what a rush... Either way, we belted down stairs toward the orb and... and actually why don't you take over, Morgan?"

"What?" the young man replied. "Nah, man. You go ahead and finish."

"No, Morgan," Cleo smiled, "seriously. You tell Azure how she got rescued."

"If you want," he sighed. "Um... So... Well, like Rob said, there were all these e-zombies all over the place and, when we got down stairs, you were alone down there with them..."

"Honestly?"

"Yes," Cleo nodded, with a wide smile. "Go on, Morgan."

"Right," he said, clearing his throat. "Well, you screamed and attracted our attention. Fortunately, only one of the zombies was after you because the rest wanted to kill us. Anyway, everybody opened fire... well, I didn't because I didn't have a gun yet. That was before you taught me to shoot. But, either way, we killed the thing and then you came with us. In fact, you even helped us recover the orb."

"Wow!" Cleo said. "Did you just see that, Rob? That's what *humility* looks like!"

"I don't like it," Robert replied, shaking his head. "It seems *pretentious.*"

"Anyway, Azure," Cleo continued, "what Morgan didn't tell you, is that *he* saved your life. If he hadn't reacted when he did, there's no way you'd have made it. And, if you hadn't then you wouldn't be here with is now. So, Morgan is actually the reason you're here and not just another missing person."

"If he didn't have a gun..."

"Oh," Cleo giggled. "He charged it with a baseball bat."

"Baseball bat?"

"It's like a metal club," Cleo explained. "And, actually, the zombie almost killed him."

"So," Azure said, turning her eyes to Morgan, "you actually risked your life to save mine?"

"Yeah," he nodded.

"Why didn't you tell me before?"

"I..." he stammered. "I don't know... I mean; it would have seemed like bragging about doing the only thing I could have done. Ya know what I mean?"

"I think I actually do," she smiled. "And, that surprises me."

"I know," he sighed. "Sometimes I'm hard to follow."

"No," she laughed. "I mean; your reason for not telling me surprises me. I just really wish I could remember it all."

As soon as she said this, Robert shot bolt upright and snapped his fingers.

"Azure," he said, "I apologize!"

"For what?"

"For getting so distracted," he replied. "I *cannot* believe I forgot to tell you."

"Tell me what?"

"Me and Doc backed up your memories," he smiled.

"You what?" Morgan asked, swallowing as he spoke.

"We figured she might want them after she settled back in," the traveler explained. "So, we backed them up on the ship and Doc ran a quick backup with a hand scanner after the whole beach party thing. We've got 'em if you want 'em."

"I absolutely do!" she exclaimed. "That's amazing."

"It sure is..." Morgan whispered.

"One sec," Robert said, leaning over and hitting the com. "Doc, you there?"

"I am, Robert."

"Azure's ready to have her memories back."

"Excellent! Send her down to the medi-bay and I'll take care of it immediately."

"Be right back!" Azure said excitedly, rising quickly from her seat and making her way to the medi-bay as fast as those heels would let her.

"So..." Morgan said slowly as soon as she had left the room. "Rob, out of curiosity, what do you do when you get caught lying?"

"I *never* get caught," the traveler lied.

"Actually, that's a lie, Rob," Cleo pointed out.

"That's true," he nodded. "That is a lie. Well done!"

"So, what do you do when you get caught?" Morgan asked again.

"Nothing," Robert chuckled. "I've got the kind of personality where everybody just thinks it's funny when I lie to them."

"Not *everybody*," Cleo replied, gazing at him.

"Almost everybody," he admitted. "And, besides, Cleo, I *never* lie to you."

"That's also a lie," she asserted.

"You're absolutely right," he confessed. "That is a lie. I'm telling you the truth about it because I respect you so much."

"Anyway," Morgan continued, "do I have that kind of personality?"

"No…" Robert replied, shaking his head. "No, you don't. And, it's not even a close call... Why? Have you been lying?"

"No…" the young man replied defensively.

Just minutes later, Azure strutted... and I mean *strutted*... onto the bridge and made her way slowly over to Morgan's seat. She reached down, pulled him up, wrapped her arms around him, leaned forward, and kissed him. And, yeah... I mean *kissed* him... For Morgan, the moment seemed to last somewhere between *Oh! My! Goodness!* and infinity.

Although it was the single greatest experience in his life, he was a little disappointed by the fact that it was obviously a hallucination brought on by overwhelming desire or some of that second hand weed smoke. Or, in fact, he might have even died... Maybe those miniskirts really had given him a heart-attack. He knew he should have brought that defibrillator...

After several seconds of complete ecstasy, Azure brought his moment of paradise to an end.

"*That*," she said quite sexily, "was for almost getting yourself killed saving my life and then not ever bothering to brag about it."

"Well I..." he began.

He was stopped mid-sentence by Azure's forcefully flying hand. She slapped him with everything she had to give. The young man's head jerked to the side, revealing to his three companions a perfect blood-red imprint of the young lady's hand on the side of his face.

"And, *that*," she said, her tone pretty much as un-sexy as it gets, "was for the *lying*, the *bragging*, and the *manipulation*! So, now we're even, Morgan! Now, you get the chance to start over for a third time! And, the *only* reason you get that is because it's *just possible* that there's a nice guy buried somewhere inside that *moron* that you are! Cleo, can we talk?"

"Absolutely," Cleo replied, jumping from her seat, a wide smile on her face.

The two ladies stepped quickly from the bridge, leaving the young men once again alone.

"Well," Robert sighed, "that was a rather climatic end to our little *micro-date*... At least it was memorable, I guess."

"Rob," Morgan said after a few seconds. "Did you see what *just* happened?"

"Yeah," the traveler sighed. "Yeah, I did, Morgan."

"She kissed me," the young man said excitedly. "She kissed me on the *mouth*! I think she may have even used her tongue a little!"

"You know, Morgan," Robert laughed, "I really do love hanging out with you!"

"Enough to tell other people?"

"Well... No," the traveler replied. "Not that much. Well... not yet anyway..."

"I see where you're coming from," Morgan replied.

CHAPTER 11: ELECTRIC AVENUE

"Do it, Vox," Robert said after the ship stopped on the edge of Never Never Land.

"Done," Vox replied seconds later. "Twenty minutes after the last time Delmont used the machine, it took off, flew to an empty section of space, then exploded."

"That was *time delay disability*," Robert grinned.

"Man..." Morgan replied. "Y'all fit a lot into that one little box..."

"Can you check the time-lines for me?" the traveler asked.

"Sure thing," Vox nodded. "Looks like that did it. Calvin was never kidnapped and the time-lines are getting back to how they should have been."

"Awesome!"

"Where to next?" Morgan asked.

"Well," Robert replied. "As soon as the girls are done talking, we're going to have another little conference. After that, you and I have some shopping to do."

"Really?"

"Oh yeah," the traveler nodded.

Just over an hour later, all six companions were once again gathered around the conference table.

"Alright," Robert began, "this one's gonna be a little different..."

"Are they *all* going to be a *little different?*" Morgan asked.

"Probably, Morgan," the traveler replied, "just shut up and listen."

"Check."

"This time, Delmont..."

"Who is *really* good looking," Azure interrupted.

"May I continue?" Robert asked, a slight touch of annoyance in his voice.

"Please do," she smiled.

"Thank you," he replied before continuing. "The next situation is one of much more *standard time theft*, if you will. Delmont took an off-the-shelf emergency generator and sold it to a society that hadn't developed anything that advanced yet. It was very fuel efficient, but produced massive amounts of waste material."

"What did that do?" Vox asked.

"A few things," Robert replied. "First, it gave the society a slight technological and production edge; resulting in them making advancements years before they should have. It also caused the society to look at pollution as a *necessary evil*, and part of *the price of progress*. This philosophical shift completely changed their world and, hundreds of years later, it was a total mess. It also killed a number of slightly less efficient, highly Eco-friendly generators that should have been developed just a few years down the road."

"So, how do we fix it?" Doc asked.

"We sell one of their major corporations an even better generator," Robert smiled.

"That seems like a bad idea," Morgan pointed out. "I mean; we're trying to take away the technological edge the first generator gave them. Giving them a better one isn't going to do that."

"That's actually a fair point," Azure nodded.

"Yeah," the traveler chuckled. "Old Morgan's a deep thinker. But, we should be able to keep the technological damage to a minimum while completely eliminating the environmental issues."

"How?" the young man asked.

"Well," Robert explained, "we're going to sell them a generator that is even *more* efficient, and *much* cleaner, but more expensive to produce than the Delmont generator."

"What good will that do?" the young man asked.

"That's a fair question," the traveler smiled. "The answer is: It'll give the corporation we sell it to a very slight advantage. You see, the lower fuel costs will offset the cost of production so that, in the long run, our generator will be more profitable. However, our generator will also be harder to maintain and *much* more expensive than the Eco-friendly generators the society should have eventually developed anyway. And, the fact that our generator is so clean should undo that philosophical shift and make the people more environmentally aware again. The end result: both the Delmont generator and our own will eventually fall out of favor and be replaced with the generators the society should have used in the first place."

"You really are a genius, Rob," Cleo said, a look of admiration in her eyes.

"I guess I kind of am," he agreed.

"So, what's the first step?" Morgan asked.

"You and me are going to pick up a generator for Vox," the traveler replied. "Then, he and I are going to modify it a bit to make it just what we want."

"Sounds good," the young man nodded. "When do we leave?"

"Now."

A couple of minutes later, Robert and Morgan were marching down the gangway a short distance from what looked like a truly giant intergalactic bazaar.

"So, why are we here?" Morgan asked.

"I *just* explained that, like, ten minutes ago," the traveler pointed out.

"I mean," the young man explained, "why have we come here to get the generator rather than just picking one up from Never Never Land?"

"Wow..." Robert replied. "You really are full of good questions, man. But, are you sure you want to hear the answer? It'll take a few minutes."

"I got time..."

"Alright," the traveler said, taking a deep breath, "First off, Never Never Land doesn't have unlimited resources, Morgan. The generators eat up huge amounts of power; not to mention the fact that we have to keep the sun burning. Then, there's the food and production needs for day to day life on the island. You with me so far?"

"So far."

"Good," Robert replied. "Well, that means eating up resources to make something like a generator that we can easily pull out of the time-line is a bad idea."

"Why can we pull this generator out of the time-line?"

"It's a piece of junk," the traveler chuckled. "Nobody ever buys it and it just ends up dumped at a junk yard."

"Does it even get recycled?" Morgan asked.

"I don't know..."

"What?"

"This place is only about seventy-five years from the end, Morgan," the traveler explained. "So, I don't know what happened after that. But, as of the moment time stopped, it hadn't been recycled."

"Wild!" the young man replied. "So, what other junk have you collected from outside Never Never Land?"

"All kinds of stuff," Robert replied. "Most of the ship, actually."

"What?"

"You see, Morgan," the traveler explained, "time travel was universally outlawed shortly before Delmont's idiotic romp through the past. We didn't even have a working time machine when we first realized the end was coming."

"How did you even see it coming?" Morgan asked.

"We monitored the time-lines in order to attempt to enforce the law," Robert replied. "Eventually, the future began to collapse until it reached a complete stand still. We only had a few centuries to get ready. As a result, everything we had was thrown into building Never Never Land. *The Ship* doesn't even have a time drive..."

"What do you mean?" Morgan interrupted.

"*The Ship*, that giant ship in Never Never Land, doesn't have a time drive in it," the traveler replied. "We used a planet based system to open... a *time-hole* is probably the easiest way to explain it... and flew through that."

"Does *the ship* have a name?"

"Yeah," Robert nodded. "It's actually *Hope*, but nobody calls it that. Just like the island is really *Haven*. Over time, people just started calling them *the island* and *the ship*."

"It's weird that your ship doesn't have a name."

"It does," the traveler chucked.

"Oh yeah," Morgan nodded, "*The Time Machine*."

"Nah," Robert replied. "I lied about that."

"Then what's it called?"

"*Cleo*."

"Yeah... that makes sense, I guess."

"It does," the traveler nodded. "She put a lot of work into it, along with me and Vox. And, being a ship, it needed a lady's name. Cleo was far and away the obvious choice."

"I can certainly see that," Morgan agreed. "So, what all did you collect for the ship?"

"The ship..."

"What do you mean by that?"

"I started out all alone with a time-pod, Morgan," the traveler replied. "I picked up enough stuff to expand it to carry two. After that, we searched the time-lines and found Vox. I went back and introduced myself to him when he was around twelve. I'd leave and show up six months down the road or so. By the time he was sixteen, he realized I really was a time traveler and hopped into the pod with me to head to Never Never Land. Since then, he's been a vital member of my team."

"What about Cleo?"

"She's actually kind of a new addition," Robert replied. "It was a little over seven years ago when she helped me and Vox finish the ship. That is to say: get it in the state it's pretty much in now. It's not really *finished* and I don't think it ever will be."

"Why?"

"Well, for one thing, it doesn't have a pool or a bowling alley."

"I can see that. You told me you met her as a baby?"

"I did," the traveler replied. "Her people live on those islands, you know? She was lost in a storm as an infant and I went and picked her up."

"What happened to her parents?"

"She doesn't know..."

"Don't you?"

"Yep..."

"Well, then..."

"Morgan," the traveler said, turning his gaze to the young man, "you have to think about things, man. If I told her that her parents were alive, how would that make her feel? What if I told her that her parents were dead? Of course I know, Morgan, but I'm not gonna tell her. Just like I'm not going to tell you whether or not *Star Trek* is really history."

"Why not?"

"Because," Robert explained, "there are only two possible outcomes. If I say *no*, you'll be depressed for months. If I say *yes*, all I'll hear is *can we go meet Captain Kirk?* for months. And, I'm not into either one of those, man."

"I see where you're coming from," Morgan replied.

As the pair jostled their way through the crowded pathways, numerous sights attracted Morgan's attention. For one thing, there were way more scantily clad alien chicks wandering around than he had encountered up to this point. Of course, he hadn't encountered any at all up to that point... Still, they couldn't hold his attention. None of them were anything compared to Azure or Cleo; no matter how revealing their attire. It takes more than a bare midriff to make a woman hot.

There were also all kinds of weapons, tools, technology, and *as seen on TV* type items spread out on the tables that filled the market. In addition, a resplendent array of food filled the air with their scents. They seemed to have an endless variety of pork-rinds and fried batters, countless meats on sticks, and even boiled peanuts. Something rather spectacular caught Morgan's eye as he was glancing over one of these vendor's wares.

"Rob," he said, a touch of concern in his voice, "is that a giant cockroach on a spit?"

"It certainly looks that way, Morgan," the traveler replied.

"Man..." the young man said, turning his head. "How do they even hunt them?"

"They use a giant boot."

"I don't think so, man. It didn't even look crushed."

"I know. I was joking. They actually use a giant can of *Raid*."

"But, wouldn't that poison the..."

"Look, man," the traveler replied, "we're here to buy a piece of junk generator; not pick up slabs of steaming hot cockroach meat. What difference does it make how they got it? Personally, I wish they hadn't! That smell is making me sick!"

"Yeah... it is a little strong..."

Minutes later, the pair found themselves at the junk dealership they had been in search of.

"This is it," Robert said, gazing down at a generator that even Morgan thought looked like a piece of junk.

"It looks like you and Vox will have your work cut out for you."

"Yeah," the traveler agreed, "but, it'll do the job. Hey, Mac! How much for this old generator?"

"For than fine piece of re-purposed equipment?" a greasy green man in his mid-fifties asked. "Fifteen-hundred ought to do it."

"Fifteen-hundred?!?!" the traveler exclaimed. "What do you think it's made out of, supermodels?"

"Well..." the man replied thoughtfully. "As it's slightly *weathered*, we can make it fourteen-fifty."

"Are there any outstanding warrants on you for fraud?" Robert chuckled. "You're outta your mind!"

"I tell you what," he sighed. "I like your brass. Thirteen-hundred."

"I like your gall," the traveler replied. "I'll give ya two-fifty."

"Two-fifty?!" the man yelled. "You want some of my teeth with that, or just a gallon or two of blood?!?! I'll take eleven-hundred."

"You're living in a dream world!" Robert replied. "Four hundred."

"If you think you got luck like that, you need to take up gambling! Nine-fifty."

"At least you're getting down to the *I was drunk* level. Five hundred."

"Well, I admit I don't want to take you for your *entire net worth*. Seven-fifty."

"There's no reasoning with you," the traveler replied, throwing up his hands. "Morgan, let's go!"

Robert turned and began to walk away when Morgan decided to point out the obvious.

"But, we *have* to have this thing, Rob!" he exclaimed.

The traveler dropped his head and stepped back to the table with a sigh.

"How much did you say?"

"Fifteen-hundred."

"Look, man," Robert replied, gazing up at his economic adversary, "I'll level with you: I need it for parts, but it ain't the only one around. I'll give you the seven-fifty."

"Done!"

"Here ya go," the traveler said, pulling a wad of bills from his pocket and handing the man the top note.

"This is a thousand!" the man exclaimed.

"Eh, keep the change," Robert smiled. "Can you deliver it to my ship?"

"No problem!"

"If you had all that money on you," Morgan said thoughtfully as they were making their way back to the ship, "why did you make a big deal over the price?"

"I just like to haggle." the traveler explained.

In less than an hour, the generator was on board and the ship back in space. For two days straight Robert and Vox slaved away in the cargo hold in an attempt to transform their precious junk into the working piece of equipment they wanted it to be. Morgan hung out with them most of this time for two simple reasons: he was hoping to learn *anything* that might prove useful *someday*, and Azure and Cleo had spent most of this time *girl-talking*. Of course, he would have happily *girl-talked* with them, but they wouldn't let him...

"So, are dolphins really smarter than people?" Morgan mused during a moment of boredom.

"Some people, I guess," the traveler replied, not looking up from his work.

"Like who?"

"Like, people who say that dolphins are smarter than people," Robert suggested.

"But, wouldn't that mean they were right?"

"*Take me down to paradox city,*" the traveler sang.

"Okay…" Morgan replied rolling his eyes. "But, be that as it may, they still strike me as really intelligent."

"I didn't know you'd ever been *struck* by one."

"You know what I mean."

"Look, Morgan," Robert said, actually taking the time to glance at the young man, "no matter how smart they are; intellect can only do so much without thumbs. It ain't easy to write underwater with a pen in your mouth. Trust me."

"Well, monkeys have thumbs," Morgan pointed out.

"Yeah…" the traveler agreed, "but, thumbs can only do so much without intellect. You, *of all people*, should know that."

Right in the middle of these two trying to solve all the philosophical problems that have plagued the universe since it's very beginning, Cleo stepped into the cargo bay. She was once again dressed in a miniskirt, stockings, etc. Morgan put his fingers on his pulse - just to keep an *eye* on his heart rate. It was squarely within the realms of *not-a-heart-*

attack... Slowly, but surely, he was getting used to his amazing good fortune...

"Rob," she said, gazing at the back of his head, "we need to talk."

"Talk away," he said, without glancing back.

"No, Rob," she sighed. "We need to talk with you looking at me."

"Well, I do love looking at you," he said, before turning his gaze to her with a smile. "Boy, do I *love* looking at you! Anyway, what's up?"

"Well," she said, taking a deep breath, her cheeks turning slightly teal, "I feel that, as your *girlfriend*, I have the right to make certain demands of you."

"Oh," he replied, taking a step nearer her, "I *certainly* agree! What kind of *demands* were you thinking of exactly? I've got the feeling they'd be a *lot* of fun just to *hear* about."

"I'm serious, Rob," she replied, putting her hand on his chest and pushing him back.

"So am I," he said, stepping nearer in spite of her resistance.

"No, you're not," she giggled, "and, you know it! Now, be serious for a minute."

"Alright," he sighed, putting his hands up. "What are your demands?"

"I want to go on another *micro-date*." she replied.

"Okay," he replied. "No problem. As soon as me and Vox..."

"No, Rob," she said, shaking her head. "Now. Right now!"

"But me and Vox..."

"Rob," she said, rolling her eyes and refusing to look him in the face, "I haven't even *seen you* for two days now and..."

"Has it been two days?!?!" Robert interrupted.

"It has, boss," Vox replied. "Small-girl's right..."

"Yes, I am!" Cleo asserted. "And since you're my *boyfriend*, I think I have the right to ask for an hour of your time every few days."

"Well, can I just..." the traveler began, gazing into her eyes. "No. No, never mind. Vox, you got this, man?"

"I got it, brother," he instantly replied. "Have fun!"

"We'll be up there in about twenty minutes," Robert said with a smile.

"You had better be, Rob," Cleo replied before strutting... Yeah, she was strutting this time... out of the cargo bay.

As soon as she had gotten down the hall a ways, Robert turned to his companion to issue instructions.

"Okay, Morgan," he said, looking his friend in the face, "we both need to take a quick shower and throw on some clean clothes. Just jeans and a button up... no wait, a black t-shirt with an open button up over that, with the sleeves rolled up. We'll look casual, but smart. Can you handle that?"

"I believe so. You think I'll need any gum?"

"I doubt it... Let's go!"

Fifteen minutes, later the young men were stepping onto the bridge together. They were shower fresh and attired in clean, somewhat spiffier, clothes.

"You changed," Cleo observed.

"I was hoping these would do something for you," Robert replied, glancing down at his attire. "Do they?"

"A little," she giggled.

"So," he said, stepping over to her seat and gazing down at her, "what are we supposed to do on this *micro-date*, exactly?"

"Well, first," she replied with a coy smile, "go sit down."

Immediately both he and Morgan obeyed.

"Before we go any further," Azure said, shooting a quick glance at Morgan, "I just want to say that, due to minor changes in circumstance, Morgan and I are now on a unified chaperoning mission."

"Is that closer to a *date* than last time?" Morgan asked.

"By an immeasurably small amount, yes," she answered.

"Eh," he shrugged, "I'll take it."

"Rob," Cleo said, turning her seat toward the traveler, "Azure and I have decided that, since you've missed out on so many improv ice-cream parties (and, since this is our *second* date), we would have ice-cream to start."

"Sure," he agreed. "We do need to live a little."

Moments later, she was handing him a *space bowl* filled with pistachio ice-cream covered in maple syrup.

"Since you never got to try it..."

"Yeah..." he said after his first bite, "this is really good. In fact, I think it's giving me heart palpitations."

"It did the same thing to me!" Morgan confessed.

Robert glared at him a moment before taking another spoonful.

"So, Morgan," Cleo said, smiling at the young man, "do you want pistachio with maple or do you want to try the blueberry and honey."

"Actually, if you could just put all that together in a bowl..."

"Morgan will have the blueberry with no syrup," the traveler interrupted. "He's had too much maple syrup and honey lately. I got the feeling it's about to get real bad for his health."

"Rob's right," the young man nodded. "I need to cut back..."

"Way back!" Robert replied. "Actually, Morgan, now that I'm thinking about it, you might want to try the blueberry with cherry syrup."

"That seems like an odd combo," Cleo replied.

Robert simply waved his *space spoon* silently at Morgan.

"I'll try it!" Morgan exclaimed.

For the next few minutes, they sat laughing, talking, and just generally enjoying each other's company before Cleo introduced another topic of general interest.

"I have a question, Azure," Cleo said thoughtfully.

"What is it?"

"What made you kiss Morgan?"

"Actually," Morgan replied, sitting bolt upright in his seat, "I've been wondering about that myself!"

"Well," she sighed, "obviously, I wanted to shatter his teeth. I mean; what with all the lying, and boasting, and that whole *psychological angle* thing down at the gun range..."

"I can see that," Cleo nodded.

"But, then," Azure continued, "I reflected on the fact that he really had risked his life to save mine."

"Sure," Cleo replied.

"So," Azure explained, "I decided that, if I gave him what he really wanted, I'd be justified in taking what I really wanted."

"I see what you mean," Cleo admitted, "but, I'm not sure I could have done it. I'd've just had to slap him and take my chances with karma."

"I seriously considered it," Azure confessed. "I guess I'm just softhearted. Still, to be completely and totally honest, it wasn't *that* bad."

"Really?!?!" Morgan replied, sitting up even bolt uprighter.

"Really," she nodded, an almost confused look on her face. "For some reason, you tasted like cinnamon. I didn't know that about human men."

As soon as she said this, Morgan pointed a knowing finger at Robert before pulling a fresh stick of gum from his pocket.

"In fact, if I had to choose between kissing you again or getting shot in the face, I'd probably just flip a coin."

"Wow!" he exclaimed. "I'm making *serious* progress!"

A few minutes after this, while they were in the middle of yet another laugh, Robert sat up and snapped his fingers.

"That's it!" he said, jumping to his feet. "Cleo, you were right! I needed a break! I know what to do with the generator now!"

Having said this, he stepped quickly over to her seat, his body language simply screaming *I'm 'bout to seriously kiss this girl for real.* As Robert leaned down toward her, Morgan jumped from his chair drawing back his right arm, just hoping for a chance to *help*. However, a sudden burst of self-control saved the traveler - both from himself and from his friend. He paused for a moment, before leaning slowly down and kissing her on the cheek.

"Thank you," he said, staring into her eyes. "I really needed this."

"Me, too," she replied, her breath somewhat shallow.

"Let's go, Morgan," the traveler said, stepping from the room. "We got to get this thing running."

A few hours later, the generator was doing exactly what they wanted it to. And, as soon as it was, Robert and Morgan headed back to the bridge.

"Cleo," the traveler said, stepping into the chamber, "Contact Sister..."

As he said this, he noticed she was back in her normal clothes.

"You changed, again."

"Of course," she smiled. "Those are my *date* clothes. I'm not just going to sit around in them. They won't have the same effect if they're not *special*."

"Good point," he nodded. "Either way, contact Sister and tell her I need the accounting department to setup a business on our next target world about five years before the target date. We'll need bank accounts, maybe a warehouse - just have them do whatever they need to do to legitimize it. Obviously, keeping the damage to a minimum as much as possible."

"Alright," she replied.

"Then, we need the tech department to register the patents we'll need spread over that five-year period. After that, the legal department needs to draw up a contract with generous, but plausible, terms. In fact, have accounting move the money around so that I can use the *lack of liquid capital* excuse to explain why we're so ready to deal."

"No problem, Rob."

"After that, get two holo-emitters setup for you and Azure. That is, if you want to go with us."

"We do!"

"I'm glad," he replied. "Keep in mind, these guys are basically human and don't have a lot of alien contact at this point. So, me and Morgan will pass as natives. Just aim for something similar."

"Any special instructions?" she asked.

"You can still be *hot*, but not as hot as you are in real life. I don't want to attract *too* much attention."

"If you say so, Rob," she giggled.

A couple of hours later, the ship was touching down in the empty parking lot of a warehouse owned by the front company. Both Robert and Morgan we're dressed in almost Earth-like business suites; complete with cowboy hats and boots. Robert held a briefcase filled with contracts and patent information. Cleo and Azure stepped onto the bridge, looking like very attractive - but very normal - human women.

"I see you kept the violet eyes," the traveler said, smiling at Cleo.

"Well, everyone'll just think they're contacts," she replied before adding, "and besides, they're one of your favorite features."

"Oh," he said, stepping over to her, "*all* of your features are my favorites."

"What are you doing, you idiot?" she laughed, stepping away from him.

"I'm just trying to help you decide," he explained.

"Decide what?"

"Well..." he said slowly, "you girls can either pretend to be our secretaries or our *love slaves*. I was just trying to help you make up your mind."

"Well, you have," she replied, tilting her head to the side. "We're your *secretaries*."

"Suit yourself," he sighed. "I just hope you know how to take shorthand..."

"We'll pretend!"

While this rapier exchange was going on, Morgan was simply sitting and staring at Azure. Finally, he got up and started walking around her while shaking his head.

"What are you doing?" she asked.

"I don't like it," Morgan replied. "It's just not *you*."

"Well," Cleo replied, "Rob told us to turn the *hot* down."

"It's not that," he said, shaking his head. "I mean; yeah, that too. But, it's more than that."

"I thought you'd be curious to see me as a human woman," Azure replied.

"Well, I wasn't," he pointed out. "You're perfect the way you are."

"Wow, Morgan," she replied, "that's *really* sweet of you to say."

"Well, I'll tell you this," he continued, "Not once in all of my many, many fantasies about you, have you *ever* been human!"

"Wow..." she said slowly. "Two steps forward, one step back..."

"That's what I said just the other day!" Robert exclaimed, snapping his fingers.

Shortly after this observation, the four of them were crawling into the back of a rather luxurious stretched *future-space limo* that had come to pick them up. This rather epic conveyance quickly transported them to the front of a very impressive sky scraper in the center of a sprawling metropolis.

"What's the name of this town?" Morgan asked, gazing almost slack-jawed out of the window.

"*Metropolis*," the traveler replied.

"Wow..." the young man said thoughtfully. "Is that a common city name?"

"The most common in all of space and time," Robert chuckled.

As the car came to a stop, the chauffeur leapt out; instantly opening the door. The young men crawled from the back seat, immediately followed by the young ladies. They made a quick stop at the welcome desk before making their way into an empty elevator and heading for the top floor.

"Now, remember," the traveler said, staring at Morgan as he spoke, "let me do *all* the talking."

"Got ya."

"And girls," he continued, "be sure to look like you're taking notes. Your job is to make me and Morgan look important. If you hadn't picked *secretaries*, you could have just sprawled all over us, but now you've made your bed..."

"We'll look like we're taking notes, Rob," Cleo asserted.

Moments later, the elevator doors opened. A secretary had been sent to greet them and then led them to a massive boardroom. Two very well dressed men were awaiting them; along with another young man in less impressive attire.

"Mr. Hood," the older of the two gentlemen said, stepping quickly over and shaking Robert's hand. "It good to meet you at last. And, who is this young man?"

"This here's my cousin," the traveler replied. "Morgan Harker. He got all the height and muscle in the family, I got all the looks and brains; you know what I'm saying?"

At this all of the men laughed.

"It's nice to meet you as well, Mr. Harker," the man replied, before pointing to his companion. "This gentleman is Mr. Pardue. And, this other young man is Tom. He's one of our engineers."

"It's a pleasure, sir," Robert replied, shaking Mr. Pardue's hand. "I hate to be brief Mr. Steel, but Daddy Hood's waitin' on me. And, if there's one thing Daddy don't like, it's waitin'."

"I completely understand," Mr. Steel nodded. "If you gentlemen will take a seat, we can get started."

"Certainly," Robert replied, sitting down at the very head of the table. "Miss Goodstuff, make sure to take exact notes. You can be sure Daddy's gonna want to know every word we said."

"Yes, sir," Cleo sighed.

Mr. Pardue took a good long look at Cleo before slowly moving his eyes to Azure.

"And, what's your name Miss?" he asked with an *I-want-your-phone-number* tone of voice.

"I'm Miss Hurtsmen," she replied with cold indifference.

"Now," Mr. Steel began, "I'll be perfectly frank Mr. Hood. We've looked over the specs, we've read over the contracts and, all in all, the deal looks good. In fact, it looks *too* good. What's the catch?"

"Well," Robert replied, "you've been honest, sir, and if there's one thing in this life I truly admire it's honesty."

Morgan had to stifle a laugh.

"So," the traveler continued, "I'm going to be completely honest with you, as well. Daddy's... Well, let's just say Daddy's got rather *exquisite* tastes. Of course, we all love him for it. It's one of the things that makes him Daddy. *However*, sometimes having a little bit *too* fine a taste can get ya into some kinda *tricky* situations. Anyway, to make a long story short, we've had to move a little money around. At the moment - and keep in mind this is a *very* temporary situation - we could use just a tad more liquid capital. We're in the middle of a big project right now - and I mean *big* – but, we need to make sure we got the gas we need to make it to the finish line. You see where I'm coming from?"

They did see where he was coming from. For the next few minutes, they sat discussing details while the engineer poured over the patent documents.

"And, what kind of fuel you planning on burning in her?" Robert asked while they were talking technical details. "I mean, she'll run on just about anything, but the better the fuel the better the output."

As soon as he asked this, Tom rose and stepped over to what appeared to be a drinks cabinet.

"We're actually considering a number of possible fuels," Mr. Steel replied. "In fact, we're hoping to develop something that's both efficient and renewable. We feel that it would obviously be in our best interests in the long run."

The engineer pulled what appeared to be two small beakers from the cabinet and filled them from a large container using a small funnel. He then corked each of them and returned to the table handing one to Robert and the other to Morgan.

"You may want to sample that," Tom said, returning to his seat.

Immediately, Robert removed the rubber cork and carefully smelled the contents. Morgan followed his example. The liquid smelled vile, but he didn't want to offend anyone in the middle of a business meeting. And besides, it probably tasted better than it smelled.

"When in Rome," he said softly, raising the beaker to his lips.

Almost instantly, he spit the fuel all over the table.

"This tastes like fuel!" he exclaimed.

"Yeah, Morgan," Robert nodded. "It *is* fuel, boy. Tom here was letting us take a sample for the lab. What did I tell y'all? This boy's like a laugh a minute!"

The other men seemed to agree and enjoyed a hearty laugh at the young man's expense. For the next hour or so, they worked on finalizing the terms of their agreement. Mr. Pardue had gotten up to stretch his legs and just happened to wander behind Cleo.

"Hmmm," he said, gazing down at the pad she had scribbled all over. "You know that doesn't look like any shorthand... Oh! I'm sorry... I was just thinking out loud... I certainly didn't mean to..."

"Looks like Daddy's not the only one with *exquisite* tastes," Mr. Steel interrupted with a grin.

"Well now," the traveler replied with a wide smile and a knowing wink, "you might just say that!"

Minutes later, the contracts were signed and the four companions were headed back to the ship.

"Yeah..." The traveler said with a contented sigh. "I really don't think that could have possibly gone *any* better!"

CHAPTER 12: THE SWORD IN THE STONE

"Miss Goodstuff," Robert said the moment they were all back on the bridge.

"That's enough, Rob," Cleo sighed, tilting her head to the side. "We're back on the ship now."

"Alright, Cleo," he laughed. "Check the time-lines, would ya?"

"Not too bad," she replied, gazing down at the monitor. "The generator introduced a couple more technical marvels that pushed them a little further forward than they already were; but nothing major. And, it completely took care of the environmental issues. Personally, I'd give it about a ninety-seven percent success rating."

"Good enough," the traveler nodded. "How much did Hood Industries make?"

"*Hood Industries?*" Morgan asked.

"The name of the front company," Cleo replied, rolling her eyes. "Obviously, Rob wanted it named after him..."

"So your last name really is Hood?"

"Yep," Robert replied. "Anyway, how much did we make over the life of the contract?"

"Four point five million," Cleo replied.

"Four point five million what?" the young man asked.

"*Quatloos.*"

"Seriously?"

"No, Morgan," Robert replied, shaking his head.

"Then what?"

"It won't mean anything to you."

"Then, how much is it in dollars from my time?"

Robert looked up and to the side for a moment, one of his eyebrows shooting up.

"Roughly one hundred twenty-five billion."

"Wow!" Morgan exclaimed, "We're rich!"

"Yeah," the traveler agreed. "We really are, Morgan. But, we sure don't need that money. Cleo, what would the estimated effects be of spreading that money evenly amongst the planet's charities over the course of forty or fifty years?"

"I'll have to check with Sister," she replied.

"Do that," he smiled. "I know it'll never have happened once we're done, but it's still a nice thing to do."

"Yeah," she nodded. "I guess it is."

Having accomplished step one of their plan, they made their way back to Never Never Land and disabled... well, they actually blew it up, but Robert preferred the word *disabled*... Marcus Delmont's time machine, thereby defeating him for the third time. However, as the traveler pointed out himself: *there ain't no rest for the weary*. And so, within minutes, they were once again seated around the conference table.

"Alright," Morgan said, dropping into his seat, *"this one's gonna be a little different."*

"Funny," Robert laughed. "But, also quite correct."

"So, what is it?" the young man asked.

"Well..." the traveler said thoughtfully. "You might almost call it *The Sword in the Stone.*"

"Excalibur?" Morgan nodded. "Cool!"

"Not exactly," Robert corrected. "For one thing, Arthur didn't pull Excalibur from the stone; he got it from the *Lady of the Lake.*"

"No, he didn't!" the young man replied.

"Yes, he did! Don't you remember? *The Lady of the Lake, her arm clad in the purest shimmering samite....*"

"Oh yeah!" Morgan exclaimed. *"Strange women lying in ponds distributing swords is no basis for a system of government."*

"Exactly!" the traveler chuckled.

"What are you two talking about?" Azure asked.

"It's this goofy movie," Vox replied.

"Yeah," Cleo said. "We need to get you programmed with ancient human culture..."

"Anyway," Robert continued, "it's kind of the same thing. The target culture believed that a particular sword signified their kings' divine right to rule. After a couple of thousand years, a civil war drove a section of their royal family to another world. One planet had the sword, the other did without."

"And, here comes Delmont," Doc speculated.

"Exactly," the traveler nodded. "Delmont took advantage of a hole in the royal family's security system to steal the sword. It was actually fairly impressive because he only had, like, fifteen minutes. It was the closest thing he ever did to being a *jewel thief*. Of course, it was really just a matter of timing. He walked in and out while an ion storm had all their security systems shut down. It was kind of like that scene in *Groundhog Day*, when *Bill Murray* just walks up and takes all that money out of that armored car."

"Hey, fix your bra, honey," Morgan chuckled.

"Yep!"

"You're right," Azure said. "I think I could use that programming..."

"Either way," the traveler continued, "when the sword turned up missing, it kicked off a civil war that should have never happened. On top of that, the idiot sold the sword to the other branch of the royal family. That kicked off yet another civil war on their planet. And, they took such good care of it that it *never* dropped out of the time-line. At this moment, it's still in their vault; frozen in non-time. As a result, we can't just go get it like we did the orb."

"Could we make a copy?" the young man asked.

"Yes!" Robert replied. "Sometimes, Morgan, you really are on the ball. Now, this culture was capable of making a *molecular scan* - but not a *molecular imprint* - before Delmont stole the sword."

"What's the difference?"

"A *molecular scan* isn't nearly as precise as a *molecular imprint*. It can tell how many molecules are in an item as well as their disposition, but it can't specifically identify a single molecule. Because of this, we can make a fake."

"Well then, you're back in your element," Morgan pointed out. "Fire up the presses."

"I never said it was counterfeit."

"So then," Vox said, "we go back and steal the sword before Delmont does, make a copy, wait for him to steal the original, and then replace it with the copy."

"That's good," Robert nodded. "But, I think we can do better. That would take a lot of running around, even for us. And, of course, we'd have several chances to mess it up."

"Then, what do you suggest?" Azure asked.

"We make *two* identical fakes," the traveler began. "Then, we steal the original and replace it with one of the fakes. After Delmont steals that fake, we replace it with the other one. That will cut down the back and forth a little."

"Once again," Cleo said, "that's brilliant."

"Thanks!" Robert replied. "And, as I figured you'd all agree with that assessment, I went ahead and ordered the swords. They should be here in the morning. As soon as they're on the ship, we can leave Never Never Land and head for the original sword."

"Sounds good," Doc replied. "What do we have to do for the swap?"

"Well..." Robert replied. "That is going to be a tad *tricky*."

"*Exciting?*" Morgan asked.

"No!" the traveler replied. "Certainly not that *tricky*. It's just that the sword is *very* well guarded most of the time, and in the middle of some war or another the rest of the time. So, I figured the easiest thing would be to steal it out of the blacksmith's shop the night after it's finished."

"That doesn't sound so *tricky*," the young man pointed out.

"Well," Robert admitted, "it's in the middle of an ion storm, so we can't use shields, stealth fields, or energy weapons. It's going to be a matter of executing a more *classic theft*. We break in during the middle of the night and make the swap."

"Why can't we swap it out after the storm?" the young man asked.

"This storm lasts fifty years..."

"I see..." Morgan mused. "Still, that really doesn't sound all that bad."

"Comparatively, it's not," Robert agreed. "And, really, we can even take some chemical lights that the ion storm can't effect. So, it *shouldn't* be overly difficult. We just need to be careful. But, either way, it's been a rich, full day. Let's all call it an early night. We've got a lot to do tomorrow."

The party broke up and all of them headed for bed. They had gotten a lot done and really did need the rest. The following morning, the swords arrived right on time and the ship headed into non-space; making its way toward the target planet.

"I been thinkin'," Robert said the moment Morgan stepped on the bridge, "you and me ought to be able to handle the swap by ourselves."

"Sounds good," Morgan sighed, slipping down into his usual seat.

"No," Cleo replied. "Azure and I are going with you."

"Why?"

"Well," she explained, "I see one of two possibilities. One: you're lying..."

"I'm not lying," Robert replied quite seriously. "This time, it really shouldn't be a big deal. It's only slightly more dangerous than picking up Calvin was."

"Alright," she replied. "In that case, it's possibility two: you're telling the truth. So, there's no reason for me and Azure not to go."

"Cleo..."

"*Girlfriend*, Rob," she replied. "I had to go be Miss Goodstuff yesterday, I get to go break into a place and steal something with you today. It's all about *fair exchange*."

"Oh," he said, "I can think of a few things we could *fair exchange*."

"Shut up, Rob," she giggled. "You're an idiot. And you're not going to distract me. So, are you going to let us go or not?"

"Yes..." he sighed, slightly irritated. "You two just have to be careful. I don't mind taking you when I know there may be a fire fight because I know that you know what you're doing. I just don't like taking you when the hostilities are more *speculative*."

"That is *crazy*, Rob!" she pointed out.

"I guess it is," he agreed. "I just... I don't know. I get *nervous* when there *might* be a fight, but I don't *know* that there will be. Especially when taking Doc and Vox would be difficult. Between the three of us *nothing* can hurt you."

"And me!" Morgan replied.

"Four of us," the traveler corrected.

"We'll be fine," she assured him.

A little over an hour later, the four of them were getting prepped up for the mission. Morgan was *very* excited because each of them was going to carry a tranq gun and one *deadly force* weapon. He didn't want to use them, of course, but it was still fun to be *packin' heat*. They were dressed entirely in black and had even darkened their faces.

"I feel like a *ninja*," Morgan pointed out, smearing black grease under his eyes.

"I *am* a ninja, Morgan," the traveler replied.

"Seriously?"

"Metaphorically, yes!"

"I prefer *literal* to *metaphorical*..."

"To each his own..."

Shortly after this world changing snippet of conversation, the guys and girls snuck silently from the invisible interior of the loading platform. They had parked a couple of miles outside of the little hamlet where stood the blacksmith's shop that contained their prize. As they strolled along, questions filled Morgan's mind... Who'd have guessed it, right?...

"So, Rob," he said thoughtfully, "If *Star Trek* is based on history; why do they have transporters, but we don't?"

"That was a TV show, Morgan."

"I know, but it was inspired by history, right?"

"Let's say that it was; so what?" Robert asked.

"Well then, why did they have transporters?"

"Morgan," the traveler explained, "I didn't say that *everything* everyone ever thought of was based on history. Imagination is a *very* real and powerful thing. People expanded the fiction in their own ways. I mean, we may not have transporters now, but that doesn't mean we'll never have them. If we ever fix the future, then it may happen one day. That's the much more classic formula of the *past changing the future*. You see what I mean?"

"I guess..." Morgan replied thoughtfully. "So, some sci-fi is just sci-fi?"

"Some of it is," Robert said. "Take *Galaxy Quest*, for example. It was a *great* movie, but it's based on *Star Trek* more than the actual future."

"I got ya," the young man replied. "And, that brings up another question that's been bothering me."

"What's that, Morgan?"

"Seriously, Rob, am I just *Guy*?"

"*Guy*?"

"Crewman number six," Morgan explained. "I mean, honestly, am I expendable?"

"Morgan," the traveler replied, stopping and turning back to face his friend. "What would make you ask that? We're obviously friends, man. And, *none* of my friends are *expendable*."

"Well," he sighed, "there's just a lot of red shirts in my closet. I mean, I haven't worn any of them because I didn't want to tempt fate. But, I still wondered why they were there."

"Oh, that," Robert chuckled. "I just thought you'd look good in red."

"Really?"

"No. I actually put them there to mess with your head and then forgot all about it. I'm sorry if it upset you, bro. It was just a joke."

"So, I'm not expendable?" Morgan asked.

"To tell you the truth," the traveler replied, "if you died, Morgan, I would have to try to alter time to bring you back from the dead. That's how important you are to this team, man."

"I know you're lying," the young man chuckled, "but that still makes me feel better. It makes me feel like *Lois Lane*."

"What?"

"That time *Superman*..."

"Oh yeah!" the traveler exclaimed. "I didn't really like that one. I mean, flying around the world backwards? What's that supposed to do?"

"I know," Morgan nodded, "that didn't make any sense to me, either."

"You know," Azure replied, "the more I hang around you guys, the *less* sense you seem to make."

"Don't worry," Robert smiled, "when you get back to Never Never Land we'll straighten that out."

"Anyway," Morgan observed, "even if we did have transporters, they probably wouldn't work in the ion storm."

"Probably not," the traveler agreed.

"Which raises another question."

"You surprise me."

"Really?"

"No, Morgan," Robert replied, shaking his head. "What's this latest question?"

"How can the ship work in the ion storm?"

"Okay," the traveler replied, "that's a fair question. The ship's shielding is much more powerful than the personal shields or the stealth field generators. It can handle that kind of power bombardment."

"I understand," the young man replied. "I just wish we could have used the invisibility belts."

"I'm sure you do!" Cleo giggled. "It would give you another chance to *accidentally* bump into someone."

"What do you mean?" Azure asked.

"Well," Cleo replied, "the first time Morgan used one of the belts, he..."

"That was a *complete* accident," he interrupted.

"Oh, I'm *sure* it was," she giggled.

"Cleo..." he said after a few moments of silence.

"What, Morgan?" she asked.

"What did I touch?"

"Shut up, Morgan!" Robert replied.

"Well, she brought it up!" the young man said defensively.

Shortly after this, a large moon slowly rose over the horizon.

"That's beautiful," Morgan said, staring off into the distance. "It reminds me of that moonlight stroll on the beach."

"It does," Robert admitted. "Except, we were *much* less likely to get ourselves accidentally killed that night. So, shut up. We're almost on the outskirts of town."

"Azure," the young man whispered, "can I hold your hand?"

"No."

"But, we might get separated."

"I can see you in the moonlight," she pointed out.

"Better safe than sorry," he replied.

"I'll take my chances..."

Just seconds later, Robert ordered Morgan to remain silent until after they had successfully broken into the blacksmith's shop. The young man obeyed, but it wasn't easy for him. Not that he really had any more questions, he just got bored easily...

"This is it," Robert whispered, stepping up to a shadowy doorway in the middle of the little town. "And it looks like we're in luck; the door's open."

"That's odd," Cleo observed. "I mean, the owner's probably got some valuable stuff in there."

"I'm sure," the traveler agreed, "but theft is a capital offense around here. So, they don't have a lot of problems with break-ins."

"Oh, nice..." she replied softly.

Moments later, all four companions were standing inside the shop. The traveler cracked a light stick and started gazing over the merchandise in search of the weapon they sought. Morgan followed his example and was amazed at the variety of tools used to kill people that filled the building. There were also several suits of plate armor that attracted his attention.

Morgan had always had a hard time with *look but don't touch*. And, as inanimate objects couldn't slap him in the face, he often couldn't keep his hands to himself when dealing with them. As a result, the temptation to handle one of these suits of armor became overwhelming. Doing this, however, knocked it slightly to the side. He did manage to grab hold of it before it fell over completely though, so it didn't make quite as much noise as Church bells ringing out Mass would have...

"Nice, Morgan," Robert exclaimed under his breath. "Why don't you just go get one of the town guards to see if he can help us find the sword?"

"Sorry..."

"Just be quiet!"

About half a minute later two things happened simultaneously. Robert found the blade they had come to retrieve, while Morgan noticed a man stepping into the room with a crossbow aimed at Azure's head. Once again, Morgan's inner hero filled his mind with a single primitive thought: must save woman!

"Azure!" he yelled as he dove between her and the weapon.

His timing was perfect, at least from a certain point of view; the bolt struck him squarely in his left lung rather than hitting Azure in the skull. In roughly the time it takes to blink, the traveler had drawn his tranq gun and shot their adversary in the throat with a dart. The man was totally unconscious in a fraction of a second, and fell without so much as making a cry.

"Morgan," Robert said, kneeling down beside his friend.

"Rob," he gasped.

"Listen..."

"No!" the young man exclaimed. "You listen. I've only got moments, man. I just want you to know that I don't care that it ended this way! I'm still glad you came to get me! You gave my life meaning! Thank you, Rob... and goodbye..."

"You know, Morgan," the traveler replied, "that night gear is made out of armor cloth..."

"What do you mean?"

"I mean," he explained, "that the bolt didn't go through it... Well, I guess it did a little. I think you may be scratched..."

"............. So I am..." the young man replied after having looked his chest over carefully. "So... We probably need to get out of here..."

"We do..."

"Did you find the sword?"

"I did..."

"Well then, grab it and let's go, I guess..."

"Alright..."

Robert helped the young man to his feet before stepping over to the unconscious man and pulling the dart from his neck. He then took a small cylinder from his pocket and begin spraying the man all over with it.

"What's that?" Morgan asked.

"Hooch," the traveler replied.

"*Hooch?*"

"Yeah," Robert chuckled. "Hooch, booze, ardent spirits; call it whatever you want."

Having said this, he pulled a hypodermic needle from his jacket pocket and jammed it in the man's arm.

"What's that?"

"More hooch," the traveler replied. "This guy's blood-alcohol level is now DUI."

"Why do that?" Morgan asked.

"Well," Robert replied, "when he wakes up tomorrow he's going to tell everybody he can find about us. However, he's still going to be seriously drunk when he does. It'll lessen the chance that anyone will believe him."

"Where did you get a crazy idea like that?"

"That Halloween episode of *The Simpsons*."

"Oh yeah!" Morgan replied. "When *Kang* and *Kodos* ran for president."

"Yeah, they did," the traveler agreed. "Let's get outta here."

They swapped the swords and made their way out of town. As soon as they passed the last of the outlying buildings, Azure spoke.

"Morgan," she said softly, "will you hold my hand?"

"Rob!" Morgan exclaimed as loudly as he dared. "Help me! That arrow was poisoned! I'm hallucinating!"

"You're not hallucinating," she giggled. "I just want to hold your hand. May I?"

"Yes!" he exclaimed. "In fact, I'd cut it off myself and hand it to you if you wanted to hold it."

"That won't be necessary."

"I'm glad! Because I'd even be willing..."

"Morgan!" she interrupted. "Just take my hand, please!"

He did. It was awesome. Holding hands is awesome. At least, it is if you build it up with romance and take your time... Our society has gotten too jaded...

They could have gotten back to the ship much faster than they did, but they were out of danger and a huge moon was slowly rising into the sky. Morgan saw Robert glance over his shoulder before reaching out to take Cleo's hand in his. The four strolled slowly back to the ship through the moonlight, hand in hand. Well... not all four of them, but you know what I mean...

Minutes after this little improv-stroll, the ship was once again in non-space heading for their next destination. Morgan, for his part, was in a cold shower. He needed it. The last forty-five minutes or so of his life had just been chock-full of excitement.

As soon as he was dry and dressed, Morgan made his way back to the bridge.

"I'm glad you're done," Robert said, turning his seat to face the young man. "You did great saving Azure back there..."

"Thank you, Morgan!" she interjected.

He simply smiled and nodded.

"But, you messed up major with the armor, bro," the traveler continued. "No more mess ups. For real!"

"Right," the young man replied. "I'll watch it, man, honestly."

"You better," Robert chuckled. "If you don't you're going to end up getting us killed at some point. Anyway, we're almost there..."

"Already?" Morgan asked.

"Yeah," the traveler replied. "And, this time, it's just going to be me and you..."

"Rob," Cleo interrupted "I want..."

"No," he immediately replied, turning his gaze to her. "This is too..."

"We'll be fine."

"Cleo," he said, staring her in the eyes. "I've done the *boyfriend* thing already today. Now, I'm doing the *captain* thing; and you're staying here, ensign."

"You're an ensign?" the young man asked.

"No," she replied, rolling her eyes. "Rob's just nuts."

"Maybe I am," he replied, "but, you're still not going. This is almost a one-man job and I only need Morgan."

"No offense, Morgan," she said glancing from the young man to Robert, "but why do you need him?"

"I agree with her," the young man pointed out.

"For one thing," Robert replied, "I'm still showing him the ropes. Cleo; you, Doc, and Vox know what you're doing. Morgan's still learning. He needs more field time and he's going to get it."

"Well, I don't like it," she said, staring out into non-space.

"Well then, don't think about it," the traveler suggested. "Why don't you just sit there contemplating that moonlight walk we just got back from? Personally, I thought it was *very* pleasant. Didn't you?"

"Very much so..." she nodded.

"Then concentrate on that," Robert replied. "And anyway, I actually need you on the ship."

"Why?"

"Well," he replied, "their security will only be down for about fifteen minutes and there's a *small* chance that we could get trapped inside. If we are, I'll need you to help get us out."

"Alright, Rob," she sighed.

"Now, Morgan," Robert said, turning to the young man, "this time, we're taking shields, stealth fields, laser guns, and transponders. If these guys were a little less advanced, I'd even take some short range communicators, but I don't want to risk those. Besides, we're going to do our best to stick together."

"Got it."

"Good. Let's go suit-up."

After getting ready, the pair stepped from the loading platform loaded to the gills. Not only did they have the aforementioned equipment, they were still packing the tranq guns and one conventional weapon each. Morgan was in seventh heaven. He *almost* felt like *Arnold*.

"Now, keep in mind," Robert said as they marched quickly and invisibly into the city, "when the ion storm hits, it's not only going to knockout their security systems. It's also going to temporarily kill our shields, stealth fields, and energy weapons. So, if you have to grab a gun and your stealth field is off, grab the tranq gun or the standard pistol."

"Right," Morgan nodded. "It's weird, though. What are the odds that this planet would suffer from ion storms too?"

"The odds might be slim, Morgan," the traveler replied, "if this weren't the *same* planet we were just on..."

"Oh, right..." Morgan mused. "Still, it's odd that Delmont would come here during an ion storm."

"Not really, man," Robert replied, shaking his head. "Not when you consider the fact that the ion storm is what made Delmont's plan workable. He looked for opportunities, bro. Just like any other scavenger."

"Oh right..." the young man replied. "Well, on an unrelated topic: Do you think my training's going well."

"Basically."

"Good," he replied. "Because *I want to learn the ways of the Force and become a Jedi like my father.*"

"That was a movie, Morgan."

"I know," the young man said, "and I'm mainly joking."

"*Mainly?*"

"I want to learn to use the *light saber*. I think I've earned that."

"It's not..."

"Okay," Morgan interrupted. "I want to learn to use the *photon saber*."

"Morgan," the traveler sighed, "do you know what the main – nay, definitive - difference between a *light saber* and a *photon saber* is? I mean, other than the fact that one is *real* and the other isn't."

"What's that?"

"Do you know what happens when two *photon saber* blades touch?"

"They make this weird noise and kind of spark a little?"

"No, Morgan," Robert replied. "You see, that's what happens when two *light saber* blades touch in the movies. What happens when two *photon saber* blades touch in real life is that they pass right through each other like flashlights do. As a result, they're not very good defensive weapons. They don't block bullets and they can pretty much cut your limbs right off. So, people don't use them as weapons. They're tools. Trying to fight with one would be like trying to fight with a chainsaw."

"*Warhammer.*"

"Which is also not *real life.*"

"Man," Morgan sighed, "sometimes, the future is a bit of a letdown."

"Well, who knows?" the traveler said. "Maybe, after we fix the future, someone will invent a real *light saber*. Then, we'll be able to *beam up* with our *light sabers* switched on and look really cool for the girls."

"That would look awesome," Morgan admitted. "And, that brings up another question... Why weren't there any transporters in *Star Wars?*"

"Well, it was *a long time ago.*"

"Yeah... that makes sense, I guess."

For the next three hours, the pair continued marching on toward their destination.

"We should have switched these stupid things off and caught a cab," Morgan pointed out as yet another car drove past them.

"Right, Morgan," Robert replied. "And then, we explain to the cabby that we just happen to be carrying an exact replica of one of their crown jewels."

"You could've lied," the young man pointed out. "In fact, I find it hard to believe that you passed up a perfectly legitimate reason to lie. You lie for fun all the time."

"No, I don't!"

"That's a lie!"

"Crap..." the traveler admitted. "You're right... That is a lie... I've got to start cutting back. Either way, we couldn't risk a cab. But, look at it this way, once we dump the sword we can head down an ally, switch these things off, and catch a cab back out of town."

"Well, I can tell you this. I'm sick of holding your hand!"

"Trust me, Morgan," Robert replied, "it ain't exactly making my heart pound with delight either."

"You need to make it where we can see the transponders."

"You may find this hard to believe, man," Robert replied testily, "but, I didn't invent these things."

"Well then, you and Vox should perfect them!"

"Maybe we should, but we've been busy," the traveler pointed out. "I doubt the guys that invented them meant for them to be used en masse. Still... you do make a point. Me and Vox might be able to come up with something. I'll give it some thought. Either way, we'd never had to use them in groups like this before we started this whole *fix time* thing."

"Well, your palm sweats like a basketball player! We're gonna have to change hands!"

"Fine..." Robert sighed. "We're almost there anyway."

A few minutes later, they were resting invisibly on a bench across the street from the museum that held the crown jewels.

"Fortunately," Robert said with a stretch, "we got a few things really going for us. First, there's plenty of light in the building because of all of those windows. Second, they are *utterly* dependent on their high-tech security systems. Third, they use energy weapons, too. So, when the power cuts out we'll have weapons, but they won't. Of course, we *do not* want to use them. But, it's still nice to know."

"I agree," Morgan replied. "So, what's the plan?"

"Well, in about ten minutes, we're going to invisible our way into the bathroom," the traveler said. "Then, the moment our stealth fields go off, we're going to make a mad dash to the room where the jewels are on display. We wait there for Delmont to show up and steal the sword; then, we replace it and head out. He only just got out in time, so we need to be right on his heels. Then, when the power comes back on we turn on our stealth fields, walk about two blocks, and catch a cab. As the sword won't be stolen, there shouldn't even be any uproar."

"Awesome!" the young man replied. "You really think it'll be that easy?"

"I *really* hope so," Robert chuckled.

Ten minutes later, the pair were headed for the museum bathroom. A few minutes after that, the power failed and they emerged quickly, but cautiously. Crowds of people were milling around here and there as the guards were trying to figure out exactly what was happening. The traveler had carefully studied all the routes and where the guards would and wouldn't be. As a result, they were in position in less than five minutes; hiding behind priceless relics of the royal family.

The museum had been mostly emptied and the guards were standing here and there waiting for orders. After a little over five minutes, Delmont appeared right on schedule. He stepped carefully this way and that; narrowly avoiding the watchful eyes of several guards in the area. As soon as he entered the chamber, he grabbed the sword and - without catching sight of Robert or Morgan - turned and fled. His timing was perfect and he was in and out before the guards knew anything had happened.

Before he was even out of sight, Robert stepped up and put the second sword in place. He then motioned to Morgan and the two did their best to avoid the wandering guards while making their way out. They almost made it. But, not quite.

"Hey, you!" one of the guards yelled suddenly.

The pair made a mad dash for the exit.

"Grab my hand!" Robert yelled.

"No!" Morgan replied "There's no point!"

Several guards drew their non-functioning guns and tried to fire at the fleeing young men.

"Grab it, you idiot!"

"No! Get off me!"

"Morgan! Grab my hand or I'll break your legs when we get back to the ship!"

"Fine!" the young man replied, grabbing the traveler's hand.

Just as he did so, their stealth field generators switched back on. Beams of energy fired all around them, several of them even hitting their shields. The invisible companions ran a few blocks, went into a public restroom, and switched off their generators. They emerged moments later and hailed a cab.

"Let's see," the cabby said as he stopped just outside of town. "That'll be..."

"Here, Mac."

"Alright. Out of a hundred..."

"Eh, keep the change..."

"Thanks, mister!"

Minutes later, the pair were back on the ship; their mission accomplished. The time-lines had been partially corrected and the first civil war had never happened. All they had left to do for this mission was make their way back to Never Never Land and un-steal the sword in the first place. They started immediately.

CHAPTER 13: DOUBLE DATE

"I don't know," Morgan sighed, "I guess I just don't see what I've got to be confident about."

"Well, try," Robert encouraged.

"I guess I'm not as fat as I was..."

"That's it?"

"That's all I can think of at the moment," the young man confessed. "Why can't you just ask them?"

"You want me to go on your honeymoon for you, too?"

"No," Morgan replied. "I think I could handle that."

"Man," Robert replied, shaking his head, "if you can't ask Azure out on a date, there ain't no way you could handle a honeymoon with her!"

"Why?" the young man asked, his eyebrows raised. "What do you know?"

"Something I ain't tellin' you!"

"Come on, man!"

"No," the traveler insisted. "If I told you now, it would spoil the surprise! You'd *never* forgive me, man!"

"What?!?! You gonna leave me hangin' like that?"

"Looks that way, don't it?" Robert pointed out. "And anyway, we're getting off topic. We're talking about your self-confidence, remember?"

"Well then," the young man sighed, "get me started."

"Let's start with the big one," the traveler suggested. "You've saved her life *twice*. Do you have any idea how few men ever get to save a woman's life, Morgan? You're already amongst the few and the proud, man!"

"I guess..."

"*Guess*?!?!" Robert exclaimed. "That right there's half your problem. Brother, you gotta *know*! You saved her life. Twice! You do realize that, right?"

"Yes," he sighed. "It's just not a big deal. Anybody would have done the same."

"No!" the traveler corrected. "Not everybody would have; and that doesn't even matter. The point is that you *did*. And, you'd do it again! Keep that in mind!"

"I'll try... You got more?"

"Look at your..." Robert began before pausing to laugh. "Your *love list*. Not only can she be in the same room with you without puking, she can even kiss you without puking."

"That's not much..."

"Whatever, man!" the traveler smiled. "She kissed you because she wanted to. Sure, she wanted to slap you, too. But trust me, Cleo wasn't playing; she'd've slapped you and taken her chances. And, when a girl says it wasn't *that bad* she's saying she'd be willing to try it again in the future."

"She was just being nice."

"Maybe, but I'd keep gum in my mouth if I were you," Robert replied. "And dude, she was holding your hand strolling through the moonlight just a few hours ago."

"Well, I had just saved her life again."

"Exactly, you moron!" the traveler laughed again. "And honestly, Morgan, you're buffing up, beginning to tan, and you're even fairly good looking."

"Well, Cleo said..."

"Two things, man," Robert interrupted. "No man, nowhere, looks as good as I do to Cleo. And, no, you're not as handsome as I am. But, you're taller!"

"You're right! I *am* taller!"

"You can use a gun now," the traveler continued, "and *do not* forget that you're one of the saviors of the universe, man!"

"I'm just your jester."

"Stop saying that!" Robert demanded. "That was just a joke, bro! Come on! Psych yourself up!"

"Right!"

"You da man! You're over six feet tall! You done saved her life! Twice! You even threatened to stomp me once!"

"Yeah! I did!" Morgan exclaimed.

"Son!" Robert continued, his voice filled with excitement. "You are big, bad, Morgan Harker! Now, go get 'em, boy!"

"Go time!" the young man said, leaping up from his bed and charging toward the bridge.

Morgan strode into the chamber as if he owned it, crossed his arms, flexed his muscles, gazed down at the girl of his dreams, and spoke.

"Azure," he said loudly, his voice booming with confidence.

"Yes, Morgan," she replied softly, smiling up at him. "What is it?"

"Well..." he began in much quieter tones, his confidence already quaking in its boots. "Well, ya see... Me and... Rob... Me and Rob were kinda talkin'..."

"Yes?"

"Yeah," he nodded. "And we were kinda thinking that maybe... I don't know... Maybe you're hungry... or will be, I mean..."

"I probably will be at some point in the future," she asserted.

"Right..." he sighed, wiping his brow. "This is crazy... I talk to you all the time..."

"You do," she agreed.

"I mean," he continued, "I say things to you that I'm not sure won't get me slapped in the face on an almost *daily* basis."

"That's true, too," she admitted.

"So, logically, I should be able to do this, right?"

"I can't say, Morgan," she pointed out, "since I'm not positive what you're trying to do right now..."

"Well, I'm trying to ask you and Cleo out on a double date with me and Rob," he explained. "But, for some reason I can't seem to do that."

"You just did," she smiled.

"I did?"

"Well, no," she giggled. "Not exactly, but you got close enough. And, I can't speak for Cleo, but I'll go."

"Really?" he asked, his voice filled with surprise. "You do realize I meant that you'd be on the date with me, and that Cleo would be with Rob, right?"

"Yeah," she nodded. "I figured that out almost right away."

"And you'll still go?"

"I will," she smiled.

"Cleo?" Morgan asked.

"Oh, I don't know," she sighed, giving Robert a coy smile. "Is this going to be another of Rob's *micro-dates* where we don't go anywhere or do anything?"

"Oh no," Robert replied, stepping slightly nearer. "This is going to be the *real* deal. I mean, most everybody knows how great it must be to be Robert Hood, but now I want to give them something new to gawk at. I want to strut around with my *girlfriend* on my arm - who just happens to be the most beautiful woman that ever lived. And, if my boy here is out with the next most beautiful woman that ever graced the universe with her presence, so much the better. I love being good looking in large groups."

"So, we're just trophies then?" she asked, raising one eyebrow.

"Oh, I wouldn't say *just*," he replied, taking her hands in his. "But, I readily admit that you two are seriously the *trophiest*. So, how 'bout making our dreams come true by helping us become the envy of all of malekind? I mean, I do let you girls ride around in my spaceship-time-machine constantly, and Morgan is all the time bringing you ice-cream."

"I'm afraid he's right," Cleo sighed.

190

"Well then," Azure replied with a sigh of her own, "I suppose we don't really have any choice."

"So, Rob," Cleo said, trying very hard to sound essentially uninterested, "where exactly is it that you plan to take us in order to show us off?"

"How about *Paris on the Half-Shell*," Morgan suggested. "It's a pretty nice place."

"Oh," the traveler said with a wide smile, "I can see where that would be fun. Girls?"

"It's up to you, I guess," Cleo replied with feigned indifference.

"Yeah," Azure agreed. "We're doing this for you, so you guys get to pick."

"What are we supposed to wear?" Cleo asked, turning her face away from the traveler.

"Brand new dresses," Robert replied. "Order whatever you want as soon as we get back to Never Never Land."

"And, what will you be wearing?" she asked, gazing at him from the side of her eyes. "I don't want to be dressed in my best on the arm of a man in a *Van Halen* T-shirt."

"Don't worry," the traveler chuckled. "We'll be wearing our best."

"Oh," she replied, rolling her eyes, "I think you might want to do *better* than that."

"We will," he agreed.

"And, after dinner?" Azure asked.

"We'll just see what we come up with," Robert grinned.

"Cleo," she said, turning to look at her friend, "I think we should probably bring mace."

"Pepper-spray would be better," Cleo replied thoughtfully. "And, fortunately, I have some."

"That'll do then," Azure smiled. "So, when is this *date* supposed to take place?"

"Tomorrow night?" the traveler suggested.

"We'll have to check our schedules," Cleo replied, "but, we'll tentatively set it for then. That doesn't give us much time to get ready, Azure. I need to at least show you the basics of self-defense if you're going to go out with Morgan."

"That's a good point," she giggled.

Having said this, she and Cleo rose, quickly making their way from the room.

"Well done!" Robert exclaimed as soon as they left. "I knew you had it in you."

"I did do good, didn't I," Morgan said, throwing out his chest. "They never stood a chance!"

Just minutes after Morgan actually managed to setup a double date - Well, kinda... I mean, you saw what happened - the ship dropped out of non-space on the very edge of Never Never Land. Almost immediately, Delmont's time machine was exploded for the fourth time making our heroes even bigger heroes than they had been before. This action un-stole the sword, which pretty much put things back to rights with regard to that particular theft.

Cleo decided it would be best to actually go shopping for the dresses rather than trying to order them off the *space internet*. That being the case, she felt it would be a wise precaution to infect the ship's computer with a rather serious virus she had coded up over the last few months. It would keep Rob from being able to fly off without her for at least a few hours. Of course, she could disable it whenever she wanted, but, as the override password was *IWillNotActLikeAnIrresponsibleJerk* she knew Rob would have a hard time cracking it. For one thing, he would probably spend hours trying variations of *CleoLovesRobert* and *RobertHoodIsTheGreatest!* before it hit him that she had been angry when she set the password...

"Alright," the traveler said as soon as the girls were off the ship. "We're going to give them about fifteen minutes and then we're heading out."

"You're leaving them here?!?!" Morgan asked, genuine shock in his voice.

"No, you moron," Robert replied, shaking his head. "I'm *never* going to leave Cleo again, man. Well... Not for a while anyway. I'm running low on *last chances* at the moment. Anyway, you heard me tell her I'd never leave her again!"

"Yeah," the young man agreed, "but lies are your native language. You speak with forked tongue there, bro."

"True... But, *this* time, I wasn't lying!"

"Then, where are we going?"

"Well," Robert replied, "a few places really. We've got a lot to take care of in the next twenty-four hours or so."

"Like?"

"To start with, you need a real haircut," the traveler explained. "I mean; I could use a touch up, but you're a mess."

"Agreed."

"Then, we've got to pick up some serious suits," Robert continued. "I was thinking, like, blue pinstripes for you maybe, and I'll probably go with a dark gray... Actually, make that black. We can kinda match your suit to Azure and mine to Cleo's hair. Hopefully it'll come across as kind of a subtle compliment. And, they need to be custom cut..."

"Is there gonna be time for that?"

"Are you kidding, Hoss?" the traveler chuckled. "I'm Robert Hood, son. They'll make time for me!"

"If you say so," the young man laughed.

"We've also got to pick up some fresh flowers... Or, *really*, we should probably have them delivered to the ship an hour or so before we go. What do you think of blue and green roses?"

"Epic," Morgan nodded. "You know, for a guy that's never been on a date, you seem to have a lot of ideas."

"I've had a lot of time to think about this," the traveler pointed out.

"What about reservations?"

"*Reservations?*" the traveler burst out laughing. "What part of *I'm Robert Hood* don't you get?!?! Oh... actually no, that's *good*, Morgan! Then, we can tell the girls that we made the reservations. It'll give the appearance that we're responsible and not too arrogant."

"Or the *illusion*, in your case."

"You're right!" Robert replied. "And, illusions are all part of *fantasy*, Morgan."

"Oh," the young man grinned, "I know all about that! So, what else?"

"A limo?"

"*Space limo?*"

"*Future limo.*"

"Works for me," Morgan replied. "Anything more?"

"I'll have to think about it," Robert nodded. "But, one thing's for sure: we have to avoid them completely for the next twenty-four hours."

"Why?"

"Tension and suspense my friend," the traveler answered. "When we pick them up tomorrow..."

"Pick them up?"

"From their rooms," Robert explained. "Anyway, man, we want to *drop the bomb on them*, if you see what I'm saying. We want to just appear out of nowhere, haircutted, sharp suited, flower bearing, etc. Basically, we want to look like something that just stepped out of their dreams. We have to go from T-shirted slobs to GQ in the twinkling of an eye, bro."

"Candy?"

"Nah," the traveler said. "I'd be too tempted to buy Cleo honey flavored candy. And if she ate any I would *completely* lose it. I have to choose my battles, ya know?"

"I feel ya. But, what if all this prep work causes Cleo to *lose it?*"

"Mmmm," Robert replied thoughtfully. "That's actually a good point... I'm wanting to push her up to the very edge of maddening, frenzied, irresistible desire, but not *over* it... Eh, I'll take the chance. You just have to stay on your toes. If anything goes wrong, just punch me in the gut. That'll bring me 'round pretty quick."

"Can do, my friend," Morgan smiled.

With their plans made, the friends set out. They got the aforementioned haircuts, suits, ordered flowers, etc. Even Morgan had to admit that his transformation was fairly impressive. As he stood gazing at himself in the mirror of the tailor's shop, he had a hard time believing he was actually him. Having made all their arrangements and preparations, the two crept back onto the ship wearing stealth generators and went straight to bed. Robert was very serious about his intention of not letting the girls see them at all until their date.

The next day was essentially spent in hiding by the two young men. Morgan completely agreed with Robert's *drop the bomb on them* theory and hoped to leave a very lasting impression on Azure. If he played his cards just right, and got *incredibly* lucky, there could theoretically be a second date. That was something worth fighting for.

The time crawled slowly by as the two young men sat locked in Robert's room talking the day away. At last, however, the hour of preparation arrived and Morgan headed to his room to take a quick shower and get dressed. As soon as he was ready, he headed back to the traveler's quarters to wait out the few remaining minutes. Robert was still putting the finishing touches on his attire. He planned to take Cleo to within about three inches of the point of no return. And, that kind of precision took planning and effort.

As Morgan wandered around Robert's room waiting for him to finish up, something attracted the young man's attention. It was a bottle of cologne. And, as chicks clearly dig cologne, he decided to spray it all over himself.

"Geez!" Morgan exclaimed with a cough. "What is this?!?! It's *really* familiar somehow, but it smells kind of funky."

"It's *my* cologne, genius!" Robert replied, glancing over at the young man with a smile.

"I figured that! That's why I put it on." Morgan explained. "Cleo seems to love the way you smell."

"Exactly, you moron!" the traveler pointed out. "She loves the way *I* smell! I've explained this to you before, man. To her, my body odor is like pheromone filled perfume. Well... as long as I've had a shower recently."

"So…" Morgan mused. "When you say this is *your* cologne…"

"Yes! Exactly!" Robert chuckled. "It smells just like me!"

"Man! This is just…" the young man replied with a look of disgust on his face. "I need another shower now!"

"Well, we ain't got time now!" the traveler pointed out. "Just try to be glad that Cleo'll think you don't stink for change!"

"She thinks I stink?" Morgan asked defensively. "And, why would you have cologne that smells like you? You really are a megalomaniac!"

"It's just one of the weapons I use in me and Cleo's little *frustration war*."

"*Frustration war?*" the man asked.

"Yeah…" Robert chuckled again. "You see; Cleo knows what she does to me. So when she's mad… Well, she's always kinda mad… But, when she's mad enough that she wants to do something special, yet doesn't want to scratch my eyes out, she'll go down to the gym and work out for a couple of hours. Once she's finished, she'll come sit near me wherever I'm trying to work. Nine times out of ten, I end up on my bed eating honey in less than an hour…"

"Man… and that's where the cologne comes in?"

"Oh yeah!" the traveler exclaimed. "It's like *seriously* concentrated. So, when I feel like it's time for a little payback, I spray it all over myself and pretend I need something from whatever room she happens to be in."

"Rob, man…" Morgan replied, slowly shaking his head, "you guys have a really weird relationship."

"Yeah…" the traveler agreed. "But it's a lotta fun. Let's go!"

Moments later, the young men were standing just outside the girls' rooms. Each of them stepped up and knocked on one of the doors. Roughly five seconds later, both chambers opened simultaneously. Yeah… the girls had worked that out… they wanted to *drop a little bomb* themselves… And *drop a bomb* they did!

Individually, they would have been gorgeous to any male between the ages of about three and stone dead, but together they sported an almost emotionally crippling level of beauty. For one thing, they had decided to coordinate. They were dressed identically with the exception of the color of their garments. Azure was attired in green, Cleo in blue. The dresses themselves were very elegant, stopped a short distance above the young ladies' knees, and left their arms completely bare. This was unquestionably the *least* dressed Morgan had ever seen either of them.

They also each wore a pair of silver bracelets, a silver choker, and dangling silver earrings. Their shoes had just enough heel to them to raise their eyes almost, but not quite, to the level of their respective male companions. Each of them had also painted their fingernails the color of the other and they had taken a good deal of time with their hair. Although it was up, loose curls hung down beside their faces. All things considered, Morgan could have cut his own throat for not thinking to bring a camera. Or even a video camera...

Each of the young men swallowed before holding out their dozen roses to the ladies. Azure received a bouquet of green flowers, Cleo one of blue. Which, considering how they had decided to dress, made the guys look like they were mind readers or something...

"This, Rob," Cleo said, stepping from the doorway with a wide smile, running her hand slowly down his lapel. "*This* does *something* for me."

"I'll *certainly* keep it in mind," he replied, swallowing again.

"And..." she said, gently sniffing the air. "Is that... Is that you, Morgan?"

"Yeah," he confessed. "I think I may have used a little bit too much cologne."

"Not at all," she replied, smelling the air again. "You smell *good!*"

"You *do!*" Azure replied, stepping within inches of the young man and taking a few deep breaths through her nose. "You smell *really, really* good! I don't know how much you paid for that cologne, but it was worth every penny!"

"Rob," Morgan said, snapping his head toward his companion. "I hate your guts. You do know that, right?"

"I think you've mentioned it before," Robert chuckled.

"What?" Cleo asked.

"Nothing," the traveler smiled. "Me and Morgan were just messin' with each other earlier and I'm pretty sure I just won. Anyway, if you ladies will give us a couple of minutes there are a couple of things we need to take care of real quick and then we can head out."

"Okay," Cleo replied, running her hand across his chest. "But don't keep us waiting long."

"No," Azure said, taking another deep breath of Morgan's cologne. "Please don't."

"Don't worry," Robert replied, "we won't."

The two men turned and started making their way toward the medi-bay.

"I can't believe this," the young man said slightly sullenly. "I get to spend an evening with the girl of my dreams and she just *loves* the way *you* smell. I think I'm gonna be sick..."

"I wouldn't worry about it," Robert laughed. "The truth is..."

"The cologne doesn't smell like you?"

"Of course it smells like me! However, the females of Azure's people are just naturally attracted to the musk of the human male. It would've probably done the same thing if you had sprayed concentrated Morgan all over you."

"That's some consolation, I guess," the young man admitted. "Still... I'm all covered in your *musk*. And, that don't exactly fill my heart with joy..."

"Well, I'm sure Azure'll be able to help you *deal with it*."

"That's probably true," Morgan confessed. "Anyway, what are we doing?"

"Well, Morgan," the traveler sighed, "I was mistaken. I thought I was prepared for this, but I'm not..."

"I don't see how we could have..."

"I mean," Robert interrupted, "I'm not emotionally or psychologically prepared. We went from riding around on Segways to flying down the highway in Ferraris in one step! We should have staggered it or something. I almost *lost it* back there, for real. I mean, only for a second, but it was a close call."

"*Lost it?*"

"Yeah," the traveler said, stopping to look his companion in the face. "Like, really lost it. Like, I almost *jumped her* right there in front of you and Azure and everything."

"*Jumped her?*"

"Do you need me to draw you a diagram, Morgan?"

"Please!"

"Funny," Robert replied, his brows knitted. "But, I'm sure you can imagine... No, wait! Don't try to imagine! Just take my word for it, man. Remember the *bad things*. We have to stop anything like that from happening again."

"So you want to call off the date?"

"Are you insane?!?!" the traveler asked, raising his voice. "Whoa... See what I mean, Morgan. I've already lost the *why not just call off the date* battle. I can't afford to lose any more battles tonight."

"So, what do we do?"

"We're going to grab a tranq-gun..."

"*Tranq-gun?*" the young man interrupted.

"Yes!" Robert nodded. "The way I'm feeling right now; I might hurt you if you tried to stop me."

"I really don't think..." Morgan began with a chuckle.

"I'd kill ya, Morgan," the traveler interrupted. "I'm at least a third degree black-belt in several different forms of martial art."

"Seriously?"

"Dangerously seriously, bro," Robert nodded. "Normally, of course, I wouldn't dream of hurting you! I mean you're trying to help me!"

"I am!"

"Right," the traveler agreed. "But, man, I feeling squirrelly! I just wasn't ready for *that!*"

"Imagine if they were a couple of years older," Morgan mused. "You know, when they hit that..."

"No!" Robert barked. "No, Morgan! That's the opposite of helping!"

"Sorry..."

"So," the traveler continued, "you're going to carry a tranq-gun on you. If I step out of line, shoot me. Oh... and, if it goes that far she might not stop even if I'm unconscious. If that happens... shoot her, too."

"Shoot her?"

"Trust me, she'll thank you later."

"Rob, this is *crazy!*"

"No, it's not," Robert disagreed. "Look! I *know* I don't want to get shot with a tranq-gun. So, if I *know* you've got one, it will help me control myself. Okay?"

"Okay..."

"Good!" the traveler exclaimed. "Oh, and we also need to make sure that none of the four of us break a sweat until we're in a crowd! You know, just to be safe!"

"Right!"

The young men grabbed the tranq-gun and quickly explained the situation to Doc. He agreed with Rob's precaution and, in a matter of minutes, had even mixed them up a little special tranquilizer just for the occasion. As soon as Morgan was packing his Stop-Rob-Juice they returned for the girls. Each of them led their respective dates down the gangway and helped them into the luxurious *future limo* that was waiting on them.

"Rob," Cleo complained as they rode along, "you're freezing us to death. We're not wearing three piece suits; you know?"

"I know," he replied, pretending to mess with the air conditioning. "I think it must be broken."

"Well, then put your arm around me!" she demanded.

"Let me see if I can fix this air..." Robert replied, tinkering with the controls again.

"Azure..."

"I guess, Morgan," she replied with a coy smile.

The young man didn't need to be told twice. He instantly slipped his arm over Azure's shoulders, feeling as if he had died and gone to heaven. For her part, she nudged a little closer and took a deep breath of that epic cologne. For one thing, Rob really was about to freeze her and Cleo to death...

"Fix the air after you've put your arm around me!" Cleo insisted. "I wouldn't have come if I had known you just planned to murder me with cold!"

"Alright," he replied as soon as he had turned the air up a bit. "I was just trying to make sure everyone was comfortable."

Having told this lie, he slipped his arm around Cleo; who instantly snuggled up to him for warmth, laying her head against his chest.

"Can you reach the gun?" Robert mouthed silently to Morgan.

In response, the young man gave the traveler a quick wink and a slow nod. For a few minutes, the young men rode along - one in the purgatory of paradise, and the other in the plain old paradise of paradise - before the limo came to a stop at *Paris on the Half-Shell*. All four of them exited the car and made their way inside.

"We made reservations," Robert pointed out, already feeling much more in control due to the presence of the large crowd that filled the restaurant.

"You *did?*" Cleo asked.

"We *did*," the traveler replied.

"Yeah," Morgan added. "We didn't want to risk *anything* lessening you girls' enjoyment of the evening."

"That was really thoughtful," Azure replied with a smile.

"*Surprisingly* thoughtful," Cleo laughed. "Morgan, that was your idea, right?"

"Kind of," he replied.

"Totally and absolutely," Robert admitted.

Their party was almost instantly shown to a table, well before the time they had reserved. Which was hardly surprising, really, considering the fact that they were out with *The Robert Hood*. In mere moments, a very attentive server was waiting patiently for their orders.

"What's Ratatouille like, Azure?" Morgan asked thoughtfully, glancing over the menu.

"I don't actually know," she replied.

"You don't know what the native dish of your home world is like?" He asked incredulously, in spite of the fact that he didn't know what the word *incredulously* meant.

"About that, Morgan," Robert chuckled.

"About what? Ratatouille?"

"Well, no," the traveler replied. "Who told you all the names of those planets?"

"You did."

"Right," Robert nodded. "And, if you had to pick a single word to describe..."

"Liar," Morgan interrupted.

"Right," the traveler continued. "Now, keeping those things in mind: what conclusion do you draw when you see a bunch of planet names listed on a menu at French restaurant?"

"Well," the young man said thoughtfully, "since you mentioned it, it's probably a safe bet that *point one* is *you lied.*"

"Good so far."

"And, that would mean *point two* probably runs along the lines of *those names were just the names of French foods.*"

"Correct."

"Clearly making *point three*: you indirectly tricked me into eating a dead snail."

"Well, Morgan," Robert laughed, "I couldn't say. Since I haven't heard anything about that."

"Well, you did," the young man nodded. "I wanted to taste what Cleo's people ate, so I ordered escargot. And, I only did that because you tricked me."

"We do eat escargot, though," Cleo pointed out.

"I know that," Morgan nodded, "but that's not really the point."

"Escargot is good, man," Robert added.

"I know that, too," the young man said. "In fact, it's really good. I'm probably just going to end up ordering it again. But, that's not my point either."

"Okay," the traveler replied. "Then, what is your point?"

"I guess I don't really have one..." Morgan mused, still staring at his menu. "I was just making an observation... Of course, one could draw the conclusion that Rob needs to think about all the possible repercussions of all his many lies."

"Wow," Cleo said. "That's a little deep."

"Well," Morgan replied thoughtfully, "I'm just trying to save someone else from having to eat, like, an octopus or a whale's head or some other crazy thing because Rob didn't think his lie out all the way to the end. That's all. Well, that and, now I wonder what all those planets are really called..."

"Do you think he should stop lying?" Cleo asked, sincerely curious.

"What?" Morgan chuckled. "If he did that, he wouldn't be *Rob*, would he? And besides, he's always saving the day with some lie or another. I'm just saying he needs to put more thought into them sometimes."

"I'm not sure I agree," Azure replied. "Personally, I really value honesty."

"So do I," Cleo agreed, shooting a glance at Robert.

"I do, as well," the traveler smiled. "I just tend to value it most in other people."

This was met with laughter of agreement from all three of Robert's companions. Just minutes later, they had all selected their meals. As he predicted himself, Morgan ordered escargot. He figured that, when you're sitting in a restaurant where you can unwittingly order a plate of dead, steaming snails, you had better stick with what you know... Robert also ordered two bottles of their finest, non-alcoholic champagne. Being the future and all, it was *really* good in spite of the fact that it was non-alcoholic. And, of course, he wasn't about to chance alcohol at that table. The last thing any of the four of them needed was to start losing inhibitions... Particularly himself and Morgan...

"Cleo," the traveler said shortly after they'd finished eating. "There's a pretty good crowd in here and the music's not bad. Would you like to dance?"

"Yes," she said with a sweet smile, "very much so."

The two of them immediately left the table and made their way to the dance floor.

"So, Azure," Morgan said after taking a moment to brace himself. "I don't suppose you'd like to dance?"

"Actually, I would," she replied.

"Oh, crap!" he exclaimed. "I just remembered! I don't know how to dance!"

"That's not a big deal, Morgan," she replied with a smile.

"Yes, it is!" he disagreed. "I mean, I would *gladly* carve my own heart out at this very table ten minutes from now in order to know how to dance at this very moment!"

"I meant," she replied, shaking her head, "I think I can teach you."

"Honestly?"

"I taught you to shoot didn't I?"

"Well, yeah," he replied. "I guess you did at that."

"And then, you taught me to shoot."

"True."

"So," she said with a coy smile. "It's my turn anyway."

"I can see that," he said, standing up and taking her by the hand.

He helped her from her seat and the couple strolled to the dance floor, taking up a position near their friends.

"Now," she said, "you take one of my hands, and put your other hand in the small of my back."

"Well," he observed, sliding his hand into position, "I *really* like dancing so far."

"I'm sure you do," she smiled.

After an hour so, he was actually doing fairly well. And it was very obvious, even to Morgan, that Azure really was enjoying herself. That alone was enough to keep him happy for the evening; if not for the rest of his life.

"You know, Morgan," she said, as they danced slowly together cheek to cheek. "You saved my life again the other day."

"I suppose so," he agreed.

"And, you haven't bragged about it even a little," she continued.

"Nothing to brag about," he replied. "Anyone who knew you would risk their life to save yours. It's as simple as that."

"Maybe," she said, drawing back to gaze into his eyes, "but that's not really my point."

"Then, what is," he smiled, a slight blush on his face.

"That I owe you one," she replied.

"You don't owe me..." he began.

His thought was interrupted by her warm lips being pressed against his. And this time, she certainly didn't seem to be in such a rush to get it over with. There were really several reasons for this, but the main one was the fact that she wasn't just counting off the seconds until she could justifiably slap his teeth out. As the moments of paradise ticked off through Morgan's mind, he finally understood why Robert had almost collapsed when he had kissed Cleo. There was something truly epic about suddenly, and unexpectedly, satiated desires. He felt his own knees weakening as she pulled slowly away.

"Now, we're even," she smiled, before resuming their dance once again.

She laid her head on his chest and took a deep breath. This encouraged the young man enough to speak.

"I don't suppose," he said softly, "I could get another one on credit."

"No," she giggled, before gently nudging him with her shoulder. "Well, not tonight, anyway."

"Are you just being nice or should I be encouraged?"

"Well, I'm a very nice girl," she pointed out. "But, you should definitely be encouraged. You've certainly gotten from *nowhere* to *somewhere*, Morgan."

"I'm glad," he replied, taking a deep breath and trying to determine whether or not he was actually just dreaming.

"I am, too," she admitted. "I honestly did wish you luck, even when I didn't think you had the slightest chance."

"What changed that?" he asked, sincerely curious.

"A few things," she explained. "Obviously, the big one was saving my life *twice*."

"Yeah."

"But, there really is more," she continued. "I mean; you're clearly an idiot, but I *think* you really do have a good heart. For instance, it's obvious that you talked to Rob for Cleo."

"How did you know that?"

"It was just a matter of me not being an idiot," she replied.

"Oh yeah..."

"And..."

"Yeah?"

"Well," she sighed, blushing a slightly purplish hue, "that suit looks good on you, and your hair's not such a mess, and you smell *really*, *really* good tonight. I mean; I know that stuff doesn't really matter, but it's nice just the same. I know you like the way I look, but there's more you like about me than just that, right?"

"There is," he replied, somewhat surprised that he was telling the truth, "There *really*, *honestly* is. You're a genuinely good person. Did you know you had tears in your eyes when you helped save your people's home world?"

"I know," she said. "I remember now, remember?"

"Oh yeah," he replied. "Well, my point is that anyone that can feel that strongly about people they've never met... Well, they're special. And, that makes you special."

"Thank you," she said, pulling back to look at him, a wide smile on her face. "Oh, and one last thing: I really like cinnamon, so that's a genuine plus."

"Anytime you want another taste..."

"I'll let you know," she interrupted, before laying her head back on his chest and continuing the dance.

The two couples actually decided to spend the rest of the evening dancing. Robert felt safe in the crowd and Cleo felt happy in his arms. Azure was enjoying the dancing itself as well as smelling Morgan basically non-stop throughout the night. Morgan was so happy about what was going on that he was pretty sure something in the restaurant had activated that second hand weed smoke again and that this was all just another *trip*...

They finally dragged themselves home in the early hours of the morning. As they stood just outside the girls' rooms they all agreed that they needed to do something like this again very soon. With thoughts of just what that *something* might be, they all quickly fell asleep.

CHAPTER 14: YOU MANIACS

"Permission to leave the ship, sir?" Morgan said, stepping onto the bridge.

"Morgan, what are you..." Robert chuckled, spinning his seat around to face young man. "Morgan... What have you done to Azure?"

"I've rewound her to thirteen," the young man replied.

"Okay..." the traveler replied, his brows knitted. "How did you do that?"

"Doc helped."

"Okay... Why did you do that?"

"If it wasn't for a good reason, Doc wouldn't have let me do it," Morgan pointed out.

"I agree," Robert nodded. "But, the question still stands: why did you do that?"

"So I could live my fantasy," Azure explained. "Morgan thought of it last night after our date."

"So you're going to buy a monster truck?" the traveler asked.

"Don't be goofy, Rob," Morgan replied.

"Well then..."

"Oh, right," the young man interrupted. "There's a monster truck park on the island. I looked it up on the *future internet* early this morning."

"Really?" Robert asked before adding, "And, we don't call it the *future internet* here in the future, Morgan."

"Got ya," the young man nodded. "And, yes, really. They even let you crush cars."

"Really?"

"Indeed," Morgan replied confidently. "Of course, it ain't free. I'm going to need an advance or some of that *play money* of yours."

"I never said it was counterfeit," the traveler pointed out. "And, you two are going alone?"

"We don't need a chaperone, Rob," Morgan asserted.

"That's a fair point."

"And, she's thirteen."

"That's a better point."

"And, Doc's coming with us."

"That's the best point," Robert agreed. "But, what with Azure being a kid and you not needing a chaperone, why is Doc going?"

"He just likes monster trucks," Morgan explained.

"Really?"

"Is that going to be your word for the day?"

"Maybe..." the traveler admitted, pulling a wad of bills from his pocket and handing it to the young man. "Anyway, since you've already put so much effort into this, you can go. But seriously, bro, we got to get back to work this afternoon. Oh, and don't go nuts. And, bring me back my change."

"I know," Morgan replied. "I ain't gonna blow all your... *cash*, I guess... on a second date."

"This isn't a date, Morgan," Azure corrected.

"Right."

"I mean, I'm thirteen," she continued. "Well, obviously I'm not really, but you know what I mean."

"I do," the young man agreed. "And, I really meant *outing*. Just think of me as your older brother."

"Ugh!" she exclaimed. "No! That's awful!"

"Oh yeah..." he said thoughtfully. "I see what you mean. Especially since last night..."

"Ugh!" she interrupted. "Shut up, Morgan! You're making it worse. Are you trying to kill this for me?"

"No!" Morgan replied. "Not at all. Forget I said that! I've already spent hours getting all this ready for you. Today is all about you, and we're going to go enjoy crushing cars. You as a young teenage girl. Me as your older brother's best friend - who you secretly have a desperate crush on!"

"Wow..." she replied. "I think you *actually* managed to make my fantasy even better... Could you put on more of that cologne?"

"Yes..." he sighed, hanging his head. "Rob?"

"Sure," the traveler chuckled. "Help yourself."

"Thanks..."

"Oh, and Morgan," Robert added. "The next time we're here we'll get you your own. I just don't have time to deal with it today."

"I would *sincerely* appreciate that," Morgan admitted.

A short time later, the heavily cologned young man was escorting his imaginary best friend's little sister - if you see what I mean - down the gangway; followed closely by Doc. For hours on end, each of the three companions enjoyed a fantasy all their own. Doc had honestly always wanted to crush a car; he'd just never told anybody because it had seemed *beneath his dignity* somehow. Azure was having *almost* the time of her life as an underage monster truck driver flying around a dirt track by the side of the older guy she had a serious crush on. And Morgan, well, believe it not, he had always wanted to do something for a woman that didn't involve any syrups, creams, or oils; he'd just never told anybody because it had seemed *beneath his dignity* somehow...

The three made their way back to the ship fairly exhausted, but very contented. The first thing they did, of course, was get Azure back to the right age. This restored a few important checks on Morgan's *love list* that had gone missing for a few hours. That made the young man feel very good, as they were part of some other fantasies he hoped - one day in the distant future - to experience.

With the entire crew back on board, Rob fired up the engines and pointed the ship toward their next destination.

"So," Morgan said, sliding into a seat as soon as the ship was underway. "I been thinking about the underwear elastic."

"Doesn't surprise me," the traveler admitted.

"No, I mean about the *underwear elastic factor.*"

"We've got to start calling it something else."

"Maybe…" the young man replied, "but my point is: that bear could have found something else to eat."

"What bear?" Robert asked.

"That bear that tried to kill us."

"Oh…" the traveler chuckled, "that bear. What about it?"

"You didn't need to feed it my clone," Morgan pointed out.

"Yeah, I know."

"Well then, why did you go to all the effort?"

"I thought it was funny," Robert confessed. "A man's got to have hobbies, Morgan."

"I see where you're coming from," the young man replied.

"Your hobby seems to be going well, by the way," the traveler observed.

"Hobby?"

"Your pursuit of Azure."

"Oh," the young man replied. "Yeah! It actually is! She kissed me again you know."

"I saw," Robert nodded. "Congratulations."

"Thanks! It was the best... however many seconds it was... I lost count... of my entire life."

"I'm sure!"

"She *definitely* used her tongue a little last night."

"That's great, Morgan," Robert replied, "but, I think we may be straying into the realm of *too much information* at this point."

"I got ya," the young man nodded. "Gentlemen don't kiss and tell; that kind of thing."

"Well... Gentlemen don't get descriptive about just how much tongue they *did* or *did not* get."

"Right. Anyway, it was great. I taste like cinnamon, you know?"

"Your gum tastes like cinnamon," Robert corrected. "So, be sure to keep chewing."

"Be prepared..."

"I'm beginning to believe that myself," the traveler chuckled.

"So..." Morgan said, rotating his seat back and forth. "You *didn't* kiss Cleo last night..."

"No... No, I didn't."

"Didn't you want to?"

"You know, Morgan," Robert replied, turning his seat toward the young man, "for a guy that constantly asks insightful questions, that's possibly the stupidest thing you've ever asked me."

"Then, why didn't you?"

"Because, Morgan," the traveler replied, a tone of defensive annoyance clearly in his voice, "I can't *just* kiss her. If my lips touch hers, I'll end up going *completely nuts*. Then, who knows what might happen... Nothing good... You can't jam holes in the dike if you're not ready for the flood..."

"Well, I was looking forward to it," Morgan admitted. "It would have made the evening complete."

"My kissing Cleo would have *made the evening complete* for you?"

"No..." Morgan replied, shaking his head. "My shooting you with the tranq-gun would have."

"Oh," the traveler laughed. "Yeah, I guess I can see that. Especially after the cologne thing..."

"All joking aside," the young man replied thoughtfully, "I think you should try kissing her again at some point."

"You what?"

"Seriously, bro, you should be able to kiss your not-exactly-fiancé once a week or so without being completely overcome by uncontrollable passion."

"It's not just me!"

"Oh, I know," Morgan replied. "I'm talking about both of you. I mean; honestly, Rob, a man that's a million years old - or whatever you are - ought to have a little more self-control."

"Well, I'm not *a million years old* to start with."

"How old are you?"

"I don't remember," Robert confessed. "However, physically, I'm twenty-five. And I have all of the everything that comes with that. When you couple that with the fact that I'm *completely* in love with Cleo (*and* the fact that she's literally my biologically perfect mate), you can see how resisting temptation takes a bit of doing."

"Sure," the young man replied, "but you could build up a tolerance."

"What do you mean?"

"I mean," Morgan continued, gazing directly into his best friend's eyes, "like building up an immunity to poison. You take small doses until your body gets used to it."

"I don't know..." Robert sighed. "I mean; I do see what you're saying, but it sounds risky."

"Well, I'll tell ya this, Rob: had I been out on a date with my dream man I would have wanted a kiss goodnight at the end of it. I mean; I guess I would... I sure don't feel nothing like that for ya, but I'm fairly certain Cleo does."

"You make a point," the traveler replied, gazing out into non-space. "But, I'm doing it as much for her as I am for me."

"In my opinion, brother, you need to work on your *close sailing/ edge dancing* a bit more. I mean, last night was the *perfect* opportunity and you didn't even make the attempt. We were in the middle of a huge crowd and I was all prepped to stop you if anything went too far. I wouldn't have even shot you if you'd've just *a little tongue* kissed her..."

"Yeah..." Robert sighed. "You're right again, man... It's just, I try not to think about what I'm missing. Ya know?"

"Sure," Morgan replied. "Well... No, actually, I don't. I work hard to think about every possible detail of what I'm missing. But, I guess I can see why you wouldn't want to do that..."

"Okay," the traveler said with a tone of definite resolve. "I'm *going* to kiss her again."

"Good man!"

"Right," Robert nodded. "But, don't rush me! I've got to work up to this man. And, I've got to put a limit on it somehow."

"What about, like, a once a week thing?"

"I don't know... Scheduling a kiss seems weird..."

"Well, don't *schedule* the kiss, then. Schedule a date or something."

"What exactly are you suggesting?" the traveler asked.

"What I'm saying," the young man explained, "is that we try to get a weekly double date or something going on. Then, at the end of each date, you kiss her. If you go nuts, I shoot you. Everybody wins."

"I guess I can see that, actually... Really, Morgan, that is a pretty good idea."

"Thank you, thank you. Honestly, I wouldn't mind if you went nuts every week. I think I could get used to shooting you on a fairly regular basis. Especially as long as that cologne thing is going on..."

"Thanks, man."

"No problem! In fact, the more I think about it, the more I'm looking forward to shooting you!"

"No, moron," the traveler chuckled. "I mean, thanks for the talk. You really are insightful at times, man."

"Glad to be of help."

Mere minutes after this soul-searching conversation, the entire crew was once again gathered around the conference table.

"Go ahead and say it, Rob," Morgan said, dropping into the seat beside Azure.

"What do you mean?"

"You know what I mean."

"No, I don't."

"You want me to say it?" Morgan asked.

"Say what?"

"*Alright*," the young man replied, doing his best *Robert*, "*this one's gonna be a little different.*"

"I don't always open these meetings that way."

"You do."

"I didn't last time," the traveler pointed out.

"You didn't?"

"No. You said it last time, remember?"

"Oh yeah," the young man nodded. "Anyway, am I right?"

"Yes..." the traveler sighed.

"I knew it! Alright, lay it on us."

"This mission is a case of text-book time-abuse. Delmont took a piece of junk Inter-Continental-Ballistic-Missile and sold it to a planet in the past on the edge of a world war."

"Why would he do something like that?" Azure asked with disgust. "Didn't he care about the lives that would cost?"

"Actually Azure, as far as we can tell, Delmont was never actually trying to do damage. He was just a complete idiot! If you look at his thefts, the only one that stands out as truly blackguard-esque was the kidnapping of Calvin Rex. And, really, that one was a little personal."

"How so?" Morgan asked. "And, you didn't mention that before."

"We weren't discussing the morality of the thing before," the traveler pointed out. "Either way, the company Delmont sold Rex to developed weapons that his home world purchased for their military. He was actually trying to do something patriotic *for the greater good*; but he was a complete fool. The weapon he helped develop cost millions of his own people's lives years after his death. Delmont wasn't always a bad guy; he was just a complete moron that didn't understand what the repercussions of his actions would be."

"How did a guy like that get a time machine?" Cleo asked.

"We can go into that later, love, we're already off topic enough. The point is that Delmont had two motivations for this sale. First, he just so happened to have a junk ICBM laying around..."

"Why would..." Morgan interrupted.

"Because, Morgan," the traveler counter-interrupted, "Delmont was an intergalactic junk dealer. He had all kinds of stuff just sitting around. Including weapons. Anyway, his second motivation was actually that a well-placed ICBM can help bring a war to a speedy conclusion."

"I don't believe that," Azure replied.

"Well," Doc said, shaking his head. "I'm afraid it's true my dear. History can more than prove it. Killing millions can sometime save billions."

"It's still monstrous," she exclaimed.

"I didn't say whether it was right or wrong," Doc pointed out, "only that it *is* effective."

"Well, fortunately for us, this ICBM didn't shorten the war. It extended it for about twenty years."

"Why, exactly, is that fortunate for us?" Cleo asked.

"Well, dear," he replied, "imagine that the weapon had undone the war and we had to *undo* that."

"I guess I do see your point, love," she admitted.

"Love?" Robert asked with a smile.

"Well..." she replied, instantly turning a dark shade of teal. "Yeah..."

"Exactly how did it extend the war, Rob?" Vox asked.

"Good question! You see, Delmont actually had a bit of a conscience. He sold it to the *right* side instead of the most powerful side. Had he done it the other way, there's a good chance the war would never have happened."

"Wow..." Morgan replied. "I didn't expect that."

"Yeah," Robert nodded. "You can never tell about people."

"Either way," Vox observed, "I know this one can't be as simple as it looks. If it was just a matter of un-selling them the ICBM, we could have *disabled* Delmont's machine again back in Never Never Land."

"Right," the traveler agreed. "The problem is that this one missile not only extended the war, it also led to a technological revolution that made serious changes to the time-lines."

"So, what can we do?" Vox asked. "This seems like a pretty much *all or nothing* proposition, Rob. I mean; we take the missile or we don't."

"At first glance, I agree," Robert replied. "But, I want to stagger our changes as much as possible. We're going to create paradoxes with this one. There's nothing we can do. However, if we break the changes up, it may be enough for the *random elements* to correct it."

"Okay," Vox nodded. "Then, what's the plan? We take the missile from the good guys and give it to the bad guys?"

"Good idea," the traveler admitted, "but, I think it's too risky. I want to try something else first."

"Like what?"

"I want to give the good guys a little more of a moral conscience. I want to stop them from ever firing their missiles."

"Exactly how do we do that, Rob?" Cleo asked, her skin tone having returned to normal.

"Well, fortunately, these guys had developed something incredibly similar to television at this point in their history. I want to setup a small satellite system that can hijack all of their signals."

"That should be doable," the green maiden agreed.

"Then, we're going to broadcast a dubbed and subtitled version of the greatest military conscience movie ever made: *Planet of the Apes*!"

"*You Maniacs!*" Morgan yelled leaping to his feet. "*You blew it up!*"

"*Little Dr. Zaius*," Azure smiled.

"That was actually from *Rocket Man*," the young man pointed out.

"I know," she replied. "But, I like it better than *Planet of the Apes*."

"How do you know about either of those?" Robert asked.

"Oh," the blue maiden replied, "Cleo got me programmed with all that crazy Earth stuff before we went shopping. I'm actually glad she did. You guys make a lot more sense now."

"I'm sure we do," the traveler agreed.

"Either way," Cleo said, shaking her head, "this is *crazy*, Rob. There is no way..."

"Cleo," he said smiling at her, "think about Earth history. At one point, two truly massive and terrible powers stood locked on the edge of war for decades. One of the reasons war never broke out was because of the evolving moral conscience of the people. And that conscience expressed itself in television, movies, and music. We can share some of that wisdom - the wisdom *not* to push the button - with these people. Their weapons technology has been pushed unnaturally forward. I think we can undo some of the damage by pushing their cultural evolution forward enough to match it. They need the wisdom to not use the power they've been given. It may not work, but I think it's where we should start."

"I agree," Doc nodded.

"So do I," Azure said. "It's certainly worth making the attempt, at least."

"Yep," Robert nodded, "Besides, if it doesn't work, we can always just blowup Delmont's machine from Never Never Land and take our chances."

"Well, I'm glad to see you've got a backup plan," Cleo replied, rolling her eyes.

"Indeed! Now, let's get started."

And, get started they did. Fortunately for the crew, Robert had Sister assign a special team to the project a year earlier. As a result, they had everything they needed - ranging from *Planet of the Apes*, to *Enemy Mine*, to *Steppenwolf's Born to be Wild*, all the way out to *M.A.S.H.* After all, he didn't want to depress the people into mass suicide...

With the media they needed for their saturation campaign already in hand, they focused their attention on the satellite system. For Cleo, hijacking the target signals was about as difficult as finding the remote and turning on the TV would be for most people... Well, maybe not quite that difficult... Especially not if the remote has made its way under the cushion of the chair you *never* sit on... Vox didn't even have to pay attention when he was prepping the satellites themselves. In fact, he let Morgan sit there quoting just about every movie they were going to play for the people from beginning to end without interruption. Due to the ease of their tasks, they were prepped up in less than two days.

"Alright, Honey-lamb," Robert said, turning gaze to Cleo. "Pump up the volume."

"*Honey-lamb?*" she replied, tilting her head to the side.

"Yeah," he nodded. "*Honey-lamb*. That's my new pet-name for you."

"Well, you'd better come up with a different new pet-name," she demanded.

"Sweet-thing?" he suggested.

"No."

"Hot-lips?"

"Don't be stupid!"

"Miss Goodstuff?"

"Rob!"

"Right," he chuckled. "Do it, Cleo."

"Thank you," she said before pushing a number of buttons on the console. "We're broadcasting."

"Good," he replied with a wide smile. "And, I like *Cleo* best anyway. It's one of the most beautiful names there ever was."

"Liar..." she giggled.

"No, I'm serious," he replied. "There's only *one* possible way I can think of to make your name any better than it is."

"What's that, Rob?" she sighed.

For a moment, the traveler said nothing. He just stared into her eyes with a half-smile on his face.

"I'll tell ya later," he finally replied.

"So, what's the plan now?" Morgan asked.

"We're going to fast forward a week and pick the satellites up," the traveler replied. "There's no reason to trash 'em and a solid week of non-stop..."

"Rob," Cleo interrupted, gazing down at one of the monitors. "Something's wrong."

"What is it?"

"They seem to think the broadcast is some kind of propaganda attack... They've fired one of their missiles."

For a few seconds, the traveler stood in silent contemplation.

"Shoot it down," he said after taking a deep breath.

"We can't be sure what the effects will be," she pointed out.

"We'll take our chances," he replied. "We're not going to sit here and watch that thing hit."

"You're the captain," she replied, quickly pushing buttons.

"So you are..." Morgan began.

"No," the traveler interrupted. "She's just humoring me. She does that sometimes."

"I do that way too often," Cleo asserted. "And... the missile is down."

"Good!" Azure exclaimed.

"Let's hope so," Robert sighed. "We'll give them a few minutes and see if they try again. If not, we'll go grab the satellites."

They didn't try again.

"That's the last one, Rob," Vox said. "We're done here."

"Great!" the traveler replied. "Cleo, what are the results?"

"Hmmm," she said thoughtfully. "It looks like you did *too* well, Rob."

"How so?"

"Well," she replied, "the war never took place, which kept millions of people alive that should have died. Needless to say, that had countless other ramifications."

"I was afraid of something like that," he sighed. "What were the long term effects?"

"Not as bad as they could have been," she replied. "It seems that the time-lines have an easier time dealing with people living that should have died than they do with people that should have lived dying. Overall, things are definitely better than they were. Still, they're not as good as they could have been."

"It'll have to do," the traveler replied. "Back to Never Never Land."

"Yes, sir."

"I love it when you humor me."

"I know, sir," she giggled.

"Still... don't overdo it. Fighting with you keeps me young."

She didn't overdo it and just minutes later, Robert and Morgan were sitting alone on the bridge.

"Well," Morgan sighed, "that didn't go quite like I had hoped..."

"How so?" Robert asked.

"Well," the young man explained. "I had hoped that something *crazy* would happen and I would get to save Azure's life again."

"Ah," the traveler nodded. "She hasn't kissed you again, then?"

"No, she hasn't. No saving her life, no kissing. At least, that's the way it seems to be..."

"Did you try asking for an advance?"

"I did," Morgan nodded. "She said she only did *cash on delivery.*"

"I'm sure she was just joking," the traveler laughed.

"Actually, I'm basically positive of that, too," the young man admitted. "At least she was giggling a lot when she said it."

"She probably just wants to keep it special, bro."

"Maybe," Morgan replied. "But, whatever the reason, I can't get her to kiss me no matter what I do."

"Yeah, about that," Robert replied. "You're gonna have to cut back on that cologne, man."

"I guess," he sighed. "It's not getting me the results I want, anyway. Of course, Azure will just walk up, jam her face to my chest, and take a few deep breaths before she lets me go."

"Really?"

"Oh yeah! She's done that like *twice* just this morning. I've got to admit I like it a lot, even if she's basically just *doin' lines of Rob* right off my chest."

"Now, that's funny!" the traveler laughed heartily.

"Maybe to you!"

"Well, let me tell you something that should be funny to you then."

"Okay. Shoot."

"Have you noticed Cleo lately?" Robert asked.

"Not really," the young man admitted. "I've been preoccupied."

"I can understand that. Either way, she's been avoiding you."

"Why?"

"Well, it ain't because she thinks you *stink*, I can tell you that."

"Oh," Morgan chuckled. "I got ya."

"Yeah," the traveler replied. "Between my looks and you being constantly coated in *Rob* cologne, she's pretty much been ready to climb the walls lately."

"Funny," the young man admitted. "But, not very nice."

"No, I agree. I've been meaning to tell you for days. It's just that I didn't want to throw off *your game*."

"I appreciate it. But, I think the cologne has run its course."

"Agreed," Robert replied. "That's why we're going to get you a bottle of *Morgan* before we leave Never Never Land. We should have done it before. I just didn't think about all the ramifications of you strolling around the ship smelling like a dozen *Robs*."

A few hours later, the ship was once again on the very outskirts of Never Never Land. A couple of minutes after that, the team had - for the sixth time - KABOOMed Delmont's machine. Although it didn't completely repair all the paradoxical damage, Robert had high hopes that finishing their next job would take care of it completely.

The two young men then took the time to make an emergency visit to *Ye Olde Perfumery*... It wasn't really old. After all it was in the *future*. The owner just felt that calling it *old* made it seem like it had a long history of successful business. And he was right. Sorry, I seem to have gotten off topic... With their new *Morgan* cologne in hand; (as well as a refill of the *Rob*), they made their way back to the ship. Then, Robert got the ship back in non-space while Morgan got himself into the first of five hot showers.

Four and a half hot showers later, the young man strutted on the bridge simply reeking of his new cologne.

"Man!" Robert exclaimed. "How much of that stuff did you use? I think I can taste it! You smell like a musk ox!"

"Just be thankful I didn't walk up here and spray it all over you," Morgan pointed out. "I was sorely tempted to after having to wander around for days smelling like you."

"You didn't *have* to," the traveler corrected. "And, it's not my fault my scent drives all the ladies wild."

"Whatever!" the young man replied. "You're about to witness the awesome power that is *Eau du Morgan*."

"Maybe we will," Robert laughed. "I've got to say, you're new self-confidence is pretty impressive."

"Well, it's about half bluff," the young man admitted. "I learned that from you!"

"You're welcome! And the other half?"

"The other half," Morgan explained, "is having one of the most beautiful women who ever lived kiss me *twice*."

"Yep," Robert nodded. "That's a shot in the arm to the old confidence, there."

"It is," the young man said with a contented sigh. "Anyway, I been thinking..."

"You surprise me!" the traveler interrupted.

"How often are you going to use that joke?"

"About as often as you use the cliché *I've been thinking*, I guess."

"Either way," Morgan replied, turning his seat to face his companion, "there's no way we're going to be able to reliably take the girls out once a week. I mean, how many days has it been since the first date?"

"Three? Or is it four? You got up the following..."

"Look, Rob, the point that you don't even know is good enough," the young man interjected. "What I'm saying is that we're not about to do *Paris on the Half-Shell* again in the next two or three days."

"Probably not..." the traveler admitted.

As the pair were talking, Vox strode onto the bridge to check a few things. He was, however, wise enough to refrain from getting involved in the young men's inane conversation. Well, mostly...

"So, we need to be able to do dinner *here*, on the ship," Morgan continued. "And we ain't gonna be able to do that with them crappy MREs of yours."

"They ain't so bad," Vox replied without glancing up from the screen.

"Well no, they're not," Robert agreed. "But, the MREs aren't exactly *dinner with a girl* quality either."

"No," Vox agreed. "They sure ain't that."

"Of course, Morgan," Robert continued with a grin. "You could try one of our dehydrated meals."

"We have dehydrated meals?"

"I just had 'em delivered to the ship right before we left!" the traveler exclaimed. "So, you should invite Azure to have a dehydrated five course meal with you. Just add water and you'll have everything you need: starter salad, hot soup, steak and baked potato, burning candles, and your choice of chocolate cake or apple pie."

"How does it know which one you want?"

"You tell it before you add the water," Robert explained.

"Yeah," Morgan replied thoughtfully. "I guess that makes sense."

"Oh, and it comes with a dehydrated bottle of champagne."

"Really?"

"Absolutely."

"Rob," Vox chuckled.

"Okay… It's really just red wine."

"That's probably good enough for a second date," Morgan mused.

"Oh, it is," the traveler assured him.

"Rob," Vox laughed again, "come on, man, you're trying to *help* him get the girl, remember?"

"You're right," Robert sighed. "I just couldn't resist temptation."

"You don't seem to try all that often," Vox observed.

"True," the traveler nodded.

"Except in *one* very specific area," Morgan observed.

"True," Vox laughed, before stepping once again from the room.

"So, no dehydrated food then?"

"Nope," the traveler confessed.

"Well, can we pick up food to cook?"

"Why?" Robert asked. "You want to be ship's cook?"

"If it means not eating those MREs all the time then, yes!"

"Congratulations," the traveler said with a salute. "You've just been promoted."

"Actually," the young man said, scratching his chin, "that leads me to another question."

"You *astound* me!"

"Right…" Morgan said slowly. "Anyway, since this is the *future*…"

"Well, it depends on when we are at the moment," Robert interrupted. "But go on."

"Where is *R2D2*?"

"I keep telling you…"

"No, no," Morgan continued. "I just mean: where are all the droids? Like, shouldn't they have become sentient by now? We could sure use *Data* on some of these missions. Or at least a robot cook."

"You ever see *Terminator*?"

"Oh yeah!" the young man replied excitedly. "But, I didn't like it as well as *Conan*. And, really, I liked *Conan the Destroyer* better than *Conan the Barbarian*. I know a lot of people didn't, but I did. The chick was hotter and it wasn't so dark. I guess I just prefer comedy really. Of course, *Terminator 2* was really good. Maybe I just don't like the *Governator* as a bad guy..."

"Right..." Robert replied, nodding his head slowly. "Not really my point... I was actually trying to mess with you, but your short attention span caused me to miss my shot."

"That'll happen sometimes," the young man admitted.

"Anyway, Morgan," the traveler replied. "The simple fact is that droids just aren't as good as people. Once we learned to unlock about fifty percent of our brain's potential, they just couldn't keep up. For instance, I can do mathematical equations in my head thousands of times faster than the fastest computers from your time."

"Right," the young man nodded. "And, you use all that brain power to make dehydrated bottles of red wine."

"No, I'm serious," the traveler chuckled. "This time, I'm for real, man. And, as you unlock more of your potential, you'll realize it. For now, just accept that droids were a fad and we've outgrown them as a culture."

"So, no ship's cook droid, then?"

"Not at the moment..."

"Okay... We got a stove?"

"Not at the moment..."

"Then, we ain't likely to get no hot cooked food around here..."

"Not at the moment..."

CHAPTER 15: IF YOU CAN'T TAKE THE HEAT

"Morgan, what is that smell?" Cleo asked as the girls stepped onto the bridge.

"Yeah," Azure said, taking a deep breath, "what *is* that smell?"

"It's just a new cologne I picked up," the young man replied.

"It's kinda strong, isn't it?" Cleo asked with a cough.

"Oh," Morgan replied. "You want me to keep using that other stuff instead?"

"No!" she exclaimed. "No, this is more *you*, I think. I just have to get used to it."

"Stand up, Morgan," Azure said, stepping over to the young man and pulling him to his feet.

The lovely young lady put her face almost to his chest before taking several deep breaths.

"Cleo's right," she asserted. "This is *definitely* more *you*... That other stuff was good, but this is *incredible*. Whatever you paid for it, you cheated the guy."

"Rob," Morgan said, jerking his head to look at his companion. "I love you and I want to have your babies."

"I think you've mentioned it before," Robert chuckled.

"What?" Azure asked.

"Nothing," the traveler smiled. "Me and Morgan were just messin' with each other earlier and I'm pretty sure he just won. Anyway, we gotta make a quick detour. He and I need to go pick something up."

"Can we come?" Cleo asked.

"Not unless you're into wandering around in a dusty warehouse before doing some heavy lifting."

"Pass," she laughed.

"We won't be but, like, twenty minutes," Robert replied. "We just so happen to be going near the place and time where what I want is, so we're going to go grab it on the way to our next target."

"Sounds good," Morgan said. "What is it?"

"I'll show you when we get there."

About twenty minutes after this, the ship touched down on the dark side of a world Morgan had never been on before. He didn't bother asking Robert what its name was. For one thing, he was certain Robert would say it was Crêpes Suzette or something like that. And since he had taken a menu from *Parish on the Half-Shell* as a souvenir, he could make up idiotic planet names without Robert's help from now on.

The two walked up to a warehouse with a large lock on its door; Morgan pulling a floating dolly behind him.

"You gonna pick this lock, too?" the young man asked.

"Sort of," the traveler replied before drawing a laser pistol and shooting the lock off.

"That's vandalism," Morgan pointed out. "I hope you know that."

"If anyone complains, I'll pay for it."

The pair threw open the door and made their way inside. The large building was completely full of *future* appliances that looked much like regular electrical appliances, but ran on *future electricity*. Robert wove his way through the maze of massive machines with Morgan following on his heels. Finally, they reached an area that was just packed with stoves. After taking a good look at several of them, the traveler turned to Morgan and spoke.

"This one'll do," he said. "Let's get it on the dolly."

"What?" Morgan asked.

"Put *the stove* on *the dolly*," Robert replied, pointing from one to the other. "It ain't rocket science, bro."

"Are we paying for it?"

"There's no one here to pay," the traveler replied, waving his hand around. "Let's get it on the dolly and get out of here."

"I'm not taking this stove, Rob," Morgan replied, shaking his head. "We're not time-bandits, we're time-un-bandits ... or whatever that would be."

"It just so happens, Morgan," the traveler said gazing out from under knitted brows, "that this stove is out of the time-lines. It just sits in this warehouse until this system's sun explodes or something."

"That doesn't mean I'm gonna help you steal it."

"It's not stealing if it doesn't belong to anyone, man," the traveler pointed out.

"Well, I'm still not comfortable with it!"

"Do you know what my middle name is, Morgan?"

"No, what is it?"

"Nathaniel!" the traveler replied. "I'm Robert Nathaniel Hood! Rob N. Hood."

"You're full of crap!" Morgan speculated.

"No, I'm not!" Robert replied. "Ask Cleo! Either way, the time has come to rob from the rich to feed the poor. You never wondered why they call me Rob?"

"Well, I just assumed..."

"That's right!" the traveler exclaim-interrupted. "And, also because sometimes I have to *rob*. There are *five hundred* stoves in this warehouse and *not one* on the ship. From the point of view of stoves, they are the *rich* and we are the *poor*. And, unless we take one the only thing the poor are going to eat is more MREs."

"Let's get it on the dolly," Morgan sighed. "But, I still don't like taking something we didn't pay for."

"Well, I don't like waste!" Robert replied, grabbing the sides of the stove.

"Well..." the young man said as soon as they had lifted it in place. "That's true, too. I guess it's better for us to take it, than for it to die in a supernova."

"Exactly, Morgan," Robert agreed. "Now let's get it back to the ship.

After getting the stove on board and placing it in an empty room that would henceforth be known as the *galley*, they decided to go back and grab a freezer and fridge as well. After all, it seemed a shame to just let them get killed in a supernova when they could live on with a purpose... Once all of these food related items were in place, Robert felt it necessary to point out that his ship was *not* going to become the *USS Grocery Store* and that these things were *only* to be used in preparation for *date night*. Of course, since they were keeping all of this secret from the girls for the moment, the ladies weren't privy to all of these high-pressure decisions the young men had to make.

About an hour and a half after this appliance related adventure, the party gathered around the conference table.

"This is the big one!" Robert said before Morgan had a chance to sit down.

"Well done!" Morgan said. "You've broken the habit. It'll be easier from here on out."

"Thank you," the traveler replied. "I certainly hope so. In any event, our next target is the first thing Marcus Delmont did and the last one we have to undo. After this, it really will be smooth sailing until the very end of the job."

"What is the end of the job?" Morgan interrupted.

"Making sure Delmont never gets his machine," Robert replied. "It is a change to the time-lines, but it's justified. It's also going to be *crazy* easy. No guards, no defenses, no rush. In fact, we don't even *have* to do it - strictly speaking - I just want to. Either way, that's not what we're talking about now."

"Then, what are we talking about?"

"Well, Morgan" the traveler said, "we're talking about the time drive that Delmont stole. Just to recap..."

"Delmont went back in time and stole a prototype time drive," Morgan began. "He then sold it to a very advanced culture that didn't have time travel capabilities. This eventually kicked off an intergalactic war and dumped a number of time travelers on the time-lines that shouldn't have been there. It also caused the death of the original creator of the drive as he had a heart-attack when he found it missing. So, a number of should-have-been time travelers were simultaneously knocked out of existence. This basically set off the time-equivalent of a hydrogen bomb and destroyed the future."

"You remembered all that?" Cleo asked, clearly stunned.

"Apparently so," the young man chuckled.

"Well, I'm impressed," she laughed.

"Well done, Morgan," Robert smiled before continuing. "Fortunately, getting to the drive shouldn't be too *exciting*. It's on a military base, but they don't have the technology to counter the stealth generators. We also have all the base's schematics and most of their security codes. Cleo, I want you to go over them forwards and backwards until you could get us in and out blindfolded and asleep."

"No problem, Rob," she smiled. "Having time to study up makes all the difference."

"We'll have to make our way to the very bottom of the complex to reach the vault. Again, fortune has smiled on us, as there's a *very* high security elevator that leads straight to it. If we can crack the code on it, we've got a direct passage. Well, we'll also have to bypass several other security systems to make it look like the elevator isn't moving."

"I'm sure me and small-girl got that," Vox replied.

"I am, as well," the traveler said. "We also need to be ready to disable their communications - just in case. If a firefight breaks out, we don't want them to be able to work as a team. We have better equipment, but only just."

"So far, so simple," Vox replied. "What's the catch?"

"Well, I guess the big thing is that the vault was sealed using the Enigma Code..."

"What?!?!" Cleo interrupted. "If that's the case..."

"It won't be a big..."

"Yes, Rob, it will be! It will be a big deal! The Enigma Code is unbreakable!"

"Unbroken," the traveler corrected.

"Unbreakable!" Cleo counter-corrected.

"What's the big deal?" Morgan asked. "We just cut through the vault."

"A brilliant idea!" Robert exclaimed. "Unfortunately, we can't."

"And why not?"

"Morgan," the traveler said, shaking his head, "don't you think if it was as simple as *shoot the lock off*, it would have occurred to me already? The vault's shielded. In fact, its shields are almost as powerful as the ship's. There's one way in: the door."

"Then, there's *no* way in, Rob," Cleo said. "I can't crack the Enigma Code!"

"I know, love," he replied. "You won't have to."

"What is the Enigma Code?" Azure asked.

"The single greatest security code ever devised," Cleo explained. "The lock is connected to a living mind. That mind is then subjected to five different random basic concepts: love, hate, lust, friendship, danger, etc. The mind will then naturally draw connections between those concepts. The Enigma Code then records the resulting brain patterns. In order to open the lock, those patterns have to be replicated - along with the desire to open the lock. That means, *only* the person that locked it can open it. And, even then, *only* if they really want to. So unless we can get whoever locked the door and convince them that they really do want to open it for us, we're sunk."

"That's not exactly accurate," Robert pointed out. "The entire locking mechanism is controlled by a computer, so the brain patterns are simplified. They don't have to be an *exact* match; they only have to be very close."

"That's a *theoretical* distinction, Rob," Cleo replied. "It doesn't make a real-world difference. The code has never been cracked."

"Well, it's about to be," he assured her. "I've spent years on this, Cleo, and I'm prepared."

"And, if we fail?" Doc asked.

"We knock out Delmont's machine and just see if the universe blows up or not," the traveler replied with a shrug. "We don't have another choice."

"Then, let's do it," Vox replied.

With the decision made, the work began. For a little over two days, Vox and Cleo poured over schematics and made plans while the rest of the crew went over maps of the base, as well as where all the guards would be when. Due to the precision of the planning, there was - as incredible as it may seem - a fairly wide tolerance for slip-ups.

They would be inside a base where they had almost complete control of the security systems and would be completely invisible to their adversaries. In addition, Robert had taken Morgan's advice and he and Vox had found a way to make the transponders visible to the team members. So, although the guards certainly wouldn't be able to see them, they would easily be able to detect each other.

Had it been a standard vault sitting at the bottom of the facility, the entire crew would have been laughing. However, the Enigma Code was more than enough to wipe the smiles from the faces of Cleo and Vox. Even Doc didn't feel that the odds of success were high. I mean; Robert said he had it, but you've seen what a liar he was...

Once their plans had been finalized, the party armed themselves to the teeth. As Robert had pointed out, this was the big one. They all took a variety of weapons, were dressed out in cloth-armor, and each carried two shield and stealth field generators, a primary and a backup. They planned to get in and out alive - if at all possible.

Finally, the ship touched down and the band piled into the car. Robert piloted them - quite invisibly and very shielded - to an empty place in a storage area on the base. Each switched on their shield and stealth generators and stepped from the car.

"Everybody remember where we parked," Robert whispered.

"Funny, Rob," Doc replied.

"I thought so, too."

"Morgan," Azure said softly, "hold my hand."

"Can't you see my transponder?" he asked.

"Yes," she replied. "I can."

"Good," he said, reaching out for her invisible form.

Fortune smiled on the young man and he actually managed to take her hand without accidentally touching anything that might have gotten him slapped later on. The band then quickly made their way from one point to another along their rather twisted and convoluted path without a single mishap. Even without being invisible, they would have probably made it inside undetected. Robert's timing was both precise and perfect and, in minutes, they were standing at the door of the elevator they sought.

Cleo pushed an exact series of buttons and the elevator rose from the depths before the door opened. The party piled inside, pushed the down button, Cleo pushed another long sequence of buttons, and the elevator began to descend. Minutes later, they were a few hundred feet under the ground; standing in a long corridor filled with a series of locked doors. Vox pulled a key-card he and Cleo had prepared from his vest pocket and opened one door after another, making their way straight for the vault and the Enigma Code.

Everything had gone perfectly and, in less than twenty minutes, they were standing at the door of the vault.

"Well," Cleo said, switching off her stealth generator, "this has been fun. Should we go now or did you bring something to eat?"

"Funny," Robert chuckled, switching off his generator.

The rest of the party followed their example and, almost instantly, all six companions were quite visibly standing in front of the vault.

"Robert," Doc said with a smile. "Perhaps now would be a good time to tell us what your plan is."

"This is," Robert replied, pulling a brain scanner from his backpack. "I've got the mind of the man that locked this door backed up on this."

"That's your big plan," Cleo laughed. "There's no way that's going to work, Rob!"

"Why not?" Morgan asked.

"Explain it to him, dear," the traveler replied. "Then I can tell you why you're wrong."

"Well Morgan," she began, "Even assuming that Rob backed up this guy's entire mind..."

"Which I did," Robert interrupted.

"It's merely a collection of data, personality traits, processing abilities, etc. Now, we could use that information to make a clone that *acted* exactly like this guy, but not one that *thought* just like him. The software that *simulates* how the man behaves works as an interface between the information that was his mind and the software that is the clone's mind. And that means, that even if the clone gave you the *exact* same answers the brain patterns would be *completely* different. That's because it's not *thought*, but *simulated thought*."

"So far, so right," Robert nodded. "So then, why won't my plan work?"

"Because," she said turning her gaze to him, "that scanner's only going to be able to simulate thinking, not think!"

"Right!"

"And, that means it won't open the door!"

"Right!"

"Then, what am I wrong about, Rob?"

"Oh," the traveler chuckled. "You're just wrong about me not being able to use it to open the door."

"...What?"

"I mean," he replied with a devilish grin, "that I plan to upload this guy's mind into Morgan's brain. Then he *will* be able to think just like him."

"Two things, Rob," she replied, very obviously excited and clearly getting angry, "that *probably* won't work, but it will *positively* kill Morgan!"

"I knew it!" Morgan replied, throwing his hands up. "I mean, I *knew* it! I'm just crewman number six! Why else would this hero from the future show up out of nowhere and drag me through space and time just to gawk at the most beautiful women that ever lived?"

"Morgan..." Robert began.

"Save it, Rob!" the young man yelled. "Save it for the next moron. Who knows how many you're going to need to go through before you're done. Either way, I told you I was glad you got me and I was willing to die for it! Well, I meant it! Mainly because I'm not a liar! Anyway, just hit me with the brain ray so I can open the door and you guys can get out of here!"

"Will you please listen to me, Morgan?" Robert asked gently.

"Et tu Robert..."

"Don't talk like that," the traveler chuckled, "you're going to make me laugh."

"I admit," Doc replied, standing up to his full height and crossing his arms, "I don't see the joke this time, Robert."

"Okay..." Robert said, throwing his hands in the air. "Let's go. Y'all done made me mad now."

"Hold on, boss," Vox said, his brows knitted. "I want to hear what you got to say whether or not Morgan does."

"I'm not saying anything if he's not gonna listen," Robert replied, shaking his head.

"I'm listening, Rob," Morgan sighed, "I ain't *believing*, but I'm listening."

"Morgan," the traveler said, stepping over to stare into the young man's eyes, "do you remember when I told you I spent years looking for you?"

"I remember that lie," he nodded. "Yes."

"Well, the more specific truth is that I spent centuries searching for you."

"Right..."

"Well, obviously I don't mean twenty-four seven, man! And, I wasn't alone. But, *we* were searching for you for centuries."

"Why?"

"Ah," Robert smiled, "that's the real question, Morgan. Why? Why are you here? If I needed a moron, bro, I could have picked one up on the island. Morons are another thing the universe is replete with. I didn't need a moron; I needed you."

"Same difference," the young man replied.

As this point, Azure stepped over and took Morgan by the hand, tears in her eyes.

"No," the traveler sighed, "not at all. Do you know why you only use five percent of your brain's potential, Morgan?"

"Yes," the young man nodded. "I'm the stupidest man that ever lived. In fact, Doc was actually able to prove that medically."

"No, Morgan," Robert replied. "You're wrong again. The fact is that the machine measures the difference between brain use and brain potential. You're not any less intelligent than the average person from your time period."

"Really?" Morgan asked.

"Of course!" the traveler exclaimed. "A person of average potential that only used five percent of it wouldn't be able to walk and chew gum at the same time, man! The reason you only use about five percent of your potential is because you have just over *twice* the brain potential of almost *every* human that ever lived!"

"Really?"

"Yes, you idiot!" Robert replied. "Why in the universe would I have dragged you all over space and time, gone to the effort to train you and get you experience, given you cash, cologne, MREs, and whatever else if all I needed was a living human brain?!?! Plus man, we're friends! Well... I thought we were!"

"Don't be like that, man," Morgan said, gazing into his friend's eyes. "It's just that all of you are *so* remarkable! It's hard to understand why in the universe we are friends. I'm a *nothing*, man!"

"You're a hero, you moron!" the traveler screamed in his face. "I've seen you charge a nano-zombie with nothing but a baseball bat, you've crept into the arms of death with us and helped us fight our way out, and you've used your body as a shield to save a friend! What is wrong with you?!?! Why can't you see what we see?!?! Even if you really were a complete and total idiot - which you're not - I would still be your friend! And, if we weren't in the middle of the most important mission we've had so far, I would seriously punch you right in the face!"

"Sorry, Rob," Morgan replied, slowly nodding his head. "So, seriously, I have more potential than most people?"

"No, Morgan," Robert sighed, his breathing heavy and his brow covered in sweat. "No, you have more potential that *anyone* who ever lived up until this point in time."

"Even you?"

"Yeah," the traveler chuckled, wiping his forehead with his hand, "even me. Of course, even if you live to be a billion years old, you still won't be as intelligent as I am. But, you really do have more potential. And, potential counts, Morgan. Plus, you're like seven inches taller than me."

"You're right," Morgan replied with a smile. "Potential does count. And, it's probably more like seven-and-a-half inches; but, in principle, you're right either way."

"So," the traveler sighed, trying to get his breathing and his disposition back to normal, "that's why I brought you here, Morgan. It would probably kill me if I put this guy's mind in my head, but your brain can handle what almost amounts to two minds at once."

"But even so, love," Cleo said softly, "there's no way he'll be able to control it."

"Yes, there is," he replied. "Right, Doc?"

"At least in theory," Doc agreed. "Robert and I did a great deal of work on that... oh maybe fifty or even seventy-five years ago now. We did develop a number of techniques that would make it possible. Robert even managed to succeed in some very simple tests with the minds of apes."

"Okay..." she replied. "But, Morgan doesn't know how to do that."

"Yes, he does" the traveler smiled. "Sister programmed him with everything I learned on the subject within minutes of him coming to Never Never Land."

"No, she didn't," Morgan replied. "She only programmed me for common. Well, that and she dumped some memories I didn't need."

"Exactly," Robert said, the devilish grin returning to his face. "One of the memories you didn't need was agreeing to do all of this before we ever started."

"What?" the young man asked, a look of sincere confusion on his face.

"Morgan," the traveler chuckled. "One of my life philosophies is; *never* let people know more than they need to."

"That's true!" Cleo, Vox, and Doc all exclaimed simultaneously.

"What good would it have done you to know that *this moment* was why you had come with me?"

"Well..."

"No," Robert interrupted. "That was a rhetorical question, Morgan. Let me give you a few possibilities: You might have gotten more and more nervous the closer we got to this. You may have started feeling like I was just using you. You might have started obsessing over what your role in the team was. You might have even started to get egotistical over your potential."

"And, we sure don't need *more* ego," Vox chuckled.

"Right," the traveler nodded. "I get to have *all* the ego."

"So, what did happen with Sister?"

"A few things," Robert replied. "First off, we programmed you for common and cleared out some memories, just like you remember. However, what you don't remember is me explaining this part of the mission to you and what you would have to do to make it happen. You also don't remember Sister clearing out even more memories we decided you didn't need and being programmed to be an information sponge when it came to anything about the mission..."

"What do you mean?" the young man asked.

"Morgan," the traveler laughed, "didn't ever strike you as odd that, before you met me, you had a hard time keeping *Merry* and *Pippin* straight in your head, but afterward you could remember completely unfamiliar planet names flawlessly..."

"They were actually French foods," Morgan interjected.

"I know that, Morgan," Robert replied. "But, isn't it just a little weird that you never got Bouillabaisse and Escargot mixed up?"

"Well, now that you mention it..."

"Or, how about the fact that you've been able to remember conversations we had from day one almost verbatim?"

"Yeah... that was kind of odd."

"That's what I'm telling you, Morgan," the traveler replied. "We prepped you for this mission and then erased the memory of us doing it. There is one thing I *really* want you to understand!"

"What's that?"

"You *agreed* to do all of this on day one! You've been a *hero* since the day we met! You agreed - not only to risk your life doing this - but also to go in blindfolded, putting your life literally in my hands."

"How did you convince me to do that?"

"Well, I lied a little..."

"Obviously!" Morgan interrupted.

"You *really* wanted to do it, Morgan," the traveler replied. "You were just nervous about the memory wipe. So, I simply told you that the machine detected a heart condition that might give you a heart-attack if you knew what you had to do. I also assured you that, when the moment of truth came, Doc would be right there with a defibrillator."

"And, I bought that?"

"Well... to be fair you didn't know me as well as you do now. If I had to do it to you again, I would have to think up a slightly better lie."

"Yeah," Morgan nodded. "I can see that... So, either way, I actually know how to do what I'm supposed to do?"

"You do."

"And, I can do it?"

"If you can't, then it really can't be done."

"Let's do it," Morgan said with complete resolve.

"Morgan," the traveler smiled, "you really are a hero!"

Instantly, Robert began punching buttons on the brain scanner. Seconds later, two minds were in the young man's head.

"What's it like?" Azure asked.

"Confusing," the young man replied, his breathing quick and shallow, "and painful... Let's hurry, Rob."

Immediately, Robert led the young man over to the vault's retinal interface and initiated it.

"Remember, Morgan," the traveler said softly, "use his mind, not yours."

Seconds ticked by that seemed like eons before one of the five displays above the vault door filled with an image.

"What does that mean?" Cleo asked.

"No idea," Robert whispered. "But, it means something to the man's mind in Morgan's head."

One symbol after another followed in rapid succession and finally the door unlocked.

"I don't believe it!" Cleo exclaimed. "Rob, you really are a genius!"

"I guess I am," he agreed, restoring Morgan's mind to normal with the scanner, "but, so is my boy here! Better?"

"Much," Morgan said with a sigh of relief. "I felt like I was about to go nuts... What's next?"

"Just cleanup," the traveler replied.

He then pulled a grenade from his side, activated it, and tossed it in the vault beside the prototype time drive. Quickly, he sealed the vault door again. Seconds later, the entire room shook with the force of an explosion.

"What was that?" the young man asked.

"You remember *thermal detonators* from *Star Wars*?"

"Of course!"

"Well, that makes a *thermal detonator* look like a firecracker."

"So, you blew up the prototype?"

"Sure," the traveler nodded. "Another of my life philosophies is; *never* climb into a vault sealed with the Enigma Code."

"Well," the young man said, his mouth hanging open in disbelief, "how are we going to replace it now that you've blown it up?"

"Oh," Robert chuckled. "We'll just replace it with a completely identical and fully functioning counterfeit, man. What difference does it make? It's not like the creator is going to check to see if his prototype has *become a fake* all of a sudden."

"Knowing you like I do I find it hard to believe that my mind didn't just leap to that conclusion..."

"I know," the traveler nodded. "But, it's been a long day for you."

"It has... Let's get out of here!"

All six of the party switched on their stealth fields and exited the base with the same timing and precision they had used to enter it. As a result, the car was once again parked in the ship just minutes later without any complications.

"Well," Robert said with a sigh of satisfaction, "In about a day and a half, a large group of military scientists are going to be very surprised."

"I'm sorry I doubted you, Rob," Cleo said, smiling at him.

"Oh, that's alright," he chuckled. "Sometimes, I really am just about too good to be true."

"But not overly humble," she observed.

"Well, no," he admitted. "I don't think you'll ever have to worry about me being all eaten up with humility."

"So I guess that's it, then," Morgan said, as he and Robert marched toward the bridge side by side.

"Almost, bro," the traveler nodded. "We still have a little cleanup to do, but..."

"No," the young man said, shaking his head. "I mean I guess I've done my job, now. So, what happens next?"

Robert brought the band to a halt, turned to face his friend, grabbed him by the shoulders, and looked him dead in the eyes.

"Morgan," he said, his voice almost stern, "you are a *long way* from *done your job*. We're saving the universe, man! How many times do I have to tell you that you're an *essential* member of one of the most elite teams ever assembled in history! Unless, of course, you're trying to tell me that you're resigning..."

"No, sir!" Morgan said, snapping to attention and giving the traveler a salute. "Not at all, sir!"

"Awesome, bro," Robert said with a wide smile. "Because I want *everybody* to know that I really love hanging out with you, man."

"I'm glad," the young man chuckled, "because I really love hanging out with you, too."

"Of course you do, boy!" the traveler exclaimed. "I'm Robert Nathaniel Hood, son!"

"Yeah," the young man nodded. "I guess you kinda are..."

CHAPTER 16: ALL'S WELL THAT ENDS WELL

"Check the time-lines, please, Cleo," Robert said the moment the party reached the bridge.

"Yes, sir," she smiled, dropping into her seat and punching buttons on the console. "It looks like that did it. There were a number of arrests and inquests to determine how, or even if, the vault had been broken into. In the end, they concluded that the time drive itself had exploded without external influence. As a result, the damage was undone and the reputation of the Enigma Code remained intact."

"Perfect," the traveler said, his eyes sparkling. "Now, to drop off our fake drive before heading back to Never Never Land for yet another *disability!*"

"You already had the duplicate prepped?" Morgan asked.

"Are you kidding me, man?" the traveler replied. "Do you know who I am?"

"You're Robert Nathaniel Hood!"

"And you're big, bad, Morgan Harker! Now, let's wrap this thing up!"

A few hours later, they had dropped off their duplicate time-drive and un-heart-attacked its creator. They then made straight for Never Never Land and blew-up-afied Delmont's beautiful time machine one last time.

"What have we got, love?" the traveler asked, his eyes turned to Cleo.

"It worked!" she almost screamed with excitement. "Time moved forward seven seconds!"

Four of the six companions cheered wildly. To Morgan and Azure, however, this didn't seem such an obvious victory.

"We did all of that for seven seconds?" Morgan asked, a disappointed tone in his voice.

"Well, no," Robert chuckled. "Not exactly. We did all of that to get time to *move at all*, Morgan. It's been a *long* time since that's happened. It means this is working! We couldn't be sure that it would until we'd actually accomplished something. But, now that we have, we *know* this will work. That's a huge victory for us."

"But, seven seconds?" the young man replied. "Shouldn't undoing all this have undone Delmont's time-bomb? Well... not *time bomb*, but you know what I mean..."

"Like I told you from the start," Robert replied, "we're not even sure why this happened, Morgan. Time travel has scrambled the time-lines until they can't self-repair. We don't know how much we'll have to undo before we fix it, but this is a real start. We just helped give the universe seven more seconds. That's a lot of time, bro! Think of how many children have been *almost born* for centuries. Now, all across the universe women are holding their newborns because of seven little seconds."

"Wow..." Morgan replied. "That's deep..."

"It is," the traveler said with a broad smile. "And, this is just the beginning, man! We still have a lot to do."

"And, we're not the only ones," Cleo laughed. "Think of all the work we just dumped on the history department. They're going to have to find out exactly what happened throughout the universe during those seven seconds."

"Wow..." Morgan said again. "That is a lot..."

"True," the traveler replied. "But, we've all got our jobs to do. I'm ready to put the finishing touches on this one and get it over with; so let's do it!"

With their end-goal in sight, they pointed the ship to the point in space-time where Delmont first acquired his time drive. Although they had already undone Delmont's damage, thereby removing the need to destroy the drive, as Robert pointed out: it was simply a matter of *class*. As they flew along through non-space, Morgan found himself thinking once again.

"I've been thinking," Morgan confessed

"You surprise me," Robert lied.

"Yeah," the young man chuckled. "Anyway, chicks dig guitars."

"Some of them do."

"Well, couldn't you and me jump back in time so I could learn to play the guitar and then bring me back here so I could impress Azure even more?"

"Maybe," the traveler replied. "But, it'd be a lot easier to have Sister program you to play the guitar. I mean, you can afford to put a little more in that brain now. We don't need all that room anymore."

"You're right!"

"Of course," Robert said thoughtfully, "you'd still need a lot of practice."

"Why?"

"Because, you have ten thumbs."

"Man..." Morgan mused. "I could be like some kind of super monkey."

"Morgan, my man, you already are."

"You're probably right. Either way, you could do it with me."

"Do what?" the traveler asked.

"Learn to play the guitar."

"What makes you think I don't know how to play the guitar?"

"Do you?" the young man asked.

"No."

"Well then..."

"Morgan, is this going somewhere?"

"Well," the young man continued, "I just figured we could go back in time, learn to play, and start a band. Then, you could impress Cleo and I could impress Azure."

"*Everything* about me impresses Cleo."

"Is that a good reason not to make the extra effort?"

"No..." the traveler said thoughtfully. "Wow! You actually made another good point. You really are forming a habit..."

"Cool! And while we're back in the past, I'm gonna grow a *ZZ Top* beard."

"No... You grow a goatee. I want the *ZZ Top* beard."

"It's going to look funny on you," Morgan pointed out, "'cause you're so short."

"I'll take my chances. What do you want to call the band?"

"*Wyld Stallyns,*" the young man suggested.

"And, you didn't get why we should call it *The Phone Booth*?"

"Oh yeah!"

"Either way, Morgan," Robert replied, "we don't have time right now."

"You have all the time."

"Maybe," the traveler admitted. "But I don't want to take the time right now. But, do remind me about it later... I have to admit you've got me intrigued with the *ZZ Top* beard thing, and I'd really like to do something for Cleo just to have done something for her."

Just hours after this conversation, the entire party was making its way toward a derelict spacecraft on an unfamiliar world.

"Delmont," the traveler began, stepping around a large piece of junk in his path, "got the time drive just like he got basically everything he ever owned. He salvaged it. This craft crashed back before time travel was made illegal and it was believed destroyed before Delmont found it. So, we're going to blow the time drive up before he can get it. Of course, he'll still make a fortune off the rest of the ship, but that's no concern of ours."

"How are we going to destroy it?" Morgan asked.

"Vox and I made a bomb using technology comparable to the ship's," Robert explained. "We're going to put it in place, along with a few other things, and then head back to Never Never Land for the finish."

After the bomb had been put in place, the traveler spent about an hour strategically placing some odd silver cylinders around a section of ground that didn't seem to have any significance to the rest of the team. Once this was done, the entire party made their way back to the ship.

"Launch four time probes, please, Vox," Robert said the moment they reached the bridge. "I want the area covered from every angle."

"Time probes?" the young man asked.

"They're specialized recording devices," Vox explained. "We send them back in time to collect data. They have their own stealth field generators and shields so they can keep themselves out of harm's way. Once they've done whatever they were sent to do, delivery pods pick them up."

"Or we pick them up ourselves," the traveler smiled. "Didn't you ever wonder how we knew exactly what was going to happen minute by minute from thousands of years in the past?"

"I did wonder," Morgan confessed.

"Well," Vox replied. "It's because we record everything using time probes before we go in."

"That's brilliant!" the young man exclaimed.

"We think so," Robert nodded.

Just seconds after the probes were deployed; Robert moved the ship just over two days into the future. With a few button presses he then collected the probes and downloaded the data on them.

"Play it, Vox," he said, staring at one of the screens on the bridge.

"What's going on?" Morgan asked.

"Wait for it..." the traveler replied quietly.

The image of Marcus Delmont appeared on the monitor. He quickly came up over a hill before stepping onto the patch of ground Robert had so carefully placed his devices around. Instantly, gray liquid began spraying from each of the cylinders, completely coating the man in fractions of a second.

"Bingo!" Robert cried with delight.

"What is that?" Cleo asked.

"Just paint," the traveler laughed. "It won't hurt him at all and I made the cylinders out of parts of the derelict ship using time-appropriate technology, so it shouldn't hurt the time-lines. That's also a custom color I had mixed up! I call it *Jackass Gray*. I actually took about a hundred pictures of donkeys and *averaged* their grays together to make it just right."

"Rob, you know you don't come across as the leader of the saviors of the universe," Morgan mused. "You actually seem a lot more like a time-clown."

"I'm like a time-ringmaster, Morgan," the traveler corrected. "If anyone's the time-clown it's you, man."

"Well, what does that make Cleo and Azure, then?"

"Ooooh," the traveler replied turning his gaze to the green maiden. "They're like a couple of time-tigresses. I feel like I need a whip and chair just looking at 'em. Cleo, come over here and let me scratch you behind the ears."

"I've said it before, Rob," she replied rolling her eyes. "You dream big."

"Yeah," he said with a devious smile, "I do. Why don't you girls go get dressed again?"

"What do you mean?" Cleo asked.

"The dresses and all that," he replied. "Would you put that stuff back on for us?"

"Why, Rob?" she asked suspiciously.

"Okay..." he sighed, punching a series of buttons on the control panel. "But I got the feeling you might regret it if you don't do it..."

"Cleo," Morgan said, turning his gaze to the young lady. "I know Rob lies basically non-stop but, from my own personal experience, I can tell you it's a good idea to take his advice when he says that."

Both of the girls sighed and left the room feigning annoyance and pretending not to be excited.

"We need showers and suits!" Robert said, as soon as the girls were out of earshot. "Oh, and by the way, you got to cut back on that cologne soon. You're going to desensitize Azure to it. And believe me, you do *not* want to do that!"

"So, should I go without now?"

"No!" the traveler assured him. "And, if I was you, I'd chew some serious gum, brother."

"Done!"

Twenty minutes later, the young man stood - freshly showered, well suited, cologne coated, and vigorously gum chewing - in the traveler's room, waiting for him to put the finishing touches on his own attire.

"Rob," Morgan said thoughtfully.

"Yeah, bro," Robert replied, stepping over to his *space dresser* and putting something in his vest pocket.

"Exactly what memories did you and Sister erase?"

"Morgan," the traveler replied, before taking a deep breath and turning around to face his friend. "To be honest with you, man, it was just a bunch of garbage you don't need."

"Yea, but..."

"Morgan," Robert interrupted, "some memories can act like a disease, bro. They can hold you back, hold you down. They can keep you trapped in the past, imprisoned in who you *were*, never giving you the chance to let you become who you *could be*."

"What do you mean?"

"I mean," the traveler continued, "didn't it strike you as odd that before you met me you couldn't even talk to a girl and then, just hours later, you were pouring your heart out to the most beautiful woman you'd ever met? It didn't seem weird that just *all of the sudden*, you could say whatever you were thinking almost without restraint? That you could take rejection as just another *bump in the road*, man?"

"Well... now that you mention it..."

"Look," Robert smiled, "you *are* big, bad Morgan Harker, one of the saviors of the universe, and Azure's not-exactly-boyfriend. That's who you *are*! Who you *were* doesn't matter. Whatever happened to poor old loser Morgan Harker simply *does not matter*! You ain't that guy anymore - and you haven't been for thousands of years."

"I guess I see what you're saying."

"It's up to you, man," the traveler said. "But, if I was in your place, I'd contact Sister and ask her to completely destroy that stuff and consider myself lucky. You know how many people from your time would have given *anything* to have their memories wiped like you have? Of course, people can do it themselves, but stuff's not always easy to let go of and put behind you... Either way, Morgan, you've been given the chance to forget without all the effort. Take my advice and let those memories go."

"You know, Rob," Morgan said, taking a deep breath, "I've learned a lot about you this trip. And, I know you're basically the lyingest thing I've ever even *heard* of. But, I also *know* that you always tell your friends what you think they need to hear. I've also noticed that you're usually right."

"Yes," Robert agreed, "I am."

"So," the young man continued, "let's contact Sister and let her know to dump that trash."

"Gladly!" the traveler said, stepping over to the young man and slapping him on the shoulder.

The young men made their way to the bridge and contacted Sister. A few minutes after that had been taken care of, the girls strutted - Yeah, they were feeling pretty *strutty* at the moment, what with helping save the universe and the guys probably taking them somewhere and what have you - into the chamber.

"So," Cleo sighed, "How's this?"

"You two," Morgan jumped in before Robert could speak, "are quite literally the loveliest creatures I have ever seen or imagined. It's a genuine pleasure to just stand here looking at you. I find it almost impossible to believe that I've actually eaten dinner with the two of you and spent the night dancing with one of you in my arms. If I died right now, I could die happy."

"Ditto," Robert replied, glancing at them over his shoulder.

"Ditto?" Cleo laughed, tilting her head to the side.

"Well, yeah," the traveler nodded. "Morgan pretty much summed it up."

As he said this, the ship appeared in real-space above the planet of Escargot. - It's not really called Escargot – but, I'm sure you've figured that out by now - I mean, I could tell you the planet's real name, but Cleo's afraid of her home address ending up on the Internet; so I've changed the name to protect the innocent.

"What are you doing, Rob," Cleo asked. "These dresses aren't exactly *beachwear*."

"I don't know that you two own anything that qualifies as *beachwear*," Morgan observed.

Both young ladies scowled at him.

"Sorry," he said sheepishly. "Old habits..."

"Don't worry," Robert replied with a grin, "I don't plan to keep us here long."

The traveler landed his ship on the same island he had on their two previous trips to Escargot before taking Cleo by the hand and leading her down the gangway and toward the beach. Morgan and Azure followed a short distance behind, also hand in hand.

"If you're curious, Morgan," Robert yelled over his shoulder, "we just picked Cleo up here about half-an-hour ago. I *love* time travel!"

Having said this, he walked to the section of beach were Cleo had been sitting when they had first arrived and surveyed the area carefully.

"There!" he said, pointing at two shallow depressions in the sand. "I was right there, Morgan."

"Okay..." the young man replied.

Robert then moved Cleo over near the spot and got her to stand just where he wanted before taking her chin in his hand and angling her head where she was staring down at the sand.

"What are you doing?" she giggled.

"What I'm *doing* is," he replied, "*it right*."

"What does that even..." she began.

Her speech was arrested, however, by Robert dropping to his knees on the sand, just where he had when they had come to pick her up. He took both of her hands in his, stared up into her face - the sunlight sparkling in his bright green eyes, the warm tropical breeze blowing around them - and spoke.

"Cleo," he said, pausing dramatically for a moment before continuing, "would you make me the happiest man that ever lived by consenting to be my wife?"

"Yes!" she almost screamed. "Yes, Rob! With everything I have, with everything I am, with every moment since the moment we first met, and with every moment that's left in time! I will *happily* become your wife!"

"Thank you," he replied softly, tears beginning to form in his eyes. "I've loved you since... I don't even know, to be honest... It seems like from the beginning of time... I'm sorry it took me so long..."

"That doesn't matter now," she said, tears streaming down her face. "Nothing matters now, except the fact that I'm yours and you're mine."

"You're right," he smiled, pulling something from his vest pocket. "And, I want *everyone* to know it. So, I got you this."

In his hand was a delicate silver ring that held a small brownish stone flecked with gold.

"That's a rather *interesting* engagement ring," Morgan observed, silently thinking to himself that, if a girl like Cleo had agreed to marry him, he would have given her a diamond the size of her head.

"It's more than that," Robert replied, slipping the ring on her finger. "It's just like Cleo, *completely unique*."

Having *put a ring on it*, the traveler leapt to his feet and pulled the fair green maiden nearer, wiping her tears away with his jacket.

"Okay, Morgan," he said with a heavy sigh. "Give me fifteen seconds then, a *loud* five second warning countdown. If I don't stop by the time you're done, you know what to do."

"Absolutely," the young man said with a wide grin.

"Just so we're clear," Robert said, gazing into his friends eyes, "that was *twenty seconds* total."

"I know!" Morgan said, confidently. "Go ahead, bro! I got your back!"

Robert didn't wait for a second invitation. He pulled Cleo back a short distance, lowered his mouth to hers, and kissed her. I mean; like, really kissed her, like, 'picking her up, spinning her around in the air, panting for breath when they were done' kissed her.

Morgan faithfully counted off the fifteen seconds in his head. Well, they were probably really more like seconds-and-a-half, but he was a generous young man and figured they had earned a little extra.

"One!" he said loudly, cracking his knuckles and almost shaking with anticipated delight.

"Two!" he continued, even more excitedly.

"Three!" he said, cracking his neck this time.

"Four!" he counted, laying his hand on Robert's shoulder, joy-filled fire in his eyes.

"Bingo!" he said, jerking the traveler back and punching him as hard as he could right in the eye.

Robert laid sprawled out on the sand, as Cleo collapsed from the overwhelming passion that was - at that moment - coursing through her veins.

"Three things, Morgan," the traveler said, sitting up and gazing at the young man through one eye. "First, thank you! Second, I had no idea you could hit that hard. The working out is paying off big time. Third, help me up. I don't want to get this suit any dirtier than it already is."

The young man immediately jumped to his friend's aid, helped him to his feet, and vigorously brushed him off.

"I have to admit," Robert said, helping Cleo to her feet with one hand and gingerly touching his eye with the other. "I didn't expect you to enjoy that quite so much."

"Yeah," Morgan nodded. "I've just wanted to do that since that whole *unrequited love* thing... Well, that and the time you made me eat the snails..."

"Escargot is good, Morgan."

"I know. I love it. That's not the point, though."

"No," the traveler laughed. "I guess it's not. Anyway, let's get back to the ship."

"Hold on there, Hoss," Morgan said, shaking his head.

"*Hoss?*" Robert said. "That's what I call *you* sometimes."

"Well, it seems it's also what I call *you* sometimes," the young man replied. "Anyway, you did your bit. Now, give me a minute to do mine."

"Knock yourself out."

"Morgan," Azure said, gazing at the young man from beneath one raised eyebrow. "What are you doing?"

"I'm doing what I'm doing," he replied, before dropping on his own knees in the sand. "Azure..."

"Morgan," she interrupted. "We haven't really known..."

"Do you mind?" he counter-interrupted. "Let me ask my question. I mean; you get to do the answering part, but I think I've earned the right to ask you a question if I want to."

"Alright," she sighed, refusing to look him in the face.

"Azure," he said, staring up at her, "would you do me the honor of going out with me, like, once a week or so?"

"What?"

"Well, me and Rob got this double-date plan; but it ain't really going work without you, so I need a little commitment here."

"Oh," she giggled. "Yeah, of course. We can certainly do like a date night once a week or something."

"Great," he said, jumping to his feet. "And, I was also wondering if you might just want to seal it..."

"Morgan," she interrupted. "A woman doesn't always want to be asked. She also doesn't always want to be the one to have to..."

Azure had no idea she had just given Morgan about fifteen times as much encouragement as he needed. If she had just assured him that she wouldn't stab him with something, he would have taken the initiative and kissed her long before. Either way, she found out pretty quick.

He grabbed her in his arms, putting his right hand in the small of her back and his left hand behind her head. Then, he kissed her with everything he had and everything he had ever seen in the movies. The young man lifted her from the ground, pressing her body gently against his while they shared a truly magical moment. And, since he was in charge of the clock this time, he sure wasn't in a hurry to bring it to an end.

"Morgan, man," the traveler said, gazing down at the ground, "come on. It's been like forty-five seconds."

"Mind your business," the young man said, pulling away for a moment before going in for seconds.

This interruption gave Azure a chance to gasp for breath, however, and put her hand to Morgan's chest.

"Wait," she said panting, gently pushing him away. "Morgan, that was a bit *more* than our normal level of kissing."

"Well, yeah," he said, "But, I figured you owed me something for that time you shot me with the tranq-gun."

"That's true," she giggled, a bit of a blush on her face, "but we're probably even now."

"No worries," he replied. "Consider this an advance."

Once more, he put his mouth to hers; giving her a three or four second *finishing touch*.

"Alright," he said, pulling her away and putting her arm around his. "Now, we can go."

The four of them headed for the ship, Azure having a bit of difficulty with balance after her experience.

"Morgan," she whispered. "You *really* are a fast learner. You know that?"

"I'm beginning to realize it," he said with a contented sigh.

As soon as they were on the ship, all four went to change. They had to go blow up the time drive and then head to Vox's house for dinner. Since it would have been hard to explain to Celeste why they had changed clothes on the way to pick up a car part, they decided put on the same clothes they had on when they picked Vox up. As the young men were making their way to their rooms, Morgan made an observation.

"You smell like honeysuckle, Rob" the young man pointed out.

"I know," the traveler replied, lifting part of his coat to his face and breathing deeply. "It's awesome, isn't it? I've always loved honeysuckle."

"Me too, Rob," the young man nodded. "Me too."

Just minutes later, Morgan stepped back onto the bridge before sliding into his usual seat.

"You need to change that shirt," the traveler said, glancing over at the young man. "That's not what you were wearing when we grabbed Vox."

"No," Morgan agreed looking down at his shirt. "It's not. Do you know why it's not, Rob?"

"Oh yeah," he said, snapping his fingers. "I dissolved those clothes for you."

"You did," the young man replied. "And, now I know enough to thank you for that."

"No problem," the traveler laughed. "Anytime."

"And what happened to your eye?"

"Doc fixed it already."

"Man! I wanted a picture of that!"

"Sorry, bro," the traveler replied, shaking his head. "Maybe next time."

"Sure..." the young man said, thoughtfully gazing out into non-space. "You know, bro, I'm pretty sure Azure planned to kiss me before we even left the ship."

"What makes you think that?"

"Well, right near the end of that first kiss," Morgan mused, "I tasted just a hint of cherry."

"Did you?" Robert asked, getting a wide grin on his face. "And what do you make of that?"

"Well, obviously," Morgan explained, "she *must* have been chewing gum before we went down there. Which *may* mean she was *planning* to kiss me. And, I think that's a good sign."

"Oh," the traveler chuckled, "I certainly agree that it *is* a good sign."

"Cool," the young man replied, growing silent for a few moments before his mind fixated on another subject. "Rob, what if someone turns all this into sci-fi?"

"What do you mean?" the traveler asked.

"I mean," Morgan explained, "what if someone from the future, I mean after we fix it, rewrites our story and takes it back into history as fiction?"

"I can't imagine anyone being that stupid, Morgan."

"I don't know," the young man replied. "I can imagine it. It would make an awesome book. Think about it! *The Chronicles of Morgan.* Or maybe: *Morgan Harker and the Rainbow Women of Time. Morgan Trek?*"

"If it ever happened," the traveler said, shaking his head, "which it won't, the book would be called: *The Last Time Traveler.*"

"You have a serious ego issue. You know that, right?"

"This from *Mr. Morganatron?*"

Shortly after this idiotic speculation about borderline impossible future events that certainly *did not* happen (no matter what that website says), the ship dropped into real-space in Never Never Land. The time drive that was the cause of all of this trouble was soon nothing but a bunch of pieces scattered through the hulk of a derelict ship, and the companions were once again on their way. Just hours later, they found themselves flying above Duck à l'orange. Minutes after this, all six companions were walking through Vox's front door.

"Hey, Celeste!" Robert called out as he strode into the room. "We brought another one for dinner. I hope that's cool."

"Always, Rob," she called from the kitchen. "Dinner's almost ready. Come on in and sit down."

All of them made their way into the dining room and sat around Vox's large, and very expensive, table.

"Celeste," the traveler said as soon as she stepped in the room, "this is Azure. *She's* Morgan's girlfriend."

"Nice to meet you," Celeste replied with a light laugh. "Robert, you should have told me the boy had a girlfriend! I was afraid he was trying to move in on your turf."

"I'm not really..." Azure began, before stopping with a blush.

"Not what, dear?" Celeste asked with a wide smile.

"I'm not really surprised Rob forgot to mention it," she replied, "Morgan and I just *officially* got together."

"Good," Celeste replied. "Maybe you two can teach Rob something about *official.*"

"I've learned, mama," the traveler replied, taking Cleo by the hand and holding out the ring for Celeste's inspection.

"Well, it's about time, boy!" she exclaimed. "But, I don't know what kind of man asks a girl to marry him on a trip to an auto parts store..."

"A man like Rob," Cleo laughed.

Moments later, Celeste was filling up and handing out plates that were quickly passed around the table.

"So, what are y'all really up to, Rob?" Celeste asked, gazing at him with a knowing smile.

"What makes you ask that?" he smiled.

"The fact that I'm not a fool," she laughed.

"Well…" he said, taking a deep breath. "Celeste, the truth is that I'm the last time traveler and we're actually an elite team of heroes trying to save the entire universe."

"Rob," she laughed again, "I just said I wasn't a fool."

"Right, right," he nodded. "Well the *real* truth is that me and Vox are building a race car."

"Yeah," she smiled. "I figured it was something like that."

The Pause
(The sequel is currently available on Amazon.com: *No Rest for The Weary*)

THANK YOU!

Dear reader, I'm Aaron J. Ethridge, the author of *The Last Time Traveler*. I want to thank you for taking the time to read the book. I sincerely hope you enjoyed it. I put a great deal of time and effort (as well as love and soul) into it. I also want you to know that this is but the first in what I plan to be a lengthy series. And, if you're interested in reading the further adventures of the last time traveler and his companions, you can do something to help me make that happen.

You see, it can be very difficult for a new author to reach readers. However, the most helpful group of people in the world for doing just that are an author's current readers. Your opinion really does matter, and a few seconds of your time could change my life for years to come. So, I ask you to take a moment to review my work or post about it on your social networks.

Also, if you like *The Last Time Traveler*, you may also enjoy my rather classical fantasy series *The Chronicles of Areon* and my light hearted fantasy series (set in a world ruled by cruel undead) *The Tales of Zanoth*. The first books in both of these series are currently available on Amazon.

The Stars of Areon – If you're a fantasy reader you may well enjoy it!

The Tower of Daelfaun – Fantasy and comedy! It's an awesome combo!!

11376353R00140

Made in the USA
San Bernardino, CA
04 December 2018